THE FOREST OF BONDAGE

The Chronicles of Lidir

THE FOREST OF BONDAGE

A Saga of Erotic Domination

Aran Ashe

First published in 1991 by
Nexus Books
338 Ladbroke Grove
London W10 5AH

Copyright © Aran Ashe 1991

Typeset by Phoenix Photosetting, Chatham, Kent
Printed and bound in Great Britain by
Cox & Wyman Ltd, Reading, Berks

ISBN 0 352 32803 7

*To Slaves
(Who Else?)*

[1]

A Tutelage is Arranged

It was around midday that outriders, cloaked in leather storm-capes which masked the distinctive bright blue livery of the Duke of Arrod's guard, came by chance upon a woman in the Forest of Lidir. The younger horseman took her for a spectre, for she was standing stock still where a rainbow struck to earth. The vision lasted but a second before the rainbow jumped again, beyond the clearing, yet in that instant she was bathed in brilliant colour and the horseman was transfixed.

When she moved, turning sunward, tossing her head back, the captive raindrops spangled through the tight curls of her sheepskin jacket; the sunlight suddenly shattered in her hair and her burnished long red locks spilled down like tongues of golden fire across her shoulders. She lifted a hand to shade her eyes and the horseman could see that the hand, like her body, was slim; all of her movements were smooth. And he could see her sunlit form in profile – the outswell of her breasts moving gently with her breathing, the soft complexion, the faint freckling of her cheeks, the fullness of her lips as they parted with incertitude and she surveyed the way ahead.

'She is beautiful,' he whispered in a tone of wonderment. He had never seen a girl so beautiful as this one, so graceful or so lithe; he was sure she must be a spirit made incarnate. The sergeant, his companion, was much more worldlywise:

'Aye lad, she is that.' Yet he nodded grimly. 'But what is she doing here?'

After all, this was a place of bandits, and here was a young woman all alone and behaving very strangely: she could be a decoy. He held his young friend back.

1

'Follow her,' he whispered. 'But keep your distance,' he warned him, for the young lad's eyes had glinted. The sergeant frowned as the enchantress walked into the clearing, hesitated, and held up something fastened round her neck. Then she set off again, on a line away from them, though he was sure they hadn't been spotted. 'She seems to be heading south,' he said. 'I'll report back to the Duke. You keep out of sight, mind.' He glanced around him warily: 'And watch your back – always mind your back – it could easily be a trap.' But his friend seemed hypnotised, and as the sergeant watched them disappear in turn beyond the clearing, he wondered if he'd made the right decision. Again he looked around, but all seemed quiet. With spring still new, the forest was fairly open, except amongst the pine trees. He waited several minutes before deciding all was well and setting off in the opposite direction.

It didn't take him long to find them; the wagons and the carriage were still laid up by the stream, just as they had been an hour ago. The horses had been watered. The sentries seemed vigilant enough – they spotted him as soon as he broke out from the trees – but the drivers and the guards sat by, beneath the trees and on the stream bank, talking, laughing, some of them whittling sticks while they watched their friends play cards. Others stretched out fast asleep and a few still hung round the wagon where the peasant girls were caged. The sergeant hated this idling; it was bad for discipline. But he knew the men had little choice; they were waiting for the order to depart, but the order was evidently delayed.

Set back a little from the rest was the Duke's carriage; the shutters were down again. Where did the old dog get his strength from? They hadn't stopped it these two days, he and that shameless one. Why did he have to bring her? It only unsettled the men, having to listen to them each night, all night – daytime too – with the cage-girls always rationed. And it made the sergeant uneasy; he was only human, after all. He hadn't been able to sleep for thinking about that doxy. Not that he liked her; give him a straight-forward buxom wench who liked a good laugh any day, or

2

better still, one of the peasants – the Surdic girl, the one with long brown hair, the shy one who would never look you in the face. . .

Now as he approached the carriage he could hear the laughter, the silly high-pitched giggling and the Duke's deep-throated chuckle. When he tethered his horse and removed his cap, the men turned to watch; some of them started sniggering. He hated having to do this; he knew there would be complaints at the interruption, especially from the doxy. The Duke, at least, understood about duty, even if he did allow himself to become waylaid by any young wench who chose to flash her eyes at him. The sergeant almost wished that he had sent the young lad back instead and had followed the mystery girl himself. But there was the question of the bounty. He looked across to the cage once more; she had been looking at him, the brown-haired one, but now she turned away. His blood surged at the memory of that first night in the forest. He shook his head, then turned and banged his gauntleted fist upon the carriage door. The carriage turned silent. The Duke coughed; the woman giggled; then there were rustling sounds. The sergeant felt his cheeks beginning to colour. At last, the door swung open.

They sat side by side, their hands upon their laps. The doxy had an air of primness; the Duke was simply sweating. He eased his collar back and began to mop his brow; his face was redder than the sergeant's, but then it always was – too much rich food, too much wine, and far too many women. He had small bright eyes which belied his age, and a swollen burning nose which would have been more at home on a brawler from the gutters of Grob than on a peer of the realm who was said to be the Prince's uncle. The sergeant knew an ox-cart driver who looked exactly like the Duke, and drank and ate as much but didn't have so many women, though not for want of trying.

The old man cleared his throat; the woman sat back, crossing her legs. A soft white ankle peeped out from beneath her petticoats.

'Sergeant!' The Duke waved his hand, then doubled up

3

and set off into a fit of coughing until his cheeks turned red enough to match his nose and his eyes began to water. His mistress never moved; she was looking straight at the sergeant. Slowly, she shifted her position, parting her lips and lifting her chin to expose her soft smooth neck and to gaze at him through half-closed eyes. The sergeant felt his face turn redder. The Duke regained his composure. 'Speak. What is it, man?' he spluttered into his kerchief.

The sergeant opened his mouth but the doxy cut in quickly:

'Not bandits again, sergeant – like the ones we had last night?' she chided. 'Not more invisible robbers come to carry us off and have their way with us?' She winked and pouted her lips and shook her shiny black curls. The sergeant scowled but she ignored it, turned to the old man and carried on undeterred. 'Just think, Willums . . . ' – Duke Wilbrid, barely recovered from the bout of coughing, winced beneath this private familiarity now laid bare – 'Just imagine it – ravished by invisible parts. Mmmm. . .' She laid her hand upon his thigh. 'Would it make you jealous?'

'Sh, Aruline, shhh. Not in front of the men, my dear.' His hand crept on to her knee to shake it playfully, which only seemed to make Aruline worse. She shut her mouth, then suddenly burst out laughing, which set the old man chuckling uncontrollably as the sergeant's normally weatherbrowned cheeks glowed ever brighter red. Last night hadn't been his fault. Something had startled the horses; he hadn't imagined it. He glowered at her. If it had been robbers and he hadn't been so alert, she wouldn't be smiling now, so she could get that silly smirk off her face. And it wasn't as if they were asleep in the tent anyway. Why did he have to take these insults from this cheeky wench? How could she twist the Duke around her finger? If the sergeant ever got the chance, he would very quickly put the hussy in her place – flashing her eyes and showing her ankle. And last night she had shown far more than her ankle. She ought to be hiding her head in shame. She had stood there, before the Duke, her bedrobe lifted up around her hips and knotted across her belly and no attempt at decency at all. It made the sergeant want to drag her from the carriage, hitch her skirts up to her armpits and . . .

'Sergeant? Your report, if you please.' The Duke was in control now. The sergeant took a deep breath and felt a little better:

'My lord,' he announced with pride, 'we have found a woman in the forest.'

Aruline's eyes widened. The Duke's lit up.

'A woman? How old? Tell us more. Was she alone? Was she armed? Did you bring her in?' The Duke edged forwards, peering over the sergeant's shoulder as if she might be concealed, like a surprise gift, behind his back. 'What did she look like?'

Aruline slapped him on the thigh. 'Wilbers, you naughty little thing!' Wilbers jumped at first, then sat back, chuckling smugly.

'Sir, she was behaving very strangely,' said the sergeant, more composed now, ignoring the questions and steering the conversation in the direction he preferred.

'Strangely – in what way?'

'She kept stopping and –'

'Yes?'

'Well, she had some kind of talisman round her neck, sir. She kept stopping to hold it up as if to offer it to the sun.'

'A witch. She could be a witch,' the Duke suggested gravely. Aruline's eyes were very wide.

The sergeant shook his head. He felt altogether better now, much more confident; the two of them were listening. And of course, so long as the enthralment was maintained, he could see the delicious vision of the brown-haired girl approaching ever closer. 'No, my lord, I doubt she is a witch. She was young – good looks too.' He had played the trump card: the Duke's eyes sparkled.

'What was she wearing?' asked Aruline.

'A sheepskin jacket and a moleskin skirt, I think, and sandals. But she carried no bag or bundle.'

The Duke began to stroke his chin. 'Then she cannot have come far. You said the girl was young and all alone and she was lost?'

'Alone, perhaps, but not lost, sir – she seemed to know where she was going; she was headed south.'

'South? But south can be a very dangerous direction for a young girl all alone. In the south there is much unrest just now.' The Duke's concerned expression melted to a smile. 'Perhaps we should talk to this young girl, find out what she is up to, offer some protection. She may not realise the dangers. We could perhaps explain.'

'I understand, sir.' And now the sergeant smiled too – at the vision within his mind, of soft brown hair and sweet shy lips and shamefast warm permissiveness.

Aruline glanced from the Duke to the sergeant and back again. 'Wilby!' she said with feigned reproof. 'What have you got planned, you very naughty boy?' She tickled him under the chin.

'But our journey is very long, my dear. We may allow ourselves some small diversion which may help to pass the time.' A slow sly smile spread across Aruline's face. The Duke began to chuckle. 'Bring the girl to me,' he commanded. 'And if she is as beautiful as you give us to believe, sergeant, you will be suitably rewarded.'

'Sir.' The sergeant bowed and withdrew, quietly closing the carriage door.

Aruline removed something from her sewing basket, then laid her head upon Duke Wilbrid's lap. She looked up into his face, her wide eyes shining with excitement. He loved her for these moments; he loved the way she seduced him to her will. Slipping her right hand beneath his shirt to tantalise his nipples, Aruline whispered: 'Let me do it to her, darling, while you watch? Mmmm. . . Let me?' Her left hand held a blue silk rope. Reaching up, she kissed him with her warm moist lips, tickling his chest curls while she did so, squeezing his nipples nervously, slipping her tongue into his mouth again and again. 'Let me, let me. . . please?' his sweet seductress begged him, and how could his soft old heart refuse her anything?

[2]

The Sport of Horsemen

Anya entered the large clearing and sat down on a fallen log. She put the folded blanket down beside her, then looked around. The forest was deserted. She had walked for several hours – the castle was far behind her now – and she hadn't seen any signs of habitation. She hadn't seen anyone at all, not that she'd expected to, for she knew that the forest was very large. Her fear had been that, once her escape was discovered, the castle might send a party in pursuit, but now she doubted that. Everything was quiet. She checked the lodestone once again; it was difficult to keep on course through the trees, but perhaps it didn't matter that much: as long as she kept going in roughly the right direction, she was sure to reach the Great River. On foot, it would probably take her days. She didn't mind; she wasn't feeling tired at all, although she was a little hungry. All the food had been finished at breakfast, when she'd said goodbye to her friend for the last time, and their ways had parted. Axine had gone back to the castle; Anya must now complete her quest alone.

But she wished she had planned things better. In the castle, the overriding dread had been that she might never escape from that terrible place and all its cruel perversions. She had managed it, with Axine's help, but where would her next meal come from? She hadn't thought of that. So now she had a journey of many days, at least, with nothing at all to eat. She put the thought to the back of her mind, stood up, then suddenly dropped to the ground as if her legs had been cut from under her. A terrifying whirring and crashing sound came through the trees behind her. She cringed, holding her breath while her heart was almost bursting through her breast. Then she saw them – and she

7

gasped for air, then slowly collapsed and heaved a sigh of pure relief as the pair of doves went beating upwards from the trees. She laughed at her skittishness; but her fist remained clenched about the lodestone pendant. Its magic had worked.

Everything fell quiet again. Anya could hear nothing but the rustle of the wind through the trees, and her own uncertain breathing. She got up cautiously. Another storm was brewing. The blackened clouds were gathering to the north. She couldn't help but think of them as rooted in the castle. In her mind's eye, she saw them, boiling up above it, then surging out in all directions like heralds of iniquity sent to search her out and strike her down with burning light-ning bolts.

She turned and set off quickly, almost at a run, towards the further trees as the first stray droplets splashed upon her face. She heard the rumble, then the sudden whoosh of the storm-wind through the bushes before she realised – far too late – that the rumbling had transformed into a beating thump, reverberating upwards through the ground beneath her feet, and masked within the whooshing sound was the panting snort of a galloping horse.

She twisted round to look over her shoulder, then tripped exactly as the rider lunged and failed to grasp her coat, but kicked out, catching her with a glancing blow across her shoulder. As she spun round, toppled and dropped the blanket, the horse thundered past above her head and she was sure she would be trampled into the earth. It was the rider's shout at missing her that galvanised her body into action. Scrambling to her feet, she dodged very quickly back the other way. She didn't look behind, but she could hear the horse protesting as the horseman wheeled it round. And then the hunt was on – the bloodchilling cries and the terrifying thumping sound of hoofbeats through the ground, approaching ever nearer. Again she tripped and now went sprawling. The stampeding beast was nigh upon her when she rolled out to the side. The horse panicked, stood upon its hind legs and tried to toss its rider to the ground. Anya saw the horseman's wild eyes suddenly widen in fear as his hands went up and he nearly overbalanced backwards. It seemed to give her strength. She jumped up, clasped the pendant and after every giant gulp of breath, she could feel its power surging through her bloodstream, making her feel light-headed, making her almost float.

The trees were less than fifty paces away; she could make it, she knew. He could never catch her in that thicket. She flew towards it, aiming at the point where the trees were densest, taking giant leaps, bounding like a deer – forty paces, thirty-five – not slowing though her lungs were burning and her heart was bursting through her chest. The hoofbeats were almost upon her again; the screams of the rider rent her ears. She kicked out harder – twenty paces – the forest would open any second now to swallow her, then close again to bar the horseman's way – fifteen paces, ten – she flung herself forwards one last time – and the trees directly before her parted in reality.

The shock was like a physical blow: a second rider emerged whose horse reared up to block her as she skidded to the ground. And now the horses circled her and Anya was transformed. It was as though all the magic in that stone had suddenly expired, as though all the driving life force that propelled her onwards had been borrowed, and the debt was now recalled. She was crouched down on her knees, unable to move. The pain in her chest was so intense she could not even breathe; the ground beneath her receded, then rose up to meet her; she could not lift her forehead from the grass; she felt so drained of energy, so devoid of hope, so hurt. She shut her eyes and when she opened them again, a giant booted foot was resting on the grass beside her cheek. Her ribs hurt as much as if the owner's fist and arm had slammed across her back and she felt as sick as if the foot had kicked her in the belly.

But she looked up sidelong at the owner of the boot.

'Good sport, my dear?' said the horseman who had chased her, then turning to his companion: 'It seems we have no ordinary gamebird here, soldier. No, indeed.' He chuckled. 'Let us hope she shows such lustiness in other sports too – to meet the Duke's requirements. Eh, my dear?'

He laid his gloved hand on her hair and she pulled away; she was very scared, but she risked another look. It was as she had thought: these weren't the castle guards. The castle guards wore suits of grey, but these men wore blue. And then there was the mention of a Duke; she had never heard tell of any Duke in the castle. There was a Countess – a very cruel woman – and there were many lords and ladies; then there was the Taskmistress, of course, who directed the slaves and arranged the wicked tortures, and the Prince – her Prince – who had won her heart with kindness, not cruelty, her Prince who had had to go away and could not know her fate. . .

'What's this?' The horseman looked down at the softly shuddering body crouched at his feet. 'Tears?' He bent down, taking Anya firmly by her long red hair and pulling her head back sharply so she was looking up into his weatherworn face. 'You do not like our sport then, my freckle-faced delight?' He smeared the tears across her cheeks with his iron-studded gauntlet. 'But, my dear, our sport has only just begun. . .' Her hair was pulled back harder. 'So wipe away these tears. Your tears can never save you if your legs can't.' The gloved fingertip was drawn down under her chin. 'Remember this lesson that your sergeant teaches you. One day it may save this pretty body.' The finger moved slowly down her breastbone. 'Though not today, I fear.' It hooked beneath her lodestone chain and effortlessly snapped it. Anya jumped up, trying to catch it, but the sergeant snatched it quickly away and held it in the air. As Anya tried to reach for it again, the sergeant simply wrapped his arm about her waist and lifted her from her feet, then threw the pendant over to his mate, laughing, 'Hang on to it lad; it seems it is a charm – it'll have the girls all over you, judging by this one, anyway.' Anya tried to push herself away from him but the horseman held her firmly. His companion grinned, examined the stone with interest and pushed it into his pocket.

Now, without the lodestone – and the sergeant was right in that respect, for she believed it her good-luck charm – Anya felt drained of all her magic strength; on top of the tiredness and defeat was a wave of helplessness; it was the same feeling that she had experienced when her husband had told her he would put her aside and sell her into slavery. She felt completely beaten. The horseman held her closely to him; her body hung limply. She should have kicked and screamed and bitten, as she'd done with the castle guards. But she no longer had the will. And Anya knew it wasn't simply these men, cruel as they appeared, that had brought it about. There was something else; something from within.

Suddenly, for the first time, she saw her quest as futile, and that terrible realisation, coming now, had made the last drops of her determination seep away to nothing. In the castle, escape was all she'd ever thought about; it was everything she'd aimed for. Now she had escaped, she had to find her lover but, even without these men waylaying her, how could she? All she knew was that he was many days ride away, across the Great River, somewhere to the south. By the time she found out where he was and how to get to him, he might easily have moved to somewhere else. And she knew he was in danger. She could feel it deep inside. She had no one to turn to now – the only two friends she had besides the Prince were back there in the castle. And that was behind it all, the weight of black hopelessness that surrounded her: if these horsemen had been from the castle, she would have been returned, and punished too, and probably very cruelly, but at least her friends, Axine and Marella, would have sought her out and helped her to bear her torment until her Prince returned to sweep her up and carry her away. But now, she had no one. . . *Have strength, you are strong*, Axine had said, but now she just felt weak.

The sergeant lowered her, then opened out her sheepskin jacket and burst the buttons on her halter, making the young horseman catch his breath as Anya's full and weighted breasts swung free. And now the raindrops fell, not driven by the wind, for there was no wind – no sound, just silence – and not freezing drops, but large warm droplets falling down, to splash upon her hair and turn it deeper copper, to mix with Anya's tears and to patter, like

11

the large henna-coloured freckles, on the tight smooth skin of Anya's breasts and, trickling down, to cling upon the velvet, upturned black-brown tips then drip upon the gently rounded belly encircled with a broad belt down below.

The sergeant's blood boiled as he looked upon this woman. Her eyes were closed, her head was tilted back to meet the falling rain; the droplets splashed upon her face, they kissed her parted lips, they ran beneath her earlobe. When she opened her eyes and looked at him with those softly pleading olive eyes with wide and deep black centres, his training almost failed him. He wanted to take her up, to lift her from the ground again and to kiss the warm and body-salted droplets from her face and lips, from underneath the velvet nipple-skin, but most of all, from the surface of her firm warm belly and from deep within the hollow of her navel. Those were the drops the sergeant's tongue would dearly love to kiss. He would love to kiss her, too, in the way he kissed the brown-haired girl, down there, amidst her murmurs, against the shame. He could not speak now, to give this new girl any instruction. He knew he could not have her fully, not yet, at least. He turned her round, placing her slender hands upon the withers of his mare. He pulled off his gauntlets and cast them to the ground, then ran his hands, a soldier's hands, grown thick with calluses, broad and rough, beneath her jacket, beneath her open halter, up her warm slim back, across her shoulders – so delicate to support such swollen breasts – then round and underneath the warm moist hollows of her armpits, down her sides and under, spreading to encompass the ribcage, then reaching up with thickened fingertips to touch – very, very lightly – only the undersurfaces of those stiff-tipped velvet teats. And his cock was hard now – harder and more sweetly painful than he ever could remember . . .

The young lad coughed. The sergeant did not want to hear, though the cough was meant for him. But he knew the rules; he knew that this one was not his; he would get the brown-haired girl, and the brown-haired girl was soft and warm and lovely, but the brown-haired girl was not this one. He had to touch this perfect body once. The young lad moved uneasily. The sergeant still ignored him. The lad would get his turn; he would change his tune then.

The rain was pouring down and dripping from the sergeant's cape. The girl's hair was deep, black-copper coloured now, gathered into long wet swaths on her sheepskin coat. Her breathing was uneven. He pinched her nipples gently. They felt like hot stones underneath the velvet. He wanted to thrust his fingers down between her belly and her belt. He dared not. But surely it was worth it, for a beauty such as this? Her belly shuddered as her nipples brushed against the mare's coat. Again the feeling came, the overpowering need to take her, the surge that made his cockstem almost burst.

'Sergeant?' the voice kept trying to distract him.

'Shh!'

He could feel her body shaking very gently. It wasn't the rain; the rain was warm. A shimmering tightness shook her; he could feel that tightness in the underbellies of her breasts, a polished smoothness feeding back to the tight incurve of the underjoin, which he lifted now to bed his little fingers to that softened skin, so now his hands supported her, taking up the weight of flesh and gently brushing the tips against the horse's coat. Again the shimmer came – just as the brown-haired girl's body shimmered at the moment when her shame turned hot and she melted into liquid pleasure. The sergeant felt his throat turn dry. He could hear the young lad's breathing. He couldn't hear the girl's, for the girl was straining now to hold her breath; finally it burst out from her body and the sergeant felt her ribcage expanding and contracting in rapid pulses, making her breasts rise and fall and brush each time against the warm soft coat of his mare. The air was strong with the scent of horse; her body was tight with passion. He trailed his fingers down her belly, across the almond well, down to where the belly kissed against the beltline, then round to the back. He gathered the moleskin skirt up, but only at the back, so it brushed against the skin hairs of her thighs, up across the goosefleshed firm and rounded bottom, exposing the deep dark well until the hemline stroked the fine pale hair at the small of her back. She shuddered as the first raindrop touched her there. He rolled the moleskin up and tucked it in the belt, so now the tension was increased, with the broad belt pressing against her belly and the pressure of the tucked-up fold of cloth against the lower part of her back.

The sergeant made her lift her ankles from the ground and stand up on her toes. It rendered her buttocks tighter. He watched the raindrops splash silently down the exposed skin. He did not touch her; he took his illicit pleasure indirectly, from the measure of her breathing – the anticipation of the touch that never came – and the vision of the raindrops running down her buttocks to the backs of her thighs, kissing her flesh in the way he was forbidden to do, tickling her intimately in the deep dark cleft of pleasured disallowance.

'Spread, my beauty . . .' he heard his voice murmur; the thighs edged uneasily apart. The sergeant drew breath quickly. He heard her whisper, 'No . . .' from shame. But she had done it all the same. And the darkness had not lightened as her buttocks opened. It had not been the shadow: her skin within the cleft was coloured deep black-brown. He crouched and looked at her. Again he dared not touch, but that tainting had not lessened his wanting, not one bit. 'Reach up and open out.' Again his cockstem felt as if it would burst right through his breeches; she had done it straight away. Her bottom was arched out towards him, tense, her buttocks opened wide. She had done it automatically, immediately she was instructed; it was as if she did these things by reflex, as if she had been conditioned to such ways. Another large raindrop struck the small of her back, then trickled down into the groove; she gasped as the tickling liquid touched the dark and secret mouth. The flesh expanded, then contracted, tight.

'Sergeant!'

The sergeant, fingertips stretched out towards the luscious well of pleasure, turned, his eyes glazed over by the vision of that wanting. 'Sergeant? We must get back. The Duke expects us.'

Anya held her breath once more against the feeling in her belly, the tightness of the beltline all around her. She was still standing on her toes, not daring to lower without being instructed; it made her feel as if she were in the air, suspended with the broad firm band around her middle, forcing pressure there, where it should not be, making her flesh excited. And when he had made her spread her legs, it had only made it worse, for the raindrops tickled her intimacy, making her want to close her legs and squeeze; the suppression of that squeeze brought on the sinking feeling. She could not help herself from bearing down between her thighs, even as the two men looked upon her. She prayed they had not witnessed it.

The sergeant's hand was at her ankle. He removed the sandal from her right foot, then lifted her foot up gently until her knee was tightly bent, but even on tiptoes she could scarcely reach the stirrup. Anya heard a murmured protest from the younger man; then all was silent. The sergeant moved closer; his breath tickled her earlobe and a shiver ran down her spine, all the way to the tip and down below it, where the cold leather surface of his cape brushed against her bareness. His fingertips touched the inner surface of her uplifted thigh; the backs of his other fingers brushed slowly up from the base of her spine; then both palms curved round her buttocks, gently lifting her again, taking her weight. The little fingers drifted into the crease. 'Spread,' he whispered, 'bear down through your bottom,' making her feel lewd. Anya's hands gripped tight about the horse's mane. Her body tensed; she tried to force her bottom hard against his fingers, to concentrate her lewdness down into the split and as she pushed, she felt his fingertip tickle her tiny pushed-out secret mouth. Her breath was caught. 'Again,' the whisper came. Again she pressed; the secret tickle touched her.

The sergeant wanted her to push down at the front. 'I want your flesh to open; I will help you,' he murmured. He stroked her mound, its softened bush still short in its regrowing; the fingers reached beneath and up to tickle her belly; the heel of his hand brushed against her swollen satin

15

sex lips. 'Push, let your body open . . .' As she tensed, and pushed again and grasped the horse's mane the harder and gripped her toes about the stirrup, his hands lifted her upper thighs. They pressed; the fingertips teased her flesh leaves open as she pushed, then a finger touched inside the hot soft living flesh, kissing against the liquid wall to one side then the other. Anya felt shudders run down inside to lick against the places that he touched. The finger then retreated, and Anya's flesh tightened in a slow delicious liquid spasm that forced a drop of inner moistness out. She could feel it dangling coolly from the left-hand burning flesh lip. 'Open,' he said again, and she tried to push until she split. The fingertips now pressed around the thickened hood of flesh that sheltered the hard little nub of pleasure. She felt it slip out easily; she was wet. The fingers did not touch it, but the pressure all around it kept it pushed out very hard. She closed her eyes; the feeling was sweet, but it did not progress as her body now needed. Instead, her skirt was unrolled, her leg was carefully lifted down and the sandal was refitted.

'Turn round,' the sergeant ordered. Now she was looking up into his weather-lined face and his hard, staring eyes. 'From now on you shall keep your legs apart.' The sinking feeling came again. 'Good. Always keep your legs apart, my dear – the first lesson for a cage-girl.' Anya flinched. It made the sergeant smile. The younger man stood back, stroking the neck of his horse, but watching Anya intently. 'Hitch up your skirt,' the sergeant said. 'Roll it up all round.' Her lip began to tremble; she did not want to do it, not when she was facing him. The shame she always felt at having her sex exposed was too intense. 'Do as I say.' He did not shout; he merely whispered, but it was a whisper which she dared not disobey. 'Spread wider; push down . . . You are learning.' He crouched down and patted her on the belly, then gave a very low whistle. She turned her head away, from shame, as he called the other horseman over.

Anya's legs were parted, wide. She wanted to cry, but now she could not; they were talking about her. The men stood up. When the sergeant stepped towards her, his storm-cape brushed her thighs. It did not brush the hairs upon her mound, for those hairs were still very short. In the castle, she had been shaved. But that shaving was not her only secret: those short hairs simply formed a soft bright copper dusting on her milk white skin, an insufficient cover to her shame. They could not disguise the prominent matt-black lips around her fleshpot. She knew the soldiers had never seen a woman like her, for she knew she was unique, and that uniqueness shamed her.

The sergeant made no comment about her blackness. He rolled her skirt down. 'Now, button yourself up,' he simply said. But she could tell he was agitated by what he had seen. Her fingers fumbled with the halter. 'Quickly!' Two of the buttons were missing on account of the way he had ripped it open.

He now took hold of the folds of Anya's skirt, below the belt at each side and firmly pulled it down her hips as far as he could until it almost hurt her. Her belly swelled out above it, leaving a line of bare flesh below the hem of her jacket, all the way round. From his saddlebag, he took a thick coarse rope, passed it round her back and knotted it tightly round her belly. It prickled against her skin. The knot hung slightly down; the sergeant was dissatisfied. He grunted, unfastened it and pulled it even tighter, jerking it so Anya was dragged towards him, almost off her feet. This time the knot surmounted her belly and did not hang down. The rope bit into her. So now, with the pressure of the belt low down about her hips, and the tightness of the rope about her belly, the feeling came again, much deeper down, between her legs, which were kept outspread, as instructed. He looked at her as he held her chin up and he shook the rope, which shook the knot and forced another sweet qualm in her belly. Suddenly he pursed his lips; his look was cruel. Anya glanced away. She could hear the strained breathing. The end of the rope was released. Two hands quickly grasped the joining of her halter, then burst the halter open. Her breasts spilled out again. The young horseman gasped. The sergeant, barely able to contain his passion any longer, brushed her nipples roughly with his thumbs.

17

'Sergeant! No! We must deliver her intact!' The sergeant gritted his teeth; the thumbtips stopped.

But now there were no buttons left to button; the halter lay uncertainly against her bosom as it swelled with every frightened breath she took. She was picturing what the cage might be like, dangling from the branch of a great oak tree, the cage-girls kept inside it with a rope about their bellies and their legs shackled wide apart – as wide as hers were now. She imagined the cage being lowered, the girls backing away and one being picked – she knew it would be her – and taken, with the sergeant's hand clasped round the rope about her belly, dragged into the woods and used according to his will. She knew he would use her long and hard. But for Anya now, with her hips and waist restrained, her halter brushing up against her nipples as she breathed, her thighs held wide and aching, pushing out her sex in lewdness beneath her moleskin skirt, that threat was laced with something else.

The riders mounted. The sergeant refitted his gauntlets, then took in some of the slack of the rope, securing it to the saddle. 'Right, my darling, off we go!' He spurred the horse into a trot and tugged on the rope. Anya had to run, holding on to the stirrup leather, to keep abreast of him as the horse was driven back across the clearing. It made the sergeant laugh to see her jumping over stumps and bushes as she tried to keep her footing. All the time, the tension in the rope was tugging at her belly. She tripped, crying out as the rope slid up her ribcage and jammed beneath the outswell of her breasts; she was dragged for several yards along the ground before she managed to grasp the rope and pull herself upright. The horsemen stopped for a few moments, but the sergeant allowed her no other concession. 'Pick your feet up this time,' he shouted and set off at a brisker trot with Anya clinging on to the rope with both hands now. She lost one sandal, then the other.

Very soon, she was out of breath, tripping as she tried to clear the obstacles in her way, fighting back the tears of humiliation, her cheeks burning ever brighter at the laughter and the coarseness of the comments which he shouted to

18

his mate. For with the buttons on her halter missing, Anya's breasts swung free and uncontrolled; as they bounced they hurt her. The sergeant did not seem to care. He slowed his horse to a walk. Anya thought at first this might have been from kindness, but without warning, as soon as she drew level, he brought his whip down sharply on her bottom. Though she was protected by the thick moleskin skirt, her buttocks smarted. 'Get those knees up in the air,' he cried, 'your sergeant wants to see those bubbies jiggle.' So now, as the horse broke into a trot, and the sharp cracks fell across her bottom, the tears came again – the tears she had been warned against – not cool this time but hot and stinging tears of cruel humiliation, worse than any physical pain. But the sergeant was pleased to see her luscious breasts bounce strongly up and down and sometimes to the side as her knees kicked up higher, as her master so required.

The sergeant's face was flushed; he could feel his blood coursing through his veins; his flesh between his thighs was stiff with his excitement. He would have his turn with this one before his lordship had his way, and nobody would stop him.

'Sergeant!' the younger horseman shouted. Anya had stumbled and was being dragged along the ground. 'She is tired; perhaps we should let her ride awhile. I could carry her behind me?'

'So! Tired and weak, is it?' The sergeant dragged her to her feet, then hauled the rope in tighter until she was standing up on tiptoes; the toe of his boot was pushed into her belly. 'Well – we do not want our cage-girls tired and weak. We want our cage-girls willing.' He bent down, twisting her body round, so her back was pressed against the horse's upper foreleg. She faced the young soldier. He had shown some concern, at least, but she knew he could not save her.

The sergeant removed his gauntlets. Her breasts were gathered in his hands; he began kneading them together, yet not roughly, as she had expected – had even hoped – for she was sure that then the young man would intercede on her behalf. She could see it in his eyes; his eyes did not seem cruel. The hands about her breasts were carefully pressing and stimulating them, squeezing until the nipples rubbed against each other, pinching until the fluid gathered to make the nipples harden. Then the sergeant took one of the reins, slinging it beneath her breasts and lifting them by that means, as if it were a halter, forcing them together tightly, then shaking till they bounced. All this while the young soldier looked upon her as her lewdness was displayed, for with all the working, the constant stimulation there, her nipples were poking out hard from her tightly bobbing mounds.

With the loose end of the other rein, the sergeant smacked each nipple. The short smacks resounded through the silence. Her nipples burned; he pulled them; his fingers slipped; her nipples were wet with rain. He smacked again, very quickly, so the whole breast shook. Now her nipples throbbed. He made her stand with her legs more definitely apart; she had to hold her breasts up, pointing them towards the other horseman while the sergeant rolled the ends between his fingers, making them more engorged, then smacked them once again. When he was finally satisfied and Anya was fully disgraced, with her breasts now capped by large deep purple-brown acorns, the sergeant pronounced: 'You're right son, this doxy needs a ride. A good one. She shall get that soon enough.' The young soldier's eyes gazed fixedly from blood-drained cheeks; Anya's belly quavered.

But the sergeant did not relent; Anya was driven on again, though now the whip did not fall so frequently as before, for she remembered to lift her knees up high. Her breasts felt tighter now; the tips felt hot and swollen; the feeling in her belly was very strange. When she stumbled again, the younger horseman caught her by the arm before she fell.

The rain had softened now to a fine lukewarm drizzle which cooled Anya's face and wet her neck but lay as a spray of tiny droplets gathered on the upper surface of her breasts, towards the teats, which remained pushed out beyond the shelter of her open halter to receive the rain directly. Her skirt was heavy with the weight of water; it kept sticking against her thighs; her legs were wet; her feet were

20

saturated. The sergeant's cape shed water onto her hair and shoulder.

As they entered a hollow ringed by dense tall pines, the horses slowed. The sergeant signalled and the men dismounted. Still fastened to the horse, Anya was left to regain her breath as best she could. The men chose a hummock at a distance of a few yards to sit on while a leather flask was uncorked and passed back and forth between them. They did not offer it to Anya; she did not care. Neither did they allow her to sit; the rope was too short for that. She leaned against the horse and found its solid warmth reassuring. The men began talking in low voices, so she could not hear them properly. But she heard the Duke being talked about, and saw the sergeant look about him nervously when the young man mentioned bandits, but there was no more laughter and they didn't refer to her at all. She hoped their game was over.

It was so quiet here; the only other sounds were her own breathing and the horses' intermittent snorts, and the dripping from the trees – she could hear that too. She liked the sound of dripping water; it usually made her shiver, but not this time, for she still felt very warm. Her heart was beating fast even now. At one point, back there, when she had been made to run very fast over difficult ground, kicking her knees up all the time, breathing harder and harder, she had felt dizzy, exhilarated almost. She hadn't enjoyed it, but neither had she hated it; the feeling had been unfamiliar. She still felt light-headed; it was as if she were aware of everything, especially the smells. She could smell her own body scent – the fear and the exertion – and, very strongly, the horse's smell – she liked that smell of horses – and the sweet sharp smell of resin all around her. The pines, so tall and dense and black – a blackness of shadow, and a pale grey mist of interlacing fine dead branches – and pink, too, a pink-brown glowing carpet of aged fallen needles. They were soft beneath her feet. There was water trickling everywhere, fed by fine straight threads from high above, running down the cracked grey trunks, dripping from the branches, forming a dark blanket down the horse's flank,

21

steaming from its neck, and trickling down between her breasts, down to the ropeline and beneath it, a wet cool clinging about the beltline of her skirt. She loved the forest; she liked the softened colours and the delicious smells in rain.

The horsemen stood out starkly as their leather capes moved and their jerkins flashed brilliant blue. The younger one was looking at her now; the two men were getting up and coming towards her, but for once it was the younger one leading. Anya's heart was beating faster.

'Here, you must be thirsty.' It was the first time he had spoken to her. He offered the flask. She had expected that he would be shy, but he wasn't. It was just that his voice and manner were gentle, not harsh as the sergeant's had been. Anya glanced to where the sergeant stood, hands on hips, a short distance behind. His stare was unflinching. 'Do not mind him. Drink,' the horseman whispered. He smiled. His eyes were soft and kind; they were like her Prince's eyes, she realised now. Her fingers fumbled as she took the flask. The liquid tasted sweet and thin, like watered wine, but it made her belly feel warm. She drank again, too quickly, and felt it overflow across her chin, then down her neck. The young man watched the line of liquid working downwards. Anya felt it tickling onto her breast. Then he lifted up his forearm automatically, as if it had been he who had dribbled and now he would wipe the drip away. He hesitated, half reaching now with his fingers as Anya's body stiffened and her breathing quickened from the anticipation of the interrupted touch. The quickness of her breathing made her bosom rise and shimmer.

The horseman looked at her, staring into her eyes. His gaze, so frank, not shy at all, made her feel strange. The pupils of his eyes expanded as his eyes caressed her face. She wanted to look away; she half wanted him to touch her. Perhaps it was the wine that had caused that feeling. Her body was excited. Perhaps it was the touching the sergeant had forced upon her; she had been stimulated then although she did not want it, but she knew this man's touch would be gentle, yet more exciting still. She would welcome this

22

touch. She said as much with her eyes, for she had not looked away at all; she had said it with the short quick breaths which shook her breasts and made her nipples tighten. His hand moved again; Anya heard a clink; the lodestone chain was slipped into her pocket, on the side away from the sergeant. The young man had secretly returned her good-luck charm.

'Forest child . . .' was what he whispered. Anya's eyes grew wide. She almost wanted him to kiss her. 'When you are a cage-girl –' his voice was soft, seductive – 'I will slip you from your cage on a warm and moon-bright night.' His fingertips touched her belly lightly, just below the rope. 'I will carry you; I will lay your bare back on a blanket of pine needles. You will point your toes up to the sky . . .' Her skirt was lifted up; the fingers pressed against her open thighs, very near the tops, so close to Anya's flesh leaves that it took her breath away. 'You will suckle me with this salted nipple in between your legs . . .' And had he chosen to touch her flesh bud then, her pleasure might well have come about without the moon, or the needles soft against her back, without the moist lip-sucking of her nubbin. She shuddered when he kissed her neck, then bending, kissed her breasts and then her belly. The kisses were pure delight. Now it was the sergeant's turn to cough, then laugh – uneasily. He had been watching, but he hadn't heard his companion's words. Yet he could tell well enough how Anya was responding.

'She can ride behind me, sergeant,' the soldier offered once again.

The sergeant merely shook his head, mounted, and hauled his new-found cage-girl up across the shoulders of his steed. He let her rest face down; they set off through the trees.

As they advanced towards the camp at a comparatively gentle trot, the blood slowly drained down to Anya's face until she thought her head would burst; the withers of the horse steadily pummelled into her belly. The sergeant lifted up her skirt once more, laying his bare hand flat upon her lower back to steady her, and instructed her, 'Keep your thighs apart, my girl.' Anya found this very difficult to do. Then later, at a point where his companion had gone ahead a little and the horses were in single file through the densely woven forest, he hitched her skirt up higher, not only at the back but also at the front, so that her open thighs pressed against the horse's shoulder. He then locked his forearm round the nearer thigh, pulling it to separate the cheeks. Anya waited for the touch to come within the spread split of her bottom, but it did not. She could hear the sergeant's controlled tight breathing. When he pulled her hand back and laid it at the joining of his thighs, she could feel the rigid cockstem; even through the thick cloth of his breeches, it felt hot against her hand. Then she felt the water droplets from the shaken overhanging branches drip upon the skin of her back, the skin of her buttocks, the skin of her open thighs. The sergeant pulled more firmly upon her thigh to open her split more fully. He stopped the horse beneath a dripping branch. He used both hands now to hold the cheeks apart. Three droplets splashed in quick succession, straight into the hollow; the third one splashed upon the tense and tiny mouth between the open cheeks. And on that third splash, Anya heard the sergeant murmur, 'Good . . .' as she felt her ticklish bud of sexual pleasure jump to kiss the horsehair. 'Very good, my girl.' A delicious overturning feeling came within her belly.

Her head was hung already, but now she wanted to cover it up from shame, for though that tickling jump between her legs felt luscious, it was the compliment, the acknowledgement of her lewdness, that had made her belly quaver.

[3]

The Blue Silk Rope

Anya heard the shouts, then felt the sergeant ease her body up from the horse's back while he straightened out her skirt. When she turned her head, she could see the wagons – three at least – and a magnificent carriage in brilliant blue and gold which looked very out of place against the forest green. On one of the wagons was the cage of women. Even though it was not, as she had imagined, attached to the branch of a tree, it made her apprehensive, but what frightened her even more was the crowd of soldiers that had cried out when they saw her; they were running up the slope towards them. She tried to bury her head against the horse's flank. The sergeant chuckled and slowed his horse to a walk as he approached the mob.

'Do not be afraid,' he said, placing his broad hand underneath her skirt, pressing it against her lower back. 'You will not be given over to our lusty lads. Not yet, at least – provided you behave. And surely you have not forgotten already?' His hand moved down to tap the backs of her thighs, where she held them pressed together. The sinking feeling came; she could feel the gooseflesh forming as she opened out her thighs. 'Wider,' he whispered. Though her face burned, she did it, then she heard the grunt of approbation. The sergeant's fingers slipped beneath her. His hand enclosed her body at the joining of her legs; with each step the horse took, her flesh leaves kissed against his palm; his thumb, lying bedded between the cheeks, caressed her bottom mouth, and as her flesh softened to the shameless intimacy of this pleasurable apposition, the sergeant murmured soft words of approval.

But now the soldiers pressed and clamoured from both

sides, reaching up to pinch her breasts and pull her hair and touch her calves and thighs. Her skirt was thrown up about her waist, and Anya blushed deep crimson at the laughter and the crude remarks, but the sergeant did not stop them. He simply warned her, as his hand was lifted away and her thighs began to close, 'Keep those buttocks open, girl, keep those legs apart,' then pointed out to all and sundry the state of Anya's blackness whilst he held her wide apart and rubbed a broad and callused finger very roughly in the crease.

The men became unruly; the younger horseman shouted at them; in the end, the sergeant had difficulty keeping them at bay and Anya's tears flowed freely as she jerked in vain to escape the nips and cruel thrusts of the many urgent hands and fingers stabbing between her thighs. Worse yet were the taunts about her colour, the hot state of her flesh, and about what they said she and the sergeant had been doing in the woods. They threatened her with accounts of what they themselves would do to her when she was encaged. Then suddenly, the shouting stopped. The hands no longer mauled her; her clothes were quickly readjusted. The sergeant coughed. 'You'd better be on your best behaviour now, my girl. No word of this, mind.' Anya went very still, but she was breathing very fast. The horse advanced again, towards the bright blue carriage.

Even now, the sergeant did not seem able to resist touching her; his hand moved furtively and urgently beneath her skirt, but to the blind side of the carriage. She felt ashamed, for her flesh was moist now; as his fingers squeezed, the flesh lips slipped between them. When the horse finally came to a halt in front of the coach, and Anya looked up to behold a man who could be none other than the Duke, her head went down again, for on the side unseen, in secret, her thighs lay open – wantonly, this lord would surely think if he but knew – taking improper pleasure from the sergeant's eager hand.

'Lift her up, sergeant. We must show our guest consideration.' The voice sounded firm, and suspicious. 'What was all the commotion?' The Duke was clad in a robe of blue and red and seemed to be wearing a short white wig. He was stoutly built. His face was very red; Anya thought perhaps he might be angry.

The horsemen had dismounted, leaving Anya now sitting astride the sergeant's horse. The soldiers' heads were bowed. Anya followed their example. For a long while, nobody answered the Duke. Then the sergeant raised his head.

'I am sorry, sir,' he said, sounding much less sure than usual, 'I fear the men were a little . . . frisky.' He smiled apologetically.

'Hmm. Well, get her down,' the Duke said abruptly. The sergeant dragged her from the horse. The Duke was annoyed by this unnecessary zeal. 'Consideration, sergeant,' he warned through gritted teeth. 'Remove the rope. Let me look at her.' Anya would not look into the Duke's face. She really did not dare, although she was curious to determine the nature of this man. She sensed he had stepped closer. 'Hmmm. It seems they were very frisky.' A warm pink finger reached uncertainly to tease at her halter top. 'She is wet, sergeant – saturated. I see she is unbuttoned.'

'Sir, it has been raining,' the sergeant offered in partial explanation.

'I hope she has not been –'

'Sir!' the sergeant protested. The younger horseman coughed.

'Hmmm.' The pink finger was pressed beneath Anya's chin to lift it. She was looking into the Duke's face – at his bright eyes and even brighter nose – and then she glanced down. 'But delicious, none the less, truly delicious.' The Duke's murmur had been barely audible. She could feel his fingers venturing down her neckline towards her breasts. Then she heard another cough, this time from within the carriage. It was a woman's voice. It seemed to stir the Duke back to his senses, for he snorted, making Anya jump, then turned sharply on the sergeant:

'The talisman – you said she wore a talisman.' Anya suddenly stiffened and her eyes went wide, for her lodestone was in her pocket.

'The young lad has it,' the sergeant said.

27

'What?' The Duke turned upon the soldier, frowning, placing his hands upon his hips and sticking his chin out strongly. Anya moved her lips to speak up in his defence, but the soldier answered calmly:

'My lord, we had to take it from her: we feared the talisman might be used against us. But it seems it was a harmless toy, a trinket such as might be given by a lover to a lass.' Anya glanced at the young soldier; his words had not been lost upon her. He was smiling – at her, she knew. She squeezed the lodestone pendant through the material of her pocket. 'I have it here, sir,' the soldier said, pretending to search his pockets. Very quickly his smile faded as the search became more urgent. Now his face looked very worried. 'Sir,' he turned his pockets out, 'I have . . .'

'You've lost it, you buffoon! Get off! Out of my sight before I . . .' The Duke raised his arm; the soldier backed away with head hung low. 'No reward for you, my lad.' Now the sergeant smiled. The smile half faded as the Duke turned to him, but very soon re-formed. 'But certainly for you, sergeant. You promised and you delivered. You have delivered us a treat.' Again the fingers descended to spread the halter open, and now to turn the nipples gently to the side. 'Hmmm. You may take your pick, sergeant, from the cage. But make it quick. We leave within the hour. Now, let us get these wet things off the creature . . . Coachman!'

As Anya was disrobed, and a warm dry blanket spread about her, she turned to witness a disturbing sight: the cage was opened and a young woman descended the steps, a girl with long brown hair. Anya's heart sank to see the sergeant shout some instruction, whereupon the girl, in front of all the laughing men, lifted up her dress about her hips to expose her thighs and buttocks. Yet this seemed insufficient degradation for the sergeant's liking. She was made to lift again until the dress was raised above her belly, over her breasts and up beneath her armpits. Then she was driven up the slope, towards the trees, her knees up in the air, with the sergeant loping along behind her. The sharp cracks of his flat broad palm upon her buttocks echoed across to torture

Anya's ears and to make her cheeks and neck flush with hot embarrassment on the girl's behalf.

The Duke sighed. 'So good to see the peasants having fun, is it not, my dear?' he said, pinching Anya's burning earlobe playfully as he helped her up to the carriage.

The interior was blue. The carpet, the seats, the curtains and the cushions were blue. Almost every surface was upholstered in a deep-piled plush of velvet. In the far corner of the carriage a woman, young and attractive, with black curly hair and a low-cut bright red dress lay, propped against silk cushions. She had been pretending to do her embroidery, but the work was set down on her sewing box immediately Anya entered. It was obvious the woman was not relaxed; she was moving all the time, readjusting her position, stroking her hair, smiling, then pursing her lips, examining her fingernails, playing with the jewelled bangles round her wrists, twisting the rings round, pulling at her earrings, and all the time looking back and forth between Anya and the Duke. She kept twitching; she made Anya feel nervous from the start. The Duke sat down, trapping the woman's bare right foot as he did so, setting her giggling as she pulled it free. Anya drew the blanket tightly round her.

'Sit down, my dear.' The Duke indicated that she should sit opposite him. The woman tucked her feet up and clasped her arms around her knees, then looked at Anya with her large bright eyes while the Duke sat back, resting one arm on her knee and tickling her ankle with his other hand. He sighed: 'Well, my dear, you haven't said much, have you?' Anya hadn't even spoken. He winked; she glanced away. 'You must tell us all about yourself.' He looked across expectantly. Anya was put off by the intensity of the two sets of eyes now fixed upon her and she felt afraid to break the depth of silence. The padded surfaces all around seemed to soak up every sound, so when the Duke had finished speaking, the silence was suddenly total. Anyhow, she didn't know what to say, or even whether she should tell these people anything at all. Perhaps they would return her to the castle if they found out she'd escaped?

'Speak up, my child. Do not be afraid. We will not harm you. Will we, Aruline?'

Aruline's face was quite impassive. 'No, my lord,' she replied, but then, as if his words had been some sort of signal, she lifted the lid of her sewing box and peeped inside, and as she snapped it shut again she flashed her eyes at Anya. Anya was very frightened by that gesture, and by the excitement in those eyes. She edged back, even as Aruline leaned towards her; she was very suspicious of the contents of the box. Aruline next looked purposefully at the Duke, who very slowly nodded. Anya now turned very pale indeed, for being drawn out from the box by Aruline's slender hand, slowly and deliberately, was a very long length of slim blue rope, a plaited silken rope, with a tassel at the end. Anya could not take her eyes away from that rope as Aruline leisurely twined it round her finger, then round her palm, then finally stretched it at arm's length between her fists. She got up slowly and placed herself beside Anya, very close. Anya pulled the blanket more tightly round her neck and shoulders. She tried ignoring Aruline and stared instead imploringly at the Duke, hoping he might come to her assistance, while her hair was being touched and rearranged by very nervous, tickling fingers.

'Come, come. Speak up.' The Duke, seemingly unperturbed by Aruline's fervent ministrations, which now extended to gentle tuggings at the blanket, had suddenly assumed a rather sterner air. 'We cannot wait all day. Who are you, my girl? And what were you doing in the forest?'

Anya hesitated, half glancing at Aruline and the rope, which was now being carefully twisted, then she bowed her head and whispered: 'I am Anya, my lord.' She looked furtively at the rope again. Aruline had lifted it up and pressed it to her lips. Her tongue, a very long slim tongue, slick and shining, pushed out and began curling around it, almost like a snake about a branch.

'Hmm. A pretty name for a pretty girl. Do you not think so, Aruline?'

Aruline's tongue slipped leisurely back into her mouth. 'Indeed, my lord,' she murmured, lifting Anya's hair, reaching underneath to touch her neck and earlobe very lightly, so it tickled, then turning Anya's head, bending and pressing her lips to Anya's, as Anya's eyes, quite wide now with dismay, looked sidelong at the Duke. 'Indeed she is,' Aruline repeated in a very deep voice, and Anya felt the soft lips yet again, more fully this time. As she closed her eyes – for she did not wish to look so closely into Aruline's face whilst this was being done to her – she felt the tip of Aruline's long warm tongue slip beneath her upper lip to stroke the skin to greater sensitivity and to deposit there a promise of seduction. Anya drew back sharply. The Duke could not have been in doubt about the nature of the kiss, so why had he permitted it? He seemed to pretend it hadn't happened.

The questioning resumed, with Aruline's hand now slipped inside the blanket, resting very precariously on Anya's belly just above her tightly pressed together thighs:

'And where have you come from, Anya?' asked the Duke.

Anya bowed her head and did not answer.

'I see.' He sounded grave. 'Look at me, my child.' He waited until she had complied before continuing: 'Where are you bound?' Again she looked down. 'Hmmm.' The Duke said nothing further for a while, but when her gaze returned, he was still staring at her intently. The keenness of his stare made her very much afraid. Aruline's fingertips moved; that made her very worried. When he began again, the Duke's voice was very soft, hardly raised above a whisper, but he spoke quickly; each phrase he uttered made Anya's heart sink further:

'My sergeant finds a girl alone in the forest – a girl of considerable beauty – no ordinary peasant; not dressed like a peasant, either. She has no baggage, no food; therefore she cannot have been on the road for long. She is travelling south. To the north of here, there is but one place of any consequence within a day's walk – or a week's. I think you know it well, my dear.' He hesitated; Anya waited for him to say it; his face moved closer; his bright eyes narrowed. 'The Castle of Lidir!'

31

She hung her head. His next words stabbed her in the heart: 'You are a slave! Admit it!'

'No!' Not any more she wasn't; she was a free woman; no one could enslave her.

'A slave, escaped and on the run!'

'No!' But her tears proclaimed her guilt, she knew it; her tears were overflowing. The woman's hand retreated from beneath the blanket, as if expressing disapproval at these revelations, and though Anya had never wanted the touch, its withdrawal now served only to make her isolation total.

'Look me in the face.' His eyes were cold now, cold and intense, as if a cold fire burned there, drawing sustenance from her tears of shame. 'Deny it all you care to; I knew it from the start. I could see it in your eyes.' His voice fell to a murmur, as if he were reliving half-forgotten memories. 'The languor, the sweet shame, the depth of sensuality . . .' Then he beset her with a fierce and piercing gaze. 'But your own lips shall admit it.' He leaned forwards again. His eyes widened. 'Before this afternoon is through, your sensuality shall be tested, and your shame, your pleasure shall be expressed – in time – and you shall admit your status as a slave to love. For I, too, have sojourned in your castle. I have tasted the delights of slaves. Be assured, my dear, though you may have passed without those walls, you can never escape your nature.' And now it seemed the last trace of kindness in his eyes had melted away beneath the rekindled memories of lustful domination to an inner core of rigid sternness. His eyes were staring; they seemed to restrain her body and impale her soul.

'Aruline,' his voice was tense now, carefully controlled, 'tie her. Proceed with the pleasuring; elicit the depths of this delectable creature's sensuality – and her shame.'

The blanket was lowered from Anya's shivering body, and then removed completely. Aruline, no longer nervous, worked with calm confidence. She directed Anya to kneel up; she ignored her tears. She held up the rope tautly in front of her, looking at her and waiting. Anya did not know what the woman wanted. In the end, she held out her arms with her wrists pressed together. Aruline smiled, but shook her head. 'No, my dear,' she whispered, placing the rope upon the seat, 'though we find this gesture quite delicious . . .' Aruline turned; the Duke, by means of a nod, concurred. She lifted Anya's wrists and kissed the inner surfaces, drawing small wet circles with her tongue. The kisses sent shivers up Anya's arms; the shivers shook her breasts. Aruline pressed her moist lips to the tips. She did not suck; she pressed the wetness against each tip and then withdrew. A cool and shining circle now enveloped each gathering black-brown nipple. The Duke expressed approval; he reached to touch. Aruline pushed his hand away. The rope was taken up.

'Lift up, my darling, lift your arms.' The rope was passed around Anya's back, high up under her arms, then drawn round and crossed above her breasts, pulled tight, then released until it slipped, then immediately re-tightened, then by this means, the tightening and relaxation, the constriction inched over the outswell of her breasts, trapping the nipples, then pushing the breasts up as it slipped beneath them. Down her body it moved, compressing and releasing, until it squeezed a tight band round her lower back and belly. With the rope held firmly in this position, Aruline gently kissed her; the kissing, with the tightness there, made Anya feel aroused. Between the kisses, Aruline murmured something that Anya could not make out. The rope was uncrossed, but not removed completely. Keeping it pulled hard against Anya's back, Aruline said, 'Lift up higher.' She fed the ends down the front, between Anya's legs, to each side of her sex, round the back of each thigh, beneath the buttock, then round the front again. She pulled it to bed it into the creases of the thighs, then knotted it tightly below the belly, so the tassel hung down and tickled Anya's sex with its lips pulled slightly open by the pressure of the rope to either side.

At this point, the Duke required that Anya be made to spread her knees until she ached and to sit back on her heels, 'in the posture of a slave,' he said. He wished to look at her; he wished to see her intimate parts. The tassel was lifted to the side to afford him a better view. He was most interested in her blackness, and in the shortness of her hair. He questioned her very closely about these things; while Aruline's fingertips returned to Anya's body, to browse through the fine red sward, then to lift away while Aruline sniffed them, he took his kerchief, shook it out, wiped away the last of Anya's tears and asked about the shaving.

'It was a punishment,' Anya whispered, making the Duke's eyes light up. 'My lord required that my flesh be rendered smooth,' she explained, and a soft shudder rippled through her lower belly at the memories of the way that place had been laid so bare, then oiled by the cruel lord's hand, of the way her flesh had been so wickedly abused.

'Punishment, you say?' The Duke was very interested. 'You were not kept shaved, then, to emphasise your blackness?' Aruline pinned Anya's arms behind her to make her belly bow out tightly, then separated her flesh lips that he might examine her more closely.

'No, my lord.' She caught her breath as the woman's fingers pressed against her.

'I see. Now tell us about the punishment. Was your pleasure withheld?'

Suddenly she looked away; the fingertips began touching very lightly, releasing, then lifting Anya's flesh leaves open each time they gently closed. 'Were you smacked – for pleasure?' Anya closed her eyes. Her flesh contracted; those words had made her lower belly quaver. Aruline carefully opened her again then stroked the silky outer skin while the flesh lips slowly curled once more until they touched to form a purse. 'Open your eyes, my child, and look at me.' The Duke's face was very close again. Aruline's hand retreated to lie flat against Anya's inner thigh. And for the first time, it was the Duke who touched her; tapping her swollen pursed-together flesh lips from side to side was the ducal fingertip. 'Did they smack you? Did it bring you pleasure?' She looked away, in shame; she could not bear it; she felt hunted. How did he know about these things? How could he? Anya's hot and weighted purse of flesh came to rest against the finger. She tensed. The fingertip did not move. Those words, the memories they stirred, were

34

whirling round her mind. 'Answer. Did they smack you, and did that smacking bring you . . .'

At that instant, Anya felt her flesh contract away from the touching fingertip. 'Hmmm . . . So be it then.' The Duke sat back. 'Rub her, Aruline. Rub the surliness out of this flesh with the flat of your hand. We shall get to the bottom of this.'

And Aruline did; Anya could not escape the degradation, nor the pleasure of that intimate rub – Aruline's soft warm hand against Anya's even softer, warmer, slowly moistening flesh between her legs. The palm allowed no concession to her shape. It pressed against her firmly, so the flesh leaves doubled over to the side and then it slowly turned until they slipped with Anya's oilings. She felt dreadful, for her body kept responding. Aruline lifted up her chin and made her look into her eyes – those wicked, flashing eyes. As Aruline's hand rubbed slowly, Anya's flesh slipped and the leaves slowly separated until it was the inner warmth that was captured in Aruline's hand and the swelling bud, in its unsheathing, touched the base of Aruline's thumb. Anya's breathing changed; her pleasure was mounting. Aruline gently nipped the flesh lips back together, lifted her palm away and inhaled the aroma captured on her skin.

The Duke then examined the palm for traces of liquid, and having observed that such transgression had indeed occurred, instructed therefore that the offending legs be separated to the point where the muscles of the upper thighs were taut and hard, and the mound was pushed out visibly, with the sex lips directed down until they nearly touched the velvet. Then, with the slave disported in this fashion, she herself was made to separate the lips, not by touching them directly, but rather by pressing her fingers against the rope to either side, and simultaneously pushing down, so the split travelled very slowly up their length before they suddenly cleaved apart.

A small firm satin cushion could now be placed between the open lips, to maintain, by virtue of the body weight bearing down, an appropriate pressure there, and to keep the sex lips open while the Duke explored further the question of the smacking. The girl was made to look directly into his face, that he might judge, on the basis of her expression, both the accuracy of her answers and, more particularly, the efficacy of his questions in stimulating her to lewd and wanton notions. At critical points, the quick flick of a finger would be the signal for Aruline to stroke the heavy silken tassel of the rope upwards, always upwards, across the place where she held the hooding of the sex lips firmly back. For the Duke had found, by long experience, that this was the most effective way to question a girl, namely with her thighs spread wide, her flesh held open, and some instrument of pleasure tickling intermittently up across her nubbin.

'You were whipped?' His eyes had glinted when he asked this. It made Anya very much afraid.

'No. No, my lord,' she whispered, and yet the shiver in her belly was triggered. Again the tassel tickled.

'Then what? The strap, the cane? Speak up, now.' She bowed her head. The Duke directed that her head be lifted up, and he flicked his finger twice. 'Well?'

'The ss . . . A strap, my lord, sometimes.' The tassel brushed upwards to each side of Anya's flesh leaves, making her want to pull away. It now began to tap her, to tap very lightly at her tip.

'Ah-ah. Do not lift.' The Duke waved a reproving finger. 'Press down upon your cushion, my child. There. Open her more fully, Aruline.' So now, with Anya's flesh lips parted wide, her knees were edged further yet apart; the cushion pressed deep against the inner walls of her open sex and her flesh bud rested on the surface of the satin.

'Did you like the strap?'

'No!' She looked to Aruline for support. Aruline's eyes were deep pools of desire; Anya had to look away.

'I see . . .' Her tiny bud of pleasure moved; she felt it brush against the satin; she could not stop it. Had he noticed?

'What about bare hands?' he asked. Anya shuddered. 'Hmmm . . .' he said. His hand touched her belly, pressing flat against it above the rope, then pressed against her inner thighs; he was watching her expression as he did this. Did he know where they had smacked her? 'Answer . . .' She hated this; she hated what the stimulation was doing to her body. She tensed; she had nearly pushed her thigh against the hand; she wanted to move against the satin; that movement would be sweet . . .

'Yes, my lord, but . . .'

'Yes?' The hand rubbed against her thigh, then stopped, but the pressure was maintained. The thumbpad brushed against her open sex lip. 'But what?'

She did not want to tell him. He made her. The pressure of his hand and the brushing of his thumb there made her; she felt more ashamed than ever to have to admit this: 'But mainly, they used fingers.'

'Fingers?' The Duke seemed surprised, though the gentle rubbing took up again. 'I see. And where did these fingers smack you?'

She could not answer that; she could not bring herself to tell anyone of that degradation.

'Aruline . . . ?' The hood of Anya's flesh was drawn fully back; the tassel cascaded in a circle round the tip of her nubbin. Her breathing came stronger. 'Well, my dear?' The feeling was delicious; the tassel was now replaced by Aruline's moistened finger, tapping very lightly at the tip. Anya's belly cramped against the feelings she was trying to hold back. 'Stop!' Her nubbin pulsed. The Duke extended a finger and thumb and very softly closed those digits round it. His voice was now a murmur. 'Did they smack you in this place?' He squeezed very, very lightly; she gasped. He released the pulsing tip. 'I see . . . Have her turn round, Aruline.'

Anya was made to lift and turn, a move which she welcomed at first, for not only did it offer her nubbin some slight respite from the lightly tickling torture, but it meant she no longer had to look the Duke in the face. However, such security was short-lived, for the cushion was folded to make it tighter than before and was reapplied between her open squatting thighs. Now the cheeks of her bottom were spread apart while her interrogators examined her. They discussed their findings in terms which were brutally frank. She could feel the hot soft ducal hands upon her cheeks and the cool slim fingers in her crease, tickling and stroking there until her flesh contracted. Anya had never heard a lady use such words as Aruline did now, as she touched Anya in that very private place. 'Hmmm,' she finally heard the ominous murmur from behind.

More ominous still, though, was the knock at the carriage door. Anya tried to lift and to close her thighs, but the hot hands held her down. 'Remain in that position,' the Duke ordered. 'Did we instruct you otherwise? Keep your knees spread wide. Push out your bottom. Now, do not dare to move . . . Come in!'

It was the sergeant. He sounded out of breath: 'My lord, everything is ready for departure. The outriders –' He must have noticed Anya; she buried her face and covered it with her hands. 'The outriders are dispatched, sir.'

'Thank you, sergeant. But wait; you may perhaps assist us. This girl you brought us is a slave on the run.'

'A slave, sir?'

'Indeed. And this slave, sergeant, now desires to experience – at first hand – the technique you use so ably on the cage-girls. We are interested to know if it will, as we suspect, warm the slave to pleasure. Aruline, arrange her.'

And so, despite the fact that soldiers, scouts, wagoners and coachmen, cage-girls, too, were set for progress on their journey, departure was delayed once more, albeit for a very significant reason: that the Duke of Arrod, a man, it must be said, of comparatively gentle disposition, but driven now by a perverse desire which seemingly could not otherwise be assuaged, wanted the slave girl spanked with a good broad hand. Any pleasure which might accrue to the girl was quite incidental to the basic requirement that her buttocks be made to burn for his amusement.

The preparations, nevertheless, were precise. Aruline understood them much more fully than the Duke, and he left such matters to her. She gently lifted Anya's hips and eased the cushion from between them. She touched her, pressing her fingertips around the still-swollen bud of flesh to ensure it poked out firmly. She moistened it to make quite sure, then flicked it quickly, then rubbed it lightly in a circle until she heard the sudden catch of breath which was the signal to proceed.

'Hurry up, my dear,' the Duke chastised her gently.

'Shh . . . Always so impatient, always in a rush.' Aruline's philosophy was quite different from the Duke's. She therefore stroked again to produce a second gasp before Anya was made to stand on the seat, facing the wall, with her hands behind her head and her legs spread apart. Now the rope could be adjusted. The knot was pulled tighter, to increase the pressure along the sensitive lines at the very tops of the thighs; these adjustments were intended to enhance the girl's anticipation. The seat, being soft, of course made it difficult to balance. However, it was essential that the thighs remained relaxed. As the girl found out in due course, if her thighs were to tense at any stage, by accident or design, Aruline would step in and call a halt in the proceedings, which would need to begin again. The point of the relaxation was very simple. Aruline explained it as she laid her hand upon each cheek of the girl's bottom in turn and very gently shook it: 'These delicious mounds must remain soft, they must not tighten. They must welcome the smacks. They must not resist. We wish to see them shaking, very softly.' Aruline kissed their softness; the girl shivered; the cheeks shook. 'There . . .' Aruline murmured.

As a final aid to Anya's education in the art of muscle control, Aruline produced from her work basket a ball of silk about the size of a small apple, but perfectly round and smooth and very light indeed. It was placed between Anya's legs so it pressed against her open sex lips, which were carefully moulded round it, not fully, with the ball pushed inside, but partially, with the lips pressed flatly to it in such a way that it was held in place not by squeezing, which would simply force it out, but by the natural oiliness of the inner surface of the flesh which would, Aruline assured her, certainly be able to cling to such a lightweight object and

39

thereby keep it in position – provided of course that the buttocks were kept at all times soft, so the shock of the slapping was absorbed and not transmitted to dislodge it.

By contrast, the instruction to the sergeant was far less intricate: 'Smack her till I tell you to desist,' Aruline said simply.

With these requirements now spelled out, Aruline could relax beside the Duke, and slip a surreptitious hand into his breeches, and the punishment could begin.

As the first sharp stinging smack of broad hand on smooth round bottom cheek was sounded, the coachman up above turned round, for the sound had passed through the open window and echoed from the trees. As the second smack came, louder, accompanied by a softened murmur from below, his fingers tightened round the reins, for he had realised what that sudden sharp sound had been. The tension was mirrored in the carriage, too, in the tight and secret grip of Aruline's hand about the Duke's hot swollen stem, and in the greater tightness in the sergeant's breeches as his hand struck home once more against the softly shaking, gently reddening, warming, deliciously separated blue-bound mounds of that lusciously perfect body.

Yet against this pervasive tightness, Anya tried to keep relaxed. The first smack took her breath away; the second made her tighten, so the ball had almost separated from her flesh; at the third, she had to will her buttocks not to tense. Cool waves of anticipation descended her inner thighs; hot prickles kissed her bottom; each time a smack descended, and the cheek vibrated, the shake transmitted as a tickle in the crease. And though her bottom stung as hot as if burning flames were licking round it, her fleshpot burned with wanting, for all the time she was thinking of the girl, the girl with long brown hair. She was thinking about what must have happened to the girl after the sergeant had made her bottom burn this way. Would it happen next to her? She was imagining, too, the sergeant's broad strong hand no longer smacking across her cheeks but reaching underneath to dislodge the ball and close round her fleshpot, touching her as he had done when she lay across his steed. And she

40

was thinking of his thick cock penetrating the girl; she knew it would be thick and tight, for her fingers had been made to touch it when she was draped across the horse's shoulders. That thick tightness would fill her flesh; it would make her want to squeeze . . .

Then, on the next smack, Anya felt it, and with her legs apart, her hands behind her head, she could not stop it, the slow delicious downward pull against her inner flesh, followed by the coolness as the silken ball half separated, clinging to the right flesh leaf, then the open-legged pleasure tremor which shook the ball free from the sticky seal and dropped it between her ankles.

'One moment, sergeant, if you please,' Aruline murmured.

Face flushed, eyes vacant now, the sergeant stood aside while she unfastened the knot, tightened the rope, followed the line with two fingertips in the creases of the thigh, picked up the ball and then reached between Anya's legs and made her stand on tiptoes while she reapplied it from behind.

Anya felt the sinking feeling in between her thighs as her flesh leaves, soft and moist and thin now, were spread back and a finger dipped inside then stroked about the inner pink to coat it with her seepage. Then the flesh hood was drawn back; a fingernail was lightly scratched across the wet and polished nubskin till she jumped, whereupon the fingertips patted the nubbin gently before the ball was placed against her, pressed, and the flesh lips drawn around it. Aruline carefully wet her fingers, sealed the joining with her own saliva, then wet the tips of Anya's nipples before allowing her to lower her ankles and the slapping was resumed.

As Anya's bottom burned with rapid smacks that seemed fiercer than before, the moisture slowly evaporated from her skin, keeping her nipples very cool and sending sticky tickles across the surface of her sex lips as the spittle mixed with seepage slowly dried. Despite these conflicting signals – the heat, cold shivers, the creeping stickiness and cool caresses which Anya's buttocks, her thighs, her belly and nipples underwent, and the lewd thoughts which tantalised her mind – the silk ball lay gripped successfully now in the delicately balanced cup. So impressed was Aruline that she set aside once more the throbbing ducal stem whose exudations she had been spreading lightly round the cap. She instructed the sergeant to desist, temporarily, while she pressed her palms, then the cool backs of her fingers to the bright red cheeks of Anya's bottom, to imbibe that special warmth; then having instructed Anya to retain the ball in place, she carefully moved her ankles further yet apart then directed two fingers of one hand in turn to the very sensitive facing surfaces of the cheeks, close against the mouth, and stroked them in a circle until the feeling that the stroking should encompass the mouth itself came on so strongly that Anya had to push. She felt her flesh leaves slip against the ball.

'Shh . . .' Aruline's voice was very soft and Anya could not help but tense as she heard at first the sound of sucking, then the two fingers, very wet now with saliva, were slowly pushed into her bottom. And though she gasped, she somehow managed not to tighten. 'Very good,' Aruline whispered. 'Now, up on your toes. There. Now doesn't that feel good?' The fingers opened out inside her; when they pressed against the inner walls on opposing sides, Anya groaned and shuddered; the ball squeezed out and dropped on the seat.

'Oh, what a shame,' Aruline said, withdrawing her fingers very gently and patting Anya on the bottom. 'But what do you think, sergeant?'

'I . . . Er . . .' The sergeant seemingly could not gather his thoughts.

'I see. My lord?'

The Duke could only choke and gurgle.

'Indeed. I agree – a lesson learned well is a lesson learned forever. She will need to get it right.' Anya's belly quaked. 'We can perhaps continue the treatment another day?' The fingers stroked her gently in the groove, touching the tiny mouth, making it pulse. 'Mmm . . .' she mused. 'So sensitive. Next time, we must make her hold these delicious cheeks apart.' Anya turned deep crimson. 'But now I think a more gentle relaxation might be called for. Kneel down, my pet.'

The sergeant was now dismissed, with the instruction for departure. Anya heard the shouts, then the crack of the coachman's whip, and the carriage jerked and swayed into a steady rolling motion. While the Duke sat back, sometimes dozing, sometimes bestowing his full attention, Aruline played with Anya for the rest of the afternoon.

She began by untying the rope. 'So hot,' she whispered, pressing her fingers against her, 'your skin here feels so hot,' as if she seemed surprised. Anya felt less anxious now that the rope had been removed. Aruline selected a small bottle and swab with which to refresh Anya. She was made to turn and kneel up facing Aruline, who knelt upon the carpet, dabbing Anya between the legs. The rope lay loosely on the seat. 'Mmm. You smell so good.' Aruline suddenly craned her long slim neck, pouted her lips and sucked Anya on the nipples. 'You taste so lovely, too.' Aruline's slim tongue formed a tube around the nipple. Her fingers, on the seat, curled up to stroke the dangling flesh leaves. She lifted the breasts and weighed them in her fingers, let them slide, then stroked up to the tips. She dipped into her workbox, removed a broad silk ribbon and passed it beneath Anya's breasts to capture the downswell in a sling which she crossed then fastened up behind Anya's neck, so the breasts were pressed together and the nipples pointed upwards. She kissed Anya, whose nipples gently brushed against the material of her dress. Her tongue slipped into Anya's mouth; her fingers tantalised her sex, coaxing the flesh leaves open, tickling the feather edges, then slipping up inside her, taking Anya's breath away.

'Delicious slave,' Aruline murmured. She sat back and looked at Anya before removing from the box a length of silk embroidery thread. She formed the end into a loop about the size of a fingertip, then wet the loop and slipped it over Anya's right nipple. The wetness kept the loop in place while Aruline carefully sucked the nipple until it swelled and hurt. The ends of the loop were slowly tightened while the sucking was maintained until the nipple was necked by the silk constriction and swelled out above it like a polished ripe red-brown berry. The silk was quickly wound round the neck for three turns, as if it were a button, then deftly knotted in position and the thread was cut. The fingers stroked between her legs again. Another loop was constructed from the length of thread, wetted, then the deep sucking performed and the loop was closed about the left nipple. Aruline gently squeezed the swollen tips.

Anya was now made to lie across Aruline's knee. She was very afraid to do this, for the rope was placed there first. It lay beneath her belly, but the end was taken up between her legs and laid loosely across the back of her thigh. Aruline kept moving it so it tickled Anya's skin while she played with her. 'Your body must be very moist,' she said, but she did not say why. She reached beneath to play with Anya's nipples, pulling and stretching them, turning them between her fingertips. She held one nipple while she touched her between the legs; she spent much time rubbing the flesh lips together and squeezing the nubbin, and pressing her fingers to the creases of the thigh. She made Anya spread, that the skin of the creases would tighten and the tickling would be enhanced. When Anya's hips began to move, she pinched the mouth of Anya's bottom, very softly and repeatedly, asking as she did so if she liked it. Anya did not wish to admit such things in front of the Duke, but that style of touching, in her outspread state, made her feel excited. Aruline seemed to know it; she stroked the inner faces of cheeks whilst she pinched her more lightly yet; she brushed the tassel of the rope within the groove; then the stroking and the pinching were transferred beneath, to the nubbin. When Anya tensed, two of Aruline's fingers held her fleshpot open and unmoving while a third one held the flesh hood firmly back until gradually the tension ebbed. The sex lips were resealed.

Anya was turned on her side and made to hold her leg up while Aruline rubbed her belly, rubbed the creases of her thighs, rubbed the outer skin of Anya's flesh leaves, working ever closer to the palpitating nubbin sealed within, until the sudden intake of breath signalled that the rope should be applied. Aruline carefully fitted it to the uppermost crease of Anya's thigh, then with one hand

44

round the back, the other at the front, gripping firmly, the tension was increased. The pressure of the rope there caused the leaves to split; the nubbin pulsed its lewdness now for all to see. Aruline lifted the rope across and applied it to the split, making Anya groan as the plaited silk touched against her tip.

'Shhhhh . . .' As Anya felt the urge to buck, Aruline used the rope to slow her. She increased the tension while she bent across Anya, kissing her, licking her lips, dripping spittle in her mouth, until the imminence of pleasure turned to a slowly bursting pain. When Anya sucked the tongue and moaned against the lips that softly kissed her, the pressure was released; the rope was laid loosely across her thigh again, and the slow massage resumed. In ways such as this, the tantalising and the squeezing till the sweet pulsations came, then the application of the tight blue silken pressure, Aruline played with Anya until a slowly welling slick lay across her lower thigh.

The rope was eased from beneath her. It was laid along her belly, folded in half, then into quarters. Aruline smiled at Anya; it made her apprehensive. She turned her on her side again so she faced the Duke and made her hold her legs apart. The rope was lifted up and slowly twisted until it formed a firm yet flexible hank. Anya's belly sank and sank as Aruline carefully opened her liquid flesh leaves and introduced the hank, slowly twisting it as she did so, so it slid inside. It filled her before a half of it had been inserted; it made her flesh feel hard and tight. Her flesh leaves had been drawn in with it. Aruline teased them out, massaged her, rubbing slowly round the mound, pressing her thighs apart, then placing her hand against her belly while she twisted once again. The Duke now reached to touch Anya; Aruline firmly moved his hand away. Anya tightened; Aruline pressed and twisted; the rope slipped further in.

Aruline encouraged Anya, murmuring softly, sucking gently on her burning earlobe, kissing the back of her neck, squeezing her bursting nipples. 'Push, my sweet,' she whispered; again she gripped the rope and twisted. Anya felt it turn inside; it made her belly ripple. Aruline wet her fingers, that she might touch her where her fleshpot gripped the rope, and caress the hard tight nubbin. Anya knew her flesh could take no more, yet Aruline reassured her. She pushed the tips of her fingers into Anya's belly, low down above her mound, and her belly yielded to the touch. 'You see,' Aruline murmured, 'this belly is so soft. We must make it smooth and hard.'

She made Anya turn over and kneel with her head down and her hips in the air. 'It will be easier this way,' she said. She stroked her thighs, massaged the belly from beneath, pulled the flesh leaves gently, then pressed her thumb between Anya's fleshpot and her bottom and rubbed. With this constant attention, the tightened flesh was rendered supple, the rope was fully introduced, the flesh leaves closed about it and the tassel dangled down. Anya's lower belly was a hard tight ball; the rope inside was pressed against her womb; the flesh about her nubbin was drawn back very sharply. Aruline wet her fingers again and stroked this flesh slowly and deliberately, commenting to the Duke, 'She is so delicious; she how hard she is, and wet too; feel her heat.'

And as Anya squirmed and tried so hard to hold back her pleasure against this persistent stimulation, two sets of fingers touched her between the legs and buttocks, the one set touching her flesh leaves, collecting up her oil and painting it round the nubbin, closing round the tassel and pulling it until she moaned, the other fingers stroking her back and thighs but returning repeatedly to explore the crease, to squeeze the velvet mouth, to rub round it in a circle and to slip the fingertip inside. They turned her on her side, that Aruline might kiss her breasts and belly while the Duke's firm hand closed about the tassel, took the strain and pulled. Anya's flesh became so excited that the touching of her nubbin had to be withheld; when Aruline held her flesh leaves wide apart, her nubbin pulsed; Aruline licked the seepage from the outer surfaces of the leaves, and stroked her tongue-tip up and down the creases; she dared not touch the tip.

The Duke suddenly became uncontrollably excited. Aruline had to intervene. Anya was turned over onto her other

46

side, so she faced the back of the seat. Her knees were drawn up tightly so her fleshpot still protruded. And while her flesh was held in abeyance with the tightly balled rope within her cramping belly, the tassel hanging down to tickle her in between the legs, her nubbin swollen up with unremitting wanting and her body slowly seeping across the back of her thigh, she was forced to listen – to the sounds of mutual pleasuring on the seat behind her, the soft, deep groans, the wicked giggles, sounds of wetness and of sucking, the murmurs, gasps and then at last the cries of pleasurable deliverance. Then when she thought that all was finished, it started up again; this time the sounds of joy were more subdued, and were mixed with furtive touchings of her back and thighs and in between her buttocks. At one point, a tongue had licked the wetness from her thigh.

Finally, Aruline appeared above her, very short of breath. She turned Anya on her back and made her hold her thighs apart. She kissed her deeply. Aruline's tongue tasted strange and salty. Her fingers stroked Anya's nubbin, drawing it to a finely pointed tip, an arrow, a shivering piercing arrow of delicious pleasure being honed between those soft wet fingers to an ever finer tip.

'Have her make the declaration.' The Duke's voice had come from nowhere. Aruline's fingertips did not release her, but she placed her lips very close to Anya's ear, so her whisper tickled: 'Tell us what you are,' she said.

Anya felt as if her body was drifting in a soft and oily sea; it was like a dream. 'But I am Anya,' she replied.

'You are a slave; your body tells us this. Admit you are a slave to love; your flesh is slave to pleasure.' The gentle fingers touched her. Anya groaned against the tongue that tried to wrap around her own and she pushed her belly up to meet the long wet fingertips. Suddenly, the tongue and fingertips were gone. Her nubbin throbbed with cruel wanting. 'Admit you are a slave.'

Aruline dipped her fingertip into her mouth and withdrew a drop of spittle. The warm thick spittle touched the tip of Anya's nubbin. Her belly bucked. 'Shh . . . Tell me.' The hand brushed against her flesh leaves as it closed round

47

the tassel, and pulled. Anya resisted; her nubbin felt as if it was being pushed out from her body. Aruline's fingertips kissed it very softly. 'Tell me . . .'

Anya's mouth was open; she could not breathe; she could only strain to meet the touch that moved away.

'I . . .' The rope slipped. She moaned.

'Yes – tell me.' The pupils of Aruline's eyes were wide; they filled Anya's vision. The rope slipped once again. The pleasure was exquisite.

Anya swallowed. 'I am a slave . . . to love,' she murmured, and even as the words were uttered, the deep drawing feeling came in her belly, the feeling of submission. Aruline smiled. The rope slid steadily now, against the luscious spasms of tightness in Anya's sex; the wetness was drawn out and up across her pulsing nubbin, up her belly to her breasts. It lay in warm wet coils upon her body. The air was heavy with the scent of Anya's inner warmth. Aruline breathed it deeply. She touched the nubbin one last time, very, very gently so as not to bring the pleasure on, then rearranged the flesh leaves neatly, removed the rope, slick with honeydew, and held it to her cheek.

She removed the satin band from round Anya's breasts, but left the silk thread wrapped around her nipples. The Duke requested that Anya sit up. She felt so hot and so ashamed that she had let these people do these things to her. But more than that, she was afraid, about the consequences of her terrible admission.

'Do not fear,' he said, 'we shall not return you to the castle. We wish only to help you, and protect you. But there is one point we must clear up. You were heading for Surdia. Why?'

Anya looked nonplussed. 'My lord?' She did not know of such a place.

The Duke sounded less patient. 'You were headed south. The province to the south is Surdia.'

'I did not know this, my lord,' she replied.

His lordship now looked pleased. His expression was more fatherly: 'Then perhaps you did not know, my dear, that you were running into danger?' His eyebrows lifted.

'Danger?' Anya became anxious, for this must mean her Prince was in danger too; she had feared this all along, but this was the first time anyone had said it outright.

'Indeed. The Surdic people are grown restless. Even now, your own Prince –' Anya flinched, for she suddenly thought she was discovered – 'is trying to intervene to calm the situation.' He shook his head. 'These are dangerous times, my dear.' He bowed his head then lifted his eyebrows and looked up at her. 'And the forest is a treacherous place for a young girl. There are bandits.' His hand wavered, then came to rest upon her knee. 'You are very fortunate, my child, to fall under our protection.' The fingers ventured up her thigh until Aruline intervened by whispering something in the Duke's ear. He frowned at Aruline; she smiled; he grunted, then reluctantly removed his hand from Anya's leg and banged his fist twice upon the side of the coach.

The coach slowed, then stopped. The coachman appeared. 'Bring her clothes; look after her,' declared the Duke. 'Feed her well. Place her with the others.' His finger came up sternly. 'Nobody shall touch her.' Then he smiled at Anya, who could only look away. 'We will resume our conversation on the morrow, my dear. It has been a pleasure talking to you. Aruline will then instruct you further in our ways.'

'My lord,' said Aruline, 'she will surely need this?'

'Ah, yes. I had forgotten.'

Aruline took the rope, still moist with Anya's seepage, and made her turn while she fastened it once round her waist then drew the end down her belly, between her thighs and up between her buttocks. She checked that Anya's flesh lips were fully separated by the plaited silk before knotting it at the back. 'In time, as she moves her limbs, this tether may unbrace,' she explained to the coachman. 'Instruct the guard to check her, to tighten this bond within her parting, but beyond this, not to interfere.' Aruline's fingers stroked the flesh leaves where they closed about the binding. When Anya was turned again, and Aruline lifted her chin and stared at Anya fixedly, Anya felt afraid.

'The seal, my dear, shall remain unbroken. Do not let me

49

down.' The voice fell to a whisper: 'The pressure shall be maintained, throughout the night, at least. It will prepare you. Then tomorrow, this delicious flesh will come the more readily to hand.' The fingers curled and closed about Anya's sex, to impart a soft fingertip squeezing. 'I will be thinking of you,' the woman sighed. 'How could I do otherwise?' She bent to kiss her, and Anya's belly liquefied.

[4]

In the Cage

At last, the night was coming. Anya clasped her hands around the smoothly carved wooden bars and looked out at the long red reflection of the setting sun upon the lake. She sniffed, even though the air was warm, for her eyes were smarting. Then she glanced round at the others once more before her gaze returned to the water. She found its stillness reassuring. They would not make her cry. She wanted to, but she would not let them see her tears. She kept her tears inside. And though her clothes had been returned, and her heart had leapt to find the lodestone still inside her pocket, and she was touching it now, the lodestone was not working. She closed her fist around it and squeezed, trying to squeeze her sadness and her pain down to a tiny point and make it disappear, but it would not work. The stone's heat burned through her palm, but it was not a heat that warmed her. It was a heat that reminded her of her failure in her purpose; it told her that her Prince was still very far away; it sent soft shivers of sadness up her arm and across her shoulders, making her feel chill.

Her nipples throbbed on account of the silken thread wound round them; she did not dare remove it. Then there was the ever-present pressure of the rope between her legs; even when she kept very still, she could feel it. If she spread her thighs it rubbed against her pushed-out bud and made it burn; if she closed them tight, her flesh lips throbbed hot against its dampness. It was a constant reminder of the way her desire had been evoked but the stimulation had been cut short before the moment of release. At the time, she did not care; she had been glad to get away from Aruline and the Duke. But they had promised her more tomorrow; she

51

knew she could never bear the torture of denial all over again. She released the stone, wrapped her arms about herself and curled up in the corner of the cage. The sunlight, reflecting up from the surface of the lake against the white ceiling of the cage, cast a deep pink glow around her. It turned to golden yellow as the campfire grew stronger and the guard walked round outside the cage, lighting the torches one by one. Within the cage now everything was bright. Anya wanted it dark. She did not wish to look upon these spiteful women.

That afternoon, when she had been put into the cage, the coachman, who kept glancing at one of the cage-girls and winking while he spoke, had told the guard: 'The Duke instructs that this one must be kept reserved.' He had lifted her skirt to show him the blue silk rope. 'She is not to be used by the men.' Anya had not been paying full attention, for at the time, she was looking at an upright post which was being erected near to the cage. She wondered what this post was for. But she realised later that by saying this out loud, the coachman had marked her out as different. This was why the others did not like her, why they ignored or taunted her.

When the meal – a thick strip of smoked meat, rough dry bread and a bowl of boarshead soup, which had lumps of jelly in it and tasted quite disgusting – had been served, a short girl, with hair the colour of pale straw, who had scowled at Anya from the start, had deliberately knocked her arm and made her spill her soup. Anya hadn't wanted it anyway, but the others had laughed at her. Then later, when all were led out to be bathed at an inlet of the lake, this blonde girl – Riga, one of the others had called her – together with her friend, the one who had been making eyes at the coachman, had tried to pull Anya under the freezing water. The guard had intervened to stop the horseplay, as they called it, but Anya knew it was no game: the two of them had been trying to drown her. She had dried off by the fire beside the cage, the guard had given her wine to drink and that had made her feel better for a while. But again she had found her gaze returning to the post. There were two short horizontal bars at the top, and the middle of the stem

52

was smooth. She had wanted to ask someone about it, but there was nobody she could talk to.

Before returning her to the cage, the guard had made her stand and hold her skirt up while he tightened the rope. It felt cold and wet against her. And now she was back with the others, those who were still left. Already, one girl had been taken for the Duke. Another two had been led off to the soldiers' camp, to entertain them by the great fire. Anya could hear the laughter and the intermittent screams.

As the rope dried, it slowly tightened, making her feel itchy. She wanted to ease the cruel pressure from the parting of her sex, but she was too afraid to do so. She kept thinking about Aruline's warning; she kept thinking about the post.

The cage door opened. A soldier, tunic half unbuttoned, a wine jug in his hand, swayed about on the wooden steps outside. He looked dirty and unkempt. As he stared vacantly at the five faces turned in his direction, the guard informed him: 'Any one, soldier. Any one at all.' Riga stood her ground, her short hair almost bristling, but Anya backed away. She felt very frightened, for the soldier's eyes had fixed, insofar as they were able to do so, upon herself. 'Except that one,' the guard said apologetically. Anya took a deep breath. Riga scowled at her. The soldier began protesting. The guard consoled him, patting him on the back. 'Well, maybe in a day or two – but not yet.' Anya felt afraid again. The soldier chose a second time. 'Ah . . . No, not that one either.' He had picked the girl with long brown hair. She was the only one who hadn't been hateful to Anya; she had kept apart from the others and had not even spoken.

'But you said –' The soldier was now insisting on his rights.

The guard shook his head slowly, 'No.' He pursed his lips, then shrugged as if he were hamstrung in this matter. 'Unfortunately, she's reserved.' The sloven protested loudly at this restriction of his choice. The guard became engaging. He put his arm about the customer's shoulder: 'Take one of the other three – they're all good wenches. I can vouch for them myself. How about the blonde – she's very sweet.' The guard tucked his tongue into his cheek. Anya looked at Riga, whose hands were at her hips. She had been glowering at the guard and now she spat upon the floor, restricting the choice by yet one more. Riga retreated to sit astride a stool beside her friend, who began stroking Riga's hair. Anya noticed that the friend's arm had something wound round it in a crisscross pattern.

The soldier chose a quiet one with short dark hair who had been sitting in the far corner. Anya watched as the girl climbed out then stood before the fire, but on the side away from the post, as if deliberately avoiding it. The soldier, swaying wildly, waited. Very slowly, the girl gathered up her skirts around her waist. Her thighs and buttocks were bathed in firelight. As she turned, tucking in the last of the material, she was silhouetted. The firelight licked around to kiss her belly and licked beneath her parted thighs. The vision of the girl exposing herself this way forced a peculiar feeling deep in Anya's belly as if she too had felt the warm kiss of the firelight there. She glanced around at the others; even Riga watched intently.

Then, with the girl's skirts still lifted up, the soldier's arm around her waist and the girl supporting him, they staggered off into the night. Anya was imagining what it might be like if she were made to do this, to expose herself in front of a stranger, in full view of these other women. Her fingers clutched the bars; she shivered at the image in her mind; the shiver cascaded up the skin of each inner thigh, as if cool hands had stroked there, very lightly. She turned and looked at Riga, for she was anxious now about what might happen if the other two were taken out and she was left alone with Riga, who kept looking at Anya as if she hated her. She never stopped looking at her. Why did she look at her that way when Anya had done nothing at all to hurt her? Why did she want to pick on her?

Another noise came from outside. Anya recognised the figure well even before he reached the wagon. So did the brown-haired girl; she had turned and closed her fists about the bars. It was the sergeant. The gate opened. He did not speak to the girl, but stared at Anya. He placed a hand upon the bars close by and Anya retreated from that hand. Then with a crooked finger, he merely beckoned to the girl while he addressed the guard:

'All quiet, guard?'

'Aye, all quiet,' the guard replied. 'I doubt we'll see trouble tonight – too still, too clear for bandits.' He pointed towards the rising yellow moon. No sooner had he said this than the stillness of the night was interrupted by an eerie sound – a hoot drifted down towards them from the upslope stand of birch trees. The sergeant's head shot round, then suddenly turned back again: the call seemed to have echoed from the lake side. 'Only owls,' the guard reassured him, but the sergeant seemed unnerved.

Anya looked out across the lake, to the blackness of the distant trees; if there was a legion out there, how could anybody know it? And if bandits were to come, and break into the cage and take her, how could that be any worse than her present plight?

The girl, who had waited patiently with eyes downcast until the men had finished talking, was taken by the arm and led down the steps, leaving only three in the cage now. Again the gesture was made. Anya watched the body, a smoother, more beautiful body this time, being outlined in silhouette against the flames as the dress was lifted high. While the sergeant stood with folded arms, she turned to the side. Some command was uttered. Her dress was lifted up to the level of her shoulders; her feet were planted wide apart. The sergeant stepped forward. Anya watched his broad hands outstretch, then press against her, front and back, rubbing up her belly, sliding over her breasts, making them shake, and gliding over the surface of her thighs and bottom, then entering the crease.

Anya jumped. Riga had left her companion and was beside her. Anya's heart was beating very fast. As the sergeant led the girl off towards the great fire, and the quick smacks began to echo and the cage-guard laughed, Riga took Anya by the hair, slowly forcing her head back and down until she was looking into her eyes.

Why did Anya not fight back? When the hand, the short small fingers, pushed down her jacket, why did she not

55

protest? Why did she let the fingers close about her nipples, still imprisoned by the silk, and hold them while they swelled to pain?

She was afraid. She did not want to fight her; she preferred this treatment to the taunts. Riga took her arm and led her to a mattress in the corner, on the side of the cage away from the fire. She sat beside her. The friend stood across from them, watching impassively. Anya looked towards the guard for help. But he had noticed nothing; he had drifted away and was settling down with a jug beside the fire. Only his head was visible. He stared into the flames and took a swig. Anya could have called out; one cry would have been sufficient, but then what would the two of them have done to her later, when the guard was out of sight?

Riga had her arm around her now. She seemed inquisitive. She asked her name. Again she touched Anya's breasts; she began picking at the silk. It made Anya doubly afraid, as she remembered Aruline's warning. But she was too scared to move the intruding hand away. It moved down; Riga lifted Anya's skirt and examined the rope with interest. The other girl came over. She didn't speak, but she watched very carefully. As Riga parted Anya's thighs, it triggered butterflies deep inside. The fingers hooked beneath the rope, where it ran down across Anya's belly, and lifted it so it impressed into the join more tightly. 'Why do you wear this?' Riga asked. 'Is it to warn the soldiers off?' Her fingers kept touching, probing, opening the flesh leaves out, examining the silk, then closing them back around it. 'The lady – does she make you come with this upon your body?' Anya didn't reply. But she knew now that this treatment to which Aruline had subjected her was unfamiliar to these women; it made her wonder if such cruel games were reserved only for herself, because she was a slave; it made her fearful of what greater degradations might be held in store for her for tomorrow.

There was a sound from behind them, on the side of the cage towards the lake. Anya panicked and almost cried out; Riga clapped a hand over her mouth and held her. When the figure appeared, it was the coachman; Anya couldn't understand why he needed to approach the cage in secret. Then she remembered the way, that afternoon, he had kept throwing knowing glances at Riga's friend. He whispered something to her now; she looked furtively out the other way, evidently checking on the guard, then ran across and helped him up. He gave her something; when she held it up to the light, it glinted; it looked like a ring. She put it quickly into her pocket, then took his hands. They began kissing through the bars.

Riga put a finger to her lips, then removed her hand from Anya's mouth. 'Shh,' she whispered, 'the guard must not get to know.' She sounded very serious. Anya looked again at the couple. The caresses were more passionate; the coachman's clothing was being unbuttoned. 'It is all right,' said Riga, 'Shira knows what she is doing. She has many visits from the coachman; he brings her many presents. See – Shira gave this to me.' Riga proudly held her arm up to show off a small gold chain fastened round her wrist. Anya's heart missed a beat at the sight of that, for though it was much smaller and finer, it reminded her of the symbols of her slavery, the gold chains she had been made to wear in the castle, the chains she had thought she had cast aside. But now, as she looked above Riga's head and saw the bars, it seemed she was still a slave, and the chain about her waist had simply been replaced by a blue silk rope, whose tightness caused her greater torment than her chains had ever done.

When she looked up again, Riga was staring at her closely. Anya felt very sad, but was less afraid now. She did not flinch when the girl began lifting her hair from her face and neck, touching her cheeks and chin, and her eyebrows, then easing her jacket back from her shoulders so she could touch her freckled skin. The touch was so open and so childlike that she did not mind it. As she watched Riga now, Anya began to see that there was much innocence in this girl she had thought so harsh.

Riga's hair was short and stiff; her eyelashes were pale and her skin appeared deeply sunbrowned. In this light, Anya could not see the true colour of her eyes, but she had seen that afternoon that Riga's eyes were violet. She had short and pointed fingers, and she kept pressing the point of her forefinger against the freckles on Anya's shoulders. Besides her chain, Riga wore earrings, very tiny gold ones, but unlike the chain, these were no recent acquisition. They were far too small now for her earlobes; they must have been fitted when she was much younger, without ever being removed, so the earlobes had expanded until the rings rested now in fine grooves impressed across their edges. It made Anya want to cut the rings, to prise them open and release the imprisoned lobes. She touched the right lobe, rubbing gently, before she even realised what she was doing, then quickly withdrew, for now she felt embarrassed. The ring had not moved, but Riga was looking at her even more intently.

She took hold of Anya's slender fingers, stretched them out and compared them with her own. She kissed their tips, then suddenly closed her eyes and slipped Anya's hand beneath her top. Anya's fingers were reluctant. The calfskin halter round the girl's small breasts felt soft. Riga pushed Anya's fingers underneath. Her skin felt very warm; it was covered with a fine, soft down. Riga turned and kissed Anya; as she did so, her breasts brushed against Anya's fingertips. Again the down was present. Though the breasts were small, the nipples felt thick and hot. The girl unfastened her halter, so her breasts were free for Anya now to stroke. Anya did not really want to do it; she felt uncomfortable; she had gone too far already. She looked over her shoulder, but the other two were oblivious. Riga's eyes were closed again; she was leaning back and resting on her arms. Anya's fingers roamed to the side and stroked beneath Riga's arms, touching the thick curls lightly. It was a very curious feeling, touching someone so intimately, like this, someone who a very short time ago had grasped her hair so cruelly. She wanted the girl to touch her, too, to lift her breasts, to touch the nipples, to unwind the silken thread and kiss, but the girl had gone very limp and compliant, allowing Anya to do all the touching, not touching Anya in return, as if aware now only of her own needs.

The loving sounds across the way had turned to sounds of lust. There was a sudden intake of breath as the coachman's cock was pushed between the bars. Anya stopped what she was doing. The man's arms were stretched out horizontally, grasping the bars to either side. The girl, Shira, was kneeling before him, working him with the fingers of both hands. Anya could see clearly now that both of Shira's arms had the crisscross pattern of leather twine wound round them from her wrists to her elbows. The coachman began to moan; a gentle thrusting action was imparted to his cockstem. Shira's tongue licked out to tantalise him as he thrust.

Riga stretched back until she leaned against the bars. The flickering glow of torchlight caught her belly, making her skin appear clothed in a golden down. Anya looked at Riga's face, at her parted lips. She realised now how young the girl must be. When she touched Riga's belly, it shivered. She touched the buckle of the belt; the belly tensed. This seemed a very different girl from the one who, this afternoon, had seemed so hard and hateful. All she appeared to want now was this physical contact.

Suddenly, Anya felt very confident; she also felt excited. It was the same kind of feeling, that delicious feeling, she had experienced when she had explored the Prince's body for the first time, all that while ago. Touching the girl in this way, when her eyes were closed, her breathing shallow, her halter top awry – when she had placed her pleasure so fully in Anya's hands – aroused Anya too; it stirred those liquid feelings in between her thighs. She would bring the girl to gasping pleasure. She would seduce her with this act of love. In the castle, Anya had learnt many things, many ways of love; she had endured many cruel stimulations, but now she would use only the ways of love. The girl would never have cause to taunt her again.

Anya felt emboldened also by the shameless abandon along the cage, though she could not understand how Shira could behave this way in public. The coachman's breeches were dropped, then kicked to the ground and Shira began to suck his cock very fully, in slow upstrokes and hard downstrokes which swallowed him completely. She held him thus whilst her fingertips tickled his belly, then she reached down to lift the bag and venture underneath. As she sucked and tickled and probed, the coachman's thighs tensed, his buttocks edged back as his cock slipped out in an effort to control the pleasure. Shira's lips tried to follow, until they were pouted out and closed about the cap. When the gasps came hard and deep, the girl withdrew her lips and held the cockstem tightly round the base with her right hand. With the left she slowly unbuttoned her top to expose her breasts, which had upturned, elongate nipples.

The coachman groaned before she even touched him with those tips. She released the cock and removed her top completely. Then she took the cock and again squeezed it very near the base. It swelled up very hard. She knelt closer, wetted the underside with her tongue, then pinched her nipple up hard before stroking it up the cock's length, to the tip. The cock was carefully angled down while the man rose up on tiptoes, whereupon Shira squeezed the end to spread the mouth, then forced the nipple in. Keeping his cockstem sleeved about her nipple, she worked him, collaring the cockhead with a rapidly vibrating finger and thumb, squeezing her teat to a hard stiff tip which the cockhead sucked upon. When the nipple was withdrawn, a long thin thread of liquid followed, glowing orange with reflected torchlight.

Neither Anya nor Riga had moved as this spectacle unfolded. Riga's eyes were open; she had remained slumped against the bars. Her breathing was quicker and shallower than before and the golden down upon her skin appeared to shimmer. Anya readjusted the open halter until it touched the sides of the breasts but left the nipples and undersides free. Then she unbuckled the thick leather belt and she opened it out on the mattress. The short leather skirt was a single piece fastened with a clasp at the side. She undid the clasp; the belly trembled; she folded back the skirt. Riga had to lift her hips before the skirt could be removed completely and her belly stood revealed. Again the golden down was present; it became denser, yet seemed to pale, towards the joining of her small slim thighs. The curls were fine and pressed flat to the skin. As Anya's fingers were laid on the surface of her belly, Riga murmured. A noise behind Anya made both women turn, but Anya did not stop her fingers stroking the fine down upon the tightening skin, and Riga began arching, spreading, moving back, encouraging Anya's fingertips to slide lower.

As Anya and Riga watched, and Anya's fingers now touched the curls impressed against the mound as she slid her nails beneath to lift the tight soft locks then caressed the flesh beneath, making Riga shudder, Shira brought across the low stool. Placing it before the man, she spread her thighs and sat astride it. She raised her chin and adjusted her position. Then she began to rock, very smoothly, keeping her legs apart, arching slightly, bending forwards, seemingly to bed her body to the seat. The cockstem twitched. With each twitch, it appeared to curve up stronger than before. The girl waited until the tip was twitching underneath her nose, then she extended her right forearm. She pulled the knot at the end of the thong fastened at her elbow and unwound the thong half way down, then paused, looking up at the man, who was breathing very loudly, before she lowered her head until the cap of his cockstem disappeared within her mouth. She did not move her head at all. She simply held him this way, with her lips pushed down over him, while she continued to unwind the thong. It detached completely from the leather wristband. She lifted her head, then whispered to the man. When he hesitated, she trailed the thong loosely around his stem for a turn or two and pulled; his cockstem was drawn through the bars until the thong slipped off him. She fastened one end of the thong around the adjacent bar then gathered up the cockstem and the bag, pulling them firmly through, whilst she wound the thong tightly round the base of the cock and beneath the bag and secured the loose end to the bar on the other side. The coachman was now trussed up so he could not move.

Shira played with him, stroking the undersurface of the stem, then wetting her fingers and rubbing, then making a tight ring with forefinger and thumb and repeatedly sliding it over him until it jammed against the outswell of the plum. She moved his legs apart. Being fastened, he had to lift up on tiptoes to ease the cutting pressure of the thong beneath his bag. Shira rewetted two fingers and reached underneath. The coachman moved up higher on his toes. Shira's wrist twisted slowly from side to side as the fingers penetrated. Her other hand closed around his plum, sliding very slowly, leaving the cap exposed for her tongue to lick round the tip at intervals. The coachman's belly was tense; he moved unwillingly against the bindings, catching his breath in protest as he did so. But his protests were ignored; the fingers continued to urge him gently from inside.

Riga became restless. She opened her thighs; she moved Anya's hand more definitely between them; her flesh lips felt hot, very hot and sticky. While Riga spread her knees wider and pushed her belly out, Anya teased the curls one by one away from Riga's sticky heat, and then she touched her bottom. She allowed the pad of her middle finger to press lightly against the small round mouth, but knew not to move the finger; the finger would only brush against it if the bottom moved, and neither would it enter, unless of course the small mouth were to push of its own accord, to open and to suck it. Riga was very tense now as Anya kept her finger very still, and very lightly touching. Her other hand did not remain still. Having moved aside the curls, its thumb stroked up and down the smooth cleared pathways in the skin to each side of the small distended sex lips, awakening that skin to greater sensitivity, until Riga's eyes widened once again and Anya felt a small contraction of the tiny mouth.

Shira had released her inner hold upon the coachman, who, apparently uncertain now of what he wanted, had protested yet again. The groan was very loud this time, and the cockstem trembled as if about to spasm. Shira removed the thong from her left arm, then pulled the end between her teeth to straighten it, then wet it, almost as if she were about to thread a needle. Anya felt a sinking feeling in between her legs when she realised what was about to happen. Shira held up the stiffened thong tip, with a droplet at the end, squeezed the twitching plum end till it split, then worked the thong tip in.

Anya suddenly wanted Riga to touch her. She wanted Riga's fingertips to caress that place on her person where the silk traversed her pleasure bud. She kept imagining Riga lifting the cord away and touching, but Riga did not move. The barely touching finger at the mouth of Riga's bottom held at bay any movement. Anya could feel the finely misting moistness at the creases of the thigh. She stroked her thumb along that moistness, then carefully applied her fingers to the softness of the sex. Riga's belly remained rigid as Anya stroked two fingers gently upwards from the junction of her flesh lips, repeatedly stroking upwards only, drawing Riga's flesh hood up again each time it sank back softer than before. Anya worked by touch alone for, like Riga, she was watching the gentle coaxing of the coachman's fleshy tube, the addition of drips of spittle, and the feeding of the thong of leather progressively within. When it would go no further, Shira allowed the remainder to dangle down below it, so the cockstem now assumed the appearance of a single-stranded whip. Once more, Shira reached beneath; the coachman murmured as the strand began to swing, and for the first time, Riga's bottom moved; the small mouth stroked against the fingertip held beneath it. Anya held the flesh hood fully back and touched the bud of flesh. Riga moved again; her bottom pressed against the fingertip.

While Shira still probed between the coachman's buttocks and simultaneously slid the outer skin of cockflesh up and down the inner tube, Anya copied that movement much more gently with the girl, by sleeving the softened flesh hood very lightly up and down across the nubbin. When Riga tensed, she tapped the nubbin slowly and evenly, then the sleeving action began again, then the tapping, until Riga groaned softly and pushed, when the fingertip was drawn by three firm pulsing sucks of Riga's bottom up into her body. As Anya stroked the hot sex lips, touched the nubbin and brushed her fingertips up across the downy belly, and the small mouth sucked her fingertip, the coachman's pleasure was finally brought about.

Shira whirled the thong until it spiralled down his stem, then tied the end in through the final loop. She adjusted her position on the stool and pushed her lips down over the cockstem very gradually, until a third of it was swallowed. As she sucked, she stroked his inner thighs until he gasped, whereupon she quickly let the plum slip out and, collaring the cockstem with her finger, pressed her thumb into the underside a little below the tip, as if the coachman were about to burst and this precaution would pre-empt it. As the ensuing groan subsided to tense and heavy breathing, the sucking was taken up again, along with the finger-tickling of the inner thighs. The bag was squeezed in a gentle milking action. It took longer the second time for the imminence of bursting to subside beneath the pressure of her thumb, before the sucking could proceed again, with a hand now pressing flat against his belly. When the groaning came a third time, followed by the violently throbbing pre-pleasure, she did not collar him, but delved beneath and stroked her fingertips firmly forwards behind the thong-bound bag until he cried out, whereupon the fingers were withdrawn. His pleasure had been triggered.

Shira sat back on her stool, clasped her hands about her knees, and watched the cockstem try to thrust itself against its bindings and through the bars to meet her. As the pulsing pleasure came, she turned her head to the side, pouted her lips and looked at the coachman coyly. Yet, violent though the pulsations and wrenching though the groans, the fluid, after a delay on account of the obstruction in the tubing, spurted as a thin and intermittent spray accompanied by a thicker milt which slowly spiralled down the stem. When the thrustings had subsided sufficiently that the coachman sagged, Shira unwound the thong and pulled it quickly out. She stripped it through her fingers to remove the gluten, then untied him from the bars. 'Until tomorrow night, my sweet,' she whispered, standing up to kiss him, lifting her leg and placing his hand between her thighs. The coachman mumbled indistinctly before disappearing over the side and off into the blackness beyond the circle of torches. Shira did not watch him go. She was concentrating on attaching the first thong to her wristband and winding it round her arm.

Anya had been touching Riga without respite, and now she felt the trickle of wetness kiss the finger slipped beneath; the whole of Riga's sex was wet, and it had overflowed. Her belly had turned rigid. When Anya kissed that belly, the mouth of Riga's bottom tightened round her fingertip. Keeping the fingertip inside, Anya now brought the palm of her hand up between Riga's legs, and pressed. Riga gasped. The legs closed around and tried to crush her hand as Riga lifted up, clasped her arms around Anya and kissed her with a breathless fervour. 'Touch me, bring me pleasure . . . There,' she pleaded, opening her thighs again, taking Anya's thumb, directing it to the burning wet bud and stroking as her belly moved against it, as her bottom opened to take the moistened middle finger very deeply. But they were interrupted by a shout which made Riga quickly pull away.

The door of the cage opened and the brown-haired girl was flung across the floor. She crouched in the corner. Riga quickly buttoned her top and began to fasten her skirt.

The disturbance had roused the guard. 'Problems, sergeant?' he enquired.

'Huh!' The sergeant puffed out his chest and his eyes narrowed as he surveyed the cage. There were marks upon his cheeks.

'You can pick another, you know.'

Anya was frightened by the fact that he was looking in their direction.

The sergeant nodded: 'I'll take that one.' Anya's heart sank to her belly.

'But, I thought you knew. The redhead – she is not to be . . .'

'Not her – the little one.' Riga looked at Anya, and Anya's heart went out to her; it was as if, in front of this man, Riga had suddenly lost her edge of fire. She got up slowly. Anya felt very afraid for her, but she could do nothing to save her. 'Hurry up, girl. We haven't got all night,' he chided. 'Come on – unless you want to take turns with that one at the post tomorrow morning.'

The mention of that thing made Anya's blood chill. She

looked out again at the black and threatening outline of the post. So, it was as she had guessed: it was an instrument of punishment after all. They would beat these girls, torture them perhaps, to procure cooperation.

The sergeant had climbed down and was standing outside. When Riga got to the door, he swept her up onto his arm as if she were as light as a doll, then pressed his hand against her belly and laughed: 'No moods from you, I hope.' He unbuttoned her top and thrust his hand beneath, then grunted with satisfaction. Now the hand pushed down her skirt. 'Wider, that's it. Mmmm, I'd say you're ready for this.' She buried her face against his neck as his hand delved deeper. 'Perhaps I should have taken this one first. Eh guard? Look at me, girl.' Again he grunted. Riga's hips moved. 'There . . .' For a second, Anya saw her face, before she turned again and hid it. 'That's the way . . . See, guard, it doesn't take the sergeant long to get them good and wet and ready.' The guard did not seem to hear. The sergeant glanced back over his shoulder at the outcast in the corner. 'Surds! Never know what's good for them, anyway,' he shouted. Then he was off into the night with his unresisting acquisition.

Anya's heart was beating wildly; she was so frightened for the girl. Perhaps Riga had done it before, perhaps she had been subjected to it many times, but how did that make it right for the sergeant to use her in that way, so callously, using threats? She hated him. She would never ever cooperate with him again. Then suddenly she realised what he had said. Surds – she had heard a word like that before. She looked at the brown-haired girl, whose face was lifted now as she stared towards the fire. The guard outside was trying to talk to her. His voice was soft and reassuring, but the girl did not reply and her face remained turned towards the fire. Eventually, the guard gave up and walked away.

Anya crept over. She sat beside her. The girl turned away, so Anya saw her in profile, then she looked once more at Anya before turning away again. She was very beautiful. Her face formed a perfect oval; her skin was smooth and dusky. She had dense dark eyebrows and full lips; the edge of her upper lip was defined sharply by a change of curve, and in the smooth concave above it was a soft dark down. But it was her eyes – large eyes which looked black – that were distinctive. And she had that way of looking at you: her eyes would meet you fully and very wide for a second and then she would glance away; then in her profile you would see the soft down on her upper lip.

Anya tried to break the ice. 'My name is Anya,' she whispered. At first, the girl made no sign that she had heard. When it came, the voice sounded disembodied; it was soft and deep, but the accent was strange and musical:

'I am Sarol-harn.' She turned to Anya, then her eyes widened as she emphasised the second part of her name: 'Sarol-harn.' She sighed and took hold of the bars, staring towards the fire again. 'Sarol-harn ni Vena,' she said very clearly and slowly, then looked at Anya once more, as if interested to witness the expression on Anya's face, which was very surprised indeed. She had never before heard a name so long as this one. Sarol-harn smiled. 'You find my name unusual?'

'It is nice. It is very long.'

'And yours is very short. You people have such short names.' Anya looked around her. Which people did she mean? Sarol-harn explored the matter further: 'You never use your family name?'

'No . . .' Now it was Anya's turn to look towards the fire. 'No. I have no family name. I have no family.'

Sarol-harn looked quizzical. 'That cannot be.'

'No. But I know nothing of my family. I never knew them.'

'You are far from home?'

Anya didn't know that either; but she had never felt at home anywhere, least of all with her former husband, who had treated her with nothing but disdain and finally had sold her into slavery. Even then, unlike her friend Axine, she had never felt the castle to be her home. She had felt truly happy only during those few short months she had spent with the Prince, but when he had gone, for Anya, the castle was just a cold and empty shell, a place of heartless cruelty. 'I suppose I am far from home,' she said.

67

'Me too. But I will get back some day.' Sarol-harn's eyes suddenly burned with fervour.

'You are from Surdia?' Anya ventured. 'I heard the sergeant say it.'

'That man! He is spineless. A coward!' It took Sarol-harn some time to calm down enough to talk about her country, as she called it, though Anya was fairly sure, from what the Duke had said, that Surdia must be a province of Lidir.

'How can I tell you?' Sarol-harn began, her eyes looking lovingly up towards the moon, almost as if her homeland lay in that direction. 'Surdia is the living rock that makes the mountains; it is the wind that stirs the long grass of the rich river plains; it is the white waves on the sea.' Now she looked straight at Anya. 'Surdia is the land of horses, teeming horses, many, many herds of wild white horses.' Anya's eyes grew wide. 'They say the white horses came up from the sea. Our ancestors braved many storms to follow them across the sea in long boats; that is how they found this land. They were the only men who were strong and brave enough to tame the great white stallions of Surdia. Ours is a very beautiful land. Our men are real men . . .'

Anya was undecided about how much of this could be true, but she could certainly picture the horses. 'How did you come to leave?' she asked.

'I lived in the north of our land. One day a party of horsemen came – not our men, not real men – but spineless fools like these,' she waved her hand in the general direction of the soldiers' fire. 'The women were taken; I was sold; I escaped; they captured me again, and punished me. Two days ago these wagons came; I was given by my master in lieu of tribute.'

'Will you escape again?'

Sarol-harn suddenly looked at Anya with suspicion. 'What is it to you?'

'I could come with you.'

'To Surdia?'

Anya nodded.

'Why?'

Anya did not wish to risk revealing her true purpose, not

until she got to know this person better. But she would have to, for it was clear that Sarol-harn did not trust her.

'My lover is in Surdia; I must seek him out.'

'Your lover is a Surd?'

'No. He is an envoy – a great lord, sent by the Council of Lidir. He has gone there to secure a treaty.'

Sarol-harn's eyes were wide in horror. 'Your lover is one of these curs,' and she spat through the bars, 'who would try to crush my people?'

'Shh! No! Do not shout.' Anya was worried the guard might hear. 'He is a good and kind lord. He would never hurt anybody. He wishes to make peace.'

'Ha! How can you say it? Lidir seeks only to destroy us, to render us as slaves. But my people are strong, they bow down to no man; the warriors of the white horses can never be defeated.'

Anya now knew that she had said too much. She shut up altogether. Sarol-harn murmured again, 'They will never defeat us, never.' Anya turned to go.

'Wait.' Sarol-harn took hold of her arm, and spoke in a very low voice, so Shira could not hear: 'I watched you this afternoon. You are not like these people. You are not hard, and yet . . .' She searched Anya's eyes. 'And yet, I think you are strong.' Those words, Axine's words, heard again, made Anya almost cry. 'You really wish to go to Surdia, to seek this man?' Sarol-harn asked, without taking her eyes from Anya's.

'No one shall stop me.' But she could feel a teardrop welling down her cheek.

Sarol-harn nodded slowly: 'Yes, you are strong, and true.' She wiped the tear away. 'Give me your hand. You have a ring. Good. Then we shall swear.'

Though Anya was reluctant to part with it, Sarol-harn took Anya's turquoise ring, then removed her own and slipped it over Anya's finger. The ring was carved from pure white stone. It was embossed with the image of a running horse. The women clasped hands. 'Good,' said Sarol-harn. 'Now we are ring sisters. We will help each other when we can.' Her voice fell to an even softer whisper:

'In time, we will escape. We will find a way; I will take you to my homeland. There you will meet some real men.'

Later, as the firelight faded, as a single torch flickered softly, all was quiet in the cage. The guard had checked her bonds; the silken cord lay bedded very deeply in the split of Anya's flesh. Shira and Sarol-harn lay asleep in opposite corners; the others were not back. Anya lay upon the mattress, thinking. Small dark clouds swept swiftly and silently across the high bright moon. Intermittent moonlight drenched the landscape with unease. Anya felt this unease very strongly. Her mind was filled with many confused visions: visions of her Prince, so far away, in danger, in a land filled with beautiful Sarol-harns; visions of strong men, real men; visions of cage-girls taking pleasure for long hours now, by the fire; visions of horses, teeming powerful white horses, surging from the moonlit billows of the deep sea waves. And behind all these visions, behind the fact that Anya's body could not sleep, was the soft burning in her belly, the softly burning need, the need for loving pleasure. For how could all these visions bring release? The need was swelling gently, rhythmically between her thighs as if her imprisoned flesh were riding on those deep and moon-drawn night-waves of the ocean. The licking flames of desire stroked up inside to warm her belly, to draw upon her silk-bound nipple tips.

She heard a noise; a hand was laid upon her shoulder. The voice was very soft indeed: 'I have come for you, as I promised, for the moon is high; the moon is right.'

[5]

On a Moon-Bright Night

Even in silhouette, she knew him, yet she did not know his name. She knew him by his words, the soft voice, the tenderness of his touch upon her neck, the gentle stroking behind her ear. She knew him from the way her belly stirred. She turned. Her lips searched out his and brushed against them. That was Anya's signal of assent. Her body was ready; she needed this deliverance; she would take it from this man. The young soldier had come to her on this moon-bright night. He would seduce her body tenderly to pleasure.

They crept out silently, yet with the surging breathlessness of lovers; the soldier's hand was clasped in sureness about her own, drawing her swiftly onwards. They passed the guard, asleep and snoring, with a jug clutched to his breast. They skirted round the murmuring group gathered round the embers of the great fire. Then, clear at last, they laughed and ran, chasing the high, scudding clouds up the hillside to a clearing which overlooked the black and silver lake. Her soldier cast his blanket to the ground.

This place was sheltered and the air was warm and still. High above, the small clouds hastened, the treetops swayed; on the blanket all was quiet, but a bridled turbulence raged within each lover. Their passion was driven by the high, bright moon.

Anya held up the lodestone. 'From a lover to a lad,' she said. The clasp was broken, so she knotted the chain around his neck. As she kissed the stone, she could feel the warmth of his skin beneath it. Then she felt shy. When she turned her head away, he folded his arms about her.

'Forest child,' he whispered. 'Will your rainbow come

71

again to wing you far away?' Anya did not understand his words, but she understood his tenderness, she understood his body pressed to hers. She stroked his hair, stroked his neck and pressed her lips to his. Then suddenly the feeling came, so powerfully that every skin hair prickled: her cheeks glowed warm; her lips felt swollen; her breasts and belly were filled with a slow delicious ache. She could sense that first touch still, where his fingertips had stroked her neck below her earlobe; she could sense his hand upon her palm, though his hand no longer touched her palm, and she could feel the soft brush of his lips against her own. She could hear his words too, those other words, soft seductive words that he had whispered in the forest glade. She could feel the drowning intensity of her passion.

He unfastened her jacket, but did not yet remove it. Her halter rested loosely against her breasts. He unfastened his tunic top and took it off completely. She could smell his scent softly on the air. It reminded her of her Prince. When he lifted aside her halter and touched the sides of her breasts in exactly the way the Prince used to do, her breathing came deeply and she shivered, even though the air was warm. His hands reached underneath her arms, his thumbtips brushed her curls and as his fingers extended over the surface of her upper back, the skin upon her shoulders was sensitised by the touch. Then his chest curls touched her silk-bound nipples.

Her hands came to rest lightly upon the soft skin of his sides. She sucked his lower lip. Her fingers moved round to tickle the tightness of his belly. She knew his flesh was stiff; the backs of her fingers, stroking up and down his belly, hardly touching him at all, ensured it. His breathing testified to this urgency. She wanted him this way; she wanted his flesh swollen hard with that same delicious pain she felt now between her thighs. She would close her soft lips round his cockstem very gently; she would touch him and caress him with her lips until he burst; warm spice would bathe her tongue.

He unbuckled his belt; her fingers moved quickly, seeking the warmth within the warm and rigid satin stem. Anya

72

would not release that stem until he was completely nude. She held him, pressing against him, steadying him, gloving the cockstem tightly while he completed his disrobing. As the final sock was removed, they toppled to the blanket. Still she held him, not moving her fingers, but closing one hand round the lower stem, pressing against the base, gathering the bag in the other hand, enclosing it, keeping him strong, tasting with her fingers the firmness of his wanting. She loved to feel this strength of urgency in her lover, and to keep the pressure concentrated there. She stroked the bag, then pressed the tips of her fingers into the yielding skin until they touched the fleshy bumps, assessing their shape, squeezing very lightly, closing round the cords within. She kissed him while she did this, kissing his belly and his chest, gently licking his lips as he craned his neck towards her, but amid the moist light touches of her lips against his skin, keeping her fingertips probing, all the while a soft threat against the pleasure, keeping the skin of the collared cockstem drawn back tightly, until he could bear the urgency no more, until he murmured, 'No . . .'

Anya now released him. She let him unfasten her skirt; she let him take her jacket. She wore only the halter now, the blue silk rope, and the thread about her nipples. When she knelt up to allow his hands to explore her breasts and to test the silken fastenings, to touch the blue cord at her belly and below, the open halter dangled loosely against the heavy-tipped outswell of her breasts, her breasts that felt so swollen that they ached. He touched her through the softness of the leather. He lifted her breasts; the leather slipped aside; her breasts shook. He moistened his lips and pressed them to the tips. She felt his tonguetip touch the polished surface of the nipple. While his fingers touched her belly, brushing the fine sward, tickling in the creases of her thighs, she felt his teeth against the silk, pulling gently, and it made her feel afraid: what would they say tomorrow if the thread had been removed?

But she did not ask him to stop. The tongue licked, the teeth nipped, and the shivers tumbled inside. As each silken collar was pulled up tightly, the pressure swelled harder to the tip. Finally the thread about her right nipple burst against the suction, and Anya could feel a burning sensation as the nipple stretched and swelled into his mouth. The sucking was repeated on the left nipple, and the bursting pressure came, followed by the drawing with the tongue.

While her breasts were sucked, the fingers tickled between her thighs. The rope that split her had forced each lip of flesh to infold as it was drawn in on her centre line, leaving two projecting rounded rims of polished skin which his fingers tickled lightly. Now he pressed his thumbs against those smooth tight rims to open them. Beneath that splitting pressure, and the urgency to push, and despite the imminence of pain, her flesh lips spread wider. When the tight silk pushed against her nubbin, with the thumbs to each side, pressing still, and his mouth still sucking round her nipple, she very nearly came.

The fingers tapped and plucked and stroked the plaited silk. Each stroke or pluck or tap carried through to Anya's nubbin. Each time she gasped, the fingers stroked her to the sides, down towards her silk-bound centre line, then returned to touch the rope. It felt as if those fingers plucked the very tip of her nubbin. The plucking and the fingertip caressing of the tight-stretched skin proceeded, accompanied by a deep sucking which seemed to elongate her nipples until they stretched along his tongue, until the urge to close her thighs against the hand was irresistible. But her soldier introduced his knees between her own to keep them wide apart. He placed her hands behind her back, crossing them, thereby throwing her shoulders back and exposing her breasts more fully. He tucked her thumbs into the rope where it passed around her waistline. That method of restraint caused a peculiar feeling, not so much at the base of her thumbs as deep within her belly. It increased the tension in the rope between her thighs. The tension was now enhanced as his hand hooked beneath the rope between her sex lips and her belly, and she was pulled towards him while he kissed her.

She was open, with her knees held apart, with the restraint encircling her belly, then concentrated in that inti-

74

mate divide, pressed against her nubbin, pressed against the mouth of her bottom, and the feeling of willing defencelessness overwhelmed her. It made her breathing shallow, made her breathing nonexistent as her tongue was slowly sucked into his mouth. Drop by honeyed drop, her body melted. The rope was becoming wet. His thumbs began to stroke her where her flesh lips joined her body. Then his hand enclosed her, cupping the blue silk split.

He turned her, with her thumbs still pinned behind her. He made her kneel up while he stroked her back and stroked her bottom. He slipped his hand between her legs, underneath the rope again as it descended from her belly. He did not pull the rope this time; his palm pressed flat against her belly. Again she gulped for air; she loved that feeling, the pressure there, low down, taking her breath away.

Her thumbs were now released. She was made to lie down on her front. The soldier took his coat and folded it as a pillow for her cheek; her jacket, doubled over, was placed between her legs to lift her belly. Her knees were now pushed up the blanket. The rope bit deep between her buttocks. The jacket was readjusted. The smooth cool waxy curls of the sheepskin tickled between her legs. She felt the rope being unknotted from her back. The dividing cord between her buttocks loosened, but the moistened silk clung to her within the groove. It was slowly peeled down to the level of her fleshpot. Her tender skin felt cool. She could hear his breathing very close. Soft shudders of premonition travelled down her back to kiss the nervous skin within her groove. A fingertip brushed lightly upwards from the end point of her spine. It was followed by a tongue. The tongue licked round and round the tip, as the fingertip worked down, ever deeper in the groove, to the mouth of her bottom. The tongue now flattened against the very sensitive place low down on Anya's spine and stroked slowly, wetly, persistently in that place, while the fingertip gently tickled the pouted mouth until it had elicited a response, in the form of a quick contraction. Now the tongue was lifted, the fingertip removed and small soft sucking kisses fell like drifting petals, over the left cheek, over the right and, with the cheeks held definitely apart, very, very lightly in the open groove. Then the game began.

The tongue would stroke leisurely back and forth across the tightening mouth, barely brushing the sensitive rim, stirring Anya's lewdness to the point where she held her breath and tensed her buttocks. Then, exactly at the moment that the flesh ring puckered, the lips would descend to draw on it quickly with a moist and sucking kiss. The tip of the tongue never entered her at all – it merely tickled back and forth, or slowly in a circle, and in due course, however much she willed her flesh to try to resist, however much she slowed her breathing, however much she tried to make her flesh relax, the constant pressure of the fingertips against the inner cheeks, keeping her cheeks apart, and the steady tonguetip tasting, the heaping of tickles upon tickles, would cause her body to turn rigid and then a fraction later, the pucker would ensue and she would have felt that sucking kiss ten times over before it was inescapably bestowed. Each time the kiss descended, her flesh felt a greater sensitivity to that touch, the pucker came more quickly until she was puckered all the time, but the lips descended slowly, applying the pleasured lewdness at a never changing pace. The sucking almost seemed to draw upon her nubbin. She wanted him to touch her there, to peel the rope from between her lips, to gather her nubbin in his fingers and hold it while his tongue pushed into her. She knew it was wrong, but that was what she wanted; she wanted to suck his tonguetip with her bottom, in the way she had done with Axine. And while she did this, while she squeezed, she wanted him to roll her nubbin between his fingers till she came. But as if he had heard her illicit thoughts, the intimate kissing stopped and she felt a hot wave, not of shame, but of interrupted wanting.

The edge of his hand was pressed into the crease between her buttocks. The palm lay fitted to one cheek. The edge of the little finger felt cool against her. Then, with the hand still in place, maintaining the pressure on her line of split, with the knuckle of the little finger resting against the rim, the kissing was resumed, soft cool kisses up the backs of Anya's thighs, then very gentle nipping with the teeth. Her bottom cheeks were spread once more, the tickling tip descended, the mouth pushed out and now, beneath the warm breath, she felt the quick nip of his teeth against her puckered rim. The sudden nip of pleasure made her belly contract. Again the tickling came and once again the tiny bite, followed by a fingertip massaging of that small and throbbing mouth. Now the cord was teased from between her flesh lips. He pulled it very slowly, so her sex lips opened and felt cold. Her thighs were moved wider apart until the muscles almost ached. The folded skirt was added to the jacket pushed beneath her belly. She waited for him to touch her sex.

When the touch came, she began to squirm, for the touch was simply the very wet tip of his tongue drawn very slowly, very lightly around the edges of her flesh lips, which were lifted, opened, pushed out by the pressure of the cushion of clothing underneath her. The touch was so light and so uncertain, it felt as if an insect were crawling round the feather edge of skin. Her cheeks were opened out again and the tongue moved back to lick the rim. That alternation of tickling from front to back made her want to plead with him to finish her. He sat up, pressing his left hand to the small of her back whilst the right hand tickled her. Two fingertips worked like tongues at the feather edges of her flesh leaves, not entering her, not closing round her leaves to stretch them, but tickling, stroking back and forth along their edges until she groaned. And then they entered. The two middle fingers pushed inside while the outer fingers lay along the creases of her thighs and the thumb pressed gently up against her bottom. The fingers of the left hand slipped beneath to work her, kneading the flesh hood, making it soft, squeezing the rigid pip. When she tried to close her thighs around him, he stopped.

He rolled the blanket aside and turned her onto her back. She gasped as the cool soft pine needles pressed against her skin. The moon lay directly up above. Her body was turned to silver in the moonlight, silver curves of belly, breast and

77

thigh which undulated softly with her breathing. 'Lift your legs,' he said. She did as she was asked, and now the scene was exactly as she had pictured it when he had given his promise in the forest glade. *You will point your toes up to the sky.* He had said that then, and more besides. Her knees crooked gently, her insteps arched, her toes pointed upwards to the high bright moon. And as her soldier planted soft kisses upon her belly, upon her breasts, upon her inner thighs, her toes reached up to try to capture the moon. She tried to keep her eyes open though they felt heavy enough to close, to concentrate upon that one thing, balancing the moon between the arches of her insteps, holding that balance gently for as long as she was able, against the waves, the deep drawing waves of sensuality as the kisses, alternating across the inner surfaces of her thighs, seduced that skin to pleasure. Every kiss caused a shimmer, every tongue lick made her want to draw her legs together. But she knew she must not do this; for then the moon would topple.

The moon shuddered softly as the kisses reached the crease. The tonguetip licked a wet cool line, like a knife against her skin, a knife that slowly, with a sweet enravishing tantalising thrill, threatened to sever her leg completely from her body. She felt the tickles in her throat, slow licking tickles that made the bright moon waver. The tickles cut the other side; the tongue was honed to a finer point; it found the very nervous skin in the centre of the crease and Anya jumped with pleasure. The soldier's palm lay against her mound now, holding her flesh lips to one side, to stretch the skin for the cutting to proceed. The tonguetip found that nerve again and the moon blacked out. Her eyes were closed; the moon must now take care of itself. She was biting her lip against the pleasure. Her legs began to shake as he spread her flesh lips open. Her belly bucked and she nearly came, for the tongue had aimed directly for the nubbin. It had stroked upon it once. The fingers squeezed the flesh around the nub, the end of the tongue entubed it and she whimpered, then the slow sucking began. *You will suckle me with this salted nipple in between your legs*, he had said. Each suck squeezed a pre-pleasure from her; it was as if his tongue was milking pleasure from her by degrees, spraying the pleasure out in tiny spurts.

And as the small bud swelled to a hard projecting pip while the flesh around it softened to a liquid salted sea each time the belly tensed and the breathing snagged and the tight thigh muscles trembled, the soldier's tongue became immobile, a tight warm tube against her nipple of desire. The tonguetip formed a rigid point which pressed against the nubbin at its base. It felt as if Aruline's silken thread were wound very tightly round it. The pressure in her flesh bud turned to pain. She moaned, and the tonguetip carefully withdrew. Her flesh lips, now softened, liquefied, lacking any resistance, were spread and held apart and the lips began again, sucking her burning salted nipple while the tips of the little fingers lay pressed against her creases.

By this means then, upon an endless time of tightness, of burning aching pleasure, of premature shudders between her thighs, of drawing sensations in her nipples, of false contractions in her belly, her pleasure was finally brought about. The fingertips stroked up her inner thighs, then downwards into the polished creases, then opened her and entered her and held her flesh apart. The tongue curled tighter round her nubbin and suddenly it felt as if her nubbin burst. The strength of pleasure sucked the breath out from her body. Her legs closed down about his shoulders, her hands closed round his head and she held him, not caring if he could even breathe at all. Her need was too insistent. Each time a pulse of pleasure was stripped down through her nubbin by his tongue, another deep suck ensued; it triggered another pulse of pleasure until her nubbin felt so sensitive she had to pull his face away. They lay there gasping, his head upon her belly, his hand between her thighs, resting his fingers within her body until the pulse ebbed away.

It seemed this fulfilment was like a potion that filled her with a sleepy sensuality, but also with a craving; it made her flesh want more. She wanted to feel his fleshcock pushed inside her. But first she wanted to kiss him in the way he had kissed her. She would suck him long and slow; she would make the pleasure hurt before it came.

As the soldier began edging up her body until she could feel his hot stem hard against her thigh, Anya turned and quickly slipped out from under him. He lay upon his side, with his cockstem arching outwards from his belly. When she touched that belly, the cockstem trembled. She framed his face with her hands and kissed him, upside down. Then her lips moved downwards, kissing his chin, his neck, his chest curls. Each nipple was taken briefly into her mouth and nipped between her teeth. Her tongue delved moistly in the navel. Her hair cascaded down between his legs to tickle him. Then his breath was drawn in sharply as she lifted the upturned cockstem on her tongue and slid it deep inside her mouth. She did not close her lips round it. She let it slide until the cockhead filled the back of her throat, until the gagging feeling came; then her lips closed down to collar him. As her head drew back, the lips slid slowly up the length and locked behind the rim. The tip of her tongue pushed into him. Her finger and thumb closed round the stem an inch below her lips, the thumb beneath, against the thickened tube, to work the outer skin gently before sliding fully down to press against the base. Now the sliding movement was performed by the lips, with the tonguetip still pushed inside the small mouth at the crown. As the lips slid down, the tongue pressure was increased until she heard a softened moan. Her mouth released the cockstem, but worked down its under-surface like a large wet sucker, drawing deeply on the underside of the plum, then shaping to the surface of the thickened undertube, sucking inch by inch down its length, then expanding once again to replace the thumb and suck on the base exactly at the joining of the cockstem and the bag.

Throughout this undersucking of the lower stem, her left hand gloved about the length, working him until he oozed. The sucker now moved up again, the lips closed round the head, and the tonguetip penetrated. The fingers pressed beneath the bag, probing the arch between his legs, testing it for firmness. As his lifted thigh began to shudder, she tasted salt, the first of many pleasured weepings. She released the stem and raised his thigh until he was forced onto his back. She knelt astride his chest, facing him, with the silken rope still tethered round her middle. When she spread her flesh, then bent to suck his lower lip, the dangling length of cool silk trailed across then trapped against him as her open wetness kissed his skin. She lifted, took the end of the rope, stretched it and forced it between his lips. Again she kissed him; their tongues searched out each other through the silk. She turned her body round and repositioned, lifting while she spread her flesh, then settling down again. The silk rope now lay heaped upon his belly. She stretched it; it would not reach beneath his stem until she had lifted his legs and made him bend his knees. Now she could fasten the cord tightly round his cockstem and his bumps. She edged her bottom back to take up the slack; the cockstem arched above the tightly stretched cord. She had him where she wanted him, constricted and defenceless.

She bent her head, kissed his belly, then took the cockstem in her mouth. As she sucked and spread her thighs and rubbed her oil against his chest, the stricture tightened and he very slowly seeped. Beneath the unyielding pressure of pleasure his body overflowed, and Anya sucked those wellings like a baby at the teat. The salted taste grew stronger in her mouth, giving way to a taste like dry and overyeasted wine. She slipped the cockhead underneath her tongue and with the back of her tongue she milked him, pressing the tonguetip very definitely, very steadily, like a tiny pulsebeat pumping the sensitive underside an inch below the tip, whilst she edged him onwards, stroking the tightly arched bridge of flesh very gently, then moving her fingers back until they entered the groove. As her fingertips spread the reluctant cheeks, then stroked around the circle, steadily round and round, while the pulsebeat pressed the cocktip, the pulsing came. She could tell it in advance, from the tightness in his belly and the slowly wrenching groans. The quick hot squirts of thickness surged against the under-surface of her tongue and mixed with her saliva. She waited until the pulsing stopped, then unfastened the cord and delivered some of the miltings onto her fingers. She let them

81

dribble down the cockstem and rubbed them round the base, then she dripped the remainder onto the bumps, massaging the liquid into them and underneath. The cockstem was still hard. She kissed it once again to keep it thus while she worked the miltings in between his buttocks.

When she was satisfied that his flesh would not go down, Anya lifted from him and snuggled up beside him, with her back pressed to his belly and his cock between her thighs. Her flesh lips spread to kiss him with her wetness. She wanted it that way for a while, arched underneath, just kissing against her, with the cocktip pressed against her nubbin. She pulled the blanket round them, then took his palm and placed it to her belly. Then she arched her back, and as he slowly gasped, she took the cockstem in. His cock felt thick and hard against her soft sea of liquidity. She wanted him pushed in to the hilt. She caught her breath as the cockhead pressed against the entrance to her womb. It felt as if the cap was moulded to her. The deep pressure was exquisite. She sighed and turned to kiss him. Then she froze. Her fleshpot tightened; he murmured with the pain.

There were figures moving across the clearing, heading straight towards them, black figures, some large, some squat, but all of them menacing.

Now her soldier had seen them too; he closed his hand over her mouth and pulled her head to the ground. They lay very still. She could feel his heartbeat against her back; she could feel his cockstem slipping out and contracting across the back of her thigh. The crouching figures advanced soundlessly past them, one of them not ten feet away. Anya was sure they would be spotted. She could see the man's hand upon the hilt of his sword, and the longbow slung across his shoulder. They seemed so frightening and stealthy, these creatures of the night. There were five at least, and they were heading for the camp.

Anya didn't wait until they had disappeared. 'Who are they? What are we going to do?' she whispered.

'Bandits.' Her soldier seemed shaken. 'They would have killed us – slit our throats.' Anya shivered. 'But we must follow them,' he said, 'see what they are up to. Then we must get back and warn the Duke. Quickly!'

They gathered up their things and hurried after the shadowy figures, towards the darkness of the further stand of trees. They moved as quietly as they could, and as quickly, but they were forced to slow as they entered the eerie blackness. Yet when they stopped to listen, they could hear nothing. As their eyes adjusted to the blackness, they could see no one. They circled round, to the side above the camp. There was no sign of anyone. They had vanished. All was quiet below them by the fires.

'Where are they?' Anya asked.

The soldier shook his head. 'They live here in the forest. They know how to hide. But they're scouts, not raiders. They'd never attack the camp itself, not with so many of us. But they'll bring more.' He surveyed the darkness all around. 'They could be watching us now.' The hairs on Anya's skin bristled; suddenly, she felt cold. 'I'd better get you back,' he said. 'I'll raise the alarm.' He made her dress and then he resecured her cord. 'There – the guard will never know.' Anya smiled, but his saying that had made her feel uneasy.

'Wait,' he said. 'Your stone.' He put the lodestone round her neck.

But she preferred to keep it hidden away; she put it in her pocket.

When they reached the camp, the guard was still asleep. They kissed goodbye and Anya slipped silently into the cage. The soldier fastened it.

Neither Riga nor the others were back. Anya hoped they'd be all right. She lay down on the smaller mattress in the corner, pulled the blanket round her and tried to sleep, but she was scared by what she'd seen. Perhaps it was true, what the Duke had said about the dangers? What if these bandits had been the first to come upon her in the forest?

Very soon, she was disturbed by sounds of voices, sounds of men moving around. Sarol-harn and Shira woke. 'What is it?' Sarol-harn asked. Shira shook her head.

'Nothing to fear, my pretty,' the guard assured her.

'Nothing to worry your head about.' But the torches were relit around the cage; more wood was thrown upon the fire until it sparked and spat. Soon afterwards, the other girls returned, most of them; Anya was sure that one of them was still missing, a girl with short black hair who had been taken out while Anya was drying off by the fire.

The sergeant carried Riga; she was asleep. He laid her on the mattress, stared at Anya briefly, then turned and left the cage. But he stood outside for a long while, talking to the guard. Anya noticed that extra sentries had been posted. She felt safer now. She drew the blanket over herself and Riga, who lay sleeping soundly with her thumb in her mouth.

[6]

The Power of Musk

Aruline stood in front of the long mirror, tying back her hair, paying tribute to her reflection. The interior of the tent was splashed with yellow morning light, which caressed her skin in soft and dappled deep lemon kisses, lighting the undersides of her breasts, brushing her thighs and belly. She stood with legs apart, drawing in her belly and pushing out her breasts, and she smiled, for even the morning sun could not light the blackness there between her thighs, the dense and matt black curls that were her pride. She kept them trimmed to a perfectly horizontal line below the navel and precisely to the creases of the thighs; she kept the skin around them smoothly shaven. Whenever she closed her legs after having held them open for a while, then in that first second when the outer curls were cool and dry and smooth, it would feel as if an animal pelt was moulded to the flesh below her belly.

But Aruline's bush was more than just delicious to the touch; it was more by far than simple decoration. Aruline's bush was functional. It distributed her musk, a musk she knew that men found irresistible. She would therefore spend long sessions fluffing out her bush, after washing, carefully removing any lingering trace of soap, and dabbing with a fresh clean towel. Then she would devote some minutes to playing with herself, brushing the moisture of her sensual heat across the surface of her curls or working it deeply in, according to requirement.

Aruline liked her body scent; she liked the scent of women. She liked men too, but she preferred the musk of women. When another woman's musk was on her skin, it made her feel excited. It made her want to do sensual things.

It was like a drug. This was why she felt excited now. The girl had done it, the girl who lay asleep beside the Duke, the girl with short black hair and a thick and curly bush, a wild bush which had never been trimmed at all. It erupted up her belly and part way down her thighs and escaped into the groove of her delectably tight-cheeked bottom. It was a bush that buried her fleshy lips so deeply that they could only be extracted with the tongue. This girl had a musk which overpowered Aruline. She had soft, gentle, shy eyes, but her musk was the musk of a wild and sensuous thing. Her musk lay upon Aruline's body now. It was infused into the skin of her breasts, her thighs, her neck and cheeks and lips. It had seeped indelibly into her fingers. Aruline was drowning in a sea of female musk, and the girl was simply sleeping. Aruline could not sleep at all. She was too excited. She had lain awake all night, touching the girl, touching the alabaster cockstem that lay bedded up inside her, the very same cockstem that had made Aruline's pleasure come.

Yet Aruline had come, not with the cockstem in herself, nor even touching her, but when she had fitted the cockstem to the girl. The girl had lain upon her side with the Duke's stem in her mouth. Aruline had looked upon her, and had then assisted the Duke to bed his cockstem deeper, to the bag. She had shown the girl how to pout her lips out very far and to take it without choking. Then she had kissed the girl on the cheek and had sucked upon her breasts. But as Aruline's open mouth moved down the belly, the scent had grown stronger all the time, until Aruline had not been able to stop herself from pressing her thighs together. She had opened the girl's legs and her own belly had quavered as the wave of sexual heat surged up to meet her. Then when she had pushed the alabaster cockstem in against the slipperiness and squeezing, and the girl had emitted a muffled murmur and had tried to close her thighs together – but Aruline had held them open, pushing the cockstem in up to the ballocks, then pulling the flesh hood back that she might suck upon the bud – it had happened. As the nib of Aruline's tongue touched the hot and musky nubbin, as the scent rolled up to overpower her, Aruline had come without touching herself at all, simply by keeping her thighs squeezed tight together as she licked upon that deliciously pulsing tip. Such was the power of musk – aided by the vision of the girl's moist pinkness spread about this thick white polished cylinder of stone.

And now, even the memory was making Aruline wet. She sighed, then drew on her skintight golden velvet riding breeches, which gloved her thighs and the cheeks of her buttocks and split her sex lips neatly. Very soon there would be a wet patch there. Did Aruline care? Of course she did – this was what she wanted. When a girl was across her lap, mere words were insufficient; the girl needed to know directly that she was giving Aruline pleasure. Aruline exhaled, then pulled the drawstring tight about her waist before fitting the matching clinging top. When she stroked, the velvet felt like a second skin about her, a soft fine furry animal skin. She drew on the calfskin knee-length boots, but she did not don the gloves. Her fingers would be needed, skin to skin, to taste again the new girl's musk as it flowed freely in her punishment. For when Aruline had chanced to pass the cage late last night, the new girl was not there. Yet, flagrant though this transgression was, Aruline was not interested in punishing the girl for punishment's sake; Aruline would interweave her punishment quite inextricably with pleasure.

She took up the riding crop, the same instrument with which she had procured the Duke's seduction. She sniffed once more the leather loop she had slipped around his ballocks while she sucked him in that quiet glade, on that stag hunt all that while ago. But now, of course, the leather smelt of women. Aruline kissed the leather loop. She crept over to the girl, who lay half on her side with the bulbs of the cockstem glowing white between her black-bushed thighs. Aruline slipped the loop around those bulbs, then slowly twisted it until the loop locked tight about the base of the stem. She took the strain and the girl began to stir. Aruline shivered. She was thinking of the girl's sex being held open, tight against the unyielding stone, throughout the night. She was thinking also of the musk infused over many hours into the alabaster.

The girl turned onto her back and opened her eyes. Aruline smiled, then took the strain again. The belly tightened. Aruline stroked it gently. As the cockstem moved, the girl murmured, for the cockstem plum was very thick, by design, to give greater satisfaction and to prevent accidental expulsion in her sleep. Aruline made the girl bend her knees, not by holding them, but rather by angling them, unsupported, gently in the air. The wave of delicious musk welled to overpower Aruline, and to make her feel warm moistness in between her thighs. As Aruline pulled, the alabaster slowly slipped out against the tightness of the upstroked belly. Aruline untwisted the loop, then laid the glistening cockstem gently upon the girl's thigh whilst she brought across her workbox. She opened it, took up the cockstem and laid it on the purple silken bands. She handled it reverently, and she left the box open, that the moistness might slowly dry and in the process steep the alabaster in its musk. She would need that stem for later. But now, with the Duke asleep still and the girl awake, though heavy-lidded, it was time for Aruline to embark upon her rounds.

The next thing Anya was aware of was the dawn. Someone was shaking her.

'Anya! She is coming,' Riga whispered urgently. In the background, Anya could hear sharp snapping sounds, like breaking twigs.

'Who?' But there was only one person it could have been. Anya didn't recognise her at first, for she was dressed in brown now, not in red. Her cheeks were pink, as if she had been running, and she held a riding crop. She kept slapping it against her thigh. Anya's eyes darted between Aruline and the women, all of whom appeared anxious, though none of them was speaking. Aruline hesitated at the wooden post. She stroked her fingers down it, then turned, with her hands on her hips, and called the cage-guard over. She eyed the women in the cage. 'No bad reports, I hope, guard?' The women were very still now. Sarol-harn was frowning.

'No . . . no, milady,' the guard sighed. 'Not really – just the one.' Anya looked round the cage. Everyone was worried. Riga put her arm round Anya. Sarol-harn bit her lip.

Aruline, striding forward, surveyed the faces arrayed before her. She seemed much sterner, more frightening than she had seemed yesterday. 'Which is it, guard?' She flexed the crop. 'Which is it to be?' Anya suddenly felt guilty as Aruline caught her eye.

The guard pointed to Sarol-harn: 'She failed to deliver the sergeant satisfaction.'

'I see. Well then, her flesh shall pay the price. Bring the sergeant. She shall deliver now – satisfaction of a different kind. Put her to the post.' And as Sarol-harn was led down the steps, Aruline delivered a vicious swipe of the crop against her bottom. 'There, my dear,' she said, 'and that is just a taster.'

Anya was aghast. Yet there was no escape. Sarol-harn was strung up, her skirts were lifted and tied around her waist. The sergeant appeared next, at a run. 'You wish the crop, sergeant?' It seemed he preferred to use bare hands.

The cracks resounded. Sarol-harn's bottom swayed, then jerked as she tried in vain to mitigate the blows. 'If you'd have moved as well as this last night, wench, there'd be no cause for complaint now,' the sergeant shouted.

'Good,' Aruline declared. 'Keep at it, sergeant. Any more, guard?' The girls backed away. 'No? But are you certain?' Her eyes roamed round the cage and came to rest on Anya, still kneeling on the bed. 'The new girl,' she announced, tapping the crop against her cheek, then pointing it accusingly at Anya. She waited. Anya's top lip trembled. 'I presume you kept the fitting tight?' The guard nodded uncertainly. 'Good. Then let us have a look . . .' Anya suddenly felt the tightness in her chest instead of round her belly. She almost could not breathe as Aruline stepped into the cage. Riga got off the bed and edged away. Aruline laid her hand upon Anya's cheek, then stroked her hair, then bent to kiss her. 'Do not be afraid, my sweet,' she whispered. Her lips closed round and sucked upon the ear-lobe. 'A girl who behaves herself has nothing to fear from me,' she added, more loudly, absent-mindedly sniffing the fingers that had stroked through Anya's hair. 'You should know that much by now. Perhaps a quiet little diversion, nothing more . . .' Aruline pouted. Anya coloured at the memories of what this woman had done to her, but Aruline lifted up her chin. 'You are very shy, still. We must work at that shyness. Have you told your friends about the little games we played?' Riga was looking at Anya, her eyebrows knitted in a frown as Anya's cheeks burned bright with shame. Aruline smiled sweetly, then the smile faded very quickly when she opened Anya's halter.

'It seems your threads have come undone. But I fastened them so securely.' She lifted Anya's nipples one by one, turning them upwards, holding the ends up as they firmed, and rubbing the up-curved undersides. 'Have these little black baubles been engaging in little games of their own? Girls' games, perhaps?' She stared about the cage slowly, analysing each and every face. 'Little girls . . . Hmmm?' Riga looked away. Aruline sighed. 'Ah, but who could blame you?' And yet the fingers still registered their disapproval as they squeezed and turned and pulled the nipples, then finally twisted them till they hurt. 'So – was it little girls, my dear?'

'No, my lady,' Anya whispered meekly.

'Then what? Not boys, I hope?' Anya could only look out to the side of the cage that faced the lake. 'Guard . . . Not boys, I hope, against our express instruction?' The slaps kept sounding in the background, from the punishment at the post. Anya knew she would be next. She could feel the teardrops welling. Why had she imagined she could get away with it?

'No. Certainly not, milady.' But the guard seemed disquieted. 'I permitted no man to take her,' he said with faint assurance.

Aruline looked at Anya's downcast expression, then lifted her chin. She took hold of Anya's lower lip and held it very tight as she looked into the tear-filled eyes. 'Then perhaps they helped themselves . . .' Aruline's nostrils dilated; she began sniffing deeply. She began sniffing at Anya's hair, her neck, her lips. Anya was mortified. She opened out Anya's halter and drew a very deep breath between her shaking mounds. Anya felt very much afraid. Aruline's expression was critical but still uncertain. At the post, the slapping had stopped. The sergeant had dropped his breeches and was taking Sarol-harn from behind amid murmurs of approval from the crowd. Aruline moved aside. 'I see that interests you, my dear. You haven't acquired a taste for it, I hope?' Now she took Anya's hand in hers and her voice fell to a whisper, as if she were chastising a favourite child: 'Can you not see that you are special? You are wasted on these creatures.' She touched her finger to her tongue to wet it, then stroked it across Anya's lips. 'My special girls are just for me,' she murmured softly, so the others couldn't hear. 'Now, turn round, my special one. Let Aruline check your fittings.'

Anya held her breath and bit her lip. Would she know? How could she tell when the guard himself had unknotted and re-fastened it twice? Her skirt was being lifted; she could hear Aruline's breathing; she could hear the thumping of her own heartbeat. When the fingertips touched the knot, she shivered. 'Oh dear,' Aruline murmured, very softly, yet in a way so charged with foreboding that Anya felt as if ice water was running down inside and out across the thighs that now were being separated so fully. 'Oh dear . . .' The fingers lifted up the knot, which now felt loose; it had felt so tight and cutting, so how could it suddenly feel so loose? Could her guilt have loosened it? It was so loose that Aruline could easily stroke the skin beneath it. 'Guard?' Anya heard him step forward, then grunt, as Aruline tapped the knot. Again the feeling came; Anya knew he was shaking his head. It had been a surprised grunt, a grunt of disavowal. 'But how could this have come about, guard?' Aruline's voice, no longer a murmur, though still calm, sounded now accusing, and firm; her tone passed judgement on the guard, called his diligence into question.

'My lady, I . . . I swear I don't know . . .' But the quaver in his voice proclaimed his laxness in this matter. 'Unless it was the girls,' he added, by way of mitigation of his failings.

'Hmm. Let us hope so, guard.'

Yet it was too late, too late for Anya, anyway. She knew

it. Her head was pushed down until her cheek lay on the mattress. The hand bearing the crop was placed against her buttocks; she could feel the loop of leather brush the end point of her spine. Aruline's words confirmed the worst: 'But let us not rush into hasty conclusions on this matter of responsibility; let us ascertain.' Anya could feel the knot being unfastened. The crop lay balanced on the left cheek of her buttocks. It swayed as Aruline's fingers worked at the knot. Finally the rope was lifted; it came away very easily, quickly pulling free from Anya's flesh and swinging between her thighs. 'Hm.' That short sound was so ominous.

Anya's flesh contracted as the cheeks were separated, then the crop was lifted from her skin. 'Turn over, my darling.' Her skirt was lifted to the level of her chin, so she could not see what Aruline was doing between her thighs. She could see only her face. Anya shivered as she felt the rope being lifted and rested on her belly. She felt the woman's hands press against her inner thighs and lift them wide apart. As Aruline looked upon her open belly, Anya looked upon Aruline's face, which suddenly seemed large and powerful.

She felt almost like a child in this woman's hands. This feeling was very strange. She did not understand how this woman, not much older than Anya and physically not much larger, could exert such power simply by her presence. It wasn't only Anya who had experienced it; the other girls were terrified. When the guard had implicated them, they had backed into the further corner of the cage. Even the guard seemed afraid.

And now Aruline's nostrils dilated once again as she drew breath deeply. Then she looked straight at Anya, who was so frightened that she dared not look away. Aruline's gaze transfixed her, even as the running chills cascaded down her widespread thighs.

Aruline smiled to see those shivers; she triggered them again and again as she touched Anya's belly and her sex, and stroked it with the crop. The guard stood by and watched. 'Oh, how this crop would dearly love to kiss these luscious sex lips,' Aruline murmured huskily, pressing it against them, making Anya want to cry. 'Mmm . . . But now, you shall hold your body open – very, very wide, my dear. Let us plumb the depths of your veracity . . . Let these fingers touch your heart.' She made Anya spread until her toes were pointing to the farther corners of the ceiling of the cage. Anya dared not move her eyes from Aruline's, but she could see the girls at the periphery of her vision; nobody made a sound. The guard stood like a statue. Beyond the bars, Sarol-harn was being led back to the cage. She stopped in her tracks; the sergeant did not push her onwards. Many soldiers were gathered round. Anya closed her eyes when she felt Aruline's fingers spread apart her flesh leaves. 'No, my darling, no. Did you learn nothing in the castle?'

Anya understood; she opened her eyes, but she tried to make her eyes unseeing as Aruline made her hold her flesh lips open while two fingers entered her, very slowly. 'There . . . Do not allow this flesh to contract. Take them into you as you did last night – as you did the living cockstem! Yes!' Aruline's eyes flashed; Anya contracted tightly. Aruline had to thrust her fingers, but she did not desist however Anya tightened, and Anya did, for her body was beyond her own control. It did not want these unloving penetrations. Yet the fingers were insistent; they pushed until the middle finger pressed against her womb. That middle finger tried to push deeper, where it could not possibly go, until Anya cried out with the pain. Aruline smiled. Her face lowered until it filled Anya's vision. The finger kept pressing very hard inside her. Aruline took Anya's lower lip between hers and sucked upon it hard, nipping it with her teeth as she sucked, drawing the blood into it, bruising.

'You are mine,' she whispered, so the others could not hear. 'The Duke has given you to me – for my amusement.' And as the thumb was pressed against her nubbin, pushing, Anya tightened so hard she could feel the joints of Aruline's fingers deep inside her. Aruline lifted up. With her free hand she removed Anya's hands from where they had held her sex lips open and she placed them instead to Anya's breasts. She made her press her breasts together very hard, until

Aruline could gather the nipples together between three fingertips and a thumb and press and try to twist them up against each other.

'Shall I have the truth my dear, or shall these nipples taste the crop?' Again Aruline smiled as Anya tightened against the fingers still inside her. She released the swollen tips then knelt on the mattress, to the side, and placed her hand on Anya's mound. With her fingers split on either side of Anya's sex, she slowly drew the bedded fingers out against the tightness. She held them to her lips then smelled them. Anya wanted to bury her head. Aruline simply looked at her, then tasted, pushing the fingers deep into her mouth. She withdrew them, licked her lips, then turned her head to one side as if undecided. 'Well my dear? The truth – is this a man upon my fingers?' Anya snapped her head to the side. She would not answer; she would never betray him, never. 'Very well. Ah, but I almost forgot . . .' Now Aruline's smile was sly. 'We have one more avenue of illicit pleasure unexplored. Turn over again, my dear.'

'No, please. I beg of you . . . not there.' She was beaten. She could not bear that degradation, the penetration of that intimate place, in front of all these people. 'It . . . It is true.' Her eyes remained downcast. 'I slipped out of the cage last night . . .'

'With a man?'

Anya nodded. When she looked up, her tears were overflowing. 'But he is not to blame. Do not punish him, please?'

Aruline's eyes lit up. 'But why would I want to punish him, my darling? It is you that has transgressed. Yet your sudden frank admission at this late stage – at this particular juncture – has intrigued me. Turn over, all the same.' So Anya was made to suffer the degradation despite her confession, with her face buried and her back arched down and her bottom in the air. And though the fingers were wet with Anya's seepage now mixed with Aruline's spittle, still the entrance was so tight on account of this shameless public persecution that with less single-minded fingers it might never have been achieved at all. But Aruline knew what she

94

wanted; in the end, Anya's body yielded. 'Good,' Aruline said, making clear to all who could not see in detail that the degradation had been brought about. The fingers were inserted to the knuckle before being drawn out much more quickly. Anya was turned over. Aruline sniffed her fingers.

'I trust your flesh showed more cooperation in your illicit escapade, my love.' Again she tasted. 'We shall have to teach this flesh a little more control. But that is for later. I will forgive this one transgression.' Anya sighed, but the respite was short-lived. 'I will punish you very gently. Take her out, guard. Strip her naked. Tie her to the stake. The girls may watch.' Aruline took up the crop and swished it. Anya began to cry out loud. 'Ah,' said Aruline, 'it is better that these pent-up feelings be allowed to run their course.' Again the crop swished quickly. She took Anya by the hair and whispered: 'My head is light, my love; my blood is coursing through my veins like wine. This is what you do to me.'

Aruline instructed that Anya be placed facing the post, with her wrists crossed around it, then drawn up and fastened to the horizontal pegs projecting from the top. That posture forced her body closely to the upright, so her breasts were separated round it. Aruline pressed the nipples to the smoothness of the wood; she wet them, then very carefully rolled them until they firmed. Now she removed the blue silk rope completely from Anya's waist and passed it in a single loop around her upper back, beneath her breasts and up between them and secured it to the pegs. Next she took a length of very fine thong and fastened the nipples together round the pole. So now Anya's shoulders and her upper body – and particularly her breasts – were held secure while her belly, legs and bottom remained entirely free to move. Anya could feel the pressure concentrated in her breasts, as they pressed against the pole, as the silk rope lifted them and squeezed beneath them, as the fine thong cut into the tightly swollen tips.

Aruline licked the smooth skin underneath the nipples, and licked around the thong. 'Move your feet back,' she murmured. Anya's feet edged back from the post as far as the loop about her upper back would permit. Her supple body arched until her lower back was almost horizontal. She felt as if her breasts were bursting. Her legs were moved apart while Aruline tested the roundness and the separation, touching her in her split. The loop end of the crop was slipped between her thighs. She shivered as her sex lips were drawn fully through this loop. Aruline then played with her until she moistened; she pulled and rubbed the sex lips till they tightened to the loop. When Aruline released the crop, it dangled down between Anya's thighs. Aruline came round the front and kissed her long and deep whilst simultaneously nipping her fingers at her teats. As Anya's body moved, the dangling crop swung and tapped against her thighs. As the kiss progressed, Aruline's fingertips wormed down Anya's belly and tickled at her nubbin, then took hold of the crop and slowly pulled it free. Anya's flesh lips now felt hot and wet. Aruline sniffed her fingers.

Once again, Aruline was at the back. 'Up on tiptoes. Quick,' she said. Though the bottom pushed further out, and the belly quaked, Aruline waited until a visible shiver ran up those thighs before two quick slashes descended, one across the buttocks, the other across the backs of the upper thighs. There was a short delay before Anya cried out. 'Up higher.' The quick cuts struck again. 'Good,' Aruline murmured. 'Good girl. Very good. Stay up.' Now Aruline's fingers were between Anya's thighs, moving urgently, stroking the smooth taut muscles, then moving forwards, spreading the flesh lips, finding the nubbin, squeezing till it slipped. 'Mmm. No, keep on your toes, my darling. There . . . So slippery. Mmm.'

Anya's ears burned at these words; she knew they were designed to shame her, and she knew that very soon, her flesh would deliver itself to shame in front of all these people. As the weals burned her bottom and throbbed across her thighs, the fingertips rolled her nubbin as if it were a tiny ball of oiled dough, which was being carefully shaped, and drawn out to a point. Then the point was tickled. The precise and inescapable insistency of the pleasure made her squirm until she whimpered, whereupon the lips were squeezed together and then the fingertips were gone. She stiffened, heard the cruel swish and the quick cuts came again. Before the gasp had cleared her throat, the lips were being separated and the nubbin worked again, this time by a rapid rubbing action, which stopped, then rubbed again repeatedly until Anya felt her belly slowly tightening towards a desperately needed yet totally unwanted very base delight. Again the hand was taken away. The throbbing in her buttocks felt warm and prickly. A single cut stung her upper thighs. She was made to spread her legs wider, for the fingers to touch, at first, and then to probe, her bottom mouth. When they were taken away, she heard them being wetted; that sound made her belly sink.

'No, do not close, my dearest. Do not be so shy. The soldiers like to see a girl take pleasure in this way.' Anya almost died with degradation as the fingers were reapplied. 'Too tight, you must relax this muscle.' And though she did not want it, she felt the tight mouth yielding to the persistent, moist and wickedly pleasurable stimulation. 'There now, is that nice?' Aruline whispered in her ear. The fingers withdrew, then found the entrance once again and quickly slipped inside. The bottom mouth had opened this time; the bottom mouth was willing. Anya detested it; she hated the pleasure mixed with pain; she hated the degradation. But her body liked the feelings deep inside, the warm ball of pressure between her legs that made her flesh expand, that made the small mouth of her bottom accept the slippery fingers. 'I will make your pleasure come, my darling.' Anya felt a lump in her thoat. 'I will wet my fingers in your mouth and rub this little nubbin till you cry out with delight.' Anya could not swallow. The sinking came again, between her legs, as Aruline's fingers, the same strongly scented fingers that had touched between her buttocks, now pushed into Anya's mouth, and her tongue disgraced her body by slipping round, then in between those fingers, not simply coating them with wet but stroking them and stretching out to press against the separating skin. When Anya opened her eyes, Aruline's face was very close. Aruline's eyes were wide. Her lips moved softly, yet she did not speak at first.

Finally the words came out. 'Delicious creature, I will have you for my own,' she said. 'For that, your pleasure shall be redoubled. I shall smack this bottom while you come.' Anya was shaking her head.

'No, please,' she whispered weakly, but Aruline's warm soft lips closed around her own to smother her dissent.

'Indeed, my love . . .' Aruline's other hand, the one that held the crop, rested lightly on Anya's buttocks. 'I shall smack this,' her little finger ventured into the joining, 'only this.' The little finger touched and Anya shuddered. When it rubbed round in a circle, Anya closed her eyes. She was imagining the pad of the finger smacking the sensitive flesh, while other fingers squeezed her yearning nubbin till she came. Now, she wanted it. Her face and neck flushed hot with delicious anticipation. 'Yes. I shall smack this small hot mouth – with the leather tip of my crop.'

'No!'

Suddenly, she didn't want it any more. But the fingertip at least was kind; the fingertip massaged her very gently. The other fingers, wet and cool, searched between her legs from the front and closed around her nubbin. Her body was trapped between the massaging whirls of pleasure and the soft squeeze of delight, and the suggestive words which bathed her skin in sweet delicious shame. 'I shall rub this bud of delectation. Your pleasure shall express between the crop-tip and my fingers. And if you do not pass out with delight, I will explore your lewdness till you do, in the comfort of my carriage, throughout the day, then in the tent, throughout the night if needs be. Be assured, your pleasure shall come repeatedly until your body swoons.'

Between the probing and the squeezing, when her back was arched down, her legs spread wide, very open to those caresses, and the seductive words so calculatingly delivered, Anya's flesh was already on the very brink of pleasure. Her flesh leaves had turned very soft and slippery. They throbbed with a delicious heat. Aruline made her bow her legs out – while remaining up on tiptoes – so the smacks could be delivered accurately, deep within the groove, to the tautly stretched sensitive rim rather than the buttocks. With two fingers and a thumb squeezed round the moistened nub, the smacking was bestowed in short quick flicks, which snapped the leather loop against the rim. 'Push out. There.' Each lick of leather made the nubbin slip against the fingers.

Though the smacks were measured and assured, the finger kissing of the nub was nervous, making Anya catch her breath and tense her thighs as the fingers worked and tapped and lightly scratched, until it felt as if the flesh around her nubbin was swollen hard and like a nut. The wetted fingers closed around this polished slippery nut and simply held it while the smacking on the mouth of the bottom echoed through to make the fingers squeeze against the nubflesh like a sucker. Soft whimpers of barely subdued pleasure counterpointed the intermittent sharp crack of the whip against her bottom mouth. The sucker sucked, the crop cracked down, the bottom mouth contracted. That was the unchanging, irresistible rhythm until Anya's thighs and belly cramped. Even then, the fingers did not move at all against the polished nut. But as the leather loop was pressed against her, in her groove, then wetted and pressed again, then slowly introduced into her bottom, her belly shuddered. And when the loop was twisted very gently round, so it kissed against her inner flesh like a trapped butterfly inside her, it felt to Anya that the small nut held gently between those fingers burst, and a wave of liquid warmth of pleasure was flooded between her thighs.

Her bottom contracted hard against the end of the crop stem pushed inside her. Her back and belly, her inner thighs were covered in perspiration; when Aruline sucked her tethered nipples, the nut swelled hard once more, the fingers closed around it, then the leather twirled, and the flooding feeling came again, more strongly than before. Her body sagged. Her legs remained bowed out; she did not close her thighs without Aruline's instruction. Aruline's hand still held her palpitating sex bud. 'Excellent, my sweet.' There were murmurs from the crowd. The leather loop was drawn from her body against the strength of another contraction. 'Mm. And I love the tightness in that bottom. I see it as a challenge.' Aruline stood behind Anya, bending, with both hands between her thighs, stroking Anya's belly, then wiping the perspiration from her with a kerchief. 'But you did not yet pass out,' she observed demurely.

While Anya's shudders fell away to an evenness of breathing, Aruline stroked her fingers against inner thighs, the cheeks of the bottom, the little tiny mouth, then pressed her hands together round the flesh lips, squeezing hard until they hurt. And yet despite the hurt, a pressured pleasure was induced by that intimate caress, and Anya's nubbin stirred again. Aruline therefore squeezed her very much tighter, until Anya cried out; then a finger and thumb closed about the hooding of the flesh leaves. The leaves were very thin and soft; the nubbin underneath was hardened up to aching.

Aruline now had Anya unfastened. She stood several yards away. When Anya turned, all the faces looked upon her. Several women expressed consternation at the incident that followed.

Aruline held her hand out, but it was cupped, and held below waist height. 'Come to me, my precious. Place your jewel in my hand,' she said. Anya did as she was bid. She walked across, lifted up and placed her thighs about the outstretched hand as if it were a saddle. As the palm enclosed her burning fleshpot and very gently squeezed, the wave of submissive pleasure threatened to drown her. Aruline made her hold her head up against the murmurs of disapproval. The women were now dismissed, all but for Riga. 'This one shall entertain the Duke,' Aruline told the guard, then whispered to Anya, 'while you and I are otherwise occupied.'

And so it was that Anya was brought once again to the carriage, to spend that day in transit, to be taken out only to be fed, to attend to her toilet and to be washed – but not soaped or perfumed – and to satisfy each of Aruline's fancies. She was required to submit willingly to these things, without coersion or restraint, and she was pleasured repeatedly until Aruline's fingers glistened wet with Anya's body juices. 'I wish to see how many times I may induce this flesh to come,' Aruline said. And it seemed the wetter

Anya's flesh became, the more insistent were Aruline's attentions. So protracted and intimate, so unrelenting were these attentions, that not only Anya's flesh lips, her inner thighs and bottom, but also her nipples, her navel, her eyebrows and her earlobes were slicked with her own distributed wetness. It had seeped into the velvet of Aruline's tights where Anya had been made to lie outspread across her knee, and Anya's nubbin itched and burned ferociously where it rubbed against the hot damp velvet. 'My darling, pleasure can still be brought about, even when flesh is tender,' Aruline explained when Anya finally pleaded for respite, 'it simply takes a little longer. Have patience, my dear.' And in due course, against the throbbing and the itching as the cruel wet fingers worked, while perhaps a lock of Anya's hair was curled or an earlobe gently rubbed, a burning pleasure would be delivered in between her wide-held thighs.

Riga had been stripped naked, apart from a red plaited cord which had been secured about her waist, and had been placed at the Duke's disposal. 'She is small and light; she will not tire my lord,' Aruline declared, and the Duke thanked her for her careful consideration.

Aruline seemed to want only to play with Anya, to make her pleasure come about in long-drawn-out and shameful ways. 'I like to watch you when you come,' she said at one point, and Anya felt the sinking feeling in her belly. 'I like to look at your expression. I like to look into your eyes.' Aruline decided that she wished to see Anya come without her body moving. Anya did not understand; Aruline elucidated. 'You shall stand. I do not wish to see you move a muscle when you come. I wish to see your depth of pleasure only in your eyes.' Aruline made her stand with her back to the carriage door for this amusement. The Duke, with Riga on his lap, watched with great absorption, holding Riga's knees together, lifting them and stroking beneath her pressed-together thighs.

While Anya stood with legs apart and hands upon her belly, Aruline closed the flesh hood round her nubbin and slid it wetly up and down, gripping it definitely between her fingertips but sliding intermittently in tiny nervous jerks. The tightness of the pleasure swelled to bursting, and Aruline therefore held the sleeved-down nubbin still. 'Breathe evenly my dear. There.' The nervous jerking began again. Anya didn't know whether she was allowed to swallow. She wanted to push her belly out. The beads of perspiration gathered beneath her breasts and in the creases of her thigh. Aruline collected up the body syrup on her finger and pasted it round the outer surface of the flesh hood. Anya's sex lips were so hot the syrup quickly dried and turned her sex lips silky. The sliding now took up again, until Anya almost gasped. Aruline carefully pressed the flesh hood back until the nubbin stood out sharply.

'Now, I want you to come – but very still, mind.' Anya knew she could never do it. Riga watched intently. Riga was moving; her bottom was moving against the Duke's hand. Aruline was moving too. 'Tense up, my dear. Push and hold. Very steady, now.' Aruline knelt and arched her tongue up to a sharp point which tickled lightly at the tip of the nubbin, touching then withdrawing, so the wet on Anya's nubbin felt like a second skin which was slowly being pulled. Aruline pressed her hands high up on Anya's thighs, then suddenly drew her head back. The nubbin pulsed. Anya had the sudden urge to squirm. Aruline stood up. 'Look into my eyes. Now, very still . . .' Her velvet suit kept brushing against the skin hairs on Anya's tight and naked body. 'You may open your mouth wide. Are you ready? Very still . . . And come.' Aruline's fingertip touched her, breaking the film of saliva, and sticking, skin to skin against her nubbin. When the fingertip pulled away, and the velvet cuff of Aruline's jacket brushed her inner thigh, she came, very slowly yet inescapably.

Aruline did not speak; her eyes were wide. Anya's eyelids were very heavy. Her body did not move. Her breathing was steady. Though nothing touched her nubbin now, the velvet cuffs kept brushing upwards to each side, stroking her silken sex lips. Yet Anya could still feel the echo of that pull about her nubbin. The pulling feeling went deeper and deeper, and stronger too, sucking through her belly and breasts and up into her throat, until it felt as if her inner flesh had liquefied and was being sucked out between her thighs.

Afterwards, she closed her eyes. Aruline's soft lips kissed her belly. Her belly gently shimmered. The deep waves drew again. It began all over again. The moist lips searched within her open fleshpot, so very soft now, so dripping wet. They gently closed about her nubbin, sucking her until the slow pulsations came. This time Anya cried out loud, for the pleasure was too intense to bear. Aruline lapped her liquid up and sucked each sweet pulsation. 'Mmm . . . So nearly, darling. You were very, very good.' And prolonged and cruel as her torture had thus far been, at these words, Anya felt a sudden surge of warmth for Aruline which she did not fully understand.

Aruline turned. Riga still sat upon the Duke's lap. Both of them were immobilised by this spectacle of pleasure. Riga's eyes were wide. 'Wasn't she good, my little one?' Riga turned her head and looked away. Aruline got up, spread Riga's legs very wide, placed her palm flat against her open fleshpot and rubbed her with the heel of her hand. She bent her head to kiss her. Before their lips touched, Riga came. 'And you're good too, my darling, so impetuous, so sweetly innocent . . .' Aruline kissed her long and slow, then lifted up her palm and licked it. Riga's eyes were full of love for Aruline, Anya could see it. It made her uneasy. She did not like them caressing one another. She did not know why. She did not understand her feelings fully. Her belly, breasts and thighs glowed with a soft and loving warmth.

But Aruline soon returned to Anya, spreading her across her lap, and now Anya found her attentions too insistent. The touching never stopped as Aruline brought her repeatedly to the brink, and Anya became sore. At one point, after rubbing which had proceeded so long that Anya's flesh had yielded up all its wet and had become dry, so when the fingertip passed very rapidly across her nubbin, she felt a hot and searing pain like a burn, she cried out so sharply that Aruline decided that Anya might be permitted to rest. But she did not wish that flesh to lose its state of awareness, as she put it, and she therefore laid Anya on her

103

back along the seat. A firm cushion was placed beneath her buttocks, but her legs were secured with bands of purple silk at the ankles and above the knees. With her buttocks raised, her fleshpot peeped between her pressed-together thighs. Aruline stroked her belly firmly upwards, to lift the fleshpot higher. She then took from her workbox a smoothly polished cockstem fashioned from white stone. She lifted Anya's head and made her throw it back.

'Open your mouth a little; pout your lips. There . . .' she whispered. Anya was made to take the plum between her lips and suck. The cockstem tasted very strongly of a woman's heat. While Aruline supported her head and sucked her neck and earlobe, she had to balance the cockstem between her lips and let it, driven by its weight, slide slowly in, until her pouted lower lip touched the surface of the bumps. Aruline carefully drew it out, then holding it horizontally with the bumps uppermost, she introduced it, with some difficulty, between Anya's tight-shut thighs. And Anya found that feeling was delicious – the thick plum trying to distend her when her thighs were fastened together, and her sex was swollen from the working, and when the stem was pushed in to the hilt, the inverted bumps held apart her flesh leaves at their joining. Each time her sex contracted, the stem was drawn within; the bumps imparted a hard round pressure to each side of Anya's nubbin to swell the flesh between. So even though her flesh was sore, she wanted to be touched. The feeling came so strongly in her belly that it hurt. Aruline seemed to recognise her wanting. She kissed the quaking belly once, exactly on the navel. She blew cool air upon the burning nubbin, then she rolled Anya's body over, so she was face down, her breasts and belly against the soft-piled seat, and the bumps pressed against her flesh to stimulate that wanting. Each time the carriage rolled or jerked, a softened pressure squeezed about her nubbin like a suck.

Whilst this gentle pleasure progressed, Anya's face was turned to the side, that she might watch Aruline pleasure Riga, who sat astride the Duke's thighs, facing Anya, with the red band about her waist, the Duke's hands about her breasts, the Duke's cockstem up inside her. But the Duke's eyes were fixed upon Anya's languorous face as Aruline by turns sucked upon Riga's lower belly at the junction of her thighs, then, when her pleasure rose too sharply, smacked her belly and smacked her inner thighs until at last Riga's pleasure was delivered upon Aruline's tongue. Then, while Riga relaxed and recovered on her side, with the Duke's appendage still within, her heavy eyelids were stimulated not to close by the treatment now bestowed on Anya.

The silk bands were removed, her legs were spread apart and as the carriage rolled, as Aruline's fingers held her buttocks wide, with Aruline's thumbs pressed against the ballocks to push the cockstem up inside. The contraction of Anya's sex around the unyielding cockstem made her cry out with the pain.

Aruline took a velvet-coated thimble from her box and fitted it to the middle finger of her right hand. The fingers of her left hand once more spread the cheeks apart. While the warm slim tongue bestowed liquid kisses at the round swirl of delight, the thimbled finger reached beneath. Velvet pleasure stroked the nubbin very lightly. Then the contractions came, repeatedly, very cruelly, and very tightly about the rigid cockstem plum as that wickedly ill-used body shuddered once again.

Aruline merely sat back, pressing her palms to those buttocks, keeping them wide apart while she watched the alabaster ballocks jump, in short delicious spasms, between the open thighs.

She was fascinated by these girls. She loved the way that, with appropriate and suitably prolonged attentions, the girls' lewdness could be elicited. And now, she would preserve that lewdness, that powerful smell of musk. She would secure it with the silk. Very carefully, she removed the cockstem and placed it in her workbox. Once again she took the blue silk rope and bound it round the waist and up between the delectable thighs, binding tightly to the creases of delight, to protect that tiny bottom and that luscious musky fleshpot and to keep the nubbin hard while Aruline helped the Duke gain satisfaction with the girl.

It was at this point that Aruline's plans were rudely interrupted.

[7]

The Excesses of Thieves

A second after Aruline's hand was lifted from her back, Anya heard a high-pitched whirr, a thud and then a scream. She jerked round. At first, she could not believe what she beheld: an arrow had passed between Aruline's fingers and was bedded in the seat. Aruline was shaking. Another arrow struck the further door. From up above them, on the roof, came a powerful thump, then grunts and sounds of scuffling. The carriage rocked. Two people tumbled past the window; they were followed by a third. Outside were cries and screams, then hoofbeats. Aruline fell to the floor. Riga cowered in the corner of the seat opposite. The Duke's face was deathly pale as he hurriedly buttoned up his clothing.

'Bandits . . .' His voice had almost failed him. The carriage suddenly speeded up and the shouts were redoubled. Through the broken shutter of the window, Anya glimpsed horsemen, not soldiers, but men clad in a great variety of garbs, men with longbows. Yet though they chased the carriage at a gallop, the horsemen were receding; the carriage was gaining speed, swaying uncontrollably, so Anya, even lying flat, could not keep her balance on the seat. 'The horses are bolting,' cried the Duke. 'They cannot hold them.' Anya knew this was because the coachman and his mate were far behind them, on the ground; she had seen them take the dive. Aruline began to wail.

But Anya was not afraid, not until the crashing sounds began. Branches started hitting the roof and sides, breaking down the shutters completely and scattering a debris of leaves and twigs inside. The horses were making wild snorting sounds; the carriage moved even faster. It creaked and groaned. Aruline's workbox spilled onto the floor, sending balls of silk, buttons, thongs and alabaster attributes in every direction. The Duke collapsed on top of Aruline. The mirror on the opposite wall shattered, showering shards all over Riga, who curled up tighter, into a ball, a soft pink ball with a red silk band around it. Then there came a dreadful bang; the carriage lurched, a wheel rolled past the window and a thick wooden stave burst through the floor a foot away from Aruline, who suddenly stopped screaming altogether. Anya could hear the horses, broken free now from their fetters, thundering off into the distance as the carriage tilted, wavered to a temporary halt then very slowly tipped onto its side, sweeping Anya, Riga and Aruline into an untidy heap which completely buried the Duke.

For a long while, all was still. Anya's knee pressed against something very warm and soft. When she moved it, she could hear the Duke groan plaintively. She moved it once again. Then she heard the arriving horses, and the cries. There were people clambering onto the overturned carriage. Above them, on the side up in the air, a face appeared, then another. The second face looked huge. There were murmurs of approval, shouts of glee.

'There's two at least,' the first voice called.

'No – three!' the giant one corrected.

Anya was suddenly very conscious of the state of her undress. She wore only the blue rope; Riga wore nothing but the bright red cord about her middle. 'And will you look at them . . . Bardin! Come and look!' the giant shouted, giving a low whistle. Then Anya caught a glimpse of a man who looked younger than the other two and sported a moustache. The door was now flung open.

'Right, everybody out!' he ordered. 'Come on! Give the girls a hand, Ulf. Let's sort the nobles from the wenches.' The huge one reached down into the carriage and hauled Riga out as if she were weightless. Then Anya felt her arm being wrenched out from its socket before she went dizzy at the speed she was pulled into the air.

Finally, the vanquished stood on the grass gazing forlornly at their captors. Anya looked at the wreckage of the blue and golden carriage, then at the creatures who had ambushed them. They were a very ragged crowd. How could the Duke's soldiers have been beaten off by these men? Some of them looked like vagabonds, others like peasants. One wore a soldier's uniform. Another was dressed like a lord, with a long purple cloak and a silk hat with a feather, though the feather was tattered and the cloak was stained. No two men were dressed alike, and like their horses, they seemed to come in every shape and size. One of them was only half as tall as Anya; another – the one named Ulf – towered above everyone; Anya had never seen a man so large. Some carried staves, others swords, but most of them had longbows. Several of the bows were drawn; the arrows pointed at the Duke, who had fallen to his knees.

Already, two wooden chests from the carriage were being plundered and Aruline's clothing was being handed round. She stood stone-faced as the men began to snigger. The man they had called Bardin, who appeared to be their leader, advanced with great assurance towards Aruline. He wore a green velvet jacket and in addition to the longbow, he wore a sword. Anya thought him handsome, except for the moustache. But now Aruline's expression had mysteriously changed from terror to timidity. Then it changed again. She looked down shyly, then looked directly at him. She lifted her head and very slightly parted her lips. He stepped towards her, pulled her head back by her hair and kissed her, long and hard. When he stepped away again, Aruline gulped for breath. The bowman beside Anya nudged her and chuckled, 'Got a good eye for the women, has our Bardin. Knows what he wants, and usually gets it . . .' All the men began to laugh. Anya was very frightened by the way this man had winked at her and leered.

'Please . . .?' the Duke began to whimper as the bowmen moved closer. But they were distracted by the shouts. A group of their companions appeared, driving Sarol-harn, Shira and the other cage-girls before them and dragging a string of roped-together soldiers and wagoners. The sergeant was among them but Anya could not see her soldier.

108

Perhaps he had got away? Then she heard the cries of surprise as Riga bolted. She had been standing next to Anya, then suddenly, she was dodging between the bowmen and running towards the trees.

Anya tried to follow her example, but she didn't get very far. Ulf's giant hand swung down behind her to grasp the rope about her waist and she was lifted, screaming and kicking, into the air. He dangled her at arm's length and shook her until her breasts bounced up and down. The howls of laughter rose to cut her more cruelly than the rope did. She felt giddy as her body slowly overbalanced and she dangled upside down, with only the tightness of the rope above her hips preventing her from crashing headlong to the ground. But it seemed this treatment was but a prelude to the degradation that ensued.

'Bottom up!' Ulf shouted, to renewed hilarity. 'It seems this missy knows what is required!' Then he smacked her bottom, with loud, deliberate slaps delivered with a hand so large that it encompassed both cheeks simultaneously. He ignored her struggles – her wild gyrations only served to shake her breasts and make the laughter even louder – and he smacked her until the cheeks were rendered bright red, though not so red as those other cheeks that burned with vanquished shame. And now, as the burly fingers began squeezing her upturned breasts, shaking them, pulling and flicking her nipples, Anya's tears flowed freely.

'Enough, Ulf!' Anya could see Bardin's laughing face beneath her, looking up. 'Surely we must treat our guests in a more gentlemanly fashion? You would not have them think us lacking in refinement?' This only seemed to cause another uproar. 'Remove her bonds.'

Ulf grunted. Anya was turned upright and cradled in a giant forearm. As her tears began to stem, she could feel Ulf's great thick fingers close about the cord around her waist. And that touch, coming so soon after the smacking – the fingers, warm from where they had made her bottom burn, but now inserted under her cord, pressing irresistibly against her belly – made her shudder. Beneath the strength of his fingers, the cord pulled apart as easily as if it were made of wet parchment, and Ulf dropped it to the ground. Yet the simple act of those powerful fingers breaking the cord that bound her sex and belly forced a shock wave through Anya's body which made her feel dizzy. It was the feeling of being completely naked in this giant's arms. And when his huge hand opened to cup her bare sex and her burning buttocks, the feeling came again, more strongly. She could not get her breath as the weight of her body spread her buttocks on his palm. His fingers extended up between her legs to spread across her belly. The middle finger pressed against her liquid sex lips. To accommodate that hand, her thighs were forced to spread so wide that the muscles almost cramped. As he pulled her to his breast and enfolded her in his other arm, with the broad hand round her head, Anya looked up into that strong and massive face, and the vision came, the vision of her being made to press her lips against the powerful cheek and chin, and again she shuddered. With that shudder, her sex lips softly pulsed against his finger. Ulf grunted. The feeling came again. It was rooted in between her open thighs; it was very strong and it was very sexual indeed.

Ulf lowered Anya gently to the grass. Her body rolled, and with her knees drawn up, the cool grass sprang against her breasts and lower belly. It tickled her open sex lips. Bardin stood above her. 'I think the missy may have taken a fancy to you, Ulf.' Her leg was suddenly lifted. She hid her face completely from the shame. 'But will you look at the colour of this . . .' And now the disgrace was double-edged, coming as it did, so soon upon those other feelings of warm arousal. When everyone had satisfied their vulgar curiosity about Anya's blackness, and her legs were permitted to close, she drew her knees up tightly and tried to curl up into a tiny ball. But Bardin would not allow her that deliverance.

'Get up! Unless you wish to be served up at the feast.' Anya did not understand the reference but she knew it to be a threat. She got up quickly, only to witness Riga being dragged back from the trees, then handed over to Ulf, who held her upside down with her legs parted while Bardin smacked her between her open thighs. 'Now, let that be a lesson – to all our very honoured guests,' Bardin declared, bowing to the women as he did so, making Anya turn very pale.

The Duke was stripped and his clothing was redistributed. He cowered in his undergarments and his short white wig. The women were herded together – all, that is, apart from Aruline. Bardin stood beside her and declared that nobody should touch her. When she whispered something into his ear, he looked across at Anya then pursed his lips. It made Anya afraid of what Aruline might have told him. His gaze was then distracted by the arrival of a wagon driven by a short barrel-shaped man in a great coat that was too large for him. Bardin directed this man to supervise the unloading of meat, salt, grain, gourds of wine and other provisions into panniers on packhorses. Anya wondered why they did not simply take the wagon. Most of the food had to be left behind.

A young man arrived, riding bareback on a piebald horse. He was clad in a deerskin jacket and a matching wide-brimmed hat, and he carried a small casket with a leather strap around it. He did not dismount, but unfastened the strap and dropped the casket at Bardin's feet. The impact caused the catch to fly open and gold coins to spill on the ground.

'Brekt!' cried Bardin, 'I knew I could rely on you! Look lads!' There were shouts of approval all around. The young man was facing Anya; he was looking at her, even as he spoke to Bardin.

'The drivers put up a fight,' he said as one of the bowmen began scooping the coins back into the casket. 'In the end, they threw it over the side, so I sent them after it. I almost lost my hat.' Brekt removed it and began reshaping it. Bardin laughed, but Brekt seemed very serious. His voice had been light, though it was clear to Anya that he had been trying to make it sound rough and stern. He was staring at Anya. He had very dark eyes, almost black, and smooth dense eyebrows, but thin lips and a small, finely featured face. He wasn't tall. Anya couldn't imagine Brekt winning a

111

struggle with the coachman. He took off his hat again and wiped his brow, then turned to look at the Duke. Brekt's hair was very dark brown, with a single long lock at the nape. There was something strange about him – the slightness of his body. He didn't look so rough and careworn as the others. When he finally slid from the horse and took a swig from the gourd of wine that Bardin offered, Anya noticed that his hands were small. When Ulf slapped him on the back, Brekt simply stared at him until he edged uneasily away. But Brekt didn't look like a bandit, Anya decided. He didn't fit in with the rest.

Once the packhorses were loaded, Bardin ordered that the women ride behind the men. He took Aruline in his arms and carried her to his horse. Riga was taken by Ulf and placed upon his carthorse. She formed a tiny doll-like figure behind him. The other women were chosen one by one. The Duke and the soldiers were tied together and left on the cart. Bardin returned and said something to Brekt; Brekt stared intently at Anya. She looked away. She knew he would choose her. When at last her gaze returned, Brekt was giving some instruction to a man who now wore the Duke's coat over his tatters. The man approached Anya, grabbed her very roughly by the arm and dragged her over to the piebald horse. She looked pleadingly towards Brekt, who simply stared. A man carrying a pannier walked past, and when he noticed Brekt staring at Anya he berated him. But Anya was very puzzled by his words:

'Not a girl again, Brekt? Why not do it properly? Get yourself a man.' As he passed, Brekt's small foot lashed out, catching him between the legs, causing him to collapse to the floor.

'Better men than you have tried it,' Brekt retorted, and as those dark eyes glinted at her, Anya suddenly knew for certain what she ought to have suspected from the first: Brekt was a woman.

The man cursed Brekt loudly, yet she totally ignored him now and he staggered away without attempting any retaliation. She was looking again at Anya. It made Anya even more uneasy. Why was she dressed like a man?

Anya jumped as the man holding her arm spoke: 'He'll be carrying his ballocks in a sling for a good while yet.' He shook his head. 'She's a tough nut, that one . . . Don't ever dare to cross her.' And with that, Anya was lifted up and slung like a pannier over Brekt's bareback piebald horse. Brekt adjusted her hat, then mounted the horse in such a way that Anya was behind her, and they fell into line with the other horses which had set off at a walk.

They travelled for a long while, during which Brekt ignored Anya. Anya might have been a blanket rather than a human being. What made it worse was that she could hear the others laughing and talking. She heard Shira's voice several times. When the horses rode three or four abreast in the clearings, she could see that the other girls had been allowed to sit up, some in front of the riders, but most of them behind, clasping their arms about the men. Anya was the only one who was treated like a chattel. There was no saddle to hold on to and she didn't dare touch the woman in front of her; it was very hard to stop herself slipping whenever they rode upslope or crossed uneven ground.

Brekt touched her only once. At the time, she was talking to Bardin who, with Aruline behind him, had drawn up beside her to consult about calling a halt. 'The horses must be rested soon,' she said. 'I feel they will need this small respite.' This seemed a strange way to put it, Anya thought, when at that moment, she felt Brekt's small hand come to rest upon the lower part of her back. 'The journey will yet be long,' Brekt said softly; the fingers curled and brushed against the skin hairs very lightly. Anya knew those words, and that gesture, to be laden with meaning; Brekt communicated to her body by that single touch, and her body was charged with tense unease She could feel the cool stroke of the small fingers for a long time after they were gone.

When they came to a watering place, the riders dismounted. There was much laughter and love-play between the couples on the grass.

'Save your strength lads, till we reach the camp,' Bardin cried. 'The feasting will be long this night.' He grasped Aruline by the waist and swept her from her feet to kiss her.

113

Ulf threw Riga playfully into the air. She giggled as he caught her. Even Sarol-harn was lain upon the ground, locked in an embrace with the man in purple silk.

Anya had to watch all of this as best she could from her position across the horse. Brekt did not command it, but Anya did not dare to dismount without the express instruction. Brekt left her while she stood talking to a group of the men. Then when everyone seemed to be preparing for departure, Brekt returned. Instead of mounting the horse, however, she stood before Anya. Anya could see only up to her waist, but Brekt spoke directly to Anya for the first time.

'I have ignored you. Forgive me.' Brekt's hand went to her belt. 'Allow me to correct that inattentiveness . . .' Anya's belly turned to ice. What she had thought was a knife tucked into Brekt's belt was the handle of a strap. Anya's belly sank and sank as Brekt pulled out the broad strap and marched round behind her. Things were happening so quickly. Brekt spoke curtly: 'Spread. Bend your knees. Press your feet together.' Anya was shaking, yet she did it – the shivers travelled up her thighs. As her soles were pressed together, a hand closed round her feet and lifted, forcing her thighs apart quite cruelly, forcing her legs up so far it seemed she would topple over forwards. 'Stand steady,' Brekt whispered, for the horse beneath Anya moved uneasily as her hands began to scrabble against the smoothness of its coat. Then with several men now gathered round, and her body held in this unsteady poise, opened, with her buttocks bunched up separately and her feet held tight together, she was leathered – quickly, relentlessly, pitilessly – beyond the point where her buttocks burned, beyond the point where hot, wet, stinging tears squeezed out from tight-shut eyes, to the point where she could not breathe. Her fingers dug into the horse's coat as Brekt examined Anya's fleshpot, spreading the lips open and drawing the hood back from the nubbin. When she had finished, Brekt would not permit Anya to close her thighs. She tucked the strap in her belt, and took from her pocket a cruel device. It was a small twig which had been split lengthwise, shaved

114

flat on one side and notched at each end, with a thong stretched tightly along the flat surface. She pursed Anya's sex lips together, then drew open the tiny bow, slipped the sex lips through and let it snap around them, so Anya's flesh was nipped between the flat stick and the thong. The pressure of the squeezing forced her flesh bud to protrude. Brekt then mounted the horse and they set off once again.

Anya had never experienced a cruelty quite like it. No tender touch was given. There was nothing in Brekt's words or actions to indicate she had any human feelings – no compassion, nothing to show that what she had done had brought even her any satisfaction. And yet as Anya's buttocks throbbed, as her body moved against the horse, her belly stirred within her. She did not like that cruel smacking, so why did the warmth seep down inside to that other place between her thighs, the place now nipped so deliciously tightly on the outside by the thong? And Anya began thinking – if Brekt was so indifferent to her, why was Anya slung across the back of Brekt's horse? Why had Brekt's hand lain upon her in that way and why did Brekt, even when separated from her and talking to the others, never take her eyes from Anya for more than a few seconds at a time?

As the ride continued through that long afternoon, it was questions such as these which whirled around in Anya's head to quell the cold viciousness of the smacking, not to render it in retrospect a pleasure – certainly it could never be that – but rather to bestow upon it the more ethereal qualities of a kind of mystery of faith, to enshroud it with a peculiar enthralment. *I have ignored you. Forgive me*, she had said. And the tiny pushed-out bead of sensual delight between Anya's legs glowed warmly with the soft spark of her wanting.

Eventually the ground began to rise and progress slowed. Anya no longer had her lodestone, yet she was aware that they had been moving towards the sun. So when they came upon a river, her heart leapt, for it was a wide river. She thought at first it must be the Great River, but it seemed too shallow; the horses forded it easily, yet Anya was not allowed to sit up. Her feet trailed in the icy water. When the

115

horse stumbled, she cried out as she felt herself slipping, but Brekt did not steady her. When they reached the further side, Anya was crying, not from fear, but from the turmoil deep inside her: crossing that water had reminded her of her Prince, of her lover far away, a gentle lover, not a cruel one.

Then Brekt's hand touched her in that same place, low down on her back, and that touch took her breath away.

Soon afterwards, they stopped. Two riders were dispatched ahead of the party, so the preparations for the feast could begin in advance of their arrival. Anya was once more left on the horse, but this time Brekt stood beside her. When Bardin came over to talk to her, Aruline was with him; Bardin did not appear to treat Aruline as if she were a captive. It was almost as if Aruline had taken over with Bardin exactly where she had left off with the Duke, and it was clear that Brekt resented this familiarity. When Aruline recounted the story of Anya's capture, adding, 'She was a runaway, a slave,' Brekt replied coldly:

'And you were a kept woman. But what she might have been does not interest me. What counts is what I make her.' As she said that, the hand, the small hand, was lifted and laid upon Anya's bare back in that very sensitive place. To Anya, the feeling was as if the hand was not on her back but was deep inside her belly.

'Are you ready?' Brekt then asked Anya. Anya shivered. Bardin and Aruline watched as Brekt took up the strap and walked round to the other side. Anya's legs were already wide; her knees were bent and her feet were pressed together. Brekt removed the clip. Anya's sex lips throbbed; her breathing came in nervous gasps. Brekt took hold of Anya's feet and raised them up so high her belly was lifted from the horse's back. Then as the falling feeling came and the smell of horse came strongly in her nostrils, the stinging slaps cracked down more cruelly than before and more closely to the crease of her buttocks. All sobs, all tears, all pleas for mercy were ignored; the leathering was delivered quite simply to the point of shuddering, gasping breathlessness. Aruline then asked to be allowed to touch Anya. Brekt refused; she tucked the strap into her belt, opened Anya's

116

sex until Anya could feel the cool air deep inside, then closed the lips, drew them firmly outwards, snapped the clip around them, then remounted. The journey was resumed. And though the smacks had been bestowed exclusively upon the cheeks of Anya's bottom, the warm glow seeped slowly downwards into her belly and her breasts. Her sex lips were distending. Her nubbin was erect.

The sun was setting as they reached the camp. They passed downslope through densely woven pine, then suddenly emerged into a dell backed by a rockface over which a small waterfall cascaded. A large flat area by the stream was lit by torches and several bright fires. The cheer went up and men clad in shades of green and red and brown came running up to them. While the horses were unloaded, the women were corralled in a stockade. Anya noticed there were other women already in the camp, some of them dressed like the men, but others more scantily attired, almost after the manner of slaves. But none of the women were shackled, and all appeared to go about their duties unrestricted. Many of these bondmaids were preparing the table, bringing wood, or plucking fowl while the men spitted pig, calf and venison for roasting.

Anya was nudged from behind. It was Sarol-harn. 'The feast will last till dawn,' she said. 'We will be brought in to serve, and for the dancing.' Then she added more quietly, 'And for the entertainment . . .'

'The entertainment?' Anya's flesh pulsed softly against the stricture gripped around it.

Sarol-harn nodded. 'Some will be selected to amuse them at the table.' Sarol-harn sounded very knowledgeable on this subject. Anya looked across at the long trestle table which was being laid with gold and silver plates and goblets. 'The rest will be passed around amongst the men on the floor.' Anya saw the heaps of furs gathered round the fires.

'Passed around?' she whispered. The thong between her legs felt very tight. Sarol-harn looked at her and nodded grimly.

'Had you not noticed? There are many more men than women. And the night is very long . . .'

Anya was very afraid at the thought of being passed around so freely between these love-starved uncouth men. Sarol-harn put her arm round Anya. 'But tomorrow,' she whispered, 'after the feast, they will not be so alert. Tomorrow, our chance will come. Trust me – and be ready.'

'You mean –?'

'Shhh!' Sarol-harn put her finger to Anya's lips.

Anya stood in line beside the fire while the carcass of the stag was turned over on the spit. The sound of music and revelry was all around. Two feet away from her, the coals glowed bright orange and sizzled as the melted fat dripped into them. The grass beside her feet was singed; her feet felt warm; the air was heavy with the delicious scent of roasting venison. From the other fires, the smell of honeyed pork and roasted goose drifted in, making her mouth water.

The cook poured something from a gourd onto the carcass as it turned, and now the air was filled with the sweet, sharp aroma of apple wine. People were dancing to the music – woodsmen and scantily clad or naked girls whirled around in a space between the heaps of furs and the long table. Riga and Shira were there, and both of them were laughing. One side of Anya's body felt the warm glow of the fire; the other side felt cool. Her feet were moving in time with the music. She wanted to join in, but she doubted they would let her: a place had been reserved for her at the table. Bardin sat in the middle, with Aruline beside him. Sarol-harn was pouring out her wine and Aruline was touching Sarol-harn while she did this. Bardin seemed to let her. Sarol-harn quickly pulled away and moved along the table. Brekt sat unmoving, staring at the dancers. She didn't seem to notice Sarol-harn at all.

Brekt made Anya very frightened; she could not understand her coldness and her cruelty. It was the place beside Brekt which had been reserved for Anya. But Brekt had instructed Anya to serve the food. 'I wish you to mix a little with the men,' she had said, making Anya part her thighs

118

while she removed the thonged clip and opened Anya's flesh leaves wide, rubbing them firmly as they ached, as they continued swelling up with blood.

Now Brekt's gaze turned from the dancers. Once more, she was looking directly at Anya. The intensity of that gaze sent a peculiar thrill through Anya's body. The fire warmed her bottom; it reminded her of that other fire that Brekt had made there with the strap that afternoon, when the jerks of Anya's body had come so strongly that her flesh leaves had burst apart and pressed against the horsehair. The feeling that came between her legs at that memory frightened Anya even more than Brekt did.

Suddenly, Anya was knocked aside by two dancers who had tripped and now tumbled at her feet. The speed of the reel was too fast for them. They were drunk. The naked girl was rolled onto her front and the man began to spank her playfully, not hard; witnessing it forced the peculiar feeling in the pit of Anya's belly. The laughter turned to grunts and gasps as the girl's cheeks were spread, her legs were moved wider apart and the gentle slapping focused on the join. Then the fingers were wetted and pushed down underneath. Anya could not bear it. When she looked up, Brekt was still staring at her. As the girl on the floor began to shudder, again the feeling came, deep in Anya's belly, at the joining of her thighs.

'Hey!' She jumped and turned round. The cook held up a giant sliver of meat, then dropped it on her tray and began to cut another. When the tray was full, Anya had to make the rounds of the men upon the floor and round the smaller fires.

It seemed the lasciviousness of the dancers had been the trigger. Anya tried to pick her way through the writhing bodies as girls were thrown onto the heaps of furs and the men fell upon them, sometimes two or more men to a girl. One girl was lifted up and held open by one man whilst she was kissed between the thighs by another; a second girl was held upside down with the man's cockstem bedded in her mouth and her legs spread about his shoulders, then was carried around that way. A third girl's body formed a bridge

119

between two men as she was lifted on one cockstem, arched backwards and made to suck upon the other. Anya found it very frightening; she was expecting that at any moment the same would happen to her. They pinched her legs and buttocks as she passed; they pulled her down and kissed her, though she tried to fight them off. When her legs were spread and rough fingers pushed between to open her swollen flesh and try to push inside, a warning shout came from the table. Anya was released. Her tray was empty. She struggled back to the fire to have it refilled.

'More meat, up here!' Bardin shouted. The cook pointed with his knife. Anya took the next trayful up to the table. Sitting at the end was the man who wore the Duke's coat, the man who had lifted Anya onto Brekt's horse that afternoon.

'Come, sit upon my knee,' he cried, jabbing his knife into the pile of meat and lifting a large slice onto his plate. Anya was apprehensive, but she did as she was asked, for she knew that Brekt was watching, though she did not understand why Brekt wanted to make her do these things. She was very conscious of her nakedness, and the way her bare skin pressed against his clothing. Then as her weight was taken fully on his lap, so the cheeks of her buttocks spread, the feeling came, the voluptuous weighted feeling between her legs. It had never really gone away since the spanking with the strap. When the man put his hand around her bare belly and pulled her more closely to him, her sex was drawn along his thigh. When he parted her legs gently, her blood-filled sex lips gaped. He kept her like that while he gave her wine, while its warmth sank down to that point between her thighs. As the dancers cavorted, and the women stripped completely and proffered their bodies for the men to touch and taste, and couples collapsed onto the floor, as the music played louder and faster, Anya's body responded to the music and the fingertip stimulation. Her nipples were pinched up to hard stiff points, her belly was stroked and her open flesh lips were touched by fingers smelling strongly of cider-roasted meat. Her inner flesh was yielding. Droplets of her love oil spilled onto his thigh.

Then there was a clap of hands. 'Let the entertainment begin!' cried Bardin. 'Bring the first one in.' It was the girl with short dark hair, the same girl who had been taken last night for the Duke. Anya did not know why she had been selected. She was breathing very quickly as the man behind her held her before the table. Her nipples had been worked to stiffness. Her lower belly was buried in a dense black bush which extended down her thighs. The girl was made to spread while Aruline whispered to Bardin then leaned across the table and touched her between the thighs. Aruline sniffed her fingers and offered them to Bardin. The girl turned her head away. A strap was thrown onto the table. It looked like Brekt's strap. Anya shivered. The fingers touched her flesh lips once again, teasing them more widely open.

The girl was made to bend over a pole supported between two men. The pole was then lifted until her feet left the ground. The man behind her took the strap and began to smack her, with her body balanced in this precarious position. Anya moved uneasily. As the cheeks of the bottom shook beneath the sharp cracks of the strap, a terrible endless sinking sensation came between Anya's thighs. Each murmur, each muffled sob that the girl made caused Anya to hold her breath. She could not take her eyes away. She was frightened and enthralled.

'Brekt will want to use you in this way,' the man beneath her whispered in her ear, and now the feeling in Anya's belly was even more profound. He lifted her and made her stand astride him as he sat, but her legs were shaking. She felt conspicuous. Several people turned to look at her, Brekt included. As the girl was spanked, and now, as her legs were separated, the hand at Anya's bottom rubbed the cheeks slowly from side to side, then opened the groove and rubbed within, then rubbed the small round mouth in slow deliberate rubs in time with the slaps.

'See – now they will smack the sex lips,' the man murmured. 'The man who gets her after this will be a very lucky one indeed.' Anya's fleshpot was dissolving as her bottom was gently rubbed.

121

He made her lower again and spread her flesh about his thigh so that her open sex lips clung to the material. He bent her forwards so her belly bowed out and he could once more touch her bottom mouth. The girl had been lowered until the tips of her outstretched toes could touch the ground. She whimpered softly as the smacks descended on her pouch and on her sex lips. Anya's back was straightened and her hands held behind her. The fingers came round the front to nip her flesh lips between a finger and thumb, then to open them and stimulate her nubbin gently while she listened to the gasps. The punishment on the pole now desisted and the strap was set aside. The girl's sex was oiled until the squeezing fingers slipped very freely around her sex lips and her nubbin. Her legs tried to close; strong hands held them open; insistent fingers held the lips apart. Her flesh was oiled more slowly; her pleasure came intermittently, it seemed, as if she did not want it yet could not prevent its spillage. Each pulse was accompanied by a sudden tightening of her belly, a spasmodic curling of her toes and a gentle increase of the fingerpad pressure at the tip of Anya's nubbin.

The onlookers at the table clapped as the girl was lifted and carried away. 'Bring the little one,' Bardin commanded and Anya's heart sank, for it was Riga he referred to. Then her anxiety was redoubled, for Brekt was beckoning Anya over. The man gave her flesh a gentle parting squeeze.

A space was cleared and Riga was deposited on the table, naked and outspread in front of Bardin and Aruline. Anya was forced to take up her place to Brekt's left on the long seat. Once Anya was seated, Brekt turned her attention to the scene on the table as, by stages, Riga was examined.

Anya glanced furtively at Brekt. She was still attired after the fashion of a man. Beneath the leather jacket was a doublet and a pure white shirt open at the neck. Around her neck was a twisted rope of leather thong. At the back, the single long lock dangled over her collar. Brekt's face was small; it reminded Anya of the face upon a finely chiselled statue she had once seen in the castle: this statue was of a small, slim-bodied young woman, her face upraised, looking out towards a far horizon. The expression on that face

122

was hard to fathom – sad perhaps, yet not tearful. Brekt had that expression now. Her eyes looked totally black; her eyelashes were very long, Anya noticed, and her lips were slightly open. Her small slim fingers held a thong. She turned to Anya.

'Kneel up,' she said. Anya was forced to sit back on her heels, with her hands behind her back. Her thumbs were tied together. Then Brekt's fingers touched her between her legs, causing a delicious shiver. The fingers were cool; they pursed her flesh leaves together and drew them down to make them project. Brekt had done this very quickly, yet still the touch was sweet. Brekt said nothing when she did this; soon afterwards, she spread Anya's knees wider apart, then pushed her forwards until her belly arched down and her breasts rested on the table. Brekt then watched Riga being pleasured as Aruline and Bardin touched her breasts and belly and between her open thighs. The examination now progressed to kisses and intimate sucks. Small pieces of meat and other delicacies were spread on Riga's flesh, on her sensitive parts, then taken up on Aruline's searching tongue. The lapping became more intimate and unashamed. Brekt's left hand was laid on Anya's breast, trapping it against the table, forcing pleasure to the tip. Riga was turned over. Brekt's fingers lightly curled around the tip of Anya's breast as Riga's bottom was spread and wine was dripped upon it and then the bottom was licked.

'You liked what he was doing to you over there?' Brekt asked. Anya jumped, though the voice was quiet. 'Or do you prefer the things I do?' Brekt lifted her left hand and laid it upon the other breast, pressing so the nipple swelled and hurt. In Brekt's right hand now was the strap; she fingered it nervously. As Aruline sat back, her fingers palpating Riga between the thighs while the wine was dripped again in the well of Riga's upturned bottom and Riga's breathing turned to gasps, Brekt rolled Anya's nipple on the table. 'Should I smack this with the strap?' Brekt tapped the swollen nipple with her fingertip. Anya shuddered and looked at her with soft submissive eyes. Brekt did not smack. She merely rolled the nipple and squeezed the breast again.

She made Anya sit up on her heels. 'Some food?' she asked. Anya nodded. But how could she feed herself with her thumbs secured behind her? Anya's hands were not required. Brekt's fingers did the feeding, selecting small slices of venison, pork and goose, or pieces of bread dipped in rich wine sauce or pork fat or delicious ripened honey. Anya's lips reached up tentatively at first, then more confidently as Brekt encouraged her to snatch those morsels from between the dripping fingers. When Anya reached too far, and the fingers slipped inside to touch against her tongue, a thrill would run down inside her to her belly. Brekt laughed to see these antics – the smooth swan-neck arching up, the soft lips begging sweetly, the gravy dripping on the skin. Anya gorged unashamedly until the melted fat ran down her neck. When Anya licked her lips, Brekt's fingertip reached again to touch her tongue. Then the golden cup of wine was lifted and tilted. Anya quaffed. The sweet strong liquid poured down her throat until a warm glow filled her belly. Brekt tipped the cup until it overflowed down Anya's breasts and over her belly, down the creases of her thighs to the seat, forming a small pool which Anya's flesh lips dipped within.

Yet despite the fact that Brekt was using Anya's body for amusement, deliberately spilling the wine and dripping gravy on her skin, Anya did not protest. Though she would have preferred that these attentions be driven by caring warmth, they were attentions all the same, and they were far removed from the blatant cruelty she had experienced that afternoon. And it was true that at intervals, Brekt's fingers would touch her, smoothing the melted fat around her nipples or pulling her sex lips gently down to dip into the wine. To Anya, the lightness of these touches was delicious.

But Brekt was also capable of indifference and great unkindness. She shouted a naked girl across – Sadine, she called her – one of the camp's bondmaids rather than a recent captive. It was obvious the girl was used to Brekt; she seemed to know exactly what to do. A plate bearing a cooked goose was brought. Sadine stood next to Brekt, who made her turn so Anya could witness what was being done. Brekt dipped two fingers of her right hand into the pool of warm fat around the carcass of the goose, then began to massage the girl between the buttocks. As the fingers rubbed, the small cheeks gently shook. Sadine began to close her eyes. The fingers were recoated with the fat and reapplied. 'There,' Brekt said as Sadine's legs gradually edged apart. Anya shuddered, for the girl had opened her eyes and turned to look at Brekt, even as the fingers suddenly slipped and bedded deeply. The look was one of longing. Sadine raised her hand and stroked Brekt's cheek. Brekt smiled. Suddenly Anya felt jealous of this girl.

A volunteer was called for. Brekt whispered to him and he stripped and lay back on the table, his cockstem already very well erect. Brekt smeared the goose-fat round the cap, the girl climbed up on the table, facing Brekt, then knelt astride and spread apart her cheeks. As her hips sank down, she closed her eyes again and the volunteer softly groaned. Brekt waited until the man was fully bedded, then she checked that Anya's flesh lips still projected firmly from her mound. As the slick and now very warm fingers touched her – the same goose-greased fingers that had been inside Sadine, but had never touched Anya in that way and had never brought her to pleasure – Anya felt a churning in her womb. She almost wanted it to be her disported on the table, her bottom gripped about the fleshy stem while those fingers touched her and stimulated her and brought about her pleasure. But Brekt's fingers left Anya's flesh leaves throbbing and frustrated, then dipped into the goose-fat again and penetrated the girl. As the girl arched further back, the fingers slipped in deeper, so she was penetrated back and front. Her belly was pushed out tightly and her knees were spread very wide. Anya watched the joining of the flesh leaves separate and the nubbin push out hard, forced by the pressure of Brekt's fingers from within. Now the fingers of Brekt's left hand smeared the goose-fat round and round the hardness of that pip, then smacked it, then oiled and rubbed again, repeatedly, until Sadine's belly went so tight that it appeared that it would split. The

125

fingertips inside her carefully withdrew and Brekt's thumbs now held Sadine open, very still against her moaning, while two index fingertips continued very gently to massage her bud; Sadine's pleasure then delivered itself in shuddering gasps and very tight contractions which immediately caused the man to buck until both bodies were lifted from the surface of the table.

Brekt acted very quickly, yet her face was calm. As Anya's breathing, already very rapid from the sights that she had witnessed, came quicker and quicker until she felt dizzy with the fear of what she knew was about to happen, everything – the goose, the girl, the goblets and the man – was swept aside, with the exception of the strap. Anya was pushed face forward out across the table until her breasts overhung the edge, until the swollen burning pouch of her sex was rested on the surface. And with her thumbs tied behind her, she was helpless. Brekt stood behind her. Anya's feet were lifted up, pressed together, and the feeling came, the delicious drowning feeling of submission. Her legs were bent tightly, then lifted until the muscles ached. The swollen pouch gaped open, the quick contractions came and Anya's sex gulped as quickly as her body gulped for air. And only then was the smacking delivered, a prolonged and measured smacking to the inner faces of the outspread cheeks, until the tiny mouth between them pulsed and her open body trickled. Like a honeycomb that had been slowly squeezed until it burst, it trickled, out across her nubbin and onto the surface of the table. Only when the slick had progressed to drip down from the edge did Brekt finally refrain.

Anya was turned over; her heart raced; her belly heaved and shook. Her thighs lay widely open; she could feel her liquid curling round and dripping down her bottom. She looked up into that calm face that had delivered her such cruel and frightening feelings. The eyelashes did not flicker, but the words made Anya's belly quaver once again. 'You have brought me great pleasure, in your submission,' Brekt said. 'A deeper pleasure than I have known. Your flesh must be rewarded.' Brekt's eyes narrowed.

'Ulf!' she cried. Anya tried to close her thighs, but Brekt held her open. 'Ulf!' Ulf lumbered across from the opposite side of the clearing. He towered above the table, above Anya's outspread form. 'She is very pretty, Ulf, is she not?' Ulf grunted. 'I trust she is not too small . . .' Brekt placed her bare palms high up on Anya's inner thighs and pressed. Anya's softness opened. She stared directly at Anya. 'You will lie with Ulf this night – for me.' Anya shivered. 'You shall refuse him nothing. This belly must take him very fully. You will do this for me. Tomorrow, I will take you into the forest, where you will please me further.' And to seal that promise, she lifted the strap and smacked it down upon each inner thigh, very near the crease. Brekt turned her to display the deep red marks upon her buttocks, hard against the groove. She then untied Anya's thumbs. 'Now get up.' As her thighs burned and the cheeks of her bottom smarted, Anya rose to her knees, then stood upon the table. Yet even then the top of her head barely reached to the level of Ulf's enormous square chin.

Though Ulf's eyes appeared warm and kind as his arms enfolded her and her face was pressed against his great warm breast, she knew her flesh would never be able to take him in that way. She was frightened by that thought, yet the swelling need between her thighs had not receded, and as her own arms stretched uncertainly to try to reach at least part way round that giant frame, the warm peculiar feeling became stronger.

Ulf lifted Anya from the table. He held her in the same way he had done that afternoon, with her sex and bottom cradled in the saddle of his hand. As she buried her face against his chest now, and that same powerful sexual feeling came between her thighs, his middle finger crooked then pressed against the pouted entrance to her sex, still moistened with her longing, and the walls spread wide apart to take it, past the first joint, past the second, until the finger filled her fuller than any cock had ever done. And as she squeezed, her sex lips pouted down to touch against the web of skin that stretched between his fingers. Brekt nodded; Anya was borne away upon the giant penetrating finger.

127

Each sway of Ulf's hand caused a deep pressure-pleasure of the fingertip against her womb. The skin of his palm pressed warmth against her bottom.

Anya was sat upon Ulf's knee and plied with strong brown wine from the pewter pot until it seemed her vision swam. Then she was laid down beneath a heap of furs by one of the fires whilst Ulf quickly removed his clothing. She saw his barrel of a chest, his giant thighs and buttocks, completely clothed in dense golden curls, and the huge cockstem, already half erect. She knew that she could never take it. As he slipped beneath the furs and pulled her body to him, and once again she felt the powerful arms, she was frightened and excited. She knew he could be gentle, but she knew he was strong, and she knew his cock was impossibly large. His skin was hot, the curls were thick all over, but very soft where they pressed against her skin. His belly curls tickled her breasts; his huge hand closed about her head and cradled her very gently. The curls on his thighs sprang against her open wetness and tickled up inside her as she spread her legs apart. When she kissed his belly, the whole of her tongue could push into the navel. His skin tasted of salted roasted meat.

Then she felt the hot weight of his cockstem up against her. She spread her thighs wider and his ballocks completely filled the space between them. The soft skin felt like satin against the walls of her open flesh. The curve of the cockstem touched her belly; the head pushed hard between her breasts to separate them. It needed both her hands to complete the closure round the cockstem at the plum.

Ulf gently pushed her head down until the thick tip of the cockstem nudged below her chin. She tried to take it in her mouth. She opened her mouth very wide and pushed. Her lips extended only half way down the cap, but she sucked as she worked the cockstem with both hands. Her tongue slipped very easily into the mouth; the tube felt warm and very smooth inside. She gripped the loose outer skin below the head, pulling it tightly while she sucked. Her tongue formed a soft plug pushed into the tube. She knew that if his pleasure were to come it would surely force that plug out and flood her mouth completely. Her tongue could taste the oily slickness of his seepage.

Ulf pulled her mouth away and turned her onto her back. He took one breast completely in his mouth and slowly sucked it; she felt his lips surrounding it, moulded to her ribcage. While he sucked, he wet his little finger in her sex then forced it up her bottom, making her gasp at the sudden strength of that distension. Then he picked her up, holding her upside down in the air above him as he lay down on his back. He lowered her until his thick warm lips enclosed both her sex and bottom and he sucked them very gently until she came.

As Anya was deposited back beneath the furs, her fleshpot very warm and very soft and sopping, she felt the head of Ulf's cockstem pushing against her, stretching her until it seemed the walls of her sex, warm and wet and slippery though they were, would split down to her bottom and her nubbin would be forced out so far that it would burst. But Ulf persisted, easing slightly whenever Anya moaned and gripped the soft skin of his belly until it bruised, then pushing again, not crushing her with his body, yet lifting her thighs very wide apart, stretching back the skin of her belly, wetting her with oil and spittle until finally, with a piercing pain, she felt her flesh give and the cockhead lodged within. The tight band of her sex about his cockhead brought him on, and Anya felt her insides suddenly flooded with hot miltings which pumped until she thought her sex would burst, then squirted out across the surface of her nubbin. When the cockhead was withdrawn, she cried out, for she thought her inner flesh would follow. Her sex felt very heavy; it lay open and dripping with his milt.

Ulf cuddled her to his breast while he played with her milt-slicked nubbin very gently till she came. The warmth of pleasure spread out and up inside, bathing her inner sex, her bottom, her womb, her belly and her breasts in a deep delicious tiredness which very soon caused her to fall asleep.

[8]

A Cure for Disobedience

In the morning, early, when a faint blue smoky haze lay above the tired remains of the campfires and the sun angled down to make the water sparkle as it tumbled over the small cascade, the women were taken down to bathe. Anya had slept very soundly, very warmly beneath Ulf's heap of furs. The wine had helped. The wine had also taken its toll. Ulf was nowhere to be seen, but jugs, gourds and small barrels, and very many snoring bodies lay scattered all around. The women had to pick their way very carefully to avoid treading on anyone.

Anya had been woken by two of the bondmaids who had helped prepare the feast. These girls now wore skirts but their breasts remained free. One of the girls wore arm thongs like Shira's. The other was strikingly beautiful; she had the same dusky skin as Sarol-harn, though she was taller and her eyes were not so wide or dark.

'You must go to the pool to wash,' she said. Her voice sounded very like Sarol-harn's. When Anya stared at her, then opened her mouth to speak, the girl frowned, then quickly moved Anya on as if she didn't want the other girl to see. Anya looked around for Sarol-harn. She suddenly remembered Sarol-harn's words, about being ready. Ready for what? It could only be escape . . .

Sarol-harn was already in the water with the others. Riga and Shira were there and several of the women of the camp, but no men. Anya was thankful for that. Three of the camp women were standing on the bank, watching the girls, probably standing guard, but the others had joined the girls in the water. Many of the girls were laughing as they splashed about and ran through the cascade. Yet even with the sun upon it, the water would surely be freezing. Anya edged into the pool very carefully from the side. When a large wave lapped against her belly it took her breath away. Then Riga and Shira, swimming up from the plunge pool, took her by her feet and pulled her under. The water was so cold she could not breathe at all. Suddenly, she was reliving the incident at the lake, and she panicked, kicking out, splashing wildly, then choking as she opened her mouth to shout and freezing water began pouring down her throat. She surfaced, coughing uncontrollably. The girls were laughing, but suddenly they realised how terrified she was. They tried to calm her. After that, Anya sat on a rock in the warmth of the sun.

Sarol-harn came over. She glanced at the women on the bank before she spoke. 'All the horses are tethered over there, on this side of the camp,' she whispered. 'Sh!' she said when Anya tried to answer. 'When we finish here, make certain we are last to leave. Sel-owina will help us.' She nodded in the direction of the tall dark girl standing on the bank.

'She is from your country?'

Sarol-harn nodded.

'Is she coming too?'

That made Sarol-harn frown. 'No. She said it is not –' Sarol-harn changed her mind: 'She said she does not want to return. Not yet.'

'Why not?' Anya was suspicious.

Sarol-harn ignored the question. 'She says we are to follow this stream to where it flows below two hills, one green, the other bare of any trees. We are to cross between these hills, then, in half a day's ride, we come upon a very wide river.'

'The Great River!' Anya shouted.

'Shhh!' Some of the women had turned. Sarol-harn glared at Anya and walked away, leaving Anya feeling quite embarrassed at her outburst.

But now her mind was racing; her heart soared. She breathed the air deeply, laughed inwardly at her squeamishness and slid once more into the cool refreshing water of the

131

pool. When she dived down, she could see the shafts of sunlight dancing, lighting up the smooth limbs above. She surfaced laughing, treading water, then her smile very rapidly faded away.

On the bank stood Brekt, staring at her. And with that stare, all of Anya's hopes expired, for Brekt had deliberately parted her deerskin jacket to reveal the straps – two straps now, a large one and a small – tucked into her belt. Somehow that small strap seemed so much more sinister than the large one. The vision in Anya's mind caused a soft qualm between her thighs. She was very aware now of the clearness of the water. Brekt was studying her body as it moved. Her breasts were floating, lifting gently with the waves, which lapped round her nipples to make them very hard. Slung diagonally over Brekt's right shoulder and under her left arm was a coil of rope. Anya could feel the deep qualm turning to a swelling pressure.

Brekt spoke to one of the women. A large cloth was brought. Brekt crooked a finger at Anya. All the women turned to look; Sarol-harn's mouth fell open. Anya experienced again the deep feeling as she ascended the bank; it was as if Ulf's hand still pressed there, from her belly to her fleshpot to her bottom.

The cloth was wrapped around her and the women began to dry her while Brekt watched. It seemed the gentle rubbing with the cloth, the coldness of the water giving way to warmth, awakened all the nerves on Anya's skin. Her breasts were gathered in the cloth and pressed together softly, then the cloth was pressed between her thighs. Brekt's eyes looked tenderly upon her. When Anya was dry, Brekt dismissed the women. She asked Anya to spread apart her legs and place her hands behind her head. Then she opened her palm; it held the small flat twig with the thong attached. 'We will go into the woods,' she said, tightening the knot at one end of the thong, then walking round Anya, assessing her from every angle before returning to the front, 'where it is quiet . . .' Brekt touched her between the legs and Anya shivered. The device was quickly slipped about her pursed-together flesh lips. It nipped them very tightly.

'Where we will not be disturbed.' Anya was very frightened by those words and by the way Brekt's fingers now touched the smaller strap. And yet she found the nipping of the thong about her swelling flesh lips made her feel aroused.

Brekt led Anya away from the stream, away from the camp, into the woods, walking very quickly. Although the woods were very open, it was difficult for Anya to keep up, for she was barefoot whilst Brekt wore leather boots. Fallen twigs and sharp stones cut into Anya's feet, making her fall behind. Brekt became impatient; she took Anya roughly by the arm and when Anya stumbled, took her by the hair. Why did she have to be so cruel? Very soon, Anya's tears were flowing. That appeared to make Brekt worse. She stood with her hands at her hips as Anya cowered on the ground.

'Kneel up,' she said through clenched teeth. 'Fold your arms behind your back.' With Anya's shoulders now drawn tightly back, her breasts were pushed out before her. As she tried in vain to stem her tears, her proffered bosom heaved and shook. She remembered the sergeant's warning about her tears and struggled to try to stop them. Brekt threatened her with the strap and the tears flowed freer than before, spreading down her cheeks and dripping from her chin.

Brekt lifted Anya, her arms still locked behind her back, and dragged her to a large oak tree. As Anya's knees sagged, Brekt still held her. She spread a hand on her shaking belly, pressing it very firmly. She lifted Anya's breasts and dropped them so they bounced, then smacked them with her fingers. Anya was turned to face the tree. The thong was pulled off her flesh and the hand was pressed against her belly once again.

'Pee,' Brekt said. 'Do it now.'

Anya's tears abated completely with the shock. She could not swallow. Her belly felt tight and swollen beneath the pressure of the hand.

'I want to see you do it,' Brekt insisted. And as the hand released her, and Brekt waited, a strange feeling came to Anya, as if a very slim forearm bedded very deep inside was being drawn very slowly out from between her open thighs. She could hear Brekt's excited breathing. She could smell the faintly musty forest air. She closed her eyes, then slowly sank until she was squatting.

'No!' She was pulled up so quickly that she went dizzy. 'Stand. Do it against the tree.'

Anya gasped: 'No . . .' She could never do it that way. Why was Brekt trying to degrade her in this way?

A hand cracked hard against her bottom. 'Now do it, or there's worse.' She was slammed forward with her body arched and her hands against the tree. Brekt stood behind her, pushing until she was curved so strongly her nipples brushed the trunk. Then her legs were spread. Brekt's hands came round the front, pressing into her belly, then slapping it, then reaching down to pull the hot fleshy droplet dangling between her thighs. She was peeled open while the fingertips kept rubbing her and squeezing. The deerskin jacket brushed against her buttocks then, as Brekt's hips became insistent, it was pressed into the crease. At the front, the fingers rubbed and nipped an itchiness into that very tender place. When Anya squirmed, the quick slaps shook her belly, then the fingers returned to rub her cruelly while Brekt murmured, 'Do it. Wet my fingers.' She thrust a forearm under from behind, cupping her hand round Anya's sex and squeezing. But excited though Anya's flesh was by the forwardness, by the intimacy, by the peculiar itchy pleasure-pain and by the thought of her hot fluid filling that small hand to overflowing while the fingertips kept playing with her, flicking her flesh lips and squeezing them tight, she could not satisfy that perverse whim. Her body just would not do it.

But Brekt was unimpressed by such proprieties. She made Anya kneel on all fours and took the broad strap to her bottom.

'Get your head down further. Lift up here,' Brekt ordered, whacking her across the buttocks cruelly. 'Now get those thighs apart.' The sinking feeling came very strongly. The next four smacks were administered between her legs, to either side of her sex lips. Brekt made her bend her knees so tightly that her body was doubled. Then she had to close her legs and squeeze until her pouch pushed out. Brekt smacked it without mercy.

She was pulled to her feet again, gasping; her back was pushed against the tree. 'Now open your body to me,' said Brekt.

With Anya's legs bowed wide apart and her buttocks spread against the bole of the tree, her mouth opened very wide indeed to take Brekt's cool small lips fully within her own and to permit Brekt's tongue to penetrate her as Brekt's small hand pushed between her legs to open her completely. All four fingers pushed inside. Brekt's palm, folding upwards, squeezed against her nubbin. And when that happened, Anya's mouth opened wider yet to let Brekt's tongue push deep towards the back of her throat. Then Brekt spoke to Anya softly.

'If you wish to ride with me, if you wish to share my bed, you must submit yourself completely, in the way Sadine does.' Anya suddenly felt a wave of jealousy at the mention of that name, at the thought of Sadine and Brekt together beneath the furs. But how could Anya be jealous when Brekt had shown her nothing but cruelty? Where was the pleasure in that? She did not know. But she did know that, with Brekt's hand inside her and Brekt's palm pressed against her nubbin and now, Brekt's lips sucking gently round her pulsing nipples, she was wet between the thighs. And with the rough bark of the tree between her open buttocks as she held herself on tiptoes, the knot inside her belly slowly tightened, the small lips sucked and the fingers reached up deeper to press against her womb.

Brekt took Anya deeper into the woods, until they came to a sunny clearing with several fallen branches and a large beech tree with a strong horizontal branch a foot or two above head height. There were pieces of wood that had been chopped or sawn. There was grass upon the ground. Brekt seemed familiar with this place. She removed the rope from over her shoulder and cast it to the ground. 'You will remember this day,' she said ominously. 'But you must not think of what befalls you as a punishment. It is a training in the pleasures of submission. The deeper your submission, the more profound will be your pleasure. I will teach you to obey.' Anya felt as if a ball was swelling inside her, weighted between her shaking legs. Her tongue felt thick. Her mouth was dry.

Brekt removed her boots, then her trousers, placing both straps carefully down, then took off her jacket, her doublet and finally, her shirt. Brekt's form was slim; the muscles of her thighs were tight. When she turned, her bottom formed two taut mounds with the bush curls clearly visible in the space between her thighs. Round her neck she wore a thong with three wooden beads. A twisted ropework thong was fastened at her belly. But the strangest thing about Brekt's appearance now was the broad long strip of very thin deerskin wrapped round her, very tightly, starting just below the armpits, swathing her breasts then finally tucked in above the slight outswell of her belly, crowned by the twisted rope. The deerskin was stretched so tightly it flattened her breasts completely. It seemed to emphasise the tight roundness of her bottom. When Brekt stood before Anya, very close, with the broad strap in her hand and her legs spread apart, Anya could smell the scent upon Brekt's body. It reminded her of burning honey, basted over roast meat and dripped upon the fire.

Brekt took her to a fallen branch about a foot thick which sloped upwards from the ground. Its upper end was trapped in the fork of a tree. Anya leaned her back against this branch and gripped it with her hands. The bark had fallen away and the aged wood felt very smooth, almost as if it had been polished. Brekt made Anya part her legs. She brushed the strap upwards between Anya's thighs, using it to tickle her skin, moving it very gently from side to side across the softness of the sex lips then up onto the belly. 'Now lift your leg astride,' she said. 'Face the wood. No – you must not use your hands. Put your hands behind you; clasp each wrist. So.' Brekt positioned Anya so her breasts as well as her thighs were separated by the sloping trunk. She bent Anya's legs and placed the soles of her feet to the sides of the trunk, so now Anya was balanced in a state of unsteady tension, unable to support herself other than with her feet. She felt she was sliding downwards. And with her knees bent, she was very exposed. Brekt enhanced the state of this exposure

136

by moving Anya's feet up the trunk, bending her knees tighter yet, spreading her buttocks widely and causing the lips of Anya's distended fleshpot to separate. Then she took the broad strap and systematically smacked her, saying, 'I will make you climb the pole. I will smack you till you drip.'

And Brekt was as good as her word. The smacking was constrained between the middle part of the back of the thighs and the lower part of the buttocks, and was administered until the skin was an even shade of redness, after which it was smacked again to render it one shade deeper. Each smack made Anya's body jerk. She tried to climb away from it by pressing with her feet. But there was no escaping; she could not use her hands; each time she tried to move, her body merely slid a fraction downwards, driven by her weight, which rendered her knees the tighter, and her buttocks that much more open to the smacking. More cruelly yet, it pulled the skin of her lower belly tightly back above her nubbin, which therefore remained throughout this punishment very erect indeed and pulsing a fraction of an inch above the polished surface of the wood.

Having basted that skin to a very even shade of cherry red, Brekt took up the smaller and more intimate strap and proceeded to smack the inner surfaces of the cheeks and then to separate them fully while she smacked the small tight mouth until the erstwhile sobs had turned to subdued moans and the emphasis had changed from the more questionable pleasure of blatant punishment to the more profound delight of carefully controlled, cruelly repressed sexual gratification – in other words, the drip. The open fleshpot slowly leaked. She waited and watched, then smacked again, pacing the smacks very evenly, directing them always at that delicious pulsing mouth, but not desisting now until the leak ran over the slowly palpitating nubbin to connect it to the smooth trunk in a narrow continuous stream that welled down to the level of the ankles. At that point Anya was instructed to dismount. She stood shaking beside the tree trunk.

'Sadine would be very jealous,' Brekt whispered, smoothing the honeydew up and down the wood. Anya looked away, from shame, and from the peculiar satisfaction that the compliment had triggered. What Brekt proposed to do next, however, made Anya very anxious. She led her to a point below the horizontal branch. 'I will tie you from this branch,' she said. 'You will keep your legs open – very straight – while I smack you till you come.' Anya was stood upon a block of wood. Brekt stood beside her, on a taller one while she looped the rope over the branch and fastened Anya by the wrists. Then the blocks were taken away. Anya hung by her wrists. 'Now stretch,' said Brekt. Anya found it very difficult. Brekt waited in front of her, her head at belly height, until her legs formed a tight vee. She took the broad strap, kissed the belly once, then smacked the inner thighs. And although Anya shuddered when the smacks struck home, she did not close her legs; she strained to push them wider than before. Brekt was very pleased. The smacks came more closely to the creases; Anya's skin was bathed in delicious stinging prickles.

'Bear down,' Brekt said. 'You must learn to keep your fleshpot open.' As Anya's arms ached and she tried to focus on the pushing in between her thighs, her flesh leaves were spread. Brekt's fingers entered, not pushing the walls of Anya's sex apart, for those walls were already held that way. The fingers took her liquid and smeared it outside, into the creases, across the upper thighs. The small strap was taken up. 'Now – very wide,' Brekt reminded her. And Anya strained to keep her muscles very tight, to keep her legs wide open to the smacking of her creases and her mound. Once more Brekt's fingers entered. As the tips stroked very lightly upwards along each open liquid wall, the small strap smacked the open sex lips. The fingers came out wet again, and reaching up, they stroked the wetness round each nipple. The hood around the nubbin was sleeved back and Brekt's small lips kissed it. A fingertip was slipped inside and the lips withdrew. A drop of honeydew was placed upon the tip of the nubbin. It was followed by a quick light smack. Anya's body jerked. And that was the unvarying rhythm, the small sucking kiss around the nub, the fingertip tickle against the inner wall, the droplet, the smack and the aching tension in that pushed-out belly and those very wide-held thighs until Anya cried out, 'Please . . .'

Brekt's dark eyes looked on her tortured belly. 'Stay open,' she whispered. The small lips this time did not release Anya, but tubed about her, held her tight, until her pleasure came. Each time the nubbin pulsed, the small lips sucked it tighter and the fingertip touched inside. Yet, open as she tried to stay, Anya could not prevent her sex from closing round and squeezing on that finger in sudden spasms which took her breath away.

As Anya was taken down, then laid in Brekt's arms, with her head pressed to the leather skin wrapped tightly round Brekt's breasts, with Brekt's cool hand between her thighs, against her softness and her wetness, she was suddenly filled with warmth for this woman. She wanted to touch Brekt, in that way.

'Brekt, I want to bring you pleasure,' Anya murmured. Brekt's fingers, wet and warmed now by Anya's liquid honey, trailed upwards over Anya's belly then closed around each nipple in turn.

'You do, my sweet,' said Brekt. 'You do.' Her fingers tickled down again and opened Anya's flesh lips. She stroked the inner walls very, very lightly. 'Tonight, Sadine will punish you,' she said, and Anya's flesh nub stirred.

Brekt lifted Anya up and led her to the tree. She spread her hands against the bole, so her body angled forward. She spread her legs and stood behind her in between her thighs. Brekt's left hand cupped the whole of Anya's sex. Her right hand cupped her breast. Brekt waited. Anya felt the shiver, then the flood of warmth, then she heard the trickle on the fallen leaves. Looking down, she saw the droplets cascading down between Brekt's fingers, on to Brekt's small wriggling toes. Then she felt the small lips kissing her very gently on the shoulders. The shiver came again; the trickling stopped. Brekt turned her round. The air was heavy with the scent of female impudence.

That night, in the small wicker shelter covered with dry bracken fronds, Anya was pleasured by Sadine in the way

Brekt had promised. As Brekt sat beside Anya and watched, Sadine knelt over her, sucking Anya's nipples, and Sadine's heavy breasts trailed circles over Anya's belly. Anya's thighs lay open, slowly melting from the fingertip touch that Brekt bestowed very lightly on her sex lips and her bottom. Then, as Sadine sat up between Anya's thighs, Brekt, with the twisted thong around her belly and the deerskin still wrapped tightly round her breasts, knelt over Anya's face and waited. She faced towards Sadine. Brekt spread her own small tight sex lips; the scent of burning honey enveloped Anya. Anya's knees were bent, her thighs were opened out until the muscles were tight, and then the smacking began–quick bare hand slaps on her thighs, on her belly, on her burning fleshpot as the honeyed scent descended. Then Anya felt her sex lips being spread and the slow licking began, slow wet upward licks of Sadine's tongue which drew her flesh hood upwards and stroked across her nubbin in a belly-melting evenness of licking. Each time the tongue pulled the flesh hood back, the flesh hood slipped back down until Sadine had to hold those thighs apart. The pressure of the pleasure came on so strongly that Anya whimpered as her tongue licked up around the small hard lips above, licking Brekt's honey, licking the tiny nubbin, pushing up inside the hot little fleshpot, until Brekt's shudders brought on Anya's first contraction. Sadine quickly took up the strap and smacked till Anya felt her nubbin burst.

Anya was put to bed, but she could not sleep, despite the delicious languid warmth that welled between her thighs. There were many murmurs, furtive movements, kisses, and sounds of slapping. And she was thinking too of Brekt's parting words, after she had stroked Anya's brow and kissed her nipples, then had turned her over, spread her legs, and tethered her throbbing sex lips with the thong. Brekt's fingertip had gently stroked this warm turgescent flesh before moving up to test the very nervous skin between the open buttocks. Then she had whispered:

'Tomorrow, I choose you to ride with me in the hunt,' and Anya had shivered with permissive pleasure as the fingertip slipped inside.

[9]

Deep Water

Next morning, after the bathing, Anya was very surprised
to be given clothing in the form of a small soft leather halter
for her breasts and a very short skirt which barely covered
the cheeks of her bottom. Brekt also fastened a small leather
rope bracelet round her wrist. Like the one round Brekt's
belly, it was made of twisted thongs. She was given long
leather boots. When Anya was dressed, Brekt brushed her
hair then tied it up.

'I like to see your neck,' she said, touching Anya's bare
neck and her shoulders, 'and I like to see your freckles.'
Anya enjoyed these attentions. Brekt placed one hand
against Anya's belly, above the line of her skirt. She slid the
other hand upwards from the backs of Anya's thighs, across
the surface of her buttocks. Anya found she liked that touch.
She parted her thighs to allow the fingertips to explore the
groove between her cheeks. Brekt's touch made her shiver.
It made her want Brekt to kiss her while she did this, but
Brekt merely looked at Anya's face while her index finger
brushed tantalisingly over the pouted mouth of lewdness in
the middle of the groove.

'Did you like the way I smacked you, in the woods?'
Brekt asked and Anya shyly looked away. Yet Brekt's
fingertip had surely felt that small pulse in the tiny pouted
mouth, the pulse that signalled Anya was excited. She had
remained excited all night long – the thong about her
swollen flesh had made certain of that – and now, as Brekt
touched her, it almost seemed the intimate tightness was
still there, squeezing her flesh bud outwards from between
the burning lips while all the pressure of wanting from the
lovemaking she had been forced to overhear surfaced once

again to taunt her with luscious thoughts of pleasure.

Later, as Anya sat by the fire, watching the curtain of porridge welling down from the lip of the cauldron after it had tipped and spilled, Brekt came again, through the thin morning mist that lingered in the dell. She stood behind Anya, dipped two fingers into Anya's bowl, then lifted them dripping, and held them up. Anya licked those fingers without shame, her head thrown back, her lips sucking, not wishing to release them as Brekt pushed a hand down her halter top and squeezed her nipples.

'On the hunt, I will take the strap,' whispered Brekt. 'I will want to smack your bottom.' A delicious fear kissed gooseflesh over Anya's skin. Brekt pinched till Anya's nipples turned painfully hard. She made her kneel and spread her thighs upon the grass, then move her heels apart, so the skirt rode up her belly and her buttocks, so the cool blades of grass, wet with morning dew, kissed between. It was while Anya was balanced in this posture of submission, with Brekt beside her, taking her breakfast of salt bacon on a spit, that Sadine passed, carrying pots and plates for washing at the stream. She looked imploringly at Brekt; she even tried to speak to her, but Brekt ignored her, taking a piece of meat from the spit and making great play of feeding it to Anya. When Sadine walked away, she was crying.

'She is upset because I have given you her things,' said Brekt, and whereas Anya had last night felt very jealous of Sadine, she now felt very guilty. Suddenly, she did not want these clothes or this leather wrist strap. Brekt became annoyed when Anya mentioned this. 'You do not wear these things for yourself, but for me,' she said, 'because they emphasise your figure. You do it to please me – for the same reason that you spread your legs and make your belly drip.' And with that, Brekt hauled her to her feet, pulled up her skirt and, standing behind her, so all could see, thrust her hand between Anya's naked thighs. 'You are hot here,' she said. 'You are wet because of the things I make you do.' Then she threw Anya to the ground, pushing her head down, throwing her skirt above her hips and making her spread her legs and squat, so her sex swelled down, exposed and vulnerable. 'Should I get the strap?' she said and smiled when Anya's belly shuddered. And though Brekt did not use the strap, nor smack Anya in any way, nor yet touch her, Anya felt the soft shivers up her buttocks and the warm feeling weighted in between her thighs as fluid gathered to her low-slung fleshpot as it gently swelled to throbbing need.

That throbbing feeling deepened when Anya was made to sit, bareback and bare-bottomed, astride the piebald horse. The hunting party comprised a dozen horses. They did not set off at a charge, as Anya had expected, but at a steady walk, following the valley downwards, into the thickened mist. Brekt and all the men carried bows and arrows. Bardin and Aruline led, accompanied by a grey horse ridden by a wiry bowman dressed in a coat of dappled brown and green. Ulf and Riga followed. Sarol-harn rode with the man in purple silk. As she passed Anya, she whispered something, but so softly that Anya could not hear; Anya tried to think what Sarol-harn might mean, but she had no way of knowing. She allowed the incident to drift to the back of her mind; she was excited by the prospect of the hunt.

As the horse moved, Anya's body gently rocked. At first, she gripped the horse's back tightly with her thighs. Very soon, her muscles ached. She relaxed her grip; the horsehair kissed and pricked her bottom. Brekt had told Anya to hold her round the waist; Anya's hands lay only lightly above the small slim hips, yet even being allowed to touch Brekt at all brought Anya pleasure. Who else was permitted to touch Brekt in this way? Sadine perhaps, but Sadine was back there in the camp. It was Anya who had been taken on the hunt.

And the touching was not one-sided. Throughout that ride, Brekt touched Anya. A hand would reach behind to tickle Anya's belly or in between her thighs. Sometimes the touching would be more prolonged. Anya, now reaching her arms forwards, would be given the reins while Brekt used the fingers of two hands to stimulate her by opening out her flesh leaves and tickling round the edges, or holding them that way while the nubbin was lightly pinched. On one occasion, Brekt placed the back of her hand flat to the horse's backbone and lifted up the two middle fingers while Anya was made to bed her flesh around them. Anya found she enjoyed the constant stimulation of this ride. Sometimes, a fingertip would be held very close to her nubbin, so as the horse moved, each rock of Anya's hips would cause the finger to slip beneath the hood and press the poked-out nubbin back into her body. Brekt would also make Anya move back, then open her flesh fully and rotate her body forwards until her inner sex was spread upon the horse. She would make her ride like that, holding her skirt up so Brekt could tickle her belly. All that time, Anya would feel the warmth of the horse against her, and the horsehair would tickle, making her feel lewd.

The first kill came unexpectedly. The scout had dismounted several times to check the trail. The party had moved off the main track and into a glade. Brekt held her longbow with an arrow at the ready. 'We may come upon the deer very soon,' she whispered. The scout was speaking to Bardin in a hushed voice. Everywhere seemed still. When the horses snorted, the warmth of their breath misted in the coolness of the air. Then Anya heard a noise which made her turn.

'Look!' she cried, and as she pointed, and the dove spread its wings to take flight from the branch, she heard the thin swish. The bird appeared to explode in a shower of feathers and fly backwards through the tree. Then it bounced down through the branches onto the ground.

'Good shot!' came the cries. Before Anya had fully realised what had happened, Brekt was off the horse and at the site of the kill. She came back waving the trophy, its head lolled back, its pure white breast feathers splashed with brilliant red, its lifeless body impaled upon the arrow. Anya turned deathly pale. Brekt simply pulled the arrow out, to the sounds of cracking bone, wiped it and replaced it in her quiver, then stowed the dove in the pocket of her coat. She licked her bloodstained fingers.

So now, as the ride continued, Anya did not hold Brekt round the waist any more; she tried to distance herself from this cruel and heartless person who would slay a beautiful and defenceless creature – the bird of purity, the bird of love – by driving an arrow through its heart. And if Brekt should cook that bird, Anya could never be made to eat it, not if she were starving. No morsel of that innocent body could be made to pass her lips, not if she should be tortured. She hated this hunt and she hated this ride, and if Brekt should speak to her, Anya would not answer.

However, Brekt did not speak. Not long afterwards, Anya's sad discomfiture turned to sweet revenge, for in a clearing they came upon some deer – a stag and several hinds. The bowmen crept onwards on foot and began to form a circle to the outside of the clearing. The others followed quietly. Anya was the only one to stay back, on the horse. She watched Bardin draw the first arrow. Carefully, she lifted up a long dry branch and began to bend it. At the instant the bowstring kissed his lips, the branch snapped with a bang which echoed round the clearing. The stag swung his head round, the arrow clattered off his antlers and the deer stampeded out of the clearing. None of the other bowmen had been fast enough. Everyone ran to the horses.

'Why did Bardin aim for the antlers?' asked Anya. Brekt laughed, then reaching up, framed Anya's face between her hands and kissed her on the chin. She didn't notice the evidence lying on the ground.

Then the chase was on – the screams, the shouts, the galloping through the trees, and the jumps which knocked the breath from Anya's body. There was no chance they could ever catch the deer now, yet nobody seemed to mind. Anya was beginning to enjoy the hunt again.

After several more false starts and misdirected arrows, the pace slowed to a canter, then a trot. As the sun rose higher, the air warmed, the mist dissolved and the ride became relaxed. There was much leg-pulling and laughter at Bardin's bowmanship. When they came to a place where the stream disappeared into a stretch of oak wood, a halt was called before they entered. The men sat on the bank, in the sunshine. Food was brought out and wine passed around. Anya, still mounted on the horse, was given bread and

145

cheese and wine. Brekt stood below her, with her hand on Anya's thigh. Some of the men came over, talking at first about the progress of the hunt, but Anya knew they were interested in her; they kept slyly glancing at her. Brekt seemed to like this; she kept edging the hem of Anya's skirt up her leg to expose her thigh and buttock. It made Anya very embarrassed indeed. She liked Brekt's touch, but she did not want it done so publicly, in front of these men. Very soon the conversation turned to Anya; the men said she was beautiful. Brekt agreed. They started asking Brekt intimate questions about Anya, as if Anya were not present. Brekt was reticent at first then, under the pressure of flattery and provocation, began replying freely. The conversation appeared to excite Brekt as much as it did the men.

'She has very nice thighs,' said one of the men, 'very pale. Yet I hear her flesh is black.' Brekt asked Anya to lift her leg over so she sat sideways rather than astride. Anya's cheeks were burning as she did it, yet she still allowed Brekt to use her in this way, to show off her body to the men. Her skirt was lifted to her navel. The men whistled. Brekt made Anya spread her legs to expose her belly. Then another of the men asked if he could touch. Brekt let him. 'She does anything I ask,' she said, then turning to Anya, 'Now hold your skirt up while he touches you.'

By now, a small crowd had gathered. The coarse thick fingers touched, stroking her short curls, separating one lip to the side, causing shivers, then trying to reach within. 'Not too far,' Brekt warned, and the man withdrew. A second man touched. Anya's thighs were lifted while he touched her bottom.

'Tight,' he said.

'I like her that way,' said Brekt. Anya's face and neck felt very hot.

'At the front here, she is very moist,' he observed, as the fingers opened her sex again and surreptitiously touched the inner walls.

'She keeps her flesh that way – for me,' Brekt answered. The men were impressed. 'She gets even wetter when I smack her. She likes the smacking very much.'

146

'No,' Anya murmured, for now her shame was tinged with fear.

Brekt glowered at her. 'You love it when I smack you.' Anya was shaking her head, but the endless sinking feeling was coming in her belly. 'Get down,' said Brekt. 'We shall see.'

As Anya was moved away from the horse, the small crowd followed. She was made to stand and pull her halter up to expose her breasts, which swelled out tightly with the pressure from above. Brekt wet her fingers, pulled Anya's head back and finger-slapped her nipples. Then Anya was made to lift her skirt, arch her belly, so her bottom pushed out, and plant her legs apart. She had to spread the cheeks of her bottom in readiness for the smacking. The women looked on from a distance. Sarol-harn was open-mouthed. Riga watched intently.

'Now pant,' said Brekt. Anya breathed very quickly. 'Pant! Very deep breaths.' Her breasts shook, her belly expanded and contracted; she began to feel light-headed. 'Faster!' Now her heart was pounding in her throat; there was a buzzing in her ears; her belly shuddered; her fleshpot pulsed; ribbons of anticipation were being drawn out of her from between her open thighs. 'Pull those cheeks wide apart.' Then the smacking started, quick cracks of the strap, not against her thighs, not against the cheeks, but against her bottom mouth. 'Keep panting. Spread those cheeks wider. Keep it tight.' Her thighs began to shake beneath the pleasure of that torture; her legs were turning to jelly. She could feel her fleshpot slowly pumping up with blood, her sex lips gradually distending from the quick quakes in her bottom. The feeling came.

'Please?' she begged, for she wanted so desperately now to be touched between the legs. The smacks simply came softer, quicker, more precisely to the mouth, making the feeling more exquisite still, until her legs buckled and she toppled to the ground. Brekt dragged her to her feet, stood behind her, pinning her body tightly as Anya gasped for breath. She kicked her legs apart. Using her fingertips to draw the flesh hood very tightly back, she began a very slow

147

massage of the poked-out nubbin, not roughly but very firmly, very wetly, until Anya could feel her pleasure coming on. When her thighs tensed hard as stone, the fingers carefully flicked her until she grunted, then she was flung belly uppermost to the ground.

'Now arch,' Brekt said. 'Dig your heels in. I want those legs spread and that belly pushed high up in the air.' Then she took the strap, smacked the upcurve of the belly – 'Keep up,' she warned – then smacked between the legs – 'Now open – hold it open' – and kept on smacking. Brekt did not stop until the strap was wet on both sides and the quick shudders of impending pleasure were replaced by a slowly burning pulse of interrupted need. 'Now kiss my boot,' said Brekt, and as Anya did it, kissing her boot and kissing her leg and attempting to kiss her belly, Brekt was pleased to see, between the soft mounds of the bottom of the crouching figure at her feet, the clear slick softly seeping down the back of the open thigh. When Anya's face was buried against her belly, before she pushed that face away, Brekt kissed the strap. As she pressed the wetness to her lips, she felt a shudder deep inside her.

When Anya finally stood up very shakily, then looked around at all the silent faces – at Aruline, wide-eyed, Riga staring, Sarol-harn standing like a statue – what did Anya feel? As she turned to face Brekt, she felt the overwhelming power of Brekt's attentions; she felt Brekt's hand against her back, low down, then the backs of Brekt's fingers tickling her nipples very tenderly, and now Brekt's lips, moist now, wetted with Anya's spillage to the strap, pressed against her own.

'Tonight, I will let you punish Sadine,' Brekt whispered. And Anya felt she was floating in a whirlpool, a roaring whirlpool sucking her down into the soft black abyss of submission. As Brekt's tongue slid smoothly into Anya's mouth and Brekt's hand closed around her softness in between her open thighs, Anya no longer wished to try to swim against this tide.

When the party entered the oak wood, Anya was half asleep, resting her head against Brekt's back. She did not

148

hear the shouts at first; they did not register. When the horse shied, it was too late. Anya toppled to the ground. Then she saw it – a squealing ball of bristle and tusks heading directly for her. She did not get to her knees before the wild boar slammed her with a glancing blow which sent her spinning into the bushes. Then the creature disappeared as fast as it had come.

Anya was so stunned that she thought she had imagined it, until she heard the screams, the arrows rattling through the branches, and felt the searing pain spreading up her thigh. When she scrambled to her feet again, the boar was racing back, driven by the horses from the other side. Brekt screamed for Anya to get out of the way. With arrows whistling past her ears, she ran into a clump of waist-high bushes, then started screaming too, for now she couldn't see the boar. She could hear the snorts and squeals, and the snapping of the branches. Suddenly it was upon her. She dived away; it missed. As she ran back towards the horses, she tripped. The arrows showered down around her, forcing the boar to skid and change direction. It careered towards the piebald horse, which did a jump-kick in the air, then tried to stand on forelegs. Brekt was forced to drop her longbow but she held on tightly while the arrows spilled from her quiver. By now, the boar had broken through the ring and all the other riders immediately set off in pursuit.

Anya sat down and began to rub her leg. The skin had started to darken to a bruise across the upper thigh and buttock. Brekt dismounted and walked over to her, but didn't seem to care. She handed her the reins and set about collecting up the scattered arrows. Then suddenly, she turned on Anya. 'I could have hit him – easily – if you hadn't been in the way. Why couldn't you hang on to the horse? Why did I bother to bring you?' Anya felt a lump in her throat. Why was Brekt not concerned about her? She could have been killed. 'Get back on,' said Brekt, 'if you can manage it without falling off again.' Anya did as she was told, but she was very upset indeed. 'And stop whimpering!' Brekt collected up all the arrows she could find. Then she turned and stared at Anya, who couldn't stop crying now. Anya was frightened by the cold cruelty in that look. 'Very well,' said Brekt through gritted teeth.

She marched over to a young birch tree and cut from it a vicious looking whippy switch. Anya sat up very straight with apprehension. Brekt, now looking fiendish, strode towards her. 'Now I'll give you something to whimper about . . .' The whip swished through the air.

'No!' The cry had come from nowhere.

Anya jumped. Brekt stopped in her tracks. Both women turned and stared. It was Sarol-harn, advancing purposefully. 'Leave her alone!' she shouted. Anya watched in disbelief, and Brekt was too stunned to prevent the switch being wrenched from her wrist. But she very quickly recovered.

'She is mine!' she cried, lunging with her foot and bringing Sarol-harn to the ground. 'I do with her as I think fit!' And although Sarol-harn fought back, she was no match for Brekt. Anya didn't know what to do.

'Stop!' she shouted. 'Both of you – stop!' She didn't want the two of them fighting over her. Why was Sarol-harn not with the others? Why had she come back?

'Anya, quickly!' cried Sarol-harn, breaking free, trying to dodge round Brekt and get to the horse. 'They will soon be back. We must get away!'

Get away? But how could they? What about Brekt? Even now Brekt was defending her as if Sarol-harn were an enemy. How could Anya convince Brekt that Sarol-harn meant no harm, that she was a friend?

'Don't you see?' Sarol-harn shouted. 'Don't you see what she is doing to you? She is only using you, like she uses Sadine.' Then she turned on Brekt. 'You are a wicked, cruel woman. Heartless – you love no one but yourself!'

Brekt spat at Sarol-harn then threw herself at her and they wrestled on the ground, Brekt kicking and biting, Sarol-harn screaming. Anya was very scared indeed. Someone would be killed. She knew it would be Sarol-harn. Brekt had her by the throat.

'Stop, I beg you – stop! Oh, please?' cried Anya. But Brekt was frenzied. Her hand had found the birch switch. It was lashed across Sarol-harn's cheek. Anya screamed. In desperation, she dug her heels into the horse's flank. The horse started towards the women. At the last second it reared up above them and Anya saw the malice in Brekt's eyes as the switch was lifted once again. And she saw too the ring – her own turquoise ring – on Sarol-harn's finger as her hand spread out to protect herself from the vicious onslaught, and something in Anya snapped.

In that instant, a vision came to her, a vision of a great white stallion rearing up, kicking out, above a nest of squirming snakes. It was a memory of a picture in the castle, in the Prince's bedchamber, a picture of braveness and of wildness and of freedom, so contrasted with her own state these last few days. And that memory, that picture, the white horse and the Prince, reminded her so vividly of her quest, the quest she had allowed her mind to be seduced into setting aside. All of those images flashed before her in that second when the horse reared and she saw the ring.

Sarol-harn had placed herself at risk to try to save her. She had done it out of loving friendship, and this was how she was being treated for that selfless act of bravery.

As Brekt fell backwards, Anya's hand swept down to take the switch. Brekt backed away. Sarol-harn jumped up. Anya broke the switch in two and flung it to the ground. While Brekt stared at Anya in total disbelief, Sarol-harn jumped up behind her onto the horse.

'Go. We must go!' she shouted. 'You are free of her at last.'

When Anya didn't move, Brekt laughed. But the laugh was hollow.

As the sound of approaching hoofbeats came, and Sarol-harn took control, turning the horse, then spurring him into a gallop up the valley side, Brekt shouted after them: 'You will never be free of me. That need – my kind of love – will haunt your flesh forever!'

Above the oak wood, in the distance, were the twin hills, one rocky, the other green. Sarol-harn slowed the horse to a walk. She was elated. Anya tried to smile with Sarol-harn, but she couldn't. She felt too sad.

'Sarol-harn, why did you risk yourself? You should have gone without me,' she said. Sarol-harn merely held up the hand that bore the ring, and Anya began to cry. Sarol-harn tried to comfort her, but it took a long time for those tears to abate to the point where Anya felt she could speak again.

At length, she wiped her eyes. 'But how did you get away from the man you rode with?' she asked.

'I just told him the truth – I was worried you were injured. And I told him he'd make better speed without me!' She laughed, and Anya laughed too, but her sadness remained undiminished. Though she was closer to her Prince now than she had been since that fatal day of his departure, she was sadder now than ever. She was thinking of Brekt's curse. She knew that Brekt was cruel, but what Anya had experienced with Brekt was not confined to cruelty. And when they had escaped, Brekt could have used her bow and arrow, but she didn't. They had taken Brekt's favourite horse; she could have sent the riders in pursuit, but again, she didn't; nobody had followed. And then there was her Prince, who, like Sarol-harn, had risked himself to save her, a Prince full of loving gentleness, not cruelty at all, a Prince with soft and gentle eyes . . .

The horse had stopped. Sarol-harn looked at her. 'You are thinking about your lover?' The tears welled freer than before. Sarol-harn put her arm round Anya. 'You must not cry. You will reach him. I am sure.'

Anya shook her head. 'What will he think of me, Sarol-harn? What will he say?'

'If he is your lover, he will love you.'

'He will never forgive me. He will hate me.'

'No!'

'He will!'

'Then it is as I told you from the start – your lover is a cur.'

The result of this frank diagnosis was that Anya's tears did not assuage completely until they had crossed between the hills, descended once more on a clear sunward track through open woodland and reached the river around the middle of the afternoon. They came upon it suddenly; one minute they were in the woods, the next, beside the river. No sound was associated with this river, no bank was visible – the forest grass and trees gave way directly to an apparently slowly moving, heavy grey-brown swell of water. There were tree branches and large tussocks of grass floating past sedately. The far side looked very distant; again it was clothed with trees.

'We had better get across,' declared Sarol-harn, standing at the edge.

Anya stared at her in disbelief. 'But the river is in flood.'

'But this is a ford. See – the trail comes down to here. It cannot be very deep.' When Anya opened her mouth to speak, Sarol-harn cut in quickly: 'We will ride. If it becomes too deep, the horse will swim. We will hold on to his mane.' Then when Anya walked to the edge and stared, Sarol-harn added, to seal their fate, 'What else can we do? Stay here? Turn back?'

At first, the water was shallower than expected. It was very cold, and the current was very strong. Soon, even on the horse, it was almost to their knees. Anya wanted to turn back, but suddenly the bottom dropped and they were floating, but moving much more quickly downstream than forwards. Neither of them saw the tree trunk until it hit them and very slowly rolled over them.

Anya grappled frantically with a branch below the water. She didn't dare open her eyes to the murk. Just at the point when anxiety turned to panic, and she felt as if her lungs were bursting, she flailed to the surface to see Sarol-harn fifty feet away. The horse had turned and was swimming back strongly for the nearer bank. Anya tried to swim towards Sarol-harn, but Sarol-harn seemed to be drifting further away. Very soon, Anya couldn't see Sarol-harn at all, and now she was exhausted. She managed to catch hold of a large piece of drifting log, but hadn't the strength to lift herself onto it. She felt very cold, and very tired. The water became very choppy; the log was moving faster and faster. The river was funnelling between very steep banks. There were boulders. She locked her arms around two forks of branches in the log just before it ploughed through two enormous waves which knocked the breath completely out of her body. After that, she didn't remember any more.

[10]

Elurial and the Inn

A mile below the gorge, perched upon a very large pedestal of rock at the highest navigable point on the south bank of the Great River, was the inn. It had grown, almost like a living thing, on this rock until it buried it completely. Its collapsed, decaying lower timbers moulded to the crannies in the stone; its ancient beams dipped, like the clawed toes of a giant bird, into the water. The inn was enormous, and haphazard. Though it had a cellar which could inebriate a regiment of men, it had a kitchen which could barely cope with a platoon. No plan of construction had ever existed; no carpenter's level had ever been used: it had narrow, uneven stairways which started upwards, then wound back down to finish in the basement; there were rooms which cantilevered out so far above the river that each footfall induced a sickening undulation of the floor; the highest bedroom in the inn was accessed through a trapdoor. And it was rumoured that there existed a room with no access at all.

The clientele of the inn was equally disjoint. It included forest dwellers – woodsmen, hunters and many of more nefarious inclinations; the bargees plying the river to the west; soldiers in transit – many of these, of late; then the itinerants, merchants and caravans traversing the mountain passes into Surdia. The inn was a trading post for news from many parts; spices, horses, furs and jewels were bartered; slaves were bought and sold; fortunes, limbs and lives were gambled on the turn of a single card. Strange happenings were everyday events. When a Surdic girl, soaking wet, half drowned, was brought in by a woodsman who had found her at the top end of the gorge, it did not raise an eyebrow.

She was bought and then immediately resold. Mild surprise was expressed in one corner of the taproom when a second girl was later reported washed up at the ferry. After that, a weather eye was kept for further windfalls, for the most marketable commodities at the inn were wine and food and women. And the most prized possession of any kind was Elurial. Elurial, however, could not be bought, nor could she be rented.

It was late into the morning when Nina, the chambermaid, drew back the curtains. Elurial bathed in the golden light. She lay upon the matt white sheets, with the coverlet folded neatly at the foot of the bed. Her back, turned to the window, formed a perfect curve – slim, with precisely drawn projecting bumps all the way down her spine, or at least, as far down as could be seen, for around her waistline was a pure white belt. Had Elurial been sitting up, her interwoven sun-gold hair would have formed a dense and wavy triangular cloak to the level of her hips. But now, with Elurial supine, her cloak of gold lay draped across her neck and breasts and belly. Elurial's face was innocent, as chaste as falling snow; her nose was small; her eyelashes were long – perfectly curved, and long and soft enough to stroke a lover's skin. Her eyes had opened now – they were as wide as innocence and just as blue. But Elurial's lips were sensual – full red, moist and swollen as if they had been sucked upon and only just released.

Elurial moved; her fingertips stretched; her limbs caressed the smoothness of the silk. When she turned, her thighs slid apart to reveal the soft white padded belt that fitted so perfectly around her waist and bedded so intimately to the crease, the belt that enfolded Elurial's tenderness each night, to flood her dreams with the sweet taunt of denial. Even now, that peculiar pleasure waxed and waned, even with Elurial's breathing: her limbs moved very slightly, the soft silk brushed her skin, her hair caressed her bright pink nipples, and the padding gently tantalised her nakedness. Elurial smiled; the delicious ritual of morning was upon her.

She looked with eyes of languid blue at the girl standing by the window, the girl whose fingertips would touch Elurial to stir the nerves upon her skin to a delicious ache of pleasure. Already Elurial could feel the gentle throb of anticipation between her outspread thighs. Nina came and sat beside Elurial, laying her fingertips upon the ivory skin of Elurial's belly. Elurial lifted up her arms and placed them underneath the pillow. Nina smiled. The fingertips tickled so lightly on the smooth bare skin of her underarms that Elurial closed her eyes. And the smoothness of Elurial's skin was unlike any other, for no downy hair, no body hair at all had ever grown there to besmirch its nudity. Soft lips gently brushed against that tender underarm skin, and kissed, then tasted, tickled with the tongue, then licked that flawless smoothness very slowly.

Nina loved to touch Elurial; she loved to brush her lips against her and to bring Elurial pleasure – not pleasure to fruition, for this was not allowed: Elurial was being trained towards a state of permanent pleasured tension which would pervade each waking moment and suffuse her every dream.

There was, of course, a purpose to this endless pleasured torturing of Elurial's perfect flesh. Demonstrations were enacted every evening for the clients. It served to stimulate them, as a prelude to their lovemaking with the other girls who, however personable and sensual in their own right, nevertheless – by comparison with Elurial – were certainly mundane. Elurial was a potion, an exquisite aphrodisiac to counteract the sluggishness of wine, to stir the faintest part to full turgidity.

The bedroom door opened; Nina stood up and backed against the wall. A stout middle-aged woman dressed in a wine-coloured frock coat lumbered in, supported by a stick and breathing heavily from the effects of the stairs. She reached the bedside, then leaned upon the stick, eyeing the chambermaid, who stood with hands clasped together and eyes downcast. The woman's hair was dyed bright red. Her eyes drew a slow circle round the room, taking in every detail, as if looking for something which might be out of place. And Elurial's room was unusual in this respect – for a room at this particular inn – for everything was spotlessly clean and perfectly arranged, from the coverlet folded neatly at the foot of Elurial's bed, to the silver tray with the small jug and the tiny brush on the table by the fire.

'Elurial, my precious,' the woman wheezed, transferring her weight more definitely to the stick as her hand came up to stroke Elurial's brow, 'and how did you sleep, my dearest? Very well, I trust?' The woman smiled benignly.

Elurial nodded. 'Yes Madam, thank you,' she answered in a voice as soft as rose water. She looked with shining eyes on the woman, whose fingertips caressed her cheek then traced the line of her lips until they parted and Elurial closed her eyes. The woman sighed.

'And did you dream again? Which dream did you dream, my precious?' Elurial's large blue eyes opened once again to bathe Madam in Elurial's sensuality. Elurial's small breasts shivered as she recounted:

'It was the dream about a tree, Madam. I was running in the forest, then suddenly I was swept up into the arms of a great tree . . .'

Madam smiled. 'Go on, my dear.' Her fingertips slid down to coax Elurial's willing nipples up to perfect points. Elurial's eyes were very wide.

'But the branches of the tree were soft and slender – like serpents. They wrapped around me, warm and slippery, round my arms and round my legs and then the serpents . . . Oh Madam!'

'Sh . . . Shhh, my precious.' Madam put her arm about Elurial's head as Elurial reached up and buried her face against the woman's thigh. 'These serpents cannot harm you,' the woman whispered tenderly. 'They are dreams; these serpents can never reach you. You are perfect, you are precious. We will protect you, always. Now lie back.'

There was a jingle as Madam removed a bunch of small silver keys fastened at her waist. Elurial shuddered softly as a key was selected and inserted into the tiny lock below the rounded belly. The belt separated into three loose ends, then Madam nervously lifted it away completely. And even

Madam, though she had beheld this vision many times before, was forced to catch her breath at this picture of soft pink nakedness, unblemished by any hair or razor-reddened roughness. For here, as in the case of Elurial's underarms, no hair had ever grown. The outer lips formed a glass-smooth shield; the inner lips, upstanding, womanly, were satin soft and deepest pink. Madam allowed her fingertips to touch that satin softness, to brush into the smoothly polished creases, and as Elurial murmured and her mouth fell open, Madam shivered. Even after all her years, she shivered at that touch. She allowed herself another touch, a gentle squeeze about the joining of the sex lips. Elurial momentarily tried to close her thighs together then, remembering, held them very wide apart. Her eyes were closed now; her mouth was pouted to an 'o'. Madam pushed the tip of a finger into that mouth and Elurial gently sucked upon it, tickling with her tongue tip as Madam's fingers gently squeezed the soft pink lips between Elurial's thighs. 'You are so delicious,' whispered Madam. Then she turned to the girl behind her.

'Elurial is hungry, are you not, my sweet? Send for Maria.' As Madam continued the gentle sexual arousal, Elurial looked up lovingly; Elurial's small teeth lightly nipped the fingertip still pushed between her lips.

Madam sat in a comfortable chair by the fire. Nina stood beside her, watching as Maria, with hair as black as ebony and eyes of deepest brown, unbuttoned her top, removing it completely, and then unlaced her bodice. As she bent to place it carefully on the chair beside the bed, her breasts, distended to overfullness, swung down like deliciously weighted brown-capped fleshy gourds. She sat upon the bed, lifting up each breast in turn, gently squeezing the swollen tip until it exuded, then wiping it with a moistened cloth. The air was pervaded with the scent of faintly yeasted milk. Maria was very young; her breasts were very heavy. Madam kept her that way for selected clients, but mainly for Elurial.

Elurial's head was laid in the girl's lap. As the girl bent

158

over her, offering the left breast, lifting it and squeezing, Elurial's tongue licked up to take the thin pale welling droplet. She opened her lips and spread them round the pear-shaped nipple, then gently sucked it in. And as the breast undulated, Maria felt the slow delicious sucking rhythm which pulled right to her belly as her bosom softly squirted; she felt the soft warm breath upon her skin and now the hand that moulded round her breast to squeeze her milk down to her teat. Maria's fingers drifted down to play with Elurial's tiny nipples, and to touch the smoothness of the belly and, as the slim thighs opened, to touch between, to rub the smooth round shield of flesh surrounding the purse of skin. Then Maria's fingertips returned. She wetted them with her milk. She used those milky fingertips to wet Elurial's sex lips, to separate them and to work the liquid around the little sexual tip until the hips began to move. She remoistened, and reapplied her warm milk to the tip until the tip was swimming, until the scent of milk and female seepage rose very strongly from between the outspread thighs, and the sucking became so intense that Madam called a halt in the proceedings. She ambled over, bidding the chambermaid follow.

Bending across Elurial, she carefully opened the sex lips wide. She indicated that Nina should take over. So now, as Madam watched and leaned upon her stick, and Elurial sucked spasmodically on Maria's nipples, Nina worked her own lips very tightly around the bud between the sex lips in between the thighs and sucked until Elurial whimpered, until Elurial no longer had the will to drink but kept tossing her head from side to side as Maria tried to feed her. Madam examined the nubbin a second time.

'Not large enough to take the ring,' she whispered. And so the sucking was taken up again, until Elurial gasped and cried out on the verge of pleasure. Madam was now more encouraged by the state of her distension. She therefore dismissed Maria. As Maria's bounteous breasts were once more laced into her bodice, Elurial was made to turn and lie upon her front. Her thighs were spread apart while Nina secured her ankles to the bottom bedposts by means of soft leather loops. The tension was adjusted until the edges of her open sex lips brushed against the silk. Madam sat upon the chair beside her. The chambermaid knelt between her thighs, stroking a single finger very slowly down the spine, down into the furrow, down across the pinkened smooth-skinned mouth, until Elurial murmured and her nubbin touched the silk. Madam passed to the chambermaid the silver tray bearing the small cylindrical sable brush, the gold rod with the tiny ring, and the little jug of honey.

The brush was used dry at first and stroked back and forth across the tiny mouth in a gentle dusting action. Then it was licked up to a point and applied beneath, very precisely, to stimulate the nubbin. Then the bottom mouth was tickled with the tip of Nina's tongue. A thick droplet of honey was poured into the well. The tongue pressed against and pushed this droplet into Elurial's body, then licked the small well clean. Throughout this treatment, the pleasured pro-tests were absorbed by Elurial's pillow. This facility was unavailable for the next part of her training.

Elurial was turned onto her back. With the pillow now beneath her hips, to raise and help to separate the flesh between her thighs, her feet were secured more tightly than before. The tiny gold ring on its supporting rod was held up to the light. Elurial swallowed. Madam stroked her brow. The tiny ring was now applied, very carefully, between her legs; yet even so, it made Elurial shudder. It slipped beneath the softened hooding of the sex lips and around the swollen bud of sexual pleasure. As Nina pressed, Elurial moaned; the nubbin squeezed through, a small bright pink polished mushroom encircled by a tiny band of gold. Nina took up the brush and dipped it in the honey. She waited. Elurial turned her head to the side, to face Madam. Very slowly, Elurial's mouth opened. Her tongue arched out. As it touched against her upper lip, then tickled very lightly, the honeyed brushtip stroked slow circles round the polished cap of her tethered nubbin until Elurial's tongue could move no more, until that tongue went rigid. Her fingers tightened round the bars of the headframe. Her legs went very stiff. Nina kept the ring in place and sucked her until she whimpered.

160

The pillow was now replaced beneath Elurial's head. Her hands were fastened to the headframe. Nina took a band of soft cloth bearing loops at one end and loose cords at the other. She fed a second, longer cord through the loops then, feeding the cloth beneath Elurial's hips, fastened the cord around her waist. The cloth band was now pulled up between Elurial's legs, tightly between her open sex lips, and fastened to the cord round her waist. Madam looked one last time on the delicious cross of Elurial's perfect outspread body. The soft cloth would press against her, absorbing her delicate exudations even as she rested. Nina drew up the satin coverlet and Madam kissed Elurial lightly on the forehead. Elurial smiled, and Nina and Madam departed.

Anya felt warm now, not cold. Her limbs still ached, but the freezing cold had turned to a soft, all-encompassing warmth. The air was no longer fresh; it was very musty. She could no longer hear the sounds of rushing water. Suddenly she was prodded into waking. She was in a bed in a small, ill-lit room. She sat up quickly. How had she got here? A large old woman with scarlet hair was standing over her with a stick. It was this stick that had been used to prod Anya. Beside the woman was a girl dressed like a servant. The woman's expression was intent, not kind. Anya was afraid.

'Where am I?' she said. 'Where is Sarol-harn?'

The woman used the stick to push her down again. 'My dear, since you ask, I will tell you plainly: this is an inn – for paying guests – and you are a piece of flotsam washed up at our door. And the first lesson a girl like you must learn is to speak when you are spoken to.' Anya was very frightened by the tone of the woman's voice, but she had to know what had happened to her friend.

'But you must tell me. Please – was someone else found too?'

The woman sighed, then turned to the servant. 'It seems the lesson must be delivered, Nina. Hold her up.' Anya began to tremble as she was dragged into a sitting position

161

and her arms were pinned behind her. 'Large breasts. Good nipples; brown ones too,' the woman observed. She took two small rings fashioned out of bone and serrated on the inner surface, and slipped one over each of Anya's nipples. The small teeth nipped her flesh and held the rings firm. The woman said, 'Now my dear, let us test the limits of your obstinacy.' She took the left nipple, pushed the ring and pulled the nipple through until Anya screamed. The woman then released the nipple, but the pain did not go away. It worsened as the nipple swelled and the teeth dug into it. The woman stroked the tight pap gently. 'Now, no more talking out of turn. Is that understood?'

'Yes . . .' Anya mumbled.

The woman then pulled the right nipple through the other ring until Anya screamed again. 'Yes Madam, if you please,' she snapped.

'Yes, Madam,' Anya replied, trying to fight back the tears as her nipples throbbed to bursting.

'Ah – tears are so sweet upon a girl, so tender and endearing,' Madam murmured. 'You must cultivate those tears, my dear – the clients love them.' Anya's mouth fell open. 'But we will keep these rings about these little pips for now – to prepare them and to help remind you of your manners. Now let me explain.' The woman motioned with a finger and Nina brought a chair. Madam sat down heavily and leaned upon her stick.

'Your friend was found safely,' she said. Anya heaved a sigh of relief. 'She has been sold,' she added, staring at Anya fixedly.

'Sold?'

The woman frowned and reached towards the nipples. 'Are you interrupting?' Anya shook her head and shrank away. 'She has been sold – as you will be as soon as we find a buyer. Trade is quiet now, with the river crossing closed. It's a pity you didn't land here when we had the soldiers; they like a girl with breasts like these. Now lie down while we look at you.'

Anya shut her eyes tightly as the cover was drawn back and she was forced to spread her legs. 'Wider,' said Madam when Anya hesitated. 'I've another device for here if needs be . . .' Anya spread until she ached, while Madam discussed her with the servant. 'She is bruised; a pity . . .' Anya shivered as her sex was slowly peeled apart. 'Black lips, see, but pink within.' She shuddered as the fingers entered. 'Squeeze,' the woman instructed her, then grunted when she complied. The fingers probed her deeply. The lips were spread back wider; the hood was lifted. The fingertips probed around her nubbin. 'Lift your legs; hold your knees apart.' Now as the fingers touched her, squeezing the burning bud, other fingers touched her bottom, pressing against the reluctant mouth, not hard but insistently. 'Very tight here,' the woman murmured. 'Too tight, perhaps.' That made Anya very anxious indeed. The fingers kept touching, not simply examining her, but touching her in such a way as to stimulate her pleasure.

The woman spoke again. 'Keep your knees held wide apart.' The hand moved up and pressed against her belly. 'Turn your head to the side. Close your eyes. Nina.'

Anya felt the servant kneel on the bed, then the warm breath between her open thighs. 'No,' she murmured.

'Oh yes, my darling,' Madam replied. 'Yes.' Her hand moved lightly over Anya's belly, then touched the creases of her thighs. 'We must see how you perform. Let Nina's tongue explore you, wet you, tickle . . .' Anya felt warm lips close about her, kiss her, draw her sex lips in. A tongue probed up inside her as the soft lips sucked. Her belly shuddered beneath the fingertip tickle in the creases. 'Move your head back. Let me see the smooth curve of your neck . . . Delicious.' Anya shuddered once again, as the tongue slipped deeply. 'Open your mouth,' the woman whispered. The tongue between her legs slid out to stroke its firm warm wetness round and round her nubbin. 'Lift up now, offer up your bottom.' Anya groaned and pulled her knees back very tightly. 'Good.' The tongue pushed against her bottom mouth, pressed against her wantonness, licked against delicious shame and entered, squirming round inside while a small wet fingertip glided very slowly round her nubbin. Madam's fingers pushed into Anya's mouth to stifle the gasps; the hand very gently slapped her belly, making her breasts shake; the fingertip circled, the tongue pushed up inside. Anya felt her belly tighten to a knot.

'Enough!' the woman said, withdrawing her fingers. 'Excellent. Let her rest.' But the nipple rings were not removed. She was laid on her back. Her feet were fastened, wide apart, to the bottom corners of the bed. Her arms were fastened to the top corners. Her sex lips were spread carefully back and a moistened finger circled round the nubbin until she groaned. While the fingertips held her flesh hood back, a small plug was pushed into her bottom. Madam made her squeeze upon it while she watched the nubbin throb. Finally, the prickly woollen blanket was drawn up over her, between her thighs, across her belly and over her very swollen nipples. It tickled against her with every small move she made.

About two hours later, Nina returned and sat her up to feed her. Her legs were not untied. When she had finished, her hands were refastened and the blanket was removed. A gag was applied between her lips. Nina knelt on the bed and licked her very slowly between the legs, licking her creases, her open sex lips and her nubbin until she whimpered into the gag. Nina then waited a few minutes, stroking Anya's belly very lightly, then reaching beneath to touch the plug, pressing until a contraction was forced, then beginning again the slow wet licking as Anya bit into the gag and her nubbin palpitated. Nina continued this treatment until Anya's underarms, breasts and belly were drenched in sweat, after which she removed the gag and kissed her with lips now smelling very strongly of Anya's sex.

'Welcome to the inn,' she said, drawing the blanket over Anya's burning body. 'But now you really must try to rest – tonight you are on duty.'

[11]

Entertaining the Guests

It was after dark when Anya was woken by Nina the maid and untied. The girl dabbed oil on Anya's nipples and worked them until the rings slipped free. The skin began to burn as the feeling seeped back in. Then the plug was removed, though with difficulty, since Anya tightened each time Nina pulled. Finally, Nina helped her from the bed.

She was led naked down some winding rickety steps, across a corridor filled with shelves of bottles and stone flagons, then down again into a large low room. She could hear the voices even from the stairs, and then she felt the wall of steam. The room was full of nude women bathing in wooden barrels of several sizes. The larger barrels had been sawn in two. Some women sat upon low wooden benches, brushing their hair. Others, on the far side, were putting on very long leather boots which reached to the tops of their thighs. The floor around the barrels was awash with sudsy water as servant girls ran back and forth with pans of water from the fires. Anya was hauled into a tub with two other women.

'I'm Oona,' said the girl next to her. She had chestnut hair which fell straight down and was cut in a fringe across her forehead. Her wide, deep brown smiling eyes looked up at Anya.

Anya nodded and smiled back. 'I'm Anya.'

Oona's manner seemed very familiar. 'I haven't seen you before,' she said, picking up a cloth and turning Anya round to wash her shoulders.

'No, I . . . I only arrived today – I think,' Anya replied uncertainly.

Oona laughed. 'You don't seem sure. I've worked here

165

six months. Faran's been here over a year.' The girl opposite Anya nodded with pride.

'A year . . ?' Anya's hopes were sinking fast. 'But have you not tried to get away?'

The two women looked horrified. 'Shh!' said Oona. She waited until the servant had passed, then whispered: 'Anyone who tries that is severely punished. Besides, it is not so bad here . . .'

Faran cut in: 'Better here than sold to a cruel master.' Oona agreed. Anya's foreboding only deepened now, as she recalled Madam's threat that she was only being kept until a buyer came forward.

The women helped Anya from the tub and began to dry her. 'What is this bruise?' asked Oona. Then she looked at Anya and her eyes widened. 'Are you the one washed up at the ferry?' Anya nodded, though she didn't know anything about a ferry. 'But that was yesterday,' said Oona, and Anya realised she must have been asleep all the previous afternoon and night, before Madam had woken her. Then she asked about Sarol-harn. The women confirmed that she had been sold.

'What happened?' Oona asked her. 'How did you fall into the river?'

As Anya began to explain, the women gathered round. She decided there was nothing to lose by telling them most of what had befallen her since her capture by the Duke. Everyone seemed very interested.

'Why did you want to cross the river once you had escaped?' Oona asked as the tale drew to a close. Anya had not mentioned the Prince.

'My friend was heading home, for Surdia. I was going with her.' This didn't seem to occasion much surprise, so Anya asked: 'Is it far?'

'It is over the mountains; only one day's journey to the border. There are many caravans for Surdia passing through here. One of them took your friend.'

'It did?' Anya was excited now, but everyone was distracted by the noise of thumping feet and raucous laughter sounding through the ceiling. It sounded as if very many

166

people were above them. Anya hadn't really noticed the noise until it had suddenly got louder. She looked up. One of the women nodded meaningfully.

'A busy night tonight,' she said.

'But the lady said it would be quiet,' said Anya.

'Quiet! Quiet for Madam perhaps – not quiet for you, my darling.' The woman advanced, moaning very loudly and began pawing Anya's breasts and belly in a very suggestive way as Anya tried to back away in horror. Everyone began to laugh. Oona put her arm round Anya, but Anya was very anxious as she was led into an adjoining cooler room where the drying was completed.

Her underarms and the creases of her thighs were perfumed with essence of sandalwood. Her hair was wrapped around and fastened up with a comb. Then she was fitted with her boots. All the women wore these boots, long boots, nothing else but boots, of various colours. Oona's boots were of black polished leather. Anya's were of a soft golden brown skin, snugly fitting. Oona laced them to the very tops of Anya's thighs. 'Press your thighs together,' she said, standing Anya before a mirror. Anya's flesh lips projected down below the top of the leather, which nearly reached up to her short red curls. 'Now stand with legs apart.' Oona gently stretched and teased the flesh lips further down. 'Madam says the masters like to see a girl this way,' she explained, 'with her purse projecting. Always stand with legs apart. Spread them if you sit upon a stool. But always keep your flesh lips pressed together, unless a master opens them. And you must not refuse a master, no matter what he asks . . .'

'But usually, they don't ask!' Faran chipped in.

Oona continued in a very serious voice: 'No. And if they smack you, never complain. Usually they do that only later on, when they take you upstairs. And always refer to them as "Master" or "Sir", however lowly they may seem. Madam gets very upset if we do not show respect.'

Oona was interrupted by a clap of hands. 'Come on girls, it's time,' the servant shouted. He wore an apron and carried a jug of wine. Though all the others hurried, Anya's feet felt as if they had turned to lead. Her throat felt tight and dry; her hands were shaking as she climbed the stairs. It was very difficult to walk at all with the boots laced up so closely; she could scarcely bend her knees. The heels of the boots were raised; they tilted her body forward and made it difficult to stand. Her buttocks felt tight. She felt ungainly; whenever she took a step, her breasts and buttocks shook and the laces brushed against her flesh lips. She was last along the corridor and through the door into the bar. 'Come along. You'll be late.' The servant slapped her on the bottom. She broke into a run and almost tripped as her heel caught in a gap between the floorboards.

And now she felt very conspicuous indeed amid all the noise and laughter. The room was full to bursting point with men banging pots upon the table, singing, and throwing their arms about the women, while servants carrying trays with overflowing jugs of beer and wine incised tortuous interlacing paths through the boiling throng. Caged chickens and pigeons hung from hooks in the ceiling; scuffles in the cages sent feathers through the air; tethered to a table leg was a goat; the floor was strewn with baskets and pack sacks. Huddled round the tiny tables were the card players – some appearing wealthy, in furs and richly coloured cloaks, others looking like shabby peasants. Most of the men in finery seemed to have women with their arms round their necks, sometimes two or three. In the corner, on a platform, was a fiddler and a boy with a pipe and tabor. It was impossible to hear the music for the shouting.

As Anya looked around, she saw the woman with scarlet hair, and she began to shake, for the woman was glowering at her. But what was Anya supposed to do? Nobody seemed to be taking any notice of her. There was nowhere she could sit; she was too afraid to approach anyone; nobody seemed to want her or even to realise she was there until a servant suddenly collided with her and scolded her when the goat kicked out at him. She knew she was about to start crying. She was floating in a hostile sea where everyone except her knew what they were about. They seemed to love it here, but she would suffocate if she had to stay another minute. She rubbed her eyes; her vision began to swim. She turned for the door but a tall man blocked her way and pointed across the room. Madam was now leaning on her stick in front of a man in a black sable coat who was sitting alone at a table. The man was looking at Anya. He had the calm assuredness of a man of substance, a nobleman perhaps.

Madam beckoned her over. Anya felt a different kind of fear now, a curious pleasure of disquiet induced by the coolness of the man's gaze.

Now Anya stood before him, and she was shaking. She was so aware of her body, and of the way she was being presented. And he seemed young, younger than her. That made it worse. His hair was blond; he had a powerful chin; his head was held up high. He was admiring her body frankly. His fingers, thick with jewelled rings, drummed upon the table as Madam spoke.

'Stand up straight now for the gentleman. Present yourself correctly.' Madam edged Anya's legs apart. 'Her name is . . .' When the woman hesitated – for she did not even know the name – Anya whispered it, just loudly enough so he could hear. The man turned his head to the side. He was interested in her, Anya knew, but there was something about him that frightened her, a cool detachedness, almost an arrogance. 'Anya . . .' Madam repeated, though the man appeared to pay her no attention. 'Now isn't she a beauty, sir?' When he didn't answer, she elaborated, palpating each part as she did so. 'Just look at these breasts . . . the thickness of the nipples. Wouldn't these be nice to suck?' Anya was trying to read his thoughts in his expression, but she couldn't. But she knew he felt desire for her. 'And these freckles . . .' Madam turned Anya round and showed him her shoulders. 'Did you ever see such freckles?'

Now he spoke for the first time. The voice sounded cool and distant: 'I don't like freckles.' Madam's lip curled almost imperceptibly as she turned Anya round again. 'And Madam, she is bruised . . .'

'But here – see. This belly. Look at the colour of her flesh.' His gaze moved down. 'Look . . .' The woman pulled at

Anya's flesh leaves, turning them to each side. 'I'll wager sir has never seen one quite this colour. And you know what they say about the colour of a woman's flesh?'

'No – what do they say, Madam?' he asked perfunctorily. Anya was feeling more and more ashamed of her body as the intimacy of this dialogue deepened.

'Why, blackness there is a sign of waywardness – fleshliness. The blacker a woman's flesh, the more she . . . You know. And you'll not find another girl in here with lips so black as this one. And not only her lips . . .' Anya's shame was now compounded as she was turned round again and made to spread and bend. 'That's why she is kept in reserve only for our most favoured guests – like the Prince.'

Anya's heart stopped. Lie or no, her heart was stopped completely, and she heard that phrase echo through her mind a hundred times before she dared to breathe again. The man's hand came to rest upon her buttocks. Her heart stopped once again. The thumb stroked inquisitorially into the crease. She shivered. The thumb was quickly taken away.

'The Prince!' the man shouted, causing a temporary hush all round him, followed by mutters of consternation. 'You would have us believe the Prince of Lidir would grace this bawdy hovel?'

'Indeed, good sir – like your venerable self. Why, only a fortnight ago – not that – ten days, his party were here, and spent the night. They made the last crossings on the ferry.' There were murmurs of agreement from around the room. Anya could not believe her ears – her Prince, here. Why hadn't the other women told her? Why hadn't she asked?

'And the Prince chose this one?' the man asked, guardedly now. 'Have her stand up.' Anya turned to face him. He looked at her intently. 'Is it true, girl? Have you lain with the Prince?' Her heart was beating wildly. She could not get her breath. She did not know what to say. She looked at Madam, who glared at her, then at the man. What was the point of lying?

'Yes,' she said. The woman sighed. But the man was unconvinced.

'Then describe him. What is he like – the Prince?'

Anya closed her eyes before she answered: 'He is handsome. He is kind. His eyes are deepest green. He is beautiful . . . He loves me, and I love him too.' Her upper lip was trembling; the teardrop rolled down to kiss it. She opened her eyes. Though she hadn't really described the Prince at all, the man's expression told that he believed her. Madam was speechless.

'Then perhaps we had better see what he finds in you to love,' said the man. His eyes narrowed. 'Kneel down before your master!' He opened his thighs. Anya was very afraid. She found it very difficult to kneel in her long leather boots. She was shaking as her cheek brushed against his inner thigh, depositing there a teardrop. His hand rubbed her face, then against her ear; it felt cool against the warmth of her trembling. She could see the smooth bulge between his legs. Now the hand rubbed her neck. She closed her eyes. 'Unbutton me,' he whispered. Her fingers were shaking as she reached to touch. The buttons were tight with the pressure from beneath; she could feel his heat. Before the last button opened, the cockstem burst free. She closed her eyes again, but she could smell his maleness very strongly. One hand enclosed her head, encircling her behind her ear; the other pressed the cockstem down into her mouth. 'Keep your lips closed about it,' he said. 'Did your Prince have a fleshcock quite so thick as this?' The cock pushed deeper, sliding over her tongue, pushing to the back of her throat. 'Take it to the balls,' he said, holding her head tightly, forcing it back, pinching her nostrils until she gasped for breath, then pushing ever deeper, not desisting until her lower lip had touched the bag, and the ballocks lay on her chin. Only when Anya had complied quite fully with his instruction did her master wrench her lips away and rest his throbbing cockstem up against her freckled cheek.

'I'll take her, Madam.' He threw a small but bulging purse. Madam caught it with one hand.

'A wise choice, sir. You will not be disappointed.' Then she inspected the contents of the bag. 'Why, sir is generous, most generous . . .'

'That is for the two.'

'What?'

He pointed to a girl astride the knee of an old man sitting two tables away. He was wearing a rich gold cloak; he looked like a merchant. The girl was Oona and she was kissing the man as his hands roved between her open thighs.

'But unfortunately sir, she is taken, as you see.'

'She is taken by me. Arrange it.' The blond man placed a small heap of coins upon the table.

'Of course,' Madam said, bowing and picking up the pile in one deft move. She moved away, collected another girl who was chatting at the bar and took her over to the merchant. The exchange was completed without incident and the woman returned with Oona and introduced her to the man in the sable coat.

Oona stood beside his chair, smiling at him, posing provocatively with one leg straight but the other angled, her knee bent casually, her thighs open. His arm went round her waist. She ran her fingers through his hair. Anya couldn't understand how Oona could be so relaxed, so free with her body, with someone she had only just met. Anya was forced to do these things, but Oona did them willingly. Even now, her eyes were closed, and her lips were parted as his hand moved down her belly to tickle her chestnut bush – as that older man had surely been doing but a few moments ago.

The blond man suddenly seemed to remember Anya, still kneeling on the floor. 'Have her stand up, Madam, and let us check her credentials further. Turn round, my dear.' Anya did so, yet she was even more afraid now that she could not see him. 'I am waiting,' came the voice. But she didn't know what he wanted next. 'Come on . . .' Then she remembered to part her legs; she was trembling as she· placed them very wide. She closed her eyes. When he touched her, tracing those cold fingers round the narrow exposed bands of thigh between the tops of her boots and her bottom, she could feel the shivers cascading down her buttocks. She was breathing very quickly now; she could sense the weight of all the eyes upon her, but especially his eyes, his piercing blue eyes looking at the cleavage of her buttocks as his fingers touched the ticklish skin at the tops of her inner thighs. And she could feel her flesh lips slowly engorging, as if Brekt's thong still nipped around them. That was what the fear, the cool proximity of that tickling, was doing to her body. It made her flesh excited to have his fingertips so near.

'Open your cheeks,' he whispered, and when Anya tensed, 'Do not refuse me, or your punishment will be worse.' Now she was terrified; her mind was racing. What had Oona said about it? Did he mean the strap? Her hands were shaking uncontrollably as her fingers spread her buttocks. 'Delicious . . .' he murmured. She was afraid to draw breath as she arched her belly down, parting the cheeks wide, holding them open. He would see her swollen sex lips between her open thighs. He would see the swirling rim of blackened lewdness, so tight now with anticipation.

'Ooh!' She could not prevent the gasp, though the fingertip stroke was light. Again it came. 'Ah . . . Please. Oh!' She bent her knees and arched her belly more tightly down; the fingertip had stroked the bottom entrance once again, more firmly. Then it pressed. It frightened her, that pressing. It flicked, and pressed again, quite hard. 'Please . . . No,' she begged very softly. *Not here*, she wanted to say – she did not want this intimacy performed in public view. She could feel the hushed silence all around. 'Please?' she whispered.

'She is tight, Madam, very tight.' His voice was loud, and coldly disapproving.

'But she is new, sir. New girls are not always familiar with . . . accustomed to such directness. We could arrange some training – before sir graces us with his next visit – to make the access freer . . .?'

'Madam – I have paid my money. The access must be freed off by tonight.' Anya began to shudder. She was very scared by the tenor of this conversation, and by the harshness of the man. It reminded her of a degradation that had been forced upon her in the castle dungeons. 'Bring oil, Madam.' And that confirmed the worst. 'Girl – bend across my knee,' he said, removing the rings from his left hand.

As her master worked two fingers into the groove, back

and forth across the puckered mouth, dripping oil upon it as he did so, that tight rim did indeed become freer. It brought her shame to have it done so publicly, with her knees splayed outwards and her legs so wide. But as the rubbing progressed, as her flesh adjusted to the rhythm, it also brought a kind of pleasure – albeit an illicit pleasure, a pleasure that she did not want and against which she was defenceless – but a pleasure nevertheless. At the instant the fingers slipped within, and Anya's flesh closed tight about them, the peculiar feeling came, as if a warm weight was pressed against her belly from inside. Her master worked the fingers in and out until they slipped quite freely, then took them out and wiped them with a cloth.

'There, Madam,' he admonished the woman. 'Is it not a pity I am obliged to do your preparations for you?'

'Thank you, sir. It will not happen next time.'

'I am very glad to hear it. And I hope not to find her remiss in any other department, though I fear that even in this quarter . . .' and he stroked a thumb upwards in the crease, 'we may not be out of the woods yet. For that was but a preliminary venture.' He therefore made Anya kneel again between his thighs while he demonstrated. His cockstem throbbed erect in front of her. He took the finger and thumb of Anya's right hand and made her grip them tightly around the two fingers he had pushed into her. When he slipped his fingers out, her finger and thumb formed a small ring which he held up by her wrist. 'There. That is where we are,' he said.

Anya was very frightened by the look in his eyes, the delight he clearly took in what he was doing to her. None of the other girls was being treated in this way. Now he took her left hand, forcing her this time to make the ring around the plum of his rigid stem. Her fingertip could barely make the closure to the thumb. Then he held the two finger rings up side by side, fastening her wrists together with his hand. 'And this, my dear,' he pointed to the left one, 'is where we are going – before tonight is through.' Anya shrank away to see it made so cruelly clear.

Her master saw the fear in her eyes; he saw the trembling

breasts and belly. He therefore pressed her freckled cheek once more against his thigh. He pulled the comb out from her hair and let the deep red curls cascade across her shoulders to those lusciously swollen black-tipped breasts and he stared into her olive eyes, glazed over now with tears. He spoke tenderly, for the first time, and perhaps for the last – he had not yet decided. 'You will do it, for me. I know . . .' he sighed. And as a single teardrop escaped to trickle down her cheek, he caught it on his fingertip, put it to his lips and tasted, then smoothed his palm across the cheek and down the soft warm neck. He gently rubbed his thumb against the lips until they opened, then pushed the cockstem in. And that feeling was delicious – it was worth a hundred purses of gold – those soft submissive lips, that moist tongue sucking, licking round the cockhead so exquisitely, and now each warm and weighted breast gathered in his hands, each nipple tip swelling hard against his squeezing fingers. And when he felt his pleasure swell almost to bursting, he very carefully lifted his boot, pressed the sole against her belly and pushed that temptress to the floor.

While the sweet girl sobbed beneath the defilement of that ill-use, he turned to the more voluptuous and freer delights of Oona, kissing her proffered belly, sucking her teats and finally kissing her lips. Her tongue pushed wetly, deep inside his mouth. Her thighs opened wider while she took his hand – he did not have to ask – and worked it ever deeper into the split of her aromatic rich brown bush, into the burning wetness of her randy little fleshpot. Then she took her wet and smeared it over his cheek, then formed her fingers into a tight wet milking glove about his cockstem, sliding, squeezing tight, and closed her thumbpad over the tip.

'Not yet, good sir,' she whispered, 'for the night is very young.'

When he could gather his wits, the man called Madam over: 'You have a suitable room?'

'Of course. At once. But we have some entertainment laid on upstairs, if you'd care to sample that before you

175

retire? It is extra – but well worth it, I assure you . . .'

They followed Madam, who made very slow progress up two flights of stairs. The man had his arm about Oona's waist, but he treated Anya very roughly, pushing her, then shouting at her when she tripped. It upset her that he abused her in this way, for no reason. She had tried to please him. She still found it very difficult to walk, let alone climb the stairs, in these high-heeled boots. Oona seemed to find it very easy; she seemed very confident, and very familiar with the man. Anya knew that was why he preferred Oona; he liked her for her forwardness, the way she kept touching him so openly. Anya could never do that with a stranger.

The room that Madam led them into was large and very warm, but very quiet, considering how many people were in there. It was a very strange place, almost like an assembly room – like the Council Chamber in the castle, but smaller and more square. The benches were arranged in tiers, and the ceiling was domed and painted white. From the middle hung a giant crystal ornament made from hundreds of dangling pieces of shaped glass. Dozens of candles burned inside it and there were candles high up, all round the room. The air was filled with the sweet scent of beeswax. A bright light showered down upon the lowest point, a deep red velvet covered bed in the centre of the room. On the bed were two nude women. One of them was Nina, the maid. The other one was singularly beautiful – slim and perfectly proportioned, with pale skin but an unusually thick mat of wavy golden hair. Though she was a woman, her figure was almost childlike. When she opened her thighs, an excited murmur travelled round the room, for her sex was totally naked. Anya looked round to see all the faces fixed upon the bed, waiting for something to happen.

Madam, however, was speaking in a hushed voice to Anya's master. He too was looking at the girl, but nodding as Madam looked at Anya. Madam then took Anya by the arm.

'You've got a ringside seat, my dear, with me,' she said ominously, beckoning to a male servant, who then helped Madam down the steps. The blond man took Oona down on the other side. Anya could not understand why she was being taken away from him. In a way, she felt relieved, but she also felt apprehensive. When they reached the lowest tier above the bed, her unease turned to dread. In front of the bench was a rail, a short length of thick wooden rail on two posts about three feet apart. She knew exactly what this rail was for: it raised many memories of punishment and degradation in the castle dungeons. As she glanced around the room, she saw several other devices of this kind. One of them was occupied: a girl had been made to sit astride it and a man was playing with her. Another girl simply lay bottom up across her master's knee, although most of the girls had been allowed to sit and watch the entertainment.

While an extra cushion was brought, that Madam might sit upon the bench behind Anya, the servant pushed Anya's belly against the bar and fastened her ankles to the uprights. Her wrists were tied behind her back. Madam then hooked her stick over the bar beside Anya. Anya found herself looking frequently at this stick, which had an upcurving handle fashioned from smoothly polished bone, until her gaze was taken by something apparently being passed around the room. It seemed to be a cloth. Its presence appeared to occasion great excitement; as each man received it, he would open it out and inhale deeply, or press it to his lips and close his eyes. Anya assumed it must be perfumed with a balm.

Directly opposite Anya was her master, with Oona on his knee. When he saw that Anya was looking, he immediately turned to kiss Oona and to squeeze her breasts gently. Anya looked away, into the well, and now she could do nothing but watch; her gaze was imprisoned by that unfolding scene.

The young girl lay on her back, her arms outstretched, palms uppermost in a gesture of submission; her legs were open and her naked sex was being stroked. Nina knelt above her, facing her feet. She began to use her tongue – the same tongue that had tortured Anya so deliciously – to stroke downwards, over the bare skin, from the belly which arched to meet it, down into the creases, then over the smoothness around the bright pink sex lips and, as the legs were lifted, round to stroke the bottom. The young girl's hips began to quake as Nina bent her legs very tightly while the tongue was pushed inside.

At that moment, Anya shuddered as a fingertip touched her bottom and very slowly wormed between the cheeks to stroke smoothly up and down the groove.

On the bed, beside Nina, a servant placed a tray bearing a jug and a short tapering candle. Anya felt her belly sinking as the jug was lifted, the bare pink sex was opened and Nina used the fingers of one hand to hold the walls apart. The girl whispered, 'No . . . Ah . . . No,' and a hush fell on the room. The girl's breathing came rapidly as Nina ignored her tender protests and the contents of the jug were poured within in a slow and heavy golden stream. The liquid looked like honey. As her fleshpot filled, the stream trailed round her sex lips and her nubbin and the girl began to moan. Anya began to shake. The stick was lifted from beside her, the stick with the smooth bone handle. Now a hand at Anya's back was pushing her gently forwards to make her bend across the bar, and she was frightened, yet excited. She heard Madam's voice, but faintly, in the distance, over the buzzing in her ears.

'Go on, my dear,' it said, 'you will have to learn these things sooner or later, and it is better sooner . . .' The fingers took her sex lips and drew them down. Below Anya, the girl's sex lips were now being sealed about her overflowing honeypot. Nina carefully licked around it, leaving the skin smooth and wet and clean. She picked up the candle from the tray. As she coated it with honey, twirling it, allowing the excess to stream into the jug, then licking her fingers, Anya felt her bottom mouth being oiled. That feeling, Madam's confident liquid fingers rubbing gently, almost made her want to move her bottom mouth against them. Then on the bed, Nina lifted the candle and held it over the upended small pink mouth below the bare, pink sealed-together sex lips, and Anya felt it – firm and smooth and cool – the bulbous upturned tip of bone being fitted to her bottom. Madam carefully searched and Anya momentarily closed her eyes. Madam gently twisted it until she found the precise angle.

'Lift my darling . . . Push. Ah there . . .' Anya gasped

with the strangeness of this pleasure as the thick cool bone plum slipped in and lodged within her bottom, distending the small mouth wide. 'There . . .' Then she felt Madam's other hand touching her in the delicious way her master had not, sleeving back her hood and holding it so her nubbin softly pulsed. And that feeling – the tight pulse of her nubbin and the pressure of distension of the horn pushed in her bottom, keeping her open – it pleasured her very deeply. Anya was held in this state of pleasured provocation while she watched what happened on the bed, watched the young girl's breathing come faster and deeper, then fragment into soft mewling sounds and subdued whimpers while the candle slowly turned as it slipped smoothly down into her bottom, causing her tight sealed sex to overflow honey in a golden stream across her nubbin, which Nina gently sucked upon and licked. And though Anya heard more sounds of pleasure and of protest, her eyes shut tight then as the horn slipped deeper, opening her bottom ever wider until the stem of the stick was pressed into the bridge of flesh between her fleshpot and her bottom. As her legs went rigid, Madam slowly slid the flesh hood up and down across her throbbing nubbin, saying: 'There my sweet, your master will be so very pleased with you tonight.'

Anya's flesh tightened hard around the horn as Madam carefully withdrew it. She bade Anya stand up and had her feet unfastened, but left her hands tied. 'We must take you upstairs now,' the woman said. Anya looked across and saw that Oona and the blond man were gone. She hadn't seen them leave.

Anya was led out and once more up some stairs, much narrower ones this time. Each time anyone passed, they would openly touch her. On one occasion, she was pinned to the wall while two men fondled her breasts and between her thighs. Madam let them do it. With her hands tied, Anya could not protect herself. She was already close to tears by the time they reached the bedroom door.

Madam knocked. There was a murmur, then a delay before the master answered. He was stripped to the waist; his chest was covered in thick blond curls. Even with his boots off, Anya only came up to his shoulders. Madam smiled and patted Anya on the bottom as she led her in:

'I think you will find her very much improved, sir.'

'Well, let us see,' he answered, rubbing his fingers, which looked oily. He turned Anya to face the wall and spread her. He stood so closely that, with her hands secured behind her, her fingertips touched the tight bulge of his crotch. 'Hmm.' She was very frightened by the thought of what he meant to do. Now her belly was pressed to the wall. A finger was wormed inside her, then withdrawn. 'Hmm. We shall see.' Finally he turned her round again to face him.

'Madam,' he said. 'One other thing – the furnishings here are incomplete . . .'

'Sir?' Madam stared round the room. So did Anya, at the large square bed with waist-high posts, the small table by the window in the corner, the cupboards and the fireplace with the chair and footstool close by, and beneath her feet, the warm thick rug. Both women wondered what it could be. Anya looked round again, then suddenly realised that Oona was face down on the bed.

The man stretched out his hand and waved it round the room. 'There is no smacking stool.'

'Oh sir, I beg your pardon. I'm sure I don't know how that could have happened. I'll have one sent up, right away.' And with that the woman departed.

Although the room was warm from the fire, the door closed with a very hollow sound, and Anya suddenly felt cold. What was a smacking stool? She could feel the churning in her belly, for she thought she could well imagine.

Now that Madam was gone, her master seemed to treat Anya even more roughly. He dragged her to the bed, lifted her bodily and lowered her so her arms slipped over the bottom corner post and she was kneeling with her back against the bedpost. Oona lay face down with her legs spread to the sides and her knees crooked to the point where her belly was slightly lifted. The man took a draught from a cup of wine and knelt on the bed beside her. In one hand he held a bottle of oil; he began applying it between Oona's legs, at the back and at the front. At intervals, Oona's hands

180

and feet would move involuntarily and she would murmur. The fingers entered her body; her toes began to curl; three fingers pushed in at the front, and then slipped up the back. He worked them until they slipped very freely through the rubbery rim, then the hand reached across to Anya. He stared at her, and waited. Anya felt her face and neck begin to colour as she slowly spread her knees apart. The oily fingertips massaged her sex lips and stroked and nipped her nubbin, then returned to penetrate Oona. The three fingers were replaced by four. 'See how freely Oona takes them,' he said. Anya swallowed. Her bottom tightened harder than before.

The man now got up from the bed and took a second draught of wine.

He pointed to the small table by the window, which stood narrowly ajar. With her hands tied, Anya couldn't move unaided. He lifted her off the bedpost and deposited her on the floor, beside the table. Even from a kneeling position she could see there was something on the table. When she looked at him imploringly, he nodded. 'For you,' he said. 'Fresh ones, thick ones. Beeswax. On the table, please.' She was shaking as she did it. 'Kneel.' She closed her eyes; she did not want to look at them; he made her. There were several candles, in a range of shapes and sizes. He picked up each one in turn and ran his fingers over it until Anya could smell the beeswax very strongly. He selected a thick one. He unfastened Anya's hands and made her use her finger and thumb to measure the candle's girth, as she had been forced to do with his cock; she was able to make the closure. 'You see, my dear – we progress by stages.'

And the degradation was performed there and then with Anya kneeling, head down, legs apart and with her hands behind her neck while the smooth and now oiled beeswax slipped coolly up inside her bottom to leave two inches of projecting stub.

'Now squeeze,' he said. Two fingers slipped beneath to nip her flesh lips round her nubbin as he worked the candle in and out.

Next, he made her stand up on the table with her legs

181

spread wide apart while he played with her. 'Keep it in. Do not let it slip,' he warned as he squeezed her sex lips and her nubbin. But with the candle being oiled, and with all the stimulation, Anya found it very hard to retain. She tried to will her bottom mouth to close about it lightly, yet she needed so desperately to close her thighs and squeeze.

Suddenly, her master was distracted by noises from outside. He opened the window wider to afford a clearer view as three closed wagons rumbled into the yard directly below them and came to a halt. But her master seemed to be looking beyond the wagons. Anya heard the sounds, then gasped at what she saw – a woman's naked body, illuminated by the light of hand-held torches, was spreadeagled in the doorway of the stables while a servant smacked her thighs and bottom with a leather belt. Anya shivered; her master's hand came to rest at the back of her thigh, just at the top of her boot, then stretched upwards, to lie against each cheek of her bottom in turn, and then to touch the candle stub very lightly, to give it a gentle turn – 'Push your bottom out,' he said – to pull it lightly and to tap it, tapping pleasure up inside her in time with the smacking in the yard. And Anya found that touching – the pleasure while she looked upon that punishment – made her feel very lewd. And it made her afraid, for it reminded her so vividly of Brekt.

Anya looked down at the man beside her, the man whose hand was touching her, the man whose face was unmoving as his eyes remained fixed upon that sight below them. What would he do with her? How would he abuse her?

A knock came at the door. 'Kneel down,' he said. 'No, not that way – face the side.' The shivers came again, up Anya's legs and across her belly: she would be clearly visible now to anyone at the door. 'Now hold your breasts in your hands. Squeeze your fingers round your nipples. Nip them. Make them hard.' Then he stood aside, a little behind Anya. 'Come in!' he shouted.

The young servant entered, looking straight at her. He would see the candle. Her cheeks were crimson with her shame, yet she did not move her fingers from her nipples.

The servant carried a stool, a very tall stool; the seat was small and shaped. Anya could not see it properly. 'Put it by the fire,' said her master. The servant almost tripped, in his nervousness and haste. Anya's master smiled. 'Come here,' he said. 'You are interested in this wench?'

'I . . . I . . . Sir?' the servant stammered.

'You find this interesting?' Her master slowly lifted first one, then the other of Anya's legs, gradually unlacing the boot, easing it off and dropping it to the floor, then carefully bending the knee tight again before replacing it on the table. Then he placed one hand on Anya's back while he took hold of the candle and tried to move it in and out. It would not move. Anya was very tight indeed and very much afraid. 'Open your eyes, girl!' Her master persisted with the candle while he addressed the servant: 'She is being trained, you see – to take a cock by midnight.' The servant looked abashed. Anya wanted to die. 'Do you think it feasible?' her master said, pushing harder. 'Or might it take till dawn?' The servant did not speak. His face turned redder than a beetroot. 'Well, my lad, it seems your presence only makes it tighter. You may leave us.' Anya closed her eyes.

With the servant gone, Anya was stood once more upon the table. She was turned. Her bottom was stroked; the candle was pulled; it slid very slowly out. He made her face him. She looked with apprehension at the stool by the fire. Noticing this, he smiled; the backs of his fingers stroked her belly.

Suddenly she was swept up and carried, with his arm beneath her bottom and her arm around his neck, over to the fireplace and she clung to him, pressing her bare breasts to his chest, for she was so frightened of that strange device, and she was frightened of his eyes.

'Do not be afraid,' he said. She saw now that the stool had a narrow seat, shaped into a kind of half cup, like a small saddle, tapering at one end. 'You know what this is for?' he asked, resting his fingertips there. She looked at it, then looked to the bed, where Oona was sitting up and watching.

'It is . . .' she faltered. Her chest felt so very tight. 'It is . . . to punish me,' she whispered. And saying that forced a soft shudder in her bosom. Her master touched that bosom very gently, touching the nipples as they firmed.

'Yes, my darling. And what part of you will fit into this cup?' As he stroked it, Anya saw that it was entirely covered in a dense, very short-piled tightly stretched skin.

'My . . . my bottom.'

He laughed, raised her chin and kissed her on the lips. 'Perhaps, my dear, if that should please me. But this cup is specially shaped for this . . .' She turned her head away in shame as he opened her thighs and closed his palm about her sex. 'No, look,' he said, turning her head that she might see within the cup a central moulded ridge. Then he opened out her flesh lips. 'See – this cup will kiss your openness. The fur will tickle you while you are punished.' She shivered. He took her finger. She did not want to touch it but he drew her fingertip along that soft skin ridge until at the end towards the rim it felt a tiny round projecting bump. She knew what that bump was for; again it made her shiver. And as her fingertip was made to stroke that soft-piled bump, his fingertip drew soft circles round her nubbin. Then he spread her legs and feigned that he would lift her astride the seat and Anya struggled like a kitten being lowered into water. Her master laughed and did not force her yet, but pulled her to his breast. He could feel her terrified heartbeat bursting through.

He lifted her and kissed that heartbeat, kissed those bulging breasts and those delicious thick brown nipples. 'Mounting this body upon the stool will be so sweet,' he murmured, and Anya felt she could not breathe at all. 'I will smack every delicious part of you: these breasts . . .' – Anya felt her nipples tighten once again – 'This belly, this hot wet place between your legs, and this tight-arsed little bottom.' His hand enclosed her sex and squeezed it very hard while his middle finger probed beneath to push into her bottom. Then he took her back and deposited her once again on the table.

'And now, an exercise in the pleasure of control,' he said, lifting a tapered candle this time and oiling it very slowly.

'Turn round, my darling.' Again, Anya felt the sinking weight deep in her belly as the coolness of the candle was slipped into her bottom. But she found this tapered candle even more difficult to hold. When he turned her to face him, her thighs were shaking. 'Remember – keep it in. But keep these legs very wide apart.' The fingertips brushed against the bare flesh of her inner thigh and her master gently kissed her quaking belly. Her thighs were wide, her sex was wet, and her belly gently quaked.

He took those wet dark lips that dangled so provocatively between her legs, closed a finger and a thumb about them and slid them very slowly up and down, very gently working her until he felt the small nub between them harden. 'Keep it in,' he repeated, edging her legs further apart, but not releasing the gently squeezed knot – enjoying the touch, the way it swelled, the way her legs shook with the pleasure – just rubbing the slippery lips about it very softly until she moaned that soft sweet moan of impending female joy, whereupon he let go of it and made the girl kneel up once more, facing him, while he removed his belt and breeches, allowing his tortured cock to spring out, thick and strong.

And now, as always, he took the belt and slowly wrapped it around his hand, watching the girl's expression as he did so – the delicious edge of sensual fear – and the heavy, perfect freckled breasts gently beginning to tremble.

He loved to smack large-breasted girls. And he had to touch those breasts that he would punish, had to feel their weighted, frightened softness gathered in his palms. He lifted each one, then dropped it, let it bounce, then softly pinched beneath the nipple. He did this three times to each breast, then smacked the nipple lightly with the belt. He found her gasp delightful. He smacked the flesh around the nipples; he lifted the tips and smacked the undersides. But he preferred to smack them while they dangled. He made the girl lean forwards. The more he smacked, the more those sweet breasts shook, the more he became excited, until he was forced to desist, for now his cockstem hurt.

But at least he had rendered those brown-black nipples

large and very hard indeed, and those heavy, rounded titties a deep warm shade of pink. He fell back into the armchair beside the bed – to relax, and to look upon that perfect body: the rounded, shaking pushed-out belly, the knees kept wide apart, and between her legs, the soft black swollen pouch protruding so invitingly, and moving so very sensually with her breathing.

'Hold your buttocks open,' he said and watched the straining tension in her belly as her sweet flesh struggled so seductively against her outspread state to keep that tapered candle deep inside. He called to the other girl, Oona. She obediently knelt between his thighs. He did not need to tell her. She was good; she always knew exactly what to do. He wanted the other girl to watch how Oona sucked his cockstem. He spread and pushed; Oona took it very deeply, until her lower lip had touched against his balls. She kept his cockstem wet and slippery; she wet her finger, pushed it beneath and slipped it up his bottom. When finally he could take no more and lay back, pulling Oona's body onto his lap, her legs closed round his cockstem; her sex lips kissed his cockhead as they cuddled, her nipples dangled down to brush against his chest, her tongue pushed deep inside his mouth. Oona was a born seductress. She fed him with her spittle, she wet her fingers between her legs, then wiped that wetness round her nipple and pushed it in his mouth. She tried to mount herself upon him, rocking until his cockhead slipped inside her hot wet pot, but he lifted her off him and deposited her on the floor before the girl.

'Suck her,' he whispered to Oona. 'Suck her till I tell you to stop.' And to the girl he said, 'Keep your cheeks spread wide, my dear, but do not let your candle slip.'

Sitting back, he smiled to see the girl's belly tense before Oona's tongue had even touched her, then shudder as the lips closed round the soft black dangling fruit and the slow sucking began, the sucking which very gradually made the belly curve the other way as the shoulders hunched, the pinkened freckle-dappled bosom shook and the mouth opened so deliciously into a silent moan, which turned into a very clear gasping shudder as Oona's tongue struck home and the belly approached deliverance.

'Wait,' he said, and the young girl groaned as Oona's lips withdrew. 'Now kiss her nipples.' As Oona's tongue reached up to suck, he got up, approached and, spreading his left palm against the young girl's belly, used the middle fingertip to draw the flesh hood back and hold it. Oona sucked, his left palm pressed; as the fingertips of his right hand caressed the tender skin in the wide-spread crease of bottom, the candle slowly slipped, the young girl whimpered, and the candle was delivered onto the table. He stroked the pulsing bottom very gently. He felt the urge of wanting very strongly.

Pushing Oona aside, he knelt between those thighs himself, to press his thumbs beside the moistened sex lips until they gaped, exposing the deep red liquid flesh within and the bright pink pulsing nubbin. Standing up, he pressed his cockhead to that cup and he felt her burning heat. She shuddered and pushed. His cockstem slipped deliciously smoothly in until her softened sex lips spread about the base, lightly sucking, wetting back the skin hairs where his cock merged with his body. He pushed; he felt her wetness kiss his balls; her nubbin touched him; his cockhead touched the entrance to her womb. Her sex contracted round him in a long slow sucking pull; his balls moved with her. His middle finger, reaching round, entered the smooth oiled tube within the crease. When he kissed her, her lips sealed tightly round his tongue; her fleshpot milked him; her bottom drew his finger up inside. She was learning, so it seemed.

Anya wanted desperately to be touched between the legs. She wanted that cock to flood her sex with miltings, while his fingertips milked her nubbin until she came. She sucked his tongue and stroked beneath it with her own; she contracted her fleshpot repeatedly about the plum. Then she felt his palm against her belly. She tensed in readiness for the gentle touch of pleasure. Suddenly the palm pushed, the cockstem withdrew, the finger slipped out of her and the tongue was wrenched away.

She was lifted down. She knew what he would do, but that knowledge did not help her. A gasping breathlessness seized her body as her bare breasts slipped against the curls upon his chest and she was lifted and carried very quickly to the stool. 'No . . .' she murmured, 'No . . .' But this time she did not struggle as her legs were lifted astride, the lips between her thighs were spread, her sex was deposited into the soft skin cup, and the small bump pressed against her swollen burning nubbin. She reached down with her toes but they could not touch the floor. Her body balanced, supported in this small skin cup fitted round her fleshpot and pressed into the bridge of flesh at the joining of her thighs. He placed her hands behind her head; she felt as if she were falling forwards. Between her legs, the pressure spread her, the soft skin pressed against her open flesh lips. Her bottom pushed out, split and bulging above the very narrow saddle. Then he took up the belt and began winding it round his fist. He brushed his fingertips over the soft leather skin where it touched her upper thigh. 'Keep your hands behind your head. Spread your legs out very wide. I will smack until this leather cup is sopping with your wet.'

And as Anya shivered and quaked and whimpered, her master did this to her. Though her thighs and buttocks and breasts burned beneath the quick smacks of the belt, delivered so as to make her breasts and buttocks bounce, it seemed to her that her sex and nubbin and nipples burned with hot desire. Each smack upon her buttocks pressed her open sex lips to the skin and the soft-piled bump pressed gently to her nubbin. Each time, before he smacked her breasts, he would play with them, squeezing the breasts together, touching the nipples gently, then wetting his fingers and wiping the wetness on her to make her nipples slip. He would tell her that her breasts were beautiful. Then he would pin her arms behind her and hold her body almost horizontally, so her breasts dangled freely and bounced against each other while he smacked. While he smacked her breasts, he had Oona lift Anya's thighs and spread her buttocks wide and stroke between the cheeks. When the short smacks were delivered to her nipples, the fingertips

188

were replaced by a tongue licking slowly upwards in the crease.

By this means then – the wet working of the nipples, the bottom licking, the all-pervasive smacking, and on occasion, the arching back of Anya's body, that her master might kiss her upturned soft submissive mouth whilst bestowing gentle squeezes on her sex lips and her nubbin – Anya's flesh was made to seep and the saddle turned very wet. Now that her breasts and buttocks burned bright red, her master decreed that it was time to smack this girl between the legs. She was lifted bodily, turned round in the air and redeposited facing backwards, so now it was her bottom that was split upon the saddle as her legs fell open to the sides. Her mound and sex lips were presented correctly, already slightly gaping, for the smacking, which in due course rendered the gape wider, the sex lips more distended and made that fleshpot weep. With her master behind her, pinning her arms and pulling tightly so her belly formed a perfect arch culminating in an exquisite gap between her thighs wherein the black lips proffered proud, she was smacked on her belly, her inner thighs and then on her sex lips until she felt as if her flesh was dipped in molten fire. Then she was sucked by Oona until she whimpered.

'Enough,' their master cried as Anya's belly began to quiver and her breasts began to shake. 'Hold her open.' He placed his palm against her squirming belly and watched her nubbin pulse. He wanted to smack it too, for its lewdness, but denied himself that pleasure and lifted her from the stool and deposited her face down on the bed. 'Oona, get the oil,' he said, but Oona did not get the chance, for the knocking at the door was very urgent.

[12]

The Merchant's Daughters

'Damn you, woman! Why must you keep interrupting?'

The master, over by the door, sounded very angry. Anya hid her face.

'Anya – Madam has found a merchant,' said Oona. 'He wants to buy you.' Oona seemed very excited, but Anya was almost too afraid to look. When she sat up she could hear background conversation, as if several people were out in the corridor, but the only person she could see was the master, barring the door with his arm, and looking very annoyed indeed.

'But Madam,' he shouted, 'have I paid good gold for treatment such as this? Why cannot you conduct your business in the morning? Why must a man be dragged from his bed in the middle of the night?'

Madam answered in very hushed tones, at which the man protested again, though not so loudly this time.

'. . . And how do I know that?' he demanded. Then he pointed at Anya. 'This one on the bed: how long have I had to spend on her?' Oona edged away from her as Anya hung her head. 'And still she cannot accommodate the most elementary of requirements. How do I know that these two you offer me will be any better?'

Yet despite the feigned uninterest, the man's arm no longer barred the access. Anya feared a bargain was being struck.

Madam was more confident now, and she angled with a silver hook: 'But sir, these girls are very experienced. See – touch them. Turn round, my dears. There . . . They know how to please a man, and how to take their pleasure too . . .'

There were soft sounds from the women, sounds of

consent. Madam whispered, 'There, you see . . .' Anya held her breath and waited. She heard another murmur of pleasure. Suddenly the door was opened fully and two girls were ushered in. She recognised both of them from earlier, at the bathing; one of them was Oona's friend. The master no longer argued. He came over, hauled Anya off the bed and deposited her beyond the door.

'Sir, I wish you luck – and perseverance,' he said. 'And I suggest you count your change with care. Now, no more interruptions if you please, Madam.' With that, the door slammed shut. Anya did not dare look up. All she could see was the hem of a yellow robe.

'Take no mind, sir,' Madam said. 'There's no pleasing some folk. Just look at her – isn't she just lovely?' The woman tapped Anya with her stick, then pulled her shoulders back and lifted her chin. While Madam rearranged her hair, Anya kept glancing up at the merchant, then looking away, for she was afraid to stare at him for too long. He was broad, a middle-aged man dressed in a bright yellow silk robe embroidered with a red dragon. His face seemed kindly. Madam stood back and waited. The man looked at Anya only once, but it was as if that single glance of those dark eyes had absorbed her every feature. He nodded slowly, then began carefully counting out very many gold coins into Madam's hand.

A little behind the merchant stood two young women. They did not belong to the inn. They looked almost Surdic, with even darker hair than the merchant, and eyes of a richer brown. Though their complexion resembled Sarol-harn's, these girls dressed very differently. They wore thick embroidered skirts and short jackets with bright silk shirts beneath. And they wore earrings, very large gold ones. Sarol-harn hadn't worn earrings. Both girls were eyeing Anya with interest, much deeper interest than the merchant seemed to have shown, then whispering to one another, and that worried Anya.

One of them, the taller of the two, lifted Anya to her feet, then turned her round and examined her while the merchant thanked Madam.

'A pleasure to do business, sir, as always,' Madam replied. 'You will stay for refreshments?'

'Thank you, Madam, no. I fear we must press on and try to make the border by noon tomorrow.' Anya's ears pricked up at the mention of the border.

'Always rushing through . . . And your two girls – it must be hard for them, too.' The woman shook her head and smiled at them, but Anya was now very worried by the intimacy of the examination. Both girls kept touching her, commenting on her freckles and the colour of her nipples, then they made her spread her thighs. The merchant took no notice of this as Madam continued with her pleasantries. 'It seems a pity you cannot stay the night at least.'

'Indeed. But time is money, Madam, and these times are troubled.' His chin rocked gravely. 'We must make the crossings while we can.'

Madam nodded sympathetically as she pocketed her gold. 'And you should get a good price for this one in the south.' Now Anya was certain the caravan must be heading for Surdia. 'Where are you bound this time, sir?' Madam asked.

'We hope to reach Karnuk.'

'The walled city itself?'

'If we can get there.' The merchant looked at Anya and pursed his lips. 'Take her down, Malindra,' he said, and turned to go. The taller girl bowed.

'Until next time, sir,' said Madam.

'I trust so, Madam.'

The two girls led Anya down the stairs and out into the stableyard, where three large covered wagons and a cart – the ones Anya had seen from the window – were waiting with drivers at the ready. Behind the last wagon was a string of horses. She was taken to the second wagon. The younger of the two girls then took her by the arm and looked at her again.

'She is not so nice as Ilona,' she said, touching Anya's breasts quite openly as Anya shivered from the cold air on her naked skin.

'Shh, Kirstal – not yet . . .' replied Malindra.

While Anya tried to absorb the significance of these

remarks, she was distracted by the disturbance as four horses thundered down the road ahead of the wagons and clattered into the yard. Anya hid her face, for they were ridden by soldiers – grey guards. She was sure they must be from the castle, but they had come the other way. One of them had a sling around his shoulder. A stable-boy came running out to take their horses, then the ostler joined the group and everyone began talking animatedly. The merchant stopped them at the door to the inn and questioned them. When he came over to the wagon, he looked worried.

'What news, father?' Malindra asked him.

He put an arm around each girl. 'My dears, it does not look good. We may not be quite so welcome as usual in the walled city. We must hurry.'

The wagon door was opened. Inside were rolls of silk and other cloths, and a very large pile of furs, but on the left side, stacked one above the other, were two very small box-shaped slatted wooden beds with sheepskins heaped upon them. As Anya was being helped up to the upper one, she could smell a faint scent, very unusual, but quite pleasant. She assumed it must be the silk.

Kirstal pulled the sheepskins over Anya's naked body, then got down and began rearranging the skins in the lower bed. Anya couldn't see what she was doing, but when she heard a murmur, a soft, tired murmur, a woman's voice, she realised there must be somebody in the bed beneath her; she hadn't seen her on account of the heap of skins. The murmur came again, then shuffling sounds. Then she heard Malindra whisper:

'No more, Kirstal. Don't give her any more. You give her too much.' The murmur came again, then Malindra's voice, more urgently: 'No, Kirstal. Enough!' Anya heard the chuckle, then she froze as Kirstal climbed up again, coming very close, so in the half-light Anya could see her full lips moving as she spoke:

'Tonight we will not tie you. But you must behave. Lie like this.' She placed Anya's arms behind her head and spread her thighs apart, then rubbed the tips of her fingers over Anya's nipples. 'Do not move. Do not be frightened by Ilona.' When Anya frowned, Kirstal laughed softly. 'Ilona has strange dreams.' Then Kirstal climbed down and the wagon door was closed and latched.

Anya was very frightened now. Who was Ilona? Why was she beginning to moan? What had Kirstal done to her? Anya's nipples throbbed very gently, almost as if a pulse were there, yet Kirstal's fingertips had touched her only gently. And the smell was there, the sharp sweet smell, more strongly in the air.

The wagons set off, rumbling over the cobbled yard, and though Anya wanted to know where they were going, she was too afraid to move. She wished she had her magic lodestone now – she needed its warm reassurance in her palm. All she could do was to lie there with her thighs spread wide and the sheepskin brushing against her as the moans beneath her turned to tiny cries – the kind of cries that lovers make – as every movement of the wagon, every bump and roll evoked a whimper or a sudden catch of breath. The girl's breathing became heavier, giving way at last to strangled gasps of sobbing pleasure. Then all fell silent down below. But it was a long time before Anya dared to move, and a still longer time before the gentle throbbing in her nipples had subsided sufficiently for the rocking of the wagon to deliver her to sleep.

The jolt woke her up. It was daylight, very bright at that, and she could hear the roar of water. Sunlight streamed through the wooden grille above the bed, lighting up the exotic colours of the rolls of silk. She looked out through the grille. The wagons had pulled up beside a raging mountain torrent. All around were rocks. The higher crags were snow covered and the sky was brilliant blue.

Then she heard a movement down below her. She took a very deep breath before climbing down.

Suddenly she was staring into a pair of very clear, very pale blue eyes which seemed almost too large for the beautiful face in which they were set. The girl had gathered the skins tightly around her as soon as Anya appeared, but her satin blonde hair had spilled out and down across her shoulders. Now Anya was ashamed that she had not had the courage to introduce herself last night, for the girl appeared very frightened.

'Are you Ilona?' Anya asked. The girl nodded but did not speak. 'I am Anya.' When Anya offered her hand, Ilona did not respond in any way. She had a very distant expression which worried Anya. The sweet sharp perfume was there; it was on the girl. Then, as Anya edged back to sit on a roll of silk, the girl took her unawares by propelling herself forwards, flinging her arms around her and holding very tightly. Anya was embarrassed by the suddenness of the gesture.

'Save me from them,' Ilona pleaded, making Anya feel even worse. 'Do not let them take me again.' And the tears rolled down her cheeks as she looked up into Anya's eyes. Anya did not know what to say. Now that the furs had fallen away, she could see that although Ilona's breasts were very full, her body was very slim indeed, slim like a willow wand, as if she were undernourished. When Ilona at last sat back, her ribs were clearly visible; her small oval belly was bedded between very bony hips; her limbs looked long; her skin was pale. Yet for all that, Ilona was very attractive, with her shining hair, her large clear eyes – so limpid with her tears – and the soft pale curls that dusted the lips between her smooth slim thighs. But most of all, it was Ilona's breasts, with their deep red, prominent, upturned nipples – breasts so full, yet on so slim a body – that made her seem desirable.

As Ilona continued to plead, Anya's anxiety could only deepen. 'It is because I have the fairest skin, the lightest hair. They never take the dark ones – only me. Why me?' Again she began to cry.

'Who does this? Those girls?' asked Anya, comparing her own skin with Ilona's as Ilona nodded. 'They take you to the master?'

'No – he is only interested in selling us to the highest bidder.'

'What –' Anya was almost too afraid to ask. She remembered very clearly the incident of last night. 'What is it that they do to you?'

195

'They . . . They force me to do things I do not want to – things that are wrong.' Anya's eyes widened. 'They use the golden dust – linnabar – on my flesh, to keep me awake and to make me. All night, they do it . . .'

Ilona was interrupted by the door being opened. Malindra frowned at her, then indicated that they should get out. A small group of women from the other wagons was already gathered on the flatter ground above the torrent. Buckets of water had been drawn and jugs had been filled so the women could wash. Anya was given clothing, but she wanted to wash herself first. She wanted to remove all traces of the man who had used her so cruelly last night.

Although the water was icy, the air was very warm, for the sun was high and this place seemed to be a hollow surrounded by the mountains. While she washed, Anya found herself looking frequently at Ilona. What was this golden dust – linnabar, she had called it? Had it been on Kirstal's fingers when she touched Anya's breasts? Had it caused the strange feeling there? Whatever the dust was, Anya was sure that it was responsible for Ilona's pale appearance. Her eyes looked so large and so distant.

What she witnessed next made Anya very much afraid. The wagon drivers were busy preparing the food, so they did not see what happened. The merchant and one of the men had taken horses and ridden ahead to check that the way was clear. None of the other women seemed to care. While Malindra stood by the wagon, watching, Kirstal approached Ilona, who began to back away. Kirstal took the cloth from her, wiped Ilona's breasts, then cast the cloth aside. Then she whispered in her ear. Ilona's wide eyes looked imploringly at Anya as Kirstal took her arm and led her up the step and into the back of the wagon. Malindra followed. Anya noticed that she had a small gold box in her hand.

Anya very quickly edged across, pretending to dry herself. She could hear nothing until she put her ear to the side of the wagon. There were faint moans, then the whispers of the girls, then more moaning – sounds of pleasure, but unwanted pleasure, Anya knew, pleasure mixed with

196

shame. Hearing those sounds made Anya feel dreadfully uncomfortable – they triggered harrowing feelings in her belly, fear for Ilona and fear of what they might be doing to her. She knew she ought to intervene, but she was too faint-hearted. Eventually the sounds died away and Anya began to dress. She was about to put her boots on when she stopped dead. The sounds were coming again, very loudly, until she could almost feel them in her belly. And this time, when the feeling came to Anya, it was not only fear; it was as if a strange hand had touched her very softly between the legs.

Her hands were shaking; her mind was racing; she was imagining what the two girls might be doing to Ilona to wring those sounds of shame and pleasure from Ilona's slender body. She could picture the deep red nipples being touched and sucked. She could picture those pale slim thighs being held apart while dusky fingertips split the soft blonde fleece and warm tongues vied to coax the moistened bud, against the pleading, against the sobs – which Anya could hear quite clearly now – to its second pleasure, a wrenching pleasure which must surely have verged on pain. She looked around, feeling very guilty now at what her ears had witnessed. Her face and neck felt hot.

Soon afterwards, Kirstal and Malindra appeared, laughing as they closed the door. Anya pretended to look away as Malindra came towards her.

'What are you doing here?' she said, laying a cool hand against Anya's burning cheek. 'Ah – I see.' She looked towards the wagon. 'You are jealous of Ilona?'

'No.' Anya wanted to tell her to stop picking on Ilona, that what they were doing was wrong, but she didn't. Her tongue sealed to the roof of her mouth.

'Perhaps you would like to join us in the wagon?' Malindra persisted. 'See what we do to her? See how Ilona likes it? For she does. Ilona loves pleasure. Do you?' Anya could not speak. Kirstal came and leaned against the wagon. 'She is nice, Kirstal – different from Ilona, but nice. We could teach her.' Malindra smiled when Anya's eyes widened in fear. When Malindra's hand came up again to stroke her cheek,

Anya backed away. 'Oh, but you are hot . . .' She separated Anya's thighs. Anya closed her eyes. 'Look. She is swollen, moist.' She touched Anya's flesh leaves very softly, then opened them so Anya could feel the coolness of the mountain air against her melting heat. 'Mmm. We will arrange it, soon. You will watch Ilona take her pleasure through the night.' Malindra touched Anya's flesh bud once. Anya shuddered. 'She is nice, Kirstal. You will see.'

At the sound of the horses returning the women moved away, leaving Anya very shaken. She stood for a long while, just drying her face, though her face was long ago dry. She stared at the snow-covered crags; she wanted to escape from here, to bathe her burning body in that snow.

When she finally summoned up the courage to look inside the wagon, she found Ilona, totally naked, curled up on the silks. The sweet sharp scent was on her body. Anya laid her hand on Ilona to comfort her, but she too felt like crying. Should she tell the merchant? Perhaps he knew. Probably he didn't care.

At the meal, Ilona hardly touched the food she was given. As the journey was resumed and the two women were allowed to sit beside the driver, Ilona fell asleep. Anya covered her with a blanket. The road descended now, winding very slowly back and forth. The mountains gradually gave way to foothills, the bare rocks to patches of green and tufts of bright spring flowers.

That night, Anya could do nothing to save Ilona. The sisters entered; Anya was made to lie face down while Kirstal took Ilona out. Malindra spread-eagled Anya, tied her to the bed and covered her upper body with the sheepskins, leaving her legs and buttocks bare. Then she touched her, stroking up the back of each thigh, spreading the cheeks and touching very lightly in the crease. The fingertips reached beneath, opened her sex lips and lay against her.

'Tomorrow you may join us,' Malindra said. The fingers slipped inside, moving very slowly in and out, wetting themselves and smearing the wet around the nubbin, then withdrawing and moistening the bottom mouth. 'Ilona will ride the Surdic saddle.' The small mouth closed very nervously around the testing fingertip.

Malindra kissed Anya's naked lower back, checked once more that the lips between her legs lay open, then tightened her bonds and left. Ilona was not returned until dawn. Anya's body ached once she had been released, but Ilona appeared worse. She looked very pale and dazed indeed. Most of that day, they travelled and Ilona slept. The border was now far behind them in the mountains.

Late in the afternoon, Anya saw a horse: a magnificent white horse galloped across in front of the wagons, then wheeled round and stood on a grassy knoll above them, calling to the horses tethered to the line. Soon after that, they entered the rolling grassy plains. They saw a herd of white horses in the distance, but never got any closer. Anya now felt for the first time that she really was in Surdia. She should have been happy but, looking at Ilona's wan figure, she experienced only apprehension.

The same evening, as they sat upon the back step of the wagon in the last warmth of the sun, and watched the two small red round tents being set up in the thick grass for the merchant and his daughters, Anya tried to encourage Ilona to talk. She had hardly spoken all day. Anya asked her what she knew of the place to which they were being taken, the walled city. It seemed Ilona had never been there, although she had heard the sisters speak of it.

'They said it is not far,' Ilona said, then looked away. When Anya turned to her, Ilona was wiping a tear from her cheek.

'Are you afraid of what will happen there?' asked Anya.

'No. They were talking, last night, Malindra and Kirstal. They do not want to let me go. They are to ask their father if they may keep me – as their slave.' She began to sob and Anya put her arm round her.

'Shh . . .' Anya did not like to see Ilona upset this way, but she needed to ask her something. 'This caravan – it goes back and forth into Surdia?' Ilona nodded. Anya took her hand before continuing: 'At the inn, they said that, not

many days ago, the Prince – the Prince of Lidir – had passed
through, on his way to Surdia.'

'Yes. Kirstal told me this. They passed his party on the
last journey: many soldiers – and nobles too – riding fast.'

'They did? Where?'

Ilona shrugged.

'Where was the caravan coming from?'

'From Karnuk, I suppose.'

'The walled city?'

Ilona nodded. 'They always work the same route: furs
this way, sometimes slaves; silks and spices back. They said
the merchant is upset because he did not sell all the silk this
time. Next time, he will carry only spices. The Surds have
many spices, shipped from across the sea.'

'The dust – linnabar – is that a spice?'

Ilona did not answer at first. She began picking her
fingernail. Then she looked at Anya. 'Linnis is a blue
flower,' she said. 'It grows here in Surdia. Linnabar is the
yellow dust. Very strong; it puts the bees to sleep, they say.
The Surds use it on their womenfolk.'

'To put them to sleep?'

Ilona smiled for the first time. 'It makes you very drowsy.
At first it is very pleasant. And it makes your pleasure good.'

'Then why do you hate it?'

'It is what they do to me. They use too much. It makes
my pleasure come and come. I cannot stop it. Sometimes,
when nobody even touches me . . .' Ilona's eyes were very
wide now, almost as wide as Anya's.

'And then it hurts?' Anya asked. 'It is no longer pleasure
then?'

'No – it is still pleasure. Very strong. It just gets stronger,
so I do not want anything else, just sleep and pleasure. And
even when I sleep I dream of pleasure. My pleasure comes
on, even in my sleep. It is in my body now; if I close my
eyes, that first feeling starts – you know?' She closed her
eyes and placed her hand on Anya's arm. Anya edged away.

As she undressed and slipped beneath the sheepskins on her
bed, Anya was still thinking about the things Ilona had told

200

her. She felt sure her Prince must be there in the walled city. But she knew there was unrest: that small party of grey guards had returned to the inn in such a hurry, and one of them was injured. Perhaps her Prince was in danger? After yesterday, she had thought to try to escape from these women as soon as possible, but now she wondered if that was wise. Perhaps she would be safer with the caravan, at least until they neared the city? Alone, she would never know how to reach it anyway. And this dust – from Ilona's description, it did not sound quite so cruel as Anya had imagined.

It was dark when the door of the wagon opened. Malindra had come for Ilona. 'Shh . . .' she said when Ilona began to murmur half-heartedly in protest, 'Take it – there . . .' The smell of linnabar was in the air. Then the door was closed and Anya was left alone. This time, she hadn't been tied. She could not settle for wondering what was happening in the tent, wondering about that strong, repeated pleasure. She tried to sleep but she couldn't; the sweet scent prevented it. She breathed it very deeply, spread her legs, laid her fingers on her belly and breathed again, and then she felt ashamed. She turned onto her side. Was it the spice? Did even its scent upon the air affect her? Or was it just the thought of Ilona being pleasured by those girls that made the warm swollen feeling come between her thighs, that made her want to touch herself to pleasure?

She did not have to ponder that problem for long, for the door opened once again and Anya's heart was beating in her throat as Malindra helped her down. Malindra did not speak, but stroked Anya's breasts and belly, looked into her face, then kissed her, cupping Anya's sex in her palm as she did so. Anya's thighs opened to let her do it. Anya felt light-headed. She felt as if her belly was melting into Malindra's hand.

In the tent, a soft warm lamp light caressed the slender bodies on the heap of pillowed silks. Ilona was naked. Kirstal wore nothing but her earrings and a string of bright green beads about her dusky belly. She lifted Ilona into a sitting position. Ilona was long-limbed and pale-skinned against Kirstal. Her ribs were clearly visible, and her breasts were full and tight. Her mouth was slightly open. Kirstal bent to kiss those breasts in gentle pulling sucks which made them shake and drew the nipples out to pointed tips.

Beside the two women was a tray with the gold box upon it, two small cups, a spoon, some coils of thong and a bottle of what looked like wine. Behind them and mounted on a low support was a magnificent saddle in polished rich brown leather inlaid with precious opal and studded with pale blue pearls. The opal had been fashioned into the shapes of galloping horses. Anya knew this must be the Surdic saddle that Malindra had referred to, and immediately she was frightened for Ilona. Ilona would ride this saddle; that was what Malindra had said. The horn of the saddle was large and smoothly polished. It was broad at the base and tapered upwards to a rounded bump. The stirrups were made of gold. Beside the saddle were jewelled reins and a small, multi-stranded whip.

Then Anya became even more afraid as Malindra collected up two pairs of rope manacles which had leather cuffs. She led Anya to the central supporting pole of the tent and stood her with her back against it so that she faced Ilona and Kirstal and could watch as Kirstal slowly bent Ilona backwards, separating her thighs to reveal the soft blonde bush. Anya's hands and feet were fastened behind her with the manacles taken round the pole. The ropes were not tight, but her movement was restricted. She could not bring her hands forward to protect her breasts; she could not fully close her thighs. Then Malindra took her by the shoulders and gently pushed her down into a crouching position, which bent her knees tightly and forced them wide apart. Now the rope between her wrists was drawn down and hooked underneath a peg in the ground behind the pole, and she could not move at all.

The tray was brought across. Malindra began rearranging the items on it then, becoming aware of Anya's anxiety, caressed her softly between the legs, taking the hot flesh leaves and very gently folding them back repeatedly, until she was satisfied that they would stay open, which only served to make Anya's apprehension deepen. Malindra placed the tray between Anya's legs and poured a little liquid into the small gold cup. The liquid was bright yellow; the scent was there, the scent of linnabar. Anya shivered and tried to close her legs but could not. She felt her flesh leaves wrinkling, cooling, curling up with fear.

'Shh,' Malindra said, opening out Anya's curled-up flesh leaves once again. 'Shhh. It is only linnis water – very weak. Do not cry. It is good. There . . .' But Anya bucked, then shuddered as the first cool drops were splashed against her open sex; she whimpered as the liquid was smeared around her nubbin; she murmured, 'No, please . . .' as Malindra wet her fingertips in the cup and pushed them up inside her sex and then into her bottom. A second cup was poured. Malindra held Anya's nose and tipped the liquid down her throat. Anya choked and coughed; the fiery liquid sprayed up the back of her nose; her eyes began to stream.

Malindra then took off her clothes and stood nude before Anya. 'You will feel it, soon. It will make your pleasure better. In time, you may try this . . .' She knelt and opened the small gold casket of linnabar, then lifted and unwound a long leather thong. A small yellow felted sliding bead was present towards one end. Malindra carefully rolled this bead in the yellow dust, shook it, then fastened the thong once round her waist and drew it down between her legs, adjusting the position of the bead, before fastening at the back. Finally, she pulled the arrangement tight, and gasped as the cord split her sex lips and the yellow bead bedded deeply at the top. When Malindra knelt closer, spreading her fingers across Anya's belly, and Anya closed her eyes, a soft delicious feeling came between Anya's legs as if she were being sucked.

'Do you feel it?' Malindra asked and Anya could only swallow. She wanted Malindra's fingers there, two fingers up inside her while Anya squeezed and Malindra stroked her nubbin with her thumb. Malindra kissed her once and then was gone. But Anya felt a warmth spreading out from her belly, where the hand had lain, and another soft pull between her thighs as if an invisible thing were there, a mouth that closed around her sex lips, drawing sustenance from her flesh, milking liquid from her body.

It was the soft moan that made Anya open her eyes. All three women were on the silks. Malindra now supported Ilona while Kirstal knelt beside her with the small gold casket. Ilona seemed so wan, so soft, so compliant to their will. Her full breasts gently rose and fell. She breathed shallowly. Then, with a sudden surge as if fear had overwhelmed her, her breasts shook, her bright red nipples tightened. Malindra lifted those tight pale breasts very gently to the sides then slowly drew her tongue across the ribs and up the small belly. The skin lifted as Malindra's tongue licked upwards; the soft blonde curls below it trembled. Ilona's head turned; her wide eyes looked beseechingly at Anya. Anya could not save her.

Kirstal carefully wetted her finger and dipped it in the casket. It came out bright yellow. Malindra whispered in Ilona's ear. Ilona's eyes closed, her mouth opened and her tongue pushed slowly out. Kirstal's finger smeared the dust upon the tongue, then carefully massaged it into its upper surface, then the underside. While this was being done, Malindra rubbed Ilona's breasts and belly and Ilona emitted little cries. Then her head was drawn back by Malindra while Kirstal pinched the tongue between her finger and thumb, lifted it up and sprinkled the dust beneath it, into the well, then licked her fingers clean. But Ilona's tongue was not released. Anya could only watch, wide-eyed, with the invisible presence drawing nectar again from between her open thighs.

Ilona was held in that position, with her hips thrust forward, her head drawn sharply back and the hand restraining her tongue, while her thighs were spread and now two separate sets of fingers touched her, working in unison, smoothing the blonde hair down, stroking in the creases, gently palpating the lips of her sex, drawing them open, one set of fingers holding them while the other touched the nubbin, pressing it, stroking upwards, wetting it – always touching very lightly – then rubbing a fingertip round it very slowly until Ilona's breathing burst. And at

that critical point, as her belly began to shudder uncontrollably, her legs were kept wide apart, small slaps were
delivered to her inner thighs, her flesh lips were pinched, her
bottom mouth was nipped, and her undulating belly was
bitten, but her head and tongue were held quite fast against
the keenness of her pleasure.

Anya was breathing very deeply with excitement. She
felt very aroused by what she had witnessed; she was imagining what it might be like to be held fast – so intimately –
by her tongue when her pleasure was delivered; she was
afraid the women might do such things to her.

Malindra came over, holding something; it wasn't the
gold casket but still it frightened Anya. It looked like a
smoothly polished piece of black wood, very slim and light
and about as long as Anya's middle finger. When Malindra
stroked Anya's inner thighs then separated her flesh lips,
Anya shuddered, for she was sure that Malindra would push
this thing inside her. However, she pressed it lengthwise
against the divide then closed the flesh around it. And with
her sex pushed out on account of her crouching posture, and
this very light slim piece of what felt like wood gripped
between the lips and pressed against her nubbin, it was a
very strange pleasure indeed. It focused the drawing feeling
there.

'You must keep this rod in place,' said Malindra, tickling
Anya's belly. 'Later, I will use it to make your pleasure
come.' Anya's mouth felt dry; her tongue felt swollen.
Malindra placed a finger at the bottom end of the rod and a
thumb at the top and pressed. As she pressed, forcing the
lips to curve, she stroked the outer surface of those lips then
kissed each of Anya's nipples and gently sucked it while the
pressure and the stroking was maintained. Then she left
Anya with the small light rod in place, sealed within the
sticky moisture of her sex lips, pressing on her ever-
swelling bud while she returned to help Kirstal pleasure
poor Ilona a second time.

A satin-covered bolster was chosen. Ilona's back was
drawn across it so that her body, moulding so compliantly
to the bolster, formed a strong arch surmounted by her

belly. Kirstal drew Ilona's arms straight back and held them at the wrists, keeping her body in tension whilst Malindra's fingertips caressed the faint blonde fleece, stroking it away from the pale pink lips of the smooth uplifted mound. Malindra then knelt between Ilona's thighs, placed Ilona's feet flat to the floor and moved them steadily apart. The belly tightened; Ilona murmured; the unresisting sex lips gaped. Malindra lifted them fully open, then very slowly licked inside, spreading one hand across the curving belly while Kirstal worked the dust into the bright red nipples. Ilona's belly gently writhed; Malindra's lips and tongue sought out the nubbin. Ilona now began to whimper. The belly lifted from the bolster. Malindra then sat up, crossed Ilona's ankles and bound them together, so her knees were bent, her thighs were open and she couldn't move. Kirstal secured her wrists and pegged them to the ground, then whispered an instruction to Ilona. Ilona's tongue pushed out. Again the dust was applied, and the tongue was gripped. This time Ilona's head was held between Kirstal's knees. Malindra stroked Ilona's belly, then smacked it sharply, once.

Anya felt the sinking feeling very strongly between her thighs; she felt the small rod move against her nubbin. She could not take her eyes from the vision now before her, as the hand was raised repeatedly and smacked down, below the tensed-up belly, between the open thighs, upon the sex lips, until Ilona grunted. Malindra then bent forwards and sucked that punished flesh until the knees jerked and the belly lifted a second time, whereupon Malindra took up the smacking of the sex lips once again.

Kirstal now released the tongue. She edged forwards, spreading her flesh above Ilona's face. The smacking was now replaced by a very gentle massage of Ilona's swollen sex. As the massage progressed, Ilona's tongue slowly arched upwards to lick Kirstal's fingers where they held her flesh lips open, then to lick inside, administering the linnabar up into Kirstal's body. Kirstal's breath snagged and she lifted away. The tongue arched up to a finely drawn point, Malindra pressed both outstretched palms against the tightness of the belly, to contain it and prevent it moving of its own volition. The palms rocked almost imperceptibly, then stopped, then rocked again; Ilona gasped; the tight-balled belly was gently shaken; Ilona's pleasure came.

But it seemed Ilona was not to be permitted release from this enthralment to desire, even though she pleaded for respite. She was untied, taken off the bolster and made to kneel. Her arms were crossed behind her back and her wrists were fastened to her ankles. The sisters then took turns to smack the full and red-tipped breasts and the small round belly. While one girl smacked, the other's fingers would enter the wet blonde fleece between Ilona's legs, holding it open throughout the smacking. Finally she was lowered backwards until her shoulders rested on the floor. Malindra slipped the sex lips fully open with a fingertip, then allowed the dust to drift down until the open pink was drenched with powdered gold. The lips were closed and pressed together to seal the linnabar within. With Ilona on her back, her legs bent, her wrists tied to her ankles, the sisters then retreated to watch and to play with Anya while Ilona's body was taken by the linnabar in its own good time.

And it was with Malindra kneeling beside Anya, gently readjusting, opening Anya's sex lips then resealing, then pressing the rod against her, taking up the drip from the end and tasting while Kirstal crouched behind Anya, gathering her breasts together and playing with the nipples, that Ilona's pleasure came while nobody touched her. Her belly shook, she groaned and sobbed and pushed against her bonds and cried out with the strength of it. She tried to close her legs and could not; no squeezing pressure could be applied to her nub-bin to assuage the wicked cruelty of that pleasure.

Anya burned with shame to be made to witness it, and to have her own pleasure brought about this way: as the stick was gently rocked against her, and now, as Malindra's fingertip stroked her bottom, Anya knew she was coming, and she would never be able to stop that feeling from sweeping her away. She gasped. Kirstal very quickly finger-smacked her nipples, Malindra drew the stick away from the moistly gripping lips, held them open, held them still, and carefully tapped the rod upon the tip of the nubbin. Anya whimpered against the first pressured surge of coming. Malindra held the flesh hood fully back. She waited; Anya felt her belly would burst. Malindra tapped again, then set the stick down on the tray. Slowly and leisurely she poured the cruel yellow liquid into the small gold cup, wet her fingertips in it, wiped them round the pushed-out flesh about the distended bud, wet them again, then wiped until the nubbin pulsed, then smacked each palpitation that the nubbin made. Anya's pleasure was delivered very fully with those quick smacks to her bud.

And though she had hated it, her pleasure had been very deep indeed. She felt very warm and swollen deep inside. Malindra opened her and slipped two fingers up inside while Kirstal kissed her, and Anya could taste the sweet strong taste of linnabar upon Kirstal's tongue. It made her feel aroused again. It made her squeeze her flesh around the fingers pushed inside her.

But now that Ilona's moans had subsided, Kirstal wanted to bring her on again. Malindra's fingers were withdrawn from Anya's sex, the linnis water was dripped within and the lips were carefully closed. Kirstal untied Ilona, lifted her to her feet and Malindra supported her swooning willowy body.

Ilona murmured, 'Please . . .' as her legs were spread and Kirstal held her small round bottom cheeks apart. Ilona was made to bend her knees and arch her belly down. The linnabar was administered deep between the open cheeks, deep into Ilona's body. Ilona's legs were kept apart with the fingers still inside her until she came. Anya wondered when this cruelty would end.

'Now we are in Surdia, Ilona, you shall ride the Surdic saddle,' Kirstal said at last, allowing Ilona's ill-used body to fall limply to the floor.

The saddle and its support were moved closer. Ilona was fitted with the reins, which resembled an ornately jewelled leather halter which buckled tightly round the shoulders. There were circular straps that collared her breasts so firmly that they looked as if they were bursting.

Malindra oiled the saddle horn and dusted it with linna-bar. Ilona was made to ride with her flesh gloved about this horn. While the ride progressed, the women played with Ilona, stimulating her with pleasure and with punishment. Her sex was licked where it split about the horn. Her nubbin was tickled with a tiny sable brush. The lips were spread back; the sex was smacked, then sealed again about the horn while the breasts were nipped and sucked. In ways such as this, Ilona's body was edged ever closer to the brink.

When at last it seemed that tortured body was prepared, Malindra drew the tray closer, filled the golden cup and placed the tiny whip beside it. Ilona murmured weakly. Malindra smiled; she arranged the leather strands into a fan, then softly stroked her fingers through the moistened fleece, whispering, 'Shh . . .' as Ilona's belly trembled. Kirstal stood behind Ilona, pulling the reins back tightly. Ilona's belly arched; her breasts poked out. Malindra continued to reassure her, and to touch her breasts and belly very gently. Ilona's head fell back; her belly seemed so tight. Malindra gently lifted back the swollen fleshy hood. She took up the cup, then dripped the linnis water. The belly moved; Ilona's mouth fell open. The yellow droplets splashed upon the swollen knot of pink; the fingertips massaged it in. The cup was tipped; the liquid trickled down the joining of the sex lips and the leather; the fingertips followed, then returned to caress the nubbin very lightly until the belly tried to lift; Malindra kissed the belly. As her soft lips planted gentle kisses, Malindra murmured, 'Shh . . .' The kissing lips moved down, a long deep moan began, then caught in Ilona's throat; Malindra's tongue retraced the line of kisses. 'Shh . . .' Malindra whispered once again.

She moved Ilona's legs back, out of the way, exposing the hard tight mound. She brushed the wetted blonde hairs back and lifted the tiny whip. Ilona whimpered when it touched her. Malindra trailed its tendrils up the creases, to the sides, then lifted back the hood and simply held it as the whimpering progressed into a moan, which deepened as the nubbin poked out tight to touch the moistened tendrils dangling down. And only when Ilona's breathing snagged a second time did the small strands lift, then whip down hard upon that focus of her sexual need, to release that snag, to castigate that tightness in Ilona's nubbin, to extract – by means of those quick thrashes in that single place – every drop of tension from her pale slim blue-eyed body, with its faint blonde belly hairs, and to render that choked-off cry a release at last from its breathlessness of pleasure.

Ilona was lifted from the saddle. Malindra turned to Anya, still fastened to the post. She looked upon her freckled face, her open thighs and, between them, the heavy dark delicious lips and the bright red belly hair, and at that sight, Malindra felt the yellow dusted captive bee between her sex lips kiss her – as if small soft lips had closed about her bud. She would make this new girl ride; she would render her bright red curls deep copper with her wet.

[13]

Real Men

As Malindra, clutching the whip, approached her, Anya
tried to wrench her body free. The peg that held her manacles uprooted and Anya, her arms and legs still fastened
round the tent pole, struggled to her feet. At her back, the
canvas flapped as if the wind had gotten up. Malindra
immediately crouched; the other women backed away;
Anya could not understand it. Why were they suddenly so
frightened of her? It gave her courage. Then she heard it
again – the canvas. This time it sounded as if it had ripped.

She turned in time to see the flash of steel and hear the
swish as the broadsword ripped a second time, then a third,
slashing the side of the tent into tatters. Now they could
hear shouting coming from outside. The women screamed,
and the tent wall suddenly burst beneath the kicking foreleg
of a great white steed. Anya fell to her knees. With a
paralysing cry, the horse and rider broke into the tent.
Before the side collapsed, Anya caught a glimpse of
stampeding horses outside. Drivers and women were running from the wagons, everyone was screaming.

In the confines of the tent, the horse appeared huge: its
giant shadow swayed across the canvas. All of the finery
was trampled underfoot. The rider, bare to the waist,
looked wild. The muscles rippled on his powerful arm as
the great sword swung, ripping the silk and canvas, hacking
pieces from the jewelled saddle, scattering all before him.
Anya could not escape. She crouched down, trying to pull
her arms out from their sockets as the sword swung again
and splinters from the tent pole descended about her ears.
Ilona, still in her reins, cowered behind Kirstal for
protection.

'Out! Out!' the rider screamed, 'Lidiran sluts get out!' Then he cut the rope that held the lamp. The oil spilled out and the silks began to burn. The three women tumbled outside, crying out for mercy. Anya began to panic. 'Out!' he growled at her. He seemed like a man possessed as he raised the sword again. She cowered further down and screamed. The blade descended twice and with the sudden jerks as her ropes were cut, she thought her hands and feet were severed. Then she was dragged up by the hair and flung out onto the grass. Behind her, the burning tent threw bright yellow flames up to the sky. In front, the wild men on white horses swarmed around the wagons, rounding everyone up. Anya knelt in awe; these men were exactly as she had pictured them from Sarol-harn's description, but in the flesh, they were far more frightening. Some of them wore sleeveless leather jerkins, but most were bare-chested. They seemed tall and strong. All of them had long dark hair flying wildly as the horses galloped. Anya had imagined these Surdic warriors' strength would be tempered with great kindness, but this did not seem to be the case at all.

At last, the women and the drivers had been collected within a ring. The merchant had been dragged out from his tent, which had then been set alight. At the far side of the ring, on a magnificent stallion, pure white except for a black blaze on its nose, was a man who must surely have been these warriors' chief. Unlike all the others, his sword remained sheathed. Ignoring the merchant's protestations, his eyes moved slowly round the group. The night breeze lifted his hair away from his face. Everyone waited for him to speak. As the merchant was thrown down before him, waving his arms and bewailing his misfortune, the chieftain's gaze returned.

'Shut up, old man,' he said, in a voice that had that same calmness and the same strange, almost musical accent, that Sarol-harn's had. He waited until the merchant's murmurs died down, then dismounted and carefully stepped around him, took out his sword, raised it high and with one quick movement that made the merchant shriek and fling himself

212

aside, the chieftain thrust the sword into the ground. He tethered the horse to the sword hilt.

'Bring the women forward,' he said.

Anya and the others were thrown to their knees at the chieftain's feet. He stared at them one by one. His eyes looked very dark but glittered with the reflected light as the fires suddenly flared up in the breeze. The merchant, aware again of what was happening to his goods, stood up and raised his arms.

'Vandals!' he cried. 'What have you done to me?' He wrung his hands. 'We are Lidirans, all of us.' The warrior beside Anya spat upon the ground; it made her very anxious. She knew from Sarol-harn what Surds thought of Lidirans. She feared that the merchant, should he persist, might get them into even deeper trouble.

Again the chieftain spoke calmly: 'Then you trespass on our land.'

'But we are traders. We come in peace; we take nothing we have not paid for . . .'

The chieftain cut him short. 'You take nothing ever again. We are here to see to that. All Lidirans must be rounded up and delivered to the castle at Karnuk.'

'But good sir – the right of free passage, a right protected by royal decree?'

'No more, old man: in Surdia, Lidiran rights are henceforth null and void, so save your breath.' His face was grim. 'Your Prince and all his company are held hostage in the castle.'

'No!' cried the merchant. 'This cannot be!'

But Anya knew it could be; she had seen it. In her mind, she had seen it from the first – the danger, the black despair that had overtaken her when he went away. As the women began to weep, as the words sank fully in, an icy hand closed tighter round Anya's heart.

She could picture him now – her Prince, in chains in a cold dark cell. She had heard of such things before: great lords held to ransom, not for weeks or months, but for years as their bodies wasted away to nothing. Who in Lidir would organise the payment of a ransom? Not the cruel Taskmistress – she would do everything in her power to prevent the

213

ransom ever being paid. Anya felt faint; her tears were rising up to blind her as she looked upon these cruel people who would do this to her lover.

The chieftain raised his head up high. 'Surdia has been taken back by its rightful owners.'

'Aye!' the cheer went up.

'Your meddling is no longer welcome. You people are interlopers on our land.' The chieftain looked around again. His eyes came to rest on Anya. He would see her tears. Anya looked away.

'By what right?' the merchant insisted bravely, yet his voice was but a croak.

'A Lidiran dares to ask about rights?' The chieftain stood tall. His closed fist struck his breast. 'I, Karrig-sarn af Vorn, have that right, sworn to me by my own countrymen. Who gave you Lidirans the right to bleed our country dry?'

'But I never – I am an honest trader.'

'Lidir! You are part of it, with your privileges, your "rights of passage". Now Lidir will pay for its abuses – in kind. We will put that blood back in our land. *This*, old man –' he withdrew the sword and held it high – this gives me the right, and I will use it, just you see . . .' Again he stared round. The merchant's face was haggard. Several of the women began to sob. Anya looked again at Karrig-sarn's face. She could see the strength of feeling there; she wondered about those cruel Lidiran abuses of his land.

'Enough of this talk,' said Karrig-sarn. 'Your caravan is impounded on behalf of the Surdic people. You and your men will join your countrymen in Karnuk, as hostages. The women will be sold.' And now he had to raise his voice above the protests and the wails. 'Chain them. Put them in the wagons.'

But as they were herded, Ilona, still very dazed, not understanding fully what was going on, remained on the ground. One of the Surds approached her.

'Get up!' he ordered. Ilona looked up at him but did not move. His hand came up, then struck Ilona a cruel blow across the cheek. She crumpled to the ground. Everybody stopped and stood in silence. He raised his foot. 'Get up!'

214

'Leave her!' Anya cried, but he ignored her. Ilona could not help herself or defend herself from this cruelty. The man's back was turned. Anya ran across and flung her weight against him. Taken unawares, he toppled to the ground. The women stood back in horror, but one of the other warriors chuckled, then others started laughing.

'Watch out, Gort-tran,' someone shouted, 'Lidir is not beaten yet!'

'But Gort-tran is,' another replied. 'And by a woman!'

When she saw the man's face, Anya backed away in fear. Tripping over the loose ropes of her ankle shackles, she fell. Now he was up again and in one giant stride was standing over her, drawing from his belt a thick, coiled, vicious whip.

'Stay your hand, Gort-tran,' the chieftain intervened, slapping him on the back and placing a firm hand on the hand that held the whip.

'She does not know her place,' said Gort-tran, pulling his hand away and threatening Anya once again.

'Then we will teach her.' Karrig-sarn turned to Anya and spoke with great sternness. 'You must mind your manners, girl – in Karnuk, you would be flayed alive for less.'

But stern as his voice had sounded, Anya knew he had intervened to save her from the whipping. He was looking at her again; those dark eyes stared at her. She glanced up at his muscular frame, the dusky skin glowing golden with reflected firelight, the tightness of the belly, the powerful arms that held the sword and kept the cruel warrior at bay. 'What is your name, girl?' he asked, planting his sword in the ground once more and extending his hand to lift her.

'Anya, my lord,' she replied uncertainly. His hand was warm; his fingers were strong. He seemed to be looking at the remains of the manacle. Suddenly his grip tightened and his thumb pressed into Anya's middle finger.

'Where did you get this ring?' It was the white ring Sarol-harn had exchanged for hers.

'It was given to me.' His hand was hurting her now.

'Did you steal it?'

'No!'

His eyes narrowed. Why would he not believe her?

Then he stood back from her a little. 'Stand straight,' he said. He touched her hair, pulling it back from her shoulders. She tensed, expecting him to touch her breasts. He hesitated, then seemed to become very angry.

'You must give this ring to me,' he shouted. 'Lidirans cannot wear Surdic rings.' She tried to free it from her finger, but it was tight, for her hands were sweating. But it was hers, given to her freely. Why did she have to give it up? She felt her throat tighten. 'Lidirans cannot own Surdic property – that is the decree.' And now she could not stop the tears. She was trembling. He wrenched it from her finger, saying ominously, 'There, you see – you will come to know your place.'

But as she turned to join the others who were being herded to the wagons, his hand came to rest upon her shoulder. She felt his skin press against her back; his arm came round, beneath her breasts, preventing her from moving forwards. Then he shouted:

'Take charge here, Gort-tran. Select five men; the rest shall ride ahead for Karnuk.' Turning Anya round, he added: 'And you shall ride with me.' He took her round the waist and simply looked at her, and Anya did not know what to make of this man. He seemed so strong, yet there was a tenderness in his hands – the way he held her – that induced in her a curious passion. She wanted to understand him. He had saved her from a whipping, then had humiliated her for a ring that meant nothing to him. He had merely cast that ring aside. Did he want her? His eyes told her that he did. But then why did he pretend to be so harsh?

And when she was lifted high astride the great white stallion and it shifted its stance beneath her, then pawed the ground, she could feel its power too. She felt exhilarated. The horse neighed, lifted his forelegs, kicked, and everyone scattered. Karrig-sarn laughed.

'He likes you, girl,' he said, slapping the horse's neck. Anya ran her fingers through the stallion's mane. The hair felt strong and wiry. Then her hand came to rest upon the smooth horn of the saddle. This saddle was large; it was not

216

jewelled like the one in the tent had been, but the leather felt smooth against her naked sex. Karrig-sarn watched her; her fingers were nervous; she lifted her hand to move it away, but he replaced it firmly against the horn, and she knew then that what had happened in the tent was not just a game invented by the sisters. His words confirmed it: 'When we ride into Karnuk, I will mount you in this way . . .' His fingers touched her bare sex at the joining of her thighs, and though the touch was but a whisper, she experienced a strange qualm of pleasure there.

The other riders, eight or ten in number, were ready. Anya was lifted and moved back. Her wrists were secured in front of her, to a loop in the back of the saddle. Karrig-sarn mounted and they set off, leaving behind the caravan.

For a long time, Anya could see the fires. She kept looking behind her, watching them gradually merge then dwindle to a single speck of light. She could feel once more the power of this noble beast, the pounding strength of its hoofbeats in the turf. She closed her eyes for a minute and she could picture once again the painting in the Prince's room. The peculiar feeling came again in her belly, spread as she was, supported on this giant beast, her wrists secured before her and her hair shaking, lifting in the cool night breeze. It seemed that, with all his strength and weight, this stallion was unstoppable: though it carried two people, it did so without effort, not slowing as the rolling downslopes gave way to steady climbs, leaping over streams, taking everything in the same strong unchanging stride. She was happy on this horse; she loved the sound of his hooves swishing through the calf-high grass; she loved the rhythm of the ride, the open freedom of this country.

As yet, she did not fully understand her status in this land.

Striking south, they rode across the dawn, not stopping until late into the morning, when they reached a wide stream flowing unhurriedly between shallow banks of bright red earth capped by the lush green grass. The men dismounted, the horses drank, but Anya was not untied. Some of the men moved upstream, spearing fish. Anya was given water from a flask that Karrig-sarn filled. She had to bend, then twist her head to drink it; even so, most of it was spilled. Her hair had fallen forward. Karrig-sarn lifted it away from her breasts and offered the flask again, watching her as she drank.

When she sat up, he raised his hand towards the manacles at her wrists; she thought he would untie her. Instead, he merely stroked her fingers. His touch was very gentle. She watched his strong fingers stroking hers so tenderly, then looked at him again, and she wondered if Sarol-harn had been right – perhaps here was a real man, after all?

Then Karrig-sarn walked up the bank, knelt down and picked three small bright blue flowers. He returned and offered them to Anya, saying:

'Our country has many flowers, but this is the best. Smell . . .' Anya knew well what it must be; she moved back as if his hand held poison. He sighed, then wrapped them carefully in a soft cloth and placed them in his saddlebag. 'We will keep them safe,' was all he said.

When the journey resumed, Anya tried to set aside her apprehensions. She became very tired. She kept dozing, then awaking to find her head was rested against the man in front. The rolling grassy plains seemed endless. Eventually the steady footfalls of the stallion rocked her fully into sleep.

That evening, they camped beside a thicket. Small fires were lit and the fish the men had caught were wrapped in fresh young leaves and roasted on the coals. Anya had not eaten since the night before. Not since she'd left the castle had she tasted anything so delicious.

The chieftain waited, until she had eaten and had licked her fingers clean, until she was relaxed. Then he took her on his knee and explained her fate. And she found that prophecy fearful. Though his voice was deep and soft, though he took her through the ordeal gently, holding her, touching her tenderly at times when she found his words too difficult to bear, the rising tide of her anxiety pressed slowly but inexorably upwards against her belly, then her breasts until it chilled against her throat.

'You are very beautiful,' he began. 'That is why I picked

you.' Anya glanced down at the fire. He saw the soft curl of her eyelashes in silhouette. 'Thus far, we have ridden through open country. Appearances – familiarities – do not matter here,' he said, curling a long lock of her hair around his finger. 'But tomorrow, we pass through a village. The people in these parts have never seen a Lidiran woman at close quarters.' Anya's breathing changed. He could see the outswell of her bosom. 'Your colouring – pale skin, red hair, freckles – is unknown in Surdia.' She bit her lip; he found that gesture sweet. 'The people will expect a display.'

'A display?' Her voice was soft, frightened. She had not looked at him. Her belly shivered. She was indeed a prize to make men covetous.

'You are a trophy of war, a sign of our success. They will want to look at you. They will wish to see how you measure up – how a Lidiran girl performs.' He watched her carefully. His fingertips touched her belly and it shivered once again, the way it had shivered when he had closed her hand about the horn upon the saddle. How he thirsted for her now: exhibiting this girl's charms would be so sweet a ploy. 'I expect you to perform well. You must not let me down.' Still she did not look at him. The firelight reflected from the round swell of her breast. Her nipples looked black. Her upper lip trembled. He wanted to kiss it. He could feel the perfect curve of her hip beneath his hand. 'Now part your thighs.'

The chieftain glanced down at the smooth slim thighs, the curls so bright in the firelight, the black and satin lips beneath, but he did not touch them yet. He simply asked her to spread wider, then rested his hand lightly against the tight thigh muscle – using that smooth hard muscle as a signal to his fingertips, a signal of her tension, of the effect his words had – while he explained about the steel belt. He told her how it would be riveted tight about her belly, and that it never would be removed. He lifted his finger and traced that line of contact deliberately, all the way round; he found her skin so sensuous, so smooth. He brushed upwards on the tight smooth skin in the grooves at the tops of her thighs: that was where the iron rings attached to the belt would bed,

219

forming tight and narrow lines of pressure there whenever she moved. He gripped his long strong fingers in a circle round the base of each breast, squeezing until the breast swelled tight: that was how her breast rings would keep her all the time – tight and pushed out hard, amusing to her master.

'Your breasts will be pierced,' he said. 'Shh.' She looked at him; her eyes were pleading. He kissed her for the first time, drawing the swollen bottom lip very gently into his mouth. 'You are delicious.' With her breast squeezed up to bursting, he gently nipped the underside of the teat, nipping until it came up hard. 'This is where your breast chain will embed. It will enhance your pleasure, you will see . . .' She shuddered when he touched the satin lips between her thighs. 'No – keep open, keep your legs apart.' The lips felt warm – living, moving, oily. 'The slave-master will pierce here too. Shhh . . .' he smothered her protest with his mouth. 'Your flesh here forms the last link in the chain – from your nipples to your belly to your pouch. Your master may use the chains in many ways – to guide you in the avenues of love, to secure your flesh to the whipping bar, to tease you open . . . to kiss you with the chains upon your flesh.'

But much as Karrig-sarn tried to allay her fears, stroking her belly, kissing her breasts and holding her sex lips open while his little finger touched inside, her anxiety was unstilled. He therefore took up the saddlebag, took out the folded cloth and removed the three small flowers, carefully peeled the petals of each one back to reveal the tuft and the small dense crown of dust and while the perfect belly shook, with legs held wide apart and sex lips fully opened, he dusted that sensual powder very precisely round the inner surface of those delicate membranes, thin with their unwanting, and gently rubbed it in until her open sex appeared like a warm pale golden flower. Then with her heels tucked tight up to her bottom, her doubled thighs bunched tight but spread until the skin in the creases was polished, he ran his fingers up and down the polished grooves, upwards across the belly, up the breasts to lift the nipples and then down again, not touching her sex at all now, allowing the linnis dust to take her very slowly, to seep its special seduction into her soul while Karrig-sarn savoured, in those lightly brushing strokes, her delicious tightness and her slowly burgeoning need.

Then he turned her onto her side, drew the blanket round her, curled her body tight, drawing her knees up to her belly, leaving her sex, with its powdered lips spread open, still available to his touch – but a touch so light it would not accelerate the precipitation of her need – while he kissed her back then finally slipped the thick plum of his cockhead into her, keeping it close to the entrance, distending her sex lips to the full, pressing a finger to each side of the sexual knot but certainly not moving, just keeping her flesh tightly open, keeping the knot pushed out, and the knees bent tight but working the nipples freely, until he finally dozed.

Then when he awoke to feel her squeezing round him very tight and trying to move against him, he simply withdrew, turned her on her back, opened her legs very wide, stroked in the creases, pressed a hand against her belly, then turned her to the other side and entered her again.

Only when she had pleaded with him several times, the embers of the fire were dead and the dawn was brightening grey, did he take pity and deliver her. He used the string of Surdic smoothstone beads. She did not protest; she welcomed that style of pleasure like a native Surdic slave. When he had done it to her, he fastened the smoothstone beads in a double loop about her upper arm.

And so it was that Anya slept once again in daylight and on horseback, until at length the steady rhythm broke, she smelt a familiar scent, and she opened her eyes. The sun was high and the horses were walking through a shallow grassy dell. No stream was visible, yet the slopes were densely carpeted in bright blue flowers. It was very warm. Insects murmured lazily. The horses moved slowly; in their wake a soft dense golden yellow haze was rising. They stopped. Anya felt the hair on the back of her neck begin to prickle as she was untied and lifted down. She was afraid to put her bare feet down amongst the flowers. The men did not seem concerned.

Karrig-sarn wanted her to smell the linnis flowers. She was scared, after the effect they had had on her last night. But he made her kneel, pushed her shoulders forward and stirred the flowerheads with his hand, then submerged her face beneath the yellow cloud. Anya coughed.

'Drink deep,' he said. 'Open your mouth. Is this not delicious?' The warm heady scent filled her mouth and nostrils, making her feel dizzy. The dust was trapped on the fine upstanding hairs of her arms; her skin tingled where it touched her. But it did smell sweet, and now the taste in her mouth was like nectar. And the feeling was coming – she felt warm inside, warm in her belly, just as she had felt last night when her knees were doubled up and her sex was open to his touch. Tendrils of warmth searched deep inside; her breasts were gathering as if they were being kissed; it was as if soft fingertips tickled her lower back, her inner thighs and belly; between her legs, her flesh was swelling.

Several of the men sat down to watch. They chatted. It was as if this dust did not affect them, yet Anya could not speak. Her limbs felt heavy. She was afraid of these feelings, frightened of what the dust would do to her. The tickling feelings came on stronger, as if her sex were being teased open, as if she were being touched inside.

Karrig-sarn held her arms behind her; he was saying something which she could not hear. It was as if she were far away, a tiny animal, looking up from deep in the grass at the giant poised above her. He had pushed her onto her side, then onto her back. The dust showered over her naked belly and her breasts. When he rubbed it into her skin, it felt like silk, as if her body were being stroked with silk. He smoothed the slippy powder around her breasts, rubbing it into the nipples, and Anya felt the fingerpad rubbing as if it were between her thighs. She whimpered softly with pleasure as the fingers crooked around the nipple, pressed and pulled until it slipped.

He rolled her over; the grass stems and the flowers tickled against her breasts then, as her legs were parted, in between her thighs. The pollen dusted in her hair; again the dizziness came, then waned. The grass felt warm. Her back was rubbed; strong fingertips massaged her shoulders, smoothing the pollen in. Her breasts were lifted outwards so the nipples could be worked. A palm stroked against her bottom and drew apart the cheeks, exposing her blackness. Her apprehension welled again. A pollen-coated finger slid into the crease, seeking the tender in-turned well, rubbing across the mouth. She wanted to close her cheeks. She was frightened of that kind of pleasure; she had seen what it had done to Ilona. The finger tried to push inside her and she tightened. The finger tried to force itself. She resisted.

He turned her onto her side. But now his eyes were angry. She attempted to cover her breasts and belly from the wildness of those eyes.

'Move your hands away,' he ordered. When Anya did not react fast enough, he took her wrists and twisted them until she cried out, then he pinched her nipples. The others now became interested and moved closer, to watch how he would deal with this disobedience. He picked a flower and began peeling back the petals to expose the densely dusted centre. Anya shrank away, for she did not want that strength of sexual wanting yet again.

'Lift your leg,' he said. Anya was very frightened. 'Lift it!' He dropped the flower and smacked his hand across her belly. 'Hold your leg up. Keep it thus – Lidiran slave.' It was as if he wanted to compound her degradation for the benefit of the men. Her leg ached. Her inner thigh trembled. 'For that, you will demonstrate your submission to your masters.' Standing at her feet, he very gradually drew his sword. The slow screech of the steel forced shivers in her belly. 'On your back. Now lift your belly; split your blackened flesh apart.'

As he held up the sword, Karrig-sarn took time to look on the woman spread before him – the face, so soft and sweet, the brilliant copper hair, the heavy black-tipped breasts which shuddered very gently with her breathing. His eyes caressed the pushed-out rounded belly, the short red curls, the open legs, the feet pressed to the ground and the very nervous fingertips which held those golden dusted black lips open to reveal the bright moist pink within. He decided then that he loved her – for a slave.

'This day, your pleasure shall be taken wantonly and publicly – as befits a Lidiran slave.' And saying that, he took the sword and placed its cold steel flat against her belly. He made her lift and kiss her open flesh against it to leave a heavy oily slick against the grey blue of the steel. When he rubbed that oil along its length, she turned her head away, and seeing her in profile, with her neck arched that way, her body slightly twisted but her legs held widely open, made him want to kiss her.

But now, he took up a second flower and knelt between her thighs. He peeled the petals back. She shuddered. 'Lift,' he said. She jerked away as the first soft dusting kissed her openness. Again he threatened her; again she complied. He made her press her feet together above her belly while he finished the dusting, dusting round the sex lips, holding the hood back, brushing the gold dust on the tight pink bud until the moaning came and then the first quick throbbing pulses. Very quickly, he lifted her onto the horse, tied her hands to the back of the saddle, drew her hips back, bending her knees very tight until her belly pressed against the horse's back and the black pouch of her sex projected. He laid a hand very firmly on her lower back so she could not move, then began to touch her very lightly, touching the split crease of her bottom, touching the pouted purse, pulling it, spreading the lips apart, laying a fingertip on the nubbin, then closing the lips again, but at all times touching very lightly until she writhed, until the sex lips reached as if to kiss against invisible flesh. Then once again he applied the dusted fingers, pushing them inside against the pleasured shivers, then gently with-drawing, then waiting. When the pulsing gave way to wrenching groans he simply held the sex lips wide apart and pinned her belly to the horse, whereupon she cramped and her belly seemed to burst. He bent her knees up very tight and forced his dusted fingers up her bottom.

As the warm feeling continued in her sex and spread now up her bottom, Anya was unfastened, lifted astride the horse once more but this time in front of Karrig-sarn with the horn of the saddle pressed below the navel, against her lower belly, and the passage across the grasslands now continued.

Soon afterwards, she felt the chieftain's hands beneath her, lifting her and she knew what he wanted; yet she was afraid to do it of her own accord. But she did not resist when he lifted her fully, edged her belly forwards, his fingertips reaching underneath to split her flesh, and lowered her gently onto the leather horn. Anya gasped as her flesh distended and her weight was taken fully. Whilst they rode, he touched her: his fingertips traced the joining of her body to the horn; her flesh was stretched and smoothed against it and stimulated in various ways. Sometimes, he would simply spread one hand around her, holding her sex, allowing his fingertips to tickle in the crease at the top of her thigh; at other times, he would stroke her until her nubbin came up very hard, then he would make the horse gallop almost to the point of her pleasure spillage, then hold her again. On one occasion, he smacked her with the reins, making her lift her legs back, out of the way, that he might smack her mound. The dust in her blood made her feel very lewd. He would make her stretch forwards and grip the horse's neck and bring her on that way, with his fingers round her nubbin and a thumb against her bottom, rubbing until her pleasure was nigh. He would take the wet up from around the base of the horn and smooth it round her bottom. When her pleasure came on strongly, he would always try to slow her, to keep her on that edge of wanting. Throughout that ride, he tried to keep her flesh in a constant state of pleasurable excitement.

They passed many herds of white horses until the open rolling plains gave way to fenced and ploughed fields dotted with scattered trees and wooden houses with low-pitched roofs covered with grass. People dressed in brightly coloured calico came out to greet the warriors, cheering them as they passed.

Finally they came to a village square. It almost seemed that news of their arrival must have sped before them, for

very quickly, most of the village turned out. 'Remember –
these people expect to see a show,' the chieftain whispered,
drawing Anya's hands behind her so her breasts pushed out
strongly, moving her legs back, that all might see the leather
horn bedded in her belly, then spurring the horse into a slow
trot around the square. After two circuits, they halted in the
centre. She was disimpaled, lifted from the horse and held
up. Seeing all the faces – young and old alike, men and
women, youths and dusky maidens – made her ashamed to
have herself displayed this way, so publicly.

It seemed the chieftain's prediction was right: the people
of this village had never seen a Lidiran woman before. They
clamoured forward, asking how she had been captured,
wanting to touch her pale skin, her red hair and her freckles.
The women wanted to know why her nipples were black-
brown, darker than their own, yet her skin was so pale. The
chieftain made her spread her legs and display the naked
flesh between her thighs. One of the women asked if all
Lidiran girls were coloured thus. The chieftain said they
were. Holding Anya's wrists together tightly above her
head, he smoothed his hand up her belly, lifting her breasts,
rubbing his fingers across her nipples until they stood out.
An old man asked how true it was about Lidiran girls and
pleasure. 'We shall see,' the chieftain replied.

She was lifted up above the crowd, on a pedestal formed
from the sawn stump of a great tree. The people jostled for
position. Anya's eyes lowered, for in front of her was a
young lad. His face, like all the others, was eager. Beside
him was a girl – very beautiful and very dark. The lad had
his arm about the girl's waist, pulling her forward as she
tried to hang back. But demure as she appeared, Anya could
see the excitement even in her eyes. The lad whispered to
her; she pushed him away. His arm closed more tightly
round her.

Anya's wrists were lifted up again and pinned above her
head. Her arms were stretched until she stood on tiptoes,
and the chieftain instructed that she part her legs. Her eyes
darted around, but she knew there was no escape. As the
chieftain's fingers teased her curls back, and he made her

bend her legs a little, a terrible foreboding enveloped her: he meant not only to display her body. Her breathing came faster. The faster Anya's breathing came, the quieter went the crowd. The chieftain would not even let her close her eyes. She felt the touch, the finger stroking of the tight muscle of her upper thigh and – despite her shame, despite the degradation, despite the faces watching – the slow down-drawing came, the slowly slipping weight inside her sex. And now his fingers stretched out tight and flat, and rubbed that sensitive place, not touching the sex itself, but just the upper thigh. The fingertips then smacked against it – well-weighed slaps of stimulation which echoed from the buildings opposite, sexual slaps which made her want to bow her legs out wide. Those quick slaps made her swelling sex lips shake. These people would see her state, she knew. They would see how she was reacting.

He cupped his hand and very gently slapped her belly, while her legs were bowed and she hung suspended by her wrists. She found the soft slapping of her belly sent gentle shudders deep inside; she could feel her nubbin firming as the soft slaps caused her sex lips, in their shaking, to tremble against her nubbin. And when he pushed her forwards and applied that soft-cupped slapping underneath her dangling breasts, then turned her round – holding her still with her wrists above her head – and likewise slapped her bottom gently, inducing in each cheek an alternating shake, then he reached beneath and rubbed her sex, his fingers came out wet. He turned her again to face the front. He made her place her hands behind her while he bent her backwards, supported on his palm and spread apart her flesh to show her wetness to the crowd. He stood her up, then called for an assistant. Anya's heart sank as the young girl pushed the lad forward, then looked shyly away as if she were embarrassed at the hastiness of her action.

'You wish to deliver this Lidiran woman's pleasure?' The lad nodded sheepishly; as the crowd murmured, the young girl looked down at her feet, then looked up again. Anya closed her legs and tried to get away. She did not want it this way, but the chieftain held her firmly. He showed no pity.

227

'In Surdia, you are nothing,' he told her plainly. 'We use Lidiran slaves as we think fit.' He held her sex lips open and pointed out the hard wet bud of flesh. 'This tiny bud is sensitive. It must be rubbed. It must be squeezed between the fingers. Try it.' And in the crowd now, the young girl backed away and looked as if she might run.

Karrig-sarn supported Anya's tense and frightened body as she tried to move her hips away, but he held her firmly, mercilessly, commanding her to move her legs apart, to lower herself that the youth's fingers might have free access to her person, and he knew that it mattered not that those fingers lacked experience in these matters. In fact, it was better that way, for each time the uncertain squeezing found her rhythm, and the belly tensed, the nipples tightened and the delicious body felt a little heavier in his hands as all the will to resist seeped out of it and the needs of the flesh took over, that very inexperience would force a break, a mistimed beat and, with a gentle moan, the girl would momentarily lose her stride. Karrig-sarn would then place his palm upon the roundness of the belly to move it and to keep it tight, gently lifting, so with each lift the flesh lips tightened round the fingertips that nervously squeezed around the nubbin and the rhythm would be re-established. And once this was the case, he could lift and pull each nipple very gently then reach below, between the cheeks and gently touch her bottom, alternating his attentions between these pleasurable extremities until her body became tense, then soft and very heavy once again, her head fell loosely to the side, her breathing shallowed, then suddenly deepened, the jaw fell slack and the sweet mouth opened to a silent moan, whereupon he could touch his lips very softly to her own, touching that soft warm moistness very gently with each and every shudder that took her tight delicious belly and delivered it finally to delight.

And after this pleasuring was completed, Karrig-sarn watched the young lad throw his arms about his sweetheart's waist and kiss her, then watched her return that kiss very deeply. Her bosom rose and fell with the sweet anticipation of pleasures yet to come, with the slow delicious lust

228

induced by having witnessed this public exposition of sexual desire and carefully controlled fulfilment. He could see it on these people's faces. For what were trophies for, if not to bring joy to the lives of humble folk like these?

Having surveyed the happy scene, he carried the soft and pliant woman draped on his arm to the table that was rapidly laid for the conqueror and his men. He thanked the villagers when the meal was done. 'But now we must ride,' he said. 'Tonight the green sod of this hallowed land shall provide our pillow. The rich red earth shall give us warmth and solace. Tomorrow we enter Karnuk.'

That evening, as the westering sun submerged blood-red beneath a soft pink pool of haze, and they looked out across the great wide shallow valley, they saw it, straight ahead – the walled city, bedded to the hillside opposite. Its granite walls were pure white; its sunlit tapered spiral towers struck skyward like glowing orange flames.

'We will make camp. We will ride at dawn,' said Karrig-sarn. He began unpacking the bedroll, but Anya could not move. She faced that vision, so wreathed with premonition: though she could not see him, Anya knew that at last she was looking upon a scene in which her lover lay, and the awesomeness of that knowledge was paralysing. She could picture him – his face, so sad – watching her from afar, not seeing her physical presence but somehow looking into her soul. And what he would see there would surely make him turn away.

Eventually, Karrig-sarn came back. He stared at her.

'Is it true?' Anya whispered. 'Is he in there? The Prince?' Her voice sounded distant, even to herself.

'They are there – the usurper and his band.'

'Will – will I get to see him?' Anya closed her eyes. She counted her heartbeats. The reply was neither disappointment nor relief. It was a deliverance to a sublime and fitting sadness:

'I think not. He is held fast in the prison tower. You will be sold in the market.'

'What will become of me?'

229

He laid his hand upon the outswell of her hips. 'Who knows? Some rich man? Even here in Surdia there are some.'

She hesitated. She looked down at the strong hand at her hip. 'Y . . . you will not keep me then?' she asked.

'Me?' He laughed softly, as if he found her question ironic. 'I deliver you, as my duty. I cannot keep you for myself.'

She took a deep breath. 'Nor would you – if you could?'

He did not answer. When he tried to take her arm, Anya collapsed to her knees. Her face was wet with tears. He lifted her and took her to the fire. She was shaking. He put the blanket round her. 'You are frightened of what will happen when you are sold?' he whispered.

She shook her head. How could she explain? She could not tell him the truth about herself; she could not explain her feelings – even to anyone.

Later, beneath the blanket, when he took his pleasure with her, Anya welcomed it – as long as he did not try to bring her pleasure too. She welcomed being taken as a slave. When he lay behind her and held her, with his fleshcock thrust between her legs and up inside her belly, she moved his hand away from her sex and instead pressed it to her breast. Then she squeezed his fleshcock with her body until she brought his pleasure on. When she felt his milt spurt deep inside her, she felt warm, as if the warmth of that milting permeated her belly. It brought an inner satisfaction that he had used her body as a vessel for his pleasure, but it did not take away her tears. As he fell asleep against her, her teardrops welled again to drip upon the grass and she cried herself to sleep.

In the night she woke, drenched in sweat. She had dreamt of Brekt – that Brekt was smacking her sex and bottom with the strap, and she was frightened and aroused by the vividness of that dream. Even now that she was awake, her fleshpot was aroused. She turned to face the man who slept beside her. She took his cockstem in her hand and milked it very quickly. It came hard, although he was asleep. She turned him on his back and mounted him, working her sex up and down him very roughly, pressing hard, pushing herself against him until he woke and moaned and thrust against her too, thrusting so hard he lifted her in the air. And again that pleasure came to Anya – not satisfaction, but the pleasure of knowing she had brought his pleasure on – the pleasure of his milt inside her belly. As she turned again to lie down, his cockstem was still hard. She took it up inside her, keeping it inside her while she dozed.

She did not sleep fully again that night. She kept squeezing the cockstem, trying to bring him on. Her nubbin felt hard and swollen. Her nubbin ached. And when she dozed, she dreamt of Brekt, Brekt smacking the strap between her legs, smacking her until she gasped, then smearing her sex with Brekt's honeydew and sucking her until she came.

While Anya spent that night in turmoil, it happened that far away, across the wide deep valley steeped in soft night haze, behind the great white granite-buttressed walls, in a small cell high up in the castle keep, a young man kept vigil as his five companions slept. His face was calm, though his mind was troubled. His shoulder stung him cruelly from the sword-slash he had failed to parry, yet that pain was but a pinprick against the anguish in his heart. That afternoon he had received the cruellest blow of all – far more piercing than the failure of his mission. But he knew he must steel himself.

He knew that she would have wanted it this way. He knew that she would have wanted him to carry on. It was his duty. He owed it to his men; he owed it to his country – even to this land, though it still rebuffed him. And he knew he must proceed with the escape. One day, he would return.

He had watched it – the ship – these last two days. He had seen it first just before sunset – a black dot in the west. He had watched it grow as it tacked closer, slowly, so as not to draw attention. And it was a ship of Surdic cut – that was deliberate too. Now it stood at anchor out beyond the headland. Tomorrow night it would move in. By then – he prayed – they would be free. Nobody – not even his lieutenant – had believed they would be imprisoned, though they had planned for the unexpected. They had swords now – their spies had seen to that – smuggled in one at a time on a fine twine dangled through the bars to the darkened street below. But they would have to make their getaway unaided from the castle. Their spies could not really help them there. And nor could the ship. It would be recognised for what it was as soon as it crossed the harbour bar. Overpowering the guards would be easiest in the daytime, in the afternoon, when they were fewest and they least expected it. Their spies would hide them in the town until dark; they would avoid the harbour altogether and slip away unnoticed on a small boat from the shore.

In five days, he would be home. He looked at the trinket in his palm and closed his hand about it. Why had she done it? Why had she tried to follow him? Why did it have to come to this? And again the sadness surged inside as he stared up at the moon.

[14]

The Closeness of Chains

They had ridden for several hours along a rutted road which took them through the dense mist of the valley and across a bridge of deep red stone. On their way, they passed many heavily laden wagons and packhorses moving in the same direction. When the ground began to rise, the mist cleared, the sun struck through, and suddenly the city was upon them. Anya was staring up at the high white walls with the spiral towers beyond. The gates were open. This place was very busy. People were erecting market stalls in the approaches and, within the walls, on the cobbled main street which wound uphill into the distance. The horses speeded up and galloped through the portal. The stallion beneath Anya stumbled: it had thrown a shoe. Karrig-sarn dismounted, but left Anya on the horse as he walked it up the hill. By now, the other riders had dispersed.

Anya's shackles had been removed; apart from the Surdic smoothstone armbeads, she was totally nude. Yet no one seemed to take much notice. Amid the throng, she saw a woman – very beautiful; with long blonde hair, she could not have been Surdic – being driven along the street by a heavy, swarthy man who must have been her master. The woman's naked body was covered in chains. Karrig-sarn's account of the chains had frightened Anya, but not so much as seeing this woman in such a state of abject misery. When the master twisted her arm, so her body was turned, Anya could see the breast chains fastened through her nipples, and those other chains, attached to the belt and running down between her thighs. Karrig-sarn stopped the horse and spoke to the man, who turned the woman around so the chieftain could examine her, then directed

Karrig-sarn up the hill. Anya felt a sinking feeling in her belly.

They passed many tightly crowded buildings, with people bustling in and out; the street seemed to narrow as they progressed upwards. Then it expanded to the right into a small blacksmith's yard. A large, red-faced man approached them. He patted the horse and began examining it.

'You have brought this one for market, sir?' he asked. Anya assumed he referred to the horse, for he had not appeared to look at her at all.

Karrig-sarn nodded. 'Is it today?'

'Tomorrow sir, the next one. The blacksmith grunted as he lifted the horse's foot and studied it closely. 'Three days a week now. Business is very good.' He pulled out a broken nail with his pliers.

'Hmm.' Karrig-sarn sounded distant. He was looking round, at the smithy and the stable block.

'I'll have him ready in a winking, sir, if you'd care to wait.' And, rubbing his palms upon his apron, the blacksmith delivered a representative wink to Anya, who once again became very conscious of her nudity.

'No hurry, smith. Is there somewhere we can use? To rest?'

The smith looked at him, then at Anya. 'There's only the stable. It's a bit of a mess, though you're welcome to take her there.' Anya looked away.

'That will do fine.'

Anya was carried through. The stable was small, only five or six stalls. It was lit by several shafts of sunlight angling down through vents in the roof. There were ponies in two of the stalls. The air in here was rich with the scent of horse and hay and bran. Down one side of the stable was ironwork – ploughshares, sickles and armoury. Beside a group of broadswords was a row of chains. They looked like the chains worn by the slave-woman in the street. Karrig-sarn sat Anya on a wide beam at the entrance to the stall at the far end. She knew what he wanted of her, even before he spoke.

234

'Our time together is drawing to a close,' he said. 'I will miss you very much.' He held her about the waist, his thumbs just brushing against her belly. 'I will not forget you – never.' Then his fingers touched her breasts, lightly, making the nipples stiffen.

The smith arrived with a giant armful of hay. He cast it down upon the straw, then went to get another. He seemed so matter of fact about it. It made Anya feel bashful. But when Karrig-sarn lifted up her chin and kissed her, her lips returned that kiss. He wanted her to part her legs. Though the smith stood watching now, though her cheeks coloured, Anya did it.

'Tomorrow – when you have been sold – you will be fitted with your steel belt and your chains,' said Karrig-sarn, stroking Anya's belly, making her feel afraid. Why did he have to keep reminding her? Why could they not spend this one last time together in tenderness and warmth, forgetting about tomorrow?

'Indeed she will, sir,' said the smith. 'More than likely it is I and my lad that will do the fitting. The slavemaster has ordered one and a half dozen . . .'

'You have them here?'

Anya's eyes darted across, like the eyes of a terrified fawn.

The smith nodded and pointed to the row of chains along the opposite wall. Karrig-sarn went over, saying, 'She is anxious, smith, about this fitting of the chains.' The blacksmith stepped forward to reassure Anya.

'What is there for her to fear? The pain is very slight.' Anya shrank away for she did not want this at all, not if it would hurt her. The smith reached – again she shied – but Karrig-sarn was back; his manner was much more stern.

'Keep still, girl, he only wants to help.' Karrig-sarn held the belt and chains and Anya now felt hunted. The skin upon her breasts turned to gooseflesh as the smith's broad fingers touched her, touching the nipples and pinching. 'Good – thick ones – they will take the chains,' he said, then pinched the skin beneath them. 'Some girls – we have to put them here. Their teat ends are not thick enough to take them. But this one, she'll be fine.' And now he was touching her belly and below. Karrig-sarn forced her to spread her thighs apart. 'She is black,' the smith observed. 'I have never seen one like that before. She should bring a good price.'

'You think so?'

Anya shivered as the thick-girthed fingers took her flesh lips and nipped them. 'Hmm. Good and broad. No problems there.' But she was so afraid of what they were proposing to do.

'I wonder,' said Karrig-sarn, 'could I perhaps borrow this set of chains for a while?' Anya's fear welled up to make a hard ball in her throat.

'Why not? But now, if you'll excuse me, I'd better attend to the horse.'

Anya could not control her breathing now as Karrig-sarn placed his arm beneath her legs, lifted her from the beam and laid her down upon the hay. Then he lowered the chains until they touched her belly. The iron felt ice-cold against the warmth of her skin. He lay beside her, trailing the chains upon her belly and her breasts while Anya shivered in the shaft of golden sunlight. He made her open her thighs while he allowed the chains to linger against her nakedness. Then he laid them fully on her belly while he kissed her. The chains sank deep into her belly. He made her press her feet together. He touched the flesh between her open thighs. He opened the lips and ran his fingertip around their edges and explained again: 'This belt – these chains – once fitted properly can never be removed. Shh . . . Keep still. Press your feet together hard. Mmm . . .' Again his fingers opened Anya's softness; they began to stroke inside. 'You will carry this burden always, as a mark of your slavery. This belt encircles your belly.' He lifted the chains and kissed her belly, pushing his tonguetip deep within the almond well, making that belly shudder. 'These chains, moulded through your flesh, become a part of you . . .'

'No . . .' she whispered.

He smiled. He found the innocence of that protest sweet. He looked upon the thighs, so open, the feet pressed sole to sole. 'Yes. And with your body locked within these

236

chains . . . Shhh . . . Yes.' Again his fingers slipped within. The inside of her sex felt soft and very warm. 'As they caress your breasts, this soft flesh here between your thighs – as they fix through you – so your pleasure will be enhanced, and your master's pleasure too . . .'

'No!' The soft contraction gently squeezed about his fingers.

'Yes – you will see. We will fit them loosely now, though only for a short while, enough for you to take your pleasure, enough for you to see.'

'No . . .'

'You doubt that I can make you cry out loud with pleasure, with these chains on your body?'

She cast her eyes down. She was frightened of just that – the closeness of chains, the profoundness of the feelings they aroused, the melding of chains and pleasure; she had experienced these frightening feelings so many times, in the castle. No, she did not doubt that he could do it – that he would – but neither did she want to take her pleasure in this way.

But his fingertips explored her gently, touched the wet between her thighs, until the feeling, the warm and weighted feeling, welled deep down inside.

And so it came about that Anya's faint resistance was swept away in the tide of Karrig-sarn's resolve and the chieftain progressively dressed the soft warm body – so slavish, so unresisting now, so sexual in its pliancy – in its chains.

The restraint was a broad chain-mail belt, attached to which were iron breast rings and thigh rings, then four narrower chains for securing through the nipples and the sex lips.

He lifted the left leg, slipped the thigh ring over the ankle, then did the same with the right, sliding them up together over her knees. Then he turned the girl to one side, then the other, lifting up the rings until they would slide no further, until they pressed into the creases at the top of each thigh. He edged the rings a little closer together, then opened out the sex lips until they touched against the rings, causing the girl to shiver and her flesh to curl away. He took those lips

237

again, moulding them to the metal, folding them until the curve of metal showed through them. Bending over her, he touched the tightly buttressed salted flesh with the tip of his tongue, tracing the smooth oiled inner pinkness of the skin, smelling her female heat.

He turned her on her belly now, leading the chains up the flowing curve of her back, lifting her, opening the chain-mail belt and letting it close about her belly. It made her murmur. He touched that belly very gently, feeding his palm beneath the open belt, stroking, fitting the fingertip to the navel, pushing, stroking again, then moving the fingers up to touch the breasts where they dangled, swollen, warm against his fingers. He would make them swell more yet.

He led the chains up her back and hung the breast loops over her shoulder, eased the rings beside her sex lips back into their grooves, then turned her on her side that he might restrain each breast within its loop. And the fit of course was tight, but the loops could be adjusted. He slackened them off and still the outswell seemed too great. The face beneath him seemed so lovesome, the full lips gently trembling. It made him want to press his lips around them, to stay them in their trembling. She protested very softly as he took the left breast, squeezed it, took it by the nipple, pulled it, forced its substance with his fingers, and worked it through the ring until the smooth cool iron lay pressed against her ribcage, until the sweet tight roundness was encircled. Then he tightened the ring – not quickly, but very gradually – stroking the breast as he did so, watching it swell, watching the skin of its underside turn polished and tight, watching pressure forced into the nipple, making the breast look full, as if she were with child. Then the right breast was en-circled, until the skin was filled so tightly it shone.

When he made her kneel, her breasts stuck out straight, pointing to the sides, the nipples poking upwards. He made her keep her hands behind her head whilst he sucked those polished titties, rolled the nipples round his tongue, then let their wetness stroke his bare chest whilst he pushed against her, kissed her, touched her belly, touched between her legs, combing through the curls then holding the distended sex lips wide until they touched the iron rings. But before he closed the belt, he made her spread and arch her belly while he kissed it. Then, with the belly still arched very tight, he bridled it within the chain-mail band while he kissed her breasts again.

That feeling – as her bursting breasts were sucked, as the chain-mail band constrained her lower back and squeezed her belly as she pushed – was more intense than what she had experienced in the castle, when she had been made to wear her chains of gold. For this belt did not yield – it constricted her belly. The feeling was so intense, so sexual: the more she arched her back, the tighter the constriction, the more the iron rings lifted her and pressed into the tops of her thighs, the more her breasts ached, the more her flesh lips swelled, the more her sex yearned to be touched, to be sucked. 'The belt will be secured. The smith will rivet it in position. These holes must line up; the iron bolts slip in through here.' The belt was drawn tighter until the holes aligned. 'There. It is better tight than slack. Your master will prefer it so – to prevent this belly spreading, and to keep this flesh in trim.' He pinned the belt with two small lengths of wooden dowelling.

And now, with the belt in place, he played with her but before proceeding further, worked her nubbin, wetting it and making it stand out hard.

'You see these?' he asked. They were the four smaller chains attached to the belt at the front. He took the outer pair and lifted them. 'These are for your breasts.' He took the end link and attempted to prise it open; it seemed very hard to do. He left her on the hay, then returned a minute later with a small pair of pliers. Taking up the pliers he placed the open jaws of the link around her nipple. 'Keep still.' But Anya could not; she could not control her breathing. He worked the breast, pulling the nipple, stretching and rubbing, softening it, then used the pliers to squeeze the ends of the link until her flesh was nipped. And though it was not tight enough to break the flesh, she cried out. His lips descended to stifle that cry, and his tongue pushed into her mouth. Then the end link of the second

239

chain was closed about the other nipple. Her nipples throbbed against the tightness of the strictures. When she sat up again, he made her turn, and each turn made the chain brush against her belly.

With Anya sitting up and leaning back on her hands, the second set of chains was led down between her thighs. She tried to close her legs against the intrusion as the coldness touched the moistness of her open warmth. But Karrig-sarn made her angle one leg to the side, to keep her belly open. He laid the chains within the pink cup of her open sex and kissed her, brushing the chains very gently against the hardness of her nubbin, then pressing them inside, closing the lips around them, then making her arch back while he reached beneath to touch the entrance to her bottom. He pushed her fully back until her shoulders touched the hay, then he sucked her sex with the chains in place, sucking her lips, sucking her nubbin through the links, drinking her wet and sucking her to the point of pleasure, to the point at which the lips became so slippery that the links could be closed around them only with great difficulty. Yet he persevered until the flesh lips were each nipped separately in the centre, tighter than her nipples.

Making her stand and walk round, he watched her, then brought her close to him, lifting each sex lip chain in turn, exposing the nubbin and playing with it while she stood there. He made her bend then played with her while the chains hung down. The chains swung and pulled her nipples and sex lips as her hips moved, as her nubbin was brought to the brink of pleasure yet again.

He made her kneel on all fours while he stripped and thrust his cock into her. And he found her flesh so delicious and so willing – so warm and slippery. With each forward thrust the weighted chains gently pressed against his balls; his fingers pulled the chained stalks of her nipples; he slipped his wrist beneath the chains affixed to her sex then opened them and laid his fingertip against the proud tip of her nubbin; very soon his pleasure was brought on. She whimpered as he pulled out, held her sex chains open and nipped her hot tip while his milt sprayed down her inner thigh and dripped on the hay. He turned her on her back again and sucked her. He bent her legs and pushed his tongue into her bottom. He made her squat and keep very still whilst he rubbed the chain against her, slowing the pressure when her pleasure nearly came.

Once he had stimulated her body to this state of total sexual awareness, he laid her down, then knelt and lifted her hips onto his lap. Her soft face looked up at him, her red hair framed by strands of yellow hay. He instructed her to bend her knees and to remove from her arm the smoothstone beads, then he watched her belly quaver as he lifted them aloft – twelve beads, each of them a slightly different shape, but all of them smoothly rounded, fashioned from a stone so rare, a stone which, when polished, slipped perfectly smoothly through the tightest of constrictions, through the most sensitive gripping skin. Twelve beads, slipping one by one – yet two nights ago, her pleasure had been brought about after only four. Last night it was two. But now he would endeavour to prolong it. The most he had witnessed a girl survive was eight.

He began by lifting the breast chains to the sides, so that as the chains slid down across her ribs, their weight might draw upon the nipples, making them stand out further from the rounded freckled mounds. Next, he straightened the chains that ran down between her thighs until the excess was gathered into two loops. He spread her legs more widely. He opened out her sex to make a black-lipped cup, pink on the interior. The excess lengths of chain he carefully placed within this cup, that the weight of the links might press against her, in due course becoming fully coated with her moistness, so that, should her sex suffer intermittent – even slight – contractions, the weighted links would slowly sink within. Then, lowering the smoothstone beads in like manner against the spread, but as yet still tightly sealed, cup between her uplifted bottom cheeks, and holding the leather string so that the weight of the first few beads might press against the black and velvet mouth, he proceeded to stimulate the bright red bud of sexual pleasure that poked between the chains between her open thighs.

He took the hood between his forefinger and his thumb and gently pulled it down over the bud, which felt to him like a hard and tiny stone as it slipped beneath the thin warm sleeve of tissue. He slid that tissue about the bud until the first qualm took her belly, arched up as it was and pushed out tight against the chain-mail belt; then he placed his finger against the first smoothstone which by design, fitted so precisely to the bottom mouth. He pushed; he held the nubflesh very lightly; the stone slipped in; the small mouth kissed his fingertip.

And thus it was that all twelve stones were slipped into the tightness of that half-reluctant bottom, with the belly kept so bowed, the thighs spread very wide and the lip chains moving very gently as her sex at intervals expanded then suddenly contracted tight. And at such times, he would hold the flesh hood back, of course, away from the bud and wait patiently until its pulsing subsided, before carefully sleeving it down again, sliding it very slowly, delighting in the feel of that nubflesh which seemed harder than before.

But delectable as this procedure proved – to both protagonists – it was but the first half of the treatment, and once these beads of love were fully inserted in their sheath to leave a length of leather thong projecting, it was time for the slow-drawing pleasure to begin. First of all, he infolded the sex lips carefully about the chains and held them thus, with his palm closed about them, while he stroked her lower belly upwards to keep the squeezing pressure tight about the nub. He lifted the breast chains and very gently pulled them until the nipples stood out hard; he stroked the tender rounded flesh upon their undersides, so polished in its tightness from the strictures, and he traced the lines of the rings that bedded against the tops of her legs. He found this part of her – the softness of the skin, the incurves, the bright red curls, the black, the tender warmth of fleshy lips, the delicious scent of female heat – exquisite.

When he took up the leather thong, she murmured. Her eyes were closed; her head was back; her mouth was slightly open. Her slender arms lay back, angled with her hands palm uppermost against the hay. Her breasts and belly lifted uncertainly with her breathing; her deliciously outspread hips lay in his lap. He took the strain; her breathing stopped, though her mouth remained open; her bottom tightened. When he touched her nub, she tried to close her thighs. He waited until they were fully open, then rearranged the sex lips until they pursed about the chains. Again, the strain was taken. The belly trembled. He sleeved the flesh hood fully back and made her hold it thus with the fingertips of one hand. He made her tense and relax these fingertips very slowly, so the pushed-out nubbin moved up and down. When he barely touched the nubbin, then lifted his fingertip a little, it remained connected by a glassy silver thread. And it was by the stretching and contraction of this thread of thickened seepage, the slow pulling at her nubskin that these minute movements bestowed, whilst every sexual part of her body was kept tight – her breasts, the nipples with their chains, the belt about her belly, the muscles of her open thighs, her flesh hood stretched back from her bud, and then the leather thong inside her, drawing the smoothstone pebble against the tightness of the slowly yielding velvet mouth – and her having to count the pebbles, out loud, one by one, that very surely brought her on.

And he simply had to maintain the tension, and the slow lifting of the silent nubbin thread and listen to her breathing, listen to the murmured count, and in-between times, watch the tonguetip slowly pushing out, watch the belly lifting as if to deliver itself so willingly to the slippage, then shuddering and sinking back again only to tighten hard once more as the next smooth pebble slipped through the round mouth of her black and satiny skin. Her nubbin pumped, her pleasure welled and as she tried to count the sixth, she could not speak the word. 'Ssss . . .' The word was cut off in her throat; as the sixth stone was delivered and her bottom tightened hard around the next stone, Anya came.

'Keep your legs spread wide,' he said to her. She did; she kept them very very wide indeed throughout those sweet contractions. 'Nnnn . . .' Her breath caught; her hips shuddered; her pleasure grunted loud; the cup of her sex that held the chains pulsated as her small mouth gently sucked upon the stone.

Karrig-sarn quickly turned her over, held her bottom cheeks apart and pulled the remaining beads out very smoothly and swiftly, then laid his hand against her to encapsulate both her sex and the mouth of her bottom. And when he kissed her back, with his hand still held against her, keeping the cheeks apart, closing her lips about the chain which pressed against her nubbin, her pleasure came again. She thrust herself hard into the hand that held her tight.

The blacksmith reappeared. 'Sir – the horse is ready.'

Karrig-sarn's hand released her. He stroked her back and bottom and the backs of her thighs, then replaced her beads about her arm. 'Good,' he said. 'I think that we are finished here. We have dallied long enough.' He unfastened the belt, released the rings, and removed the chains from Anya's body. 'Arise, girl,' he said casually. 'For duty calls – I must now report to my commander. And before that, I will need to dispose of you.'

Anya lay on her side upon the hay, stunned by such cold-heartedness, following so close upon the delivery of such sweet and drowning pleasures. Why did he want to say these things so cruelly? Then he touched her hair, stroking it from her cheek, and again the touch seemed tender. She did not understand him – what he really felt for her. 'Come,' he whispered. 'We must take you up into the marketplace, ready for tomorrow.' Then he spelled it out very clearly for the first time. 'And I must get my gold,' he said. And with that he laughed and slapped her sharply on the bottom.

Anya looked up at him, at his handsome face, at the calm, indifferent eyes. And she could see it in those eyes now: she meant nothing to him; he did not care for her at all; all of this had been just for his amusement on the journey. She felt so unloved, so drained, so hurt.

As Anya was led out, resigned now to her fate, into the open air where people were busy in the street, the sense of purpose in those lively faces seemed so otherworldly. They were free. They belonged to a world of which she would never be a part. She would spend the rest of her life in chains –

to be used for pleasure, to be abused in whatever way her masters chose – and these chains could never be cast aside as she had done with her castle chains. These chains would be bolted to her, pinned through her living flesh.

The clamour came much louder now. There was some disturbance on the uphill side of the street, but Anya did not care. She was lifted onto the horse. Again she stroked his mane; in her sadness, she drew some comfort from his power. Then she heard a different noise. She looked across the street to see a stall. Hanging outside it was a linnet in a cage. On the awning sat a free linnet calling to his mate, then flying down to her and back again. The noise Anya had heard was the stallholder jumping in an attempt to catch this bird. As he dived for it a second time, the cage was knocked to the ground, the wicker burst and the caged bird flew. Anya laughed out loud.

But now there were people running down the hill, across their path, then hesitating at the corner. Somebody shouted: 'Close the gates!' then ran to the smith. 'Has anybody passed this way?' The smith frowned, then looked down the street. It had been full of people even before the crowd appeared.

Then another voice at the corner screamed: 'Quickly! This way! They must not get away!'

Karrig-sarn wrapped the reins round the tethering ring. He stopped a man in midflight.

'What is it?'

'The Lidirans are escaped!'

Anya's eyes lit up. Escaped? How could they?

'The Prince?' she could not stop herself from shouting.

'All!'

'But how?' asked Karrig-sarn, increasing his grip about the man's arm.

The man shook himself away and threw his arms up. 'How should I know? Somehow they got past the guards – but they were seen in the marketplace. They are armed.' He glanced over his shoulder to where the crowd was disappearing round the corner. 'They must be headed for the harbour.'

245

'The harbour? But no Lidiran ship could land there . . .'

Anya could feel her heartbeat surging. She knew this was her chance, with Karrig-sarn distracted. The reins were loose about the ring. She tugged them carefully; they slipped free. She pulled them in and she could feel the power of the horse beneath her. And two things flashed through Anya's mind. She saw again the picture of the rearing wild white stallion, and she saw the Prince – in danger, pursued by this heartless mob. She turned; she thought she had heard his voice. And that was all she needed.

Where was the harbour? She did not really know. It had to be downhill – where everyone was running. She felt the blood surging through her veins. She saw Karrig-sarn's astonished face as she pulled the reins back sharply and the horse reared up so quickly that she nearly fell off backwards. She wheeled him round and she was off, downhill, scattering the crowd in every direction, through the cobbled streets.

When she came to the bend, the ground suddenly fell away and she was looking out over the sea. She pulled the horse up sharply. She had never seen the sea before; she hadn't expected it to be so close to the city. Then she saw them – a small band of men, fighting fiercely, down below her, being driven beyond where the fishing boats were docked, to the end of the harbour wall. A tiny boat was moored there. They were trying to get to it, yet it looked too small to take them. The crowd would cut them down before they even got there.

She saw him too.

In that single glimpse, she could see that he was injured. His right arm was held limply, close to his body and it was his left that held the sword. Her Prince – injured – was being driven into the sea by a raging mob of Surds. Her blood began to boil. She spurred the horse on, through the angry, stick-wielding horde that stampeded down the hill. Down into the harbour she flew, past the fishing smacks, out along the stone jetty until she met a swarming wall of yelping beasts.

The men at the back had turned when they heard the

clattering sounds. Now she could see her Prince not twenty yards away, separated from her by the seething taunting mob. And she could see his face. He had been fighting bravely, but now as he saw her, his sword hand dropped, his mouth fell open and his face went deathly pale. The soldier beside him had to put an arm around him to prevent him from collapsing. He was mortally wounded. Anya had to get to him.

A man stepped forward from the crowd and tried to grab the reins. Another raised a cudgel. A third attempted to take hold of her ankle.

Anya dug her heels in, the horse kicked up, then stood up on his hind legs, knocking the first man aside. With Anya clinging on, the horse swung round in a circle, bowling those creatures down like skittles, then lunging forwards, scattering them, pinning the ones to the right against the harbour wall and spilling the unfortunates to the left headlong into the water. Clubs and quarterstaffs, daggers and swords were no match for a wild white stallion surmounted by an even wilder woman with a purpose. No one dared approach the vicious kicking hooves. A swath was driven through the mob, then turning round, Anya drove them back. Sticks and Surds went flying. It was as if in that sudden unleashing of her fury, in the lashing out of the horse's hooves, Anya was taking a stand, fighting back against all the cruel abuses she had suffered these last few days. Repeatedly she charged them. Repeatedly she drove those wicked creatures back. The tears streamed down her face. What had they done to her Prince?

The Prince of Lidir staggered up from his knees. When he had seen her careering towards them on that giant stallion, he was sure he had been struck a mortal blow and it was her phantom come to take him. He still could not believe it – seeing her here – alive.

'Sire – the boat. Your ship is sighted. We must go quickly!' his lieutenant cried.

Suddenly Anya was off the horse and by her Prince's side. He seemed in a daze, wounded badly, but at least he was alive.

While the lieutenant held back the more venturesome of the mob who had braved the kicking horse, Anya helped her Prince down the steps. They collapsed into the boat. It cast off immediately. The lieutenant barely made it, with a flying leap.

And now, the small boat had left the pursuit craft well behind, the rescue ship loomed straight ahead, yet still the Prince could not believe it. Not until his head was cradled against the soft warmth of her breasts, not until he had smelled her skin, did he believe she was alive. 'Anya . . .' he whispered. He turned his head and looked into her shining eyes.

Then he sat up. From his pocket he took a ring and slipped it over her finger. It was her own turquoise ring.

'But how?'

'Yesterday, a young woman came to us in the prison.'

'Sarol-harn! She is safe?'

The Prince nodded. 'She did not give her name. She demanded to see the great lord – the great Lidiran chief, she said.' He smiled wistfully; his soft deep voice was tinged with sadness. 'Then she told me I must steel myself; that she was the bearer of grave news; that no one else but she could ever bring this news to me; otherwise she could never have done it. She said –' He hesitated, looking away, out across the water. 'She said the two of you had been overwhelmed in the river by a drifting tree . . . that she hadn't seen you surface . . .' He stroked her fingers gently. 'She thought that I would want to have this ring, and to know . . .' He faltered, looking into her soft and beautiful freckled face which he had expected never to see again. 'To know that you had tried so hard – so very hard – to reach me.'

The Prince could not go on. Anya threw her arms around him. Her eyes were blinded by her tears – tears of sadness at this tale, tears of relief that Sarol-harn was safe, tears of overwhelming love and joy.

[15]

The Healing

The barque had come in quickly, under full sail, flying the emblem of Lidir. It had interposed itself between the tiny boat and the pursuit craft, then had suddenly swung to landward, into attack. Taken unawares, the Surdic boats had scattered. One of them was nearly overrun: the crew panicked and abandoned ship as they saw the tall ship bearing down on them. The small craft then gave up the chase – which was fortunate, for it was many long minutes before the rescue ship was brought round and many more before the tiny boat finally nudged up to its hull and the bedraggled party clambered wearily aboard to heartfelt cheering from the crew.

The Prince presented Anya to the captain, saying: 'Captain – the Lady Anya. This woman, I owe my life to. And my heart.'

Anya became very shy. The captain chuckled gently, 'Sire – who could doubt it? I am honoured,' taking her hand and kissing it and bowing very low.

'But Captain,' declared the Prince, turning, spreading his arms wide, 'we are all of us indebted to your mastery of the sea.' He gripped the captain's forearm and shook him warmly by the hand. With a laugh and a shake of his head, the captain brushed aside his role in the proceedings:

'Would that we were sooner, Sire.' Then he cocked his head and closed one eye. 'The lookouts saw the rumpus in the harbour. We guessed it must be you. But you caught us napping – we expected you would slip away tonight, not in broad daylight.'

'Just so, but we were seen. We had hoped to make our getaway across the castle yard unnoticed, by mingling with the crowd at the slave market, but it seems we were misinformed – the market must be tomorrow.' Anya moved uneasily. 'Apart from the overseers and the few slaves in the pens, the yard was almost empty. We were spotted straight away.'

'A pity, Sire.'

'Indeed. But with your timely intervention, it worked out in the end.'

The captain smiled again and turned to Anya. 'And how did this gentle lady come to be here and to expedite this providential outcome?'

Everyone – the Prince, the captain, the lieutenant and the crewmen who had gathered close around – looked expectantly at Anya. Anya glanced from one to the other – she could not cope with all those eyes – then out across the water, looking for some escape. Finally, her eyes widened with dismay.

'Look!' she cried and pointed, 'the city is afire!' Then she ran to the upper deck, away from the crowd, and across to the rail. The sailors turned, then shook their heads knowingly, then gradually dispersed and set about their duties; the captain ordered full sail and a sunward heading. The Prince followed Anya slowly up the steps.

Anya leaned upon the side, reaching out, still pointing. 'Look,' she said, more weakly now, as the Prince drew by her side, then, 'Oh – it is the sun upon the stone,' she murmured faintly. Her eyes were full of deep disquiet. He took her hand very gently in his own, and spoke softly.

'You did not wish to tell them?'

'No,' she whispered.

'Nor me?'

How could she answer, without upsetting him further? In time – in time she would wish to tell him; she would want him to understand some things that had happened on her journey, things she could not speak about now.

Anya stared across the water, to that sun-fired city and that green, receding land, and she remembered many things; she thought of many people. Her soldier – her lover of that single night. It seemed so long ago – where was he now? She thought of the people at the inn. She thought of Karrig-sarn, and Riga, Aruline and Brekt. All of these people, a few of them kind, many cruel, all dwindled away to tiny points now, sparks within her mind. She knew those sparks would rekindle many times and grow to burning flames. And one spark glowed now, brighter than the rest. It was the memory of Sarol-harn: she had saved Anya, then when she had thought her lost, she had completed the quest on her behalf – she had delivered that remembrance to Anya's lover. That was what saddened Anya most of all – Sarol-harn not knowing that Anya had survived. Her gaze lowered and fell upon the turquoise ring upon her finger.

The Prince of Lidir looked upon the woman that he loved more dearly than his life, more dearly than his princedom; her soft and freckled face upturned again and staring out across the gulf of water, her copper hair tousled, turned to fire by the slowly sinking sun, her full lips gently trembling. He could feel her hand gripping down upon his own upon the rail – the hand so slim, the fingers so slender, yet the grip so strong and certain. She had followed him across this vast and inhospitable land – a journey on which he had been too afraid to bring her, the dangers had been so great; yet she had completed this impossible trek alone, and she had crowned it all by rescuing him and his men. *I will come with you; I will protect you*, she had said defiantly on the day of his departure all that time ago. He had refused her. Her words – so brave and true – had surfaced in his memory many times these last few days; since last night, when he had heard that fatal news, they had never gone away.

'I should not have left without saying goodbye,' he said quietly. Her full lips parted, trembling. 'I should never have left you at all.' Her head lifted higher, looking outwards still. 'Nor will I leave you – for any cause – ever again.'

And as she turned, her eyes were brimming with her tears. He put his arms about her shoulders, and kissed those soft lips tenderly. They were cool, not warm. The evening

251

chill had descended; she was shivering. He took off his cloak and put it around her shoulders; his fingertips touched the goosefleshed tightness of her breasts, and looking down, he saw for the first time the bruise upon her upper thigh. He touched it gently.

'You are hurt.'

'Shh. It is nothing. Lift me. Take me in your arms.' That was what she wanted now.

As he pulled her towards him, then swept her up and carried her down the steps to the main deck, then down again, flinging the doors of the state cabin wide, Anya's arms were round his neck. She was remembering the time he had swept her up this way and rescued her from the castle guards. And now she was looking up again into that gentle, strong face. She kissed his neck – and the earlobe with the ring – and she was happy. All the torment and the cruelties of these last few days were somehow washed away; the coolness of her skin was suffusing with the warmth of gentle love.

But when he lowered her to the floor, then called for water to fill the great tub, her Prince was rubbing his injured shoulder.

'You should not have carried me,' she said, her eyebrows furrowed with concern. 'You are wounded; you are hurt.'

'Shh. It is nothing.'

'Let me look at you.'

Carefully, she unbuttoned the Prince's tunic. She gasped when she saw the livid weal extending on his right side from his shoulder to his breast. She pressed her lips against him tenderly.

When the captain's great wooden bathtub had been filled, thick towels brought and copper jugs of scalding water placed beside the stove, Anya undressed the Prince. Her fingertips were nervous as they released the thick and supple leather belt. She placed his things on a chair beside the bed, then helped him into the tub and slipped in, facing him. She bathed him gently with a soft sea sponge, trickling water down the bloodstained, ridged and sealed-together cut, working tenderly but surely while he murmured, then tracing her lips down the line, kissing together the rough tumescent skin, touching with her tonguetip all the way down from his shoulder to the nib of the cut an inch below the nipple, then gathering up that reluctant puckered fleshy lump and sucking until it softened, until he murmured once again.

Anya was now very aware of the warmth of the Prince's body; the look was in her eyes, the look that spoke her wanting. She allowed her hands to slip beneath the small waves in the tub. The Prince took up the sponge in his left hand and squeezed the soapy bubbles down her freckled upper arms and round her breasts, then down towards her belly. Anya smiled. She parted her lips and threw her shoulders back. Beneath the water, she caught his cockstem as it moved across his thigh.

'What are these beads?' the Prince asked, rubbing his fingertips very slowly on the slippery stones on the leather thong still wrapped about her arm.

'Shh, Sire. I will tell you later. They are to do with learning how to count.'

The Prince lay back upon the soft sheets of the great bed, listening to the creaking of the timbers, looking at the woman up above him. He bathed in Anya's sensuality. He had watched her take his leather belt and leisurely flex it, then lean back while she buckled it so slowly and seductively about the round swell of her belly. And now she knelt above him, with that perfect outcurve constrained so delectably within the band of leather and crowned by the buckle of gold. His tired limbs ached pleasantly; his skin glowed warmly; the throbbing in his wound had softened. It was replaced now by a feather tickle, as Anya's fingertip followed that line again very gently, so very softly, as though that brushing touch alone would heal his skin. He found her touch was bliss. As she leaned across him, working so tenderly but so intently at that fingertip healing, he watched her long lashes flicker, and the copper locks on her shoulders move and curl. He reached with his left hand to touch those long locks, to take them up and feel their cool silk smoothness wrapped around his fingers. With each brushing fingerstroke she bestowed, her breasts moved, lifting slightly, swaying very gently, making him want to curl his tongue about their rich brown velvet nipples.

Her fingertip had reached the end of the wound; it continued downwards, brushing aside the curls on his belly, investigating the well of his navel, tantalising, not moving below. The fingertip lifted.

Anya looked at him with eyes of liquid innocence. 'Sire,' she said, 'I am afraid.' Her lips were moist and full, inviting. He wanted her to kiss him now, so he could feel those smooth locks dangle down and brush cool curves across his chest. 'I wish to love your body, but I am afraid.' Her fingertips closed tremulously about his nipple.

'Afraid?' the Prince whispered hoarsely, reaching again and lightly touching the smoothness of her belly below the belt. Anya's shoulders moved back, her breasts lifted; her brown-black perfect nipples pointed up and to the sides. She pouted her bottom lip. The Prince lifted up; he wanted so desperately to suck upon that pouted lip, and those deliciously pointed fleshy tips. Very gently, Anya pushed him down again.

'I want to –' she looked away, then her gaze returned. She looked down shyly, then spoke very quickly: 'I want to bring you pleasure – very deep and strong – to caress you with my body and to take my pleasure too, but you are wounded and I am afraid that it will hurt you.' Again her soft fingertips brushed upwards, beneath his nipples, so softly that he could almost feel that brushing much lower down, beneath the silk skin of his plum. He groaned softly with the pleasure it induced.

'See,' she said, 'it hurts you.' And it did; his cockstem throbbed up hard to aching with his wanting. Anya bent her head and closed her lips about his nipple, as if to kiss that pain away. The tip of her tongue moved wetly, warmly from side to side beneath it, then lifted it gently. Again he groaned. She raised her head a little and stared into his eyes. 'Oh, my darling – it hurts you. It is cruel. But I want so much to bring you pleasure in this way.' Those heavy smooth red locks painted satin lines of curling coolness on his chest.

'Give me leave to do this, Sire, I beg you.' Her face disappeared. He could feel the soft, moist, pouted lips moving down his belly, dabbing delectation down his centre line, then lifting up his belly hairs, brushing through them gently, sending crawling tickles deep inside. The soft lips paused; his cock tensed up, waiting for the lips to push about it. Suddenly, her face was above him once again. 'Please Sire, give me leave, I beg you.' The lips parted, the tongue peeped out bewitchingly and stroked his upper lip.

'This leave I freely give you,' he croaked.

'And the pain, Sire? What if it should become –' her voice turned very husky, 'unbearable?' She took his lower lip between her own. No ache could be worse than this ache of wanting. He could smell the delicious aroma of her skin.

'I give you leave to love me in any way you choose.'

Her eyes dilated – wanton black, sensual and guiltless.

'Then you must keep very still,' whispered the voice of delicious lechery. 'You must not move, unless I move you; you must let me do the work. Promise me this. You must do exactly as I say, no more. Promise.' Reaching back, she touched his swollen cockstem very lightly, just beneath the tip.

'I – I promise.'

'Good. But if you disobey me,' she threatened him with a finger, very firmly, 'then your punishment shall be worse.' Her hands then moved to the buckle of her belt, making the Prince begin to wonder at this gesture, combined with this rather unusual turn of phrase.

Anya began by spreading his legs. She rubbed a slender finger lengthwise along the creases of his thighs while she watched the cockstem stiffen. She stretched up beside him, keeping to the left side of his body, leaning out above him so her breasts overhung his face. She turned his head and fed her right nipple into his mouth and bade him suck. While he sucked, she played with his cockstem, rubbing it up to silk-skinned smoothness, stroking the underside, closing her hand around the plum and squeezing, drawing the skin back very tight and holding him that way, judging his progress from the tightness of his tongue about her nipple and the intermittent tremors through the roll of flesh encircled by her hand. When the tongue became too urgent, Anya would pause to stroke her thumbpad up and down each crease – 'Keep your legs apart and very still, Sire,' she would say – or she would dip her fingertips into the liquid flesh between her legs and anoint him with her clear, warm, scented flow. She would brush her moistened fingers through his hair, then return to touch his cock, to keep his flesh excited, to make it slippery with her heat. Then she would remove her nipple from his mouth, dip again and wet his eyebrows, wet his earlobes, wet his open lips. She would kiss him while her fingertips lifted up his bag of bumps and stroked the nervous skin beneath; she would taste her heat upon his lips; she would push her tongue inside to taste his spittle.

Anya now moved upwards over the Prince's body, turned his face more definitely to the side, tucked her legs up and laid his head upon her inner thigh. She placed one hand around his head to draw him close, opened her sex lips, held them back and pressed her nubbin to his lips. In this way, she suckled him with her bud of sexual pleasure, squeezing the bud out hard to let him lick. When the passion of that suckle became too strong for her to bear, she turned his head and knelt astride and dripped into his mouth, her fingertips folding the flesh sleeve back, her nubbin trembling circumscribed sexuality above his upper lip. Then she returned to the gentle stroking of the underside of his stem, the careful pulse of pressure on the plum, the tickling of his inner thigh with his legs kept wide apart and the soft wet licking in the creases to each side.

But though she tortured her Prince with exquisite stimulation, she was careful not to hurt him physically. He caught his breath – Anya's fingertips, stroking firmly upwards underneath his bag, lifting the pressured column inside him, forced the first clear droplet to well at the tip of his stem. She warned him very gently: 'My lord must stay his pleasure, save his strength. He must not let it spill.' And she nipped him underneath his tip until his pleasure had receded sufficiently for her to bring him on again.

She knelt between his legs now, to work him slowly with the skin drawn back until the pressured droplet had overflowed into a seep. As the seep welled down, her fingertips moved too, keeping the cockstem all the while in tension, moving downwards in advance of that slow leak, massaging, stroking out the path for that oily drop to follow. When the droplet reached the underside of the base, she carefully spread apart the bag and lifted with her thumbs, to make the skin there tight and polished. She transferred the fingertip pressure to a definite push around the flared-out base and watched the trickle progress slowly, fitfully, fed by gentle surges when she pushed more firmly, down into the crease between the buttocks. She released the cock and pressed her palms against his belly; the cock swayed gently, the Prince murmured. Anya bent her head and slowly sucked upon the oil-slicked curved-up underside of the plum. She tasted salt. She spread her thighs and touched herself, squeezing around her nubbin until once again she felt the urge to come, then she closed her sex lips back around her swollen bud and let it pulse. By this means, she would share her Prince's torment; that was what a friend was for.

Having prepared her lover's flesh and concentrated his mind more acutely now on pleasure by dint of transferring the ache from his injured shoulder to between his tortured thighs, Anya sat back. She waited until the Prince had opened his eyes, then she carefully unfastened from her arm the device that would in due course precipitate his release, namely the necklace of smoothstone beads. She held it up.

'Think of a number,' she announced. The Prince was confused; he hesitated. 'Quickly!' she insisted.

'Seven?' he replied, mystified.

Anya sat back again; she frowned. Then her eyes went wide. 'Seven!' Her eyes were pure amazement. 'But seven is too many.' Then her head turned to the side; she murmured in a tone of guileless awe: 'My lord is very brave.'

It was therefore with trepidation that the Prince permitted

himself to be turned onto his front with a pillow positioned underneath his belly so as to leave his cockstem curving hard an inch above the sheets. He felt his legs being spread again, but now the cheeks were being parted by slim and confident fingertips and then the soft wet pointed tongue was trailing down, dripping spittle in the well. He murmured as the stones slipped one by one, followed each time by a quick lap of the tongue.

At the fourth stone, Anya felt his body tighten hard. She waited, allowing the remainder of the necklace to dangle down whilst she massaged the firm curve between his bottom and his bag. She knew this tightness was from fluid building up inside him; she knew that seven stones were far too many for a first time, but she would help him all she could. She rubbed until a thickened droplet of this fluid began to lower from the end, then she spread his cheeks apart and massaged within the groove. It did not seem to work; the tightness simply would not go away. So she turned him on his back and rubbed his belly; she opened his legs and worked her tonguetip upwards in each crease. He groaned; his belly shuddered; his shoulder must be hurting him again. She moved upwards, spreading her thighs, spreading her sex, allowing her sex to kiss against his upturned plum, to suck upon its underside moistly while she touched his upper lip very gently with her tongue. She bore down; her sex lips spread against him. She could feel his heartbeat throbbing in his cock. His eyes were closed; he was moaning very softly with the pain. She knew she must continue with the distraction of the beads. Anya eased her body off him.

She bent his knees; again she turned him on his side. Again her fingertips pressed against the smoothstone bead; his belly shuddered as the fifth bead slipped inside. She cupped her hand around his cockstem to quell it in its trembling. He spasmed; no milt came out at first, then a thimbleful welled warmly into the cupped centre of her palm. She tipped her palm and drank, then licked the skin clean. She bent again and caught the sixth bead on her tongue; she used her tongue this time to push it deep inside

258

him. And now, with his knees still bent tight, she laid her cheek upon the sheet beside his cock, took this by the base and directed the tip against her pouted lips. As his cockstem pulsed and gulped, her fingertip pressed within the groove and the seventh bead slipped inside. She could taste the slow slippery welling of his pleasure.

She formed the end of the thong into a loop about an inch across. She placed him on his back, with the thong stretched along the surface of the bed, then knelt astride his hips, her legs locked under his and, lifting his cockstem, she lodged the tip within her fleshpot. Reaching back, she slipped the loop around her big toe. She made him push his tongue out while she sucked it.

'Now my lord must count,' she said and she made him count the progress of the slippage of the smoothstone beads as she controlled it. Her toe began the traction, she felt his belly tighten, then shudder, and his plum swelled up inside her as the first stone slipped. Her sex lips sucked upon him then advanced a fraction down his stem. Before she pulled again, she paused to stroke her nubbin with a finger and to paste her sex lips round him where they distended about his plum. She pushed her wetted fingertips into his mouth. 'Shh, Sire – keep very still. There.' Her sex lips squeezed him; the second bead slipped; his pleasure burst inside her.

As he whimpered, as his belly tightened, as his tortured body pumped, though he begged for leave to move against her, she would not give that leave, yet she softly reassured him through the ache of his deliverance: 'Shh, Sire. Even two is very good . . .'

And neither did Anya move; she held the plum of his cockstem tight inside her while her sex lips milked his tip; thick milt extruded out of her and down his stem. Anya took that milt mixed with her own honeydew and wiped it on his breast and belly; she smeared it down the line of the cut, smoothing it gently in, waiting until their conjoined fluid had evaporated fully before she would release his plum. She thought that salve would heal him; she thought that ministering to someone who really loved her would heal her too.

She removed the beads and cuddled up in front of him with his cockstem slipped between her legs and his hand below the belt about her belly. And it seemed to her that all she had to do was to close her eyes and her Prince had never been away.

Then all at once the timbers of the ship groaned loudly and Anya could feel it tilt and turn. The waning yellow moon was visible through the cabin windows. The waves seemed larger now. The bed pitched gently. At first she was afraid. A knock came at the cabin door. The Prince got up, wrapping a blanket round his waist. The messenger whispered to him at the door. The Prince returned. He turned Anya onto her back and smiled.

'We are moving south, to round the Cape. Then we shall strike north. In four days, maybe five, we shall make landfall in Lidir.' His eyes shone. 'The carrier doves have been released to take the tidings: the Princess is coming home.'

He kissed her soft lips gently; he kissed her eyelids as they closed; he kissed her freckled cheeks. He coiled a smooth red lock about his finger.

'How will we while away the time till then, Sire?' Anya murmured.

'We will surely think of something. Rest now.'

Anya thought about it very carefully; she was far too excited to sleep. The ship rolled powerfully, then suddenly seemed to drop, forcing a delicious sinking feeling deep inside. Her hand fell against the buckle of the belt; her fingertips carefully unfastened it; she shivered as the soft leather band fell away from her naked belly. Then she removed the belt completely, coiled it up out of the way and placed it by her side. But still she could not rest; she kept curling against him, pressing her back to his chest and her bottom to his belly, while the leather belt slowly unfurled beside her like a snake against her leg. Finally, she lifted up to turn to face him, and a coil of leather rolled across and trapped between their thighs. Anya looked down. The Prince's flesh was already standing hard.

Suddenly, her eyes were bright.

Her fingertips took that tense flesh nervously and touched its undersurface to the soft tongue of the belt.

'Sire?' she whispered.

'Yes, my Princess?'

'Were you ever smacked – for pleasure?'